PRAISE FOR

THE SECRET OF CLOUDS

"Long renowned as a master of historical fiction, Alyson Richman spreads her wings and soars with this contemporary story. . . . *The Secret of Clouds* is an unforgettable gift."

— Pam Jenoff, *New York Times* bestselling author of *The Orphan's Tale*

"A story of family bonds, heartbreak, healing, and hope—one that reminds us it is not how long we live but how well we live that matters most. The tenderly written ending will bring you to tears, but in the best possible way."

— Lisa Wingate, *New York Times* bestselling author of
Before We Were Yours

"A tender, captivating, and ultimately satisfying story about the emotional gifts exchanged between a caring teacher and a student in need. Thank you, Alyson Richman, for another heartrending tale."

— Jamie Ford, *New York Times* bestselling author of
Hotel on the Corner of Bitter and Sweet

"Exquisite and haunting. Richman writes with the soul of a poet, and her captivating new novel enchants while tugging ever so gently at the heart. Her story stands as a reminder to never take any day for granted."

— Fiona Davis, national bestselling author of *The Masterpiece*

"Alyson Richman weaves an emotionally rich story of love, loss, and the resilience of the human spirit. *The Secret of Clouds* will soar off the page and into your heart."

— Jamie Brenner, national bestselling author of *The Husband Hour*

MORE PRAISE FOR THE NOVELS OF
ALYSON RICHMAN

"Alyson Richman's writing sings. . . . A beautiful and compelling portrait of two women facing their unknown past and an unimaginable future as their world begins to crumble. Heartfelt and romantic."
                    —#1 *New York Times* bestselling author Kristin Hannah

"Alyson Richman deftly weaves fact and fiction to create an enthralling tale of love and sacrifice in *The Velvet Hours*. . . . A carefully wrought story of love, of what the heart chooses to give up, and what it chooses to keep. Highly recommended to readers who enjoyed Kristin Hannah's *The Nightingale*."
                    —*New York Times* bestselling author Karen White

"A book as full of treasures as the Paris apartment that inspired it. . . . A masterful mix of the glamour of the Belle Epoque and the shadows of impending war as the stories of two generations twist and twine together in delightful, heart-wrenching, and sometimes unexpected ways."   —*New York Times* bestselling author Lauren Willig

"Staggeringly evocative . . . and beautifully written."
                    —*New York Times* bestselling author John Lescroart

"Moving, unforgettable, and so expertly told—this is storytelling at its very best."   —*New York Times* bestselling author Sarah Jio

"If you love graceful, mellifluous writing, you should read this book."
                    —*New York Times* bestselling author Jenna Blum

"A meticulous profile of a man struggling against his native culture, his family, and his own sense of responsibility."
                    —*The New York Times Book Review*

BOOKS BY ALYSON RICHMAN

The Mask Carver's Son

The Rhythm of Memory

The Last Van Gogh

The Lost Wife

The Garden of Letters

The Velvet Hours

The Secret of Clouds

THE

Secret

OF

Clouds

ALYSON RICHMAN

BERKLEY

BERKLEY
An imprint of Penguin Random House LLC
1745 Broadway, New York, NY 10019

Copyright © 2019 by Alyson Richman

Penguin Random House supports copyright. Copyright fuels creativity, encourages diverse voices, promotes free speech, and creates a vibrant culture. Thank you for buying an authorized edition of this book and for complying with copyright laws by not reproducing, scanning, or distributing any part of it in any form without permission. You are supporting writers and allowing Penguin Random House to continue to publish books for every reader.

BERKLEY and the BERKLEY & B colophon are registered trademarks of
Penguin Random House LLC.

Library of Congress Cataloging-in-Publication Data

Names: Richman, Alyson, author.
Title: The secret of clouds / Alyson Richman.
Description: First edition. | New York: Berkley,
an imprint of Penguin Random House LLC, 2019.
Identifiers: LCCN 2018016371 | ISBN 9780451490773 (pbk.) | ISBN 9780451490780 (ebk.)
Subjects: LCSH: English teachers—Fiction. | Life change events—Fiction. |
Self-realization—Fiction.
Classification: LCC PS3568.I3447 S43 2019 | DDC 813/.54—dc23
LC record available at https://lccn.loc.gov/2018016371

First Edition: February 2019

Printed in the United States of America
1   3   5   7   9   10   8   6   4   2

Cover art: painted marble by oxygen / Getty Images
Cover design by Olga Grlic
Book design by Kelly Lipovich

For Zachary Wyatt

and Christina Tudisco

Nobody has ever measured, not even poets,
how much the heart can hold.

—attributed to Zelda Fitzgerald

Prologue

SHE walks the cobblestone streets, her lithe body moving quickly. Most days, she is wrapped in layers of thin sweaters with a scarf roped loosely around her neck. But today it is unseasonably warm, the sun radiating against the pale blue sky.

Everyone in the square is celebrating the surprising heat wave. Girls are wearing cotton dresses for the first time in months. Old men are playing chess in the park, their sleeves rolled up past their elbows. Young children are at the river with their parents, knee-deep in water they normally wouldn't be able to swim in until July.

The heat. The sun. The light. For a few hours before, she had soaked in the unexpected sunlight in the privacy of her garden. But now, Katya finds herself joyously leaping over a puddle of soapy water left by the street washer. Her leotard is hidden underneath a thin black blouse. Stretching from the hem of her skirt are the sculpted legs of a dancer.

She walks as if suspended from the ground, arms swinging, her bag tossed over her shoulder. Her face is bone white, her blond hair coiled into a tight bun.

As she approaches the theater, no one takes notice of Katya as she pulls open the heavy door and ascends the cement stairs toward the ballet studios. Inside, the blinds are lifted all the way up to bring in the light. As the dancers stretch, their shadows mimic their movements across the wooden floor. Like dark ghosts resurrected by the sun.

1

LET me tell you a secret. A unique kind of person exists in this world, one who radiates light even through a curtain of darkness.

As a teacher, I've seen everything in eyes staring back at me: the child who hates school and wishes to be outside; the one who aims only to please; the glassy, sleepy-eyed child; and the one who's perpetually lost in a daydream. But there are those rare moments when a student sits before you and you immediately are certain—and you can't know why, it's just a feeling in your bones—that they are different.

This child is not to be confused with the student who's the most ambitious or the one who is naturally strong at taking tests. No, this child, the one you sense is extraordinary, is the one who returns everything you give and more. He or she becomes your beacon, as every word you utter in the classroom suddenly has a destination. It's as if you are teaching toward their light.

IN the fall of 1999, I met Yuri, a student who one day would teach me lessons I could never have learned in school. I was young, just two years out of Columbia Teachers College. I had abandoned my first job after graduation as a personal assistant at a well-respected New York City PR firm, where my days had been so demoralizing and brain-sucking that I often thought eating glass might be less painful than spending twelve hours tending to my boss's Godzilla-like needs. Hoping to switch into something that could restore my faith in humanity and also give my life purpose, I followed my mother's suggestion and went back to school for a degree in teaching.

To be honest, I became nearly evangelical in my passion for teaching after I switched careers. The thrill of teaching children is that they don't edit themselves, like adults do. Truth can be found in every classroom, and I savored that purity like a refreshing glass of water. I wanted to be the teacher who read passages out loud to my students, like my own English teacher had done when I was in sixth grade, so we could all hear the music in the words. Deep down, I believed a story could change us, and that if we read it deeply enough, a good book could transform our souls.

IT was my second year teaching sixth-grade English language arts at Franklin Intermediate School, and I was full of optimism. Everything around me seemed ripe with possibility. My boyfriend, Bill, and I had just moved in together. We had spent our first four years after graduating from the University of Michigan living a few blocks from each other on the border between the Upper East Side and Spanish Harlem, where the rent was relatively cheap and the bars were plentiful. But I had grown tired of the twentysomething scene of young professionals unwinding in front of sports bar TVs and a sea of baseball caps. And the long commute from New York City to my teaching job in Long Island was killing me. I wanted fresh air and a backyard. I imagined Sunday mornings where we could spread out the newspaper and look up at each other through steaming mugs of coffee. Perhaps we'd even get a dog.

Bill resisted at first. He enjoyed the convenience of picking up a coffee and a bagel along with his copy of the *New York Post* from his favorite corner deli before hopping on the number 6 subway each morning to his Midtown office, where he sold corporate insurance. He loved the fact that there were fifty delivery places he could always choose from if he wanted something to eat after midnight. He had just started making good money and was happy to have places to spend it. He bought himself a new set of golf clubs and splurged on box seats at Mets games and concerts at Madison Square Garden.

But then, over the next few months, one by one, our closest couple friends started announcing their decision to leave the city and go where there was more grass and the lines for Sunday morning brunch weren't always an hour long. One night over Ray's Pizza, Bill observed that the migration had started. "And who am I to be the last man standing?" He wiped his mouth with a paper towel. "Maybe you're right, Maggie, let's make the move out to the burbs."

WE ended up renting a small cottage in Stony Brook, a part of Long Island that felt more like New England than the fancier towns closer to Manhattan. I had found the listing for it in my parents' local Penny-Saver and circled it in bright red ink. The location was perfect. It was close to the middle school where I was teaching, and Bill was thrilled that his Manhattan employer had a satellite office not too far away. I believed I was well on my way to becoming a full-fledged adult, at the ripe old age of twenty-six.

The new place appealed to the romantic in me. A small white clapboard cottage with red shutters and a brass door knocker, it looked as though it were lifted from the pages of a children's book. Others might have been put off by the low ceilings and the lack of closets, but I was completely sold by what the real estate agent referred to as its "old-world charm." Who doesn't love flower boxes filled with purple and magenta petunias underneath their windowsills? Who needs air-conditioning when you have tall linden trees shading a slate blue roof?

"Let's try to negotiate a little on the rent," Bill advised, the businessman in him always thrilled by the chance to get a better deal. But I ignored him. The real estate agent was pointing out the wood-burning fireplace, and I didn't want to be distracted when she was detailing the craftsmanship in the carved molding.

"That's all the heat you'll need in the winter," she laughed, pointing to the logs of cherrywood the owners had thoughtfully stacked to the side. I was sold! Already, I could imagine myself curled up underneath a blanket, reading Toni Morrison as the fire blazed on.

At the end of the tour, Bill thanked the agent and promised we'd get back to her in a few days.

I waited until he was several feet ahead of me before I pulled her aside.

"We'll take it!" I said, squeezing her arm. I had always been a sucker for "old-world charm." I could almost smell the burning cherrywood, even though it was days away from the start of summer.

WE moved in at the end of June, just after my first year at Franklin ended, and I found myself doing most of the unpacking. I wiped down the wooden shelves in the tiny living room and lined them with all my favorite novels. Ever since I had first left home, I had brought with me every one of the books I had ever loved. So even my favorite ones from eighth grade now found their way to my new shelves. My dog-eared copies of *A Separate Peace* and *A Tree Grows in Brooklyn* were lovingly placed next to more recent additions, like *The God of Small Things* and *A Suitable Boy*. Every day I worked toward making the cottage our new home, while Bill went off to work. I placed photos of the two of us in college over the mantel, and cut wild roses and arranged them in old mason jars. The fireplace hinted at all of our cozy nights to come.

In the meantime, I found a slice of heaven in the Adirondack chair under one of the trees in the garden. I knew, come September, it would be the perfect spot for me to correct my new students' papers. I couldn't wait to discover whose sparkling eyes were going to inspire me most in the coming school year.

THE Friday before Labor Day, I arrived early at Franklin Intermediate, eager to set up my classroom. I had filled my silver Toyota with boxes of supplies: folders, paper, and marking pens. My friend Suzie Price, the art teacher, was in the hallway, stapling colored paper to the bulletin board, when I walked inside. I knew it would be a full-blown art gallery of student works on display in less than two weeks' time.

"Hey, beauty," she said. In truth, Suzie was the real beauty. With bright red lips and perfect skin, and all her scarves and mix-matched separates, she had that artistic way of styling herself I so envied. Come winter, when I'd be bundled up in a practical wool cardigan, she'd be wearing one in chenille with buttons made of sea glass.

"Good summer?"

"The best! No more reverse commute from the city. Bill and I found a great new place . . . a cottage out in Stony Brook."

"That's amazing news, Maggie. I need to move out of my place one of these days. Living in a basement isn't good for the artist's soul."

"Check the PennySaver," I hollered over my shoulder as I carried my box down toward my classroom.

ROOM number 203, my classroom, was smack in the middle of Franklin's west wing. Like the majority of Long Island's public schools, Franklin's interior was devoid of any charm or architectural detail. The ceilings were low, the cement-block walls were painted a drab shade of putty, and the floors were a checkerboard of linoleum tile. But nearly all my fellow teachers relished the opportunity to defy the 1960s functional architecture and transform their surroundings into something inspiring for their students once they stepped through the threshold of their classroom.

We all prided ourselves in the various themes we used to decorate our rooms. That summer, I had deliberated over mine for weeks before finally deciding on "The mind is a powerful tool." I spent hours creating a template for a squiggly shaped brain with all its infinite coils. I then color-coded each section with an array of neon Magic Markers to highlight the two parts. I made the left side of my template orange to show the children "the logical brain," where language and analysis were generated, and then I highlighted the right side in pink for "the creative brain," the area that sparked daydreaming and imagination. I also made a miniature brain for each of my twenty-four students and wrote their names in the center with a thick black Sharpie. I hurried to my classroom, eager to begin working on setting up my bulletin board.

WHEN I entered my classroom, much to my surprise, I found a yellow Post-it note from the principal already taped to my desk.

Ms. Topper: Need to speak with you when you get a chance. I'll be in my office all day. Stop by whenever it's convenient.

Thank you,
T. Nelson

I wondered what he could possibly want to discuss on my first day back. I checked myself in the mirror, took a deep breath to calm my nerves, and prepared to go see him.

PRINCIPAL Nelson was standing over his metal filing case when I walked into his office. A desk fan was circulating warm air in the corner.

"Glad to see you, Maggie." He gestured for me to sit down. "Did you have a good summer?"

"Yes, thank you. But I'm happy to be getting back to school."

"Good to hear." He smiled as he walked over to his desk and settled into his chair. "I have an unusual request for you . . ." He leaned in closer to me.

"Maggie, I was pleased with your work here last year. You bring an enviable enthusiasm to the classroom."

I blushed and was about to deflect the praise when Mr. Nelson lifted his hand to stop me.

"No need to say anything more on that subject. I just wanted you to know that I'm looking forward to a great second year with you here at Franklin."

He cleared his throat. "And, in fact, I was *so* pleased, I thought of you right away when I got this special assignment from the superintendent."

"Sounds intriguing . . ." I felt a surge of nervous energy pass through me.

"There's a child entering the sixth grade this year who just moved into the district. He was actually slotted to be in your class, but from what I gather of the details, he was born with a heart defect that has really weakened him."

I felt my stomach tighten.

"Since he's too weak to be at school right now, the administration has agreed to send tutors to his house for him so he doesn't fall behind. And I was hoping you'd be his English language arts tutor."

He tapped his desk with two fingers as he awaited my response.

"We're obviously hoping he'll get his strength back and be able to join your class later on in the year. But in the meantime, the district will pay for you to visit him after your classes end here each day. We were thinking two days a week to start. The administration will be arranging another tutor to help him with math and science, but I don't believe he or she will be from Franklin." He folded his hands on the desk.

"Does that sound like something you'd be interested in doing, Ms. Topper?"

The excitement I'd felt only seconds before was now replaced by dread. The memory of a sick little girl from my childhood flashed through my mind, her eyes pressed to the window as the school bus passed by her house.

I could feel the color draining from my face, and my mind froze. I wanted to say something professional and well-meaning, like how wonderful it would be to teach a student one-on-one or how it would be a privilege to tutor a child who was in need, but my words failed me. I could only feel myself fidgeting nervously in my chair.

Mr. Nelson leaned forward again. "So, can I count on you, Maggie?"

I swallowed hard, desperate to do something that would at least enable me to respond, but I could not stop thinking about my childhood neighbor Ellie.

"What's the student's name?" I pushed myself to ask.

Principal Nelson lifted a sheet of paper from his desk and squinted.

"Yuri Krasny." He read the name quickly. "I have no idea if I'm pronouncing that right . . ."

"Yuri?" I said the name again. It sounded exotic and interesting. Not like all the Michaels and Jonathans who were so plentiful at Franklin Intermediate.

I felt a whirlwind of emotions rush through me—thoughts of wanting to help a child in need, and fear of the emotional baggage that I'd been carrying around for fifteen years.

"I know it would be a very special opportunity to tutor him. But would you mind if I took the long weekend to think about it? I just want to make sure I'm not spread too thin in the afternoons."

Mr. Nelson looked surprised.

"Well, sure, Maggie." He tucked his pencil behind his ear and pushed himself away from his desk, the wheels of his chair squeaking across the tile floor. "Take a look at your schedule and get back to me Tuesday. But I'll have to decide on another teacher if you're not up to it, so please don't take any longer than that."

"Of course, and I'm sorry for needing the extra time."

"But I do hope you'll see the importance of this assignment," he added. "It's unique, and I think you'd be well suited for it."

I nodded. I knew it was a vote of confidence for Mr. Nelson to have asked me, but deep down I worried if I was up to tutoring a sick child in his home. My mind kept returning to Ellie. That is the thing about memory. As hard as we try to will ourselves to forget certain events, our histories remain. I thought of those serpentine coils on the miniature brains I had made for my students. Every one of us had stories locked away in the intricate mazes of our minds. But, like most things, our stories can remain buried for only so long.

I was thirteen years old the summer that Ellie Auerbach got out of bed one morning and felt her legs go weak beneath her. She was five years old. That summer she had gotten her first bicycle, a bright pink one with a straw basket and a metal bell fastened to the handlebars. We heard her going up and down the street for hours each day, her training wheels dragging behind her, the bell ringing in the air.

I remember Mrs. Auerbach telling my mother that she thought maybe Ellie had slept in a funny position and her legs had fallen asleep. But there had also been the inexplicable fevers that had plagued her the month before, and the persistent virus that her mother thought might be a late-season flu. These were all clues that perhaps Ellie's mother had overlooked because they interfered with her refusal to waste her energy on worrying too much about things she thought would eventually pass. Yet, eventually, these events glared in a painful, telling light.

Mrs. Auerbach had always believed in the goodness of the world and that the sky changed color every sunset for a reason. "The universe doesn't want us to grow complacent in its beauty," she told me one hazy afternoon on her large white porch as she handed me a tall glass of lemonade. The condensation was cold against my fingers as I took it in hand and sipped from a paper straw. She was pregnant with Ellie then. Her abdomen was large and full against the linen of her white dress, her cheeks rosy, and her dark auburn hair in a long, single braid. She put her hands on her belly and cried, "Oh, Maggie, I felt a kick! Do you want to feel the baby?" Before I could tell her I was too squeamish, Mrs. Auerbach had put my hand over her middle. And that bright summer day, I felt a little heel or a clenched fist—round and impatient—making its needs well-known from within the confines of its womb.

THEY brought Ellie home in a straw Moses basket a few weeks later. Pink and wrinkled beneath a crocheted bonnet, her five little fingers clenched at her mouth. Mr. Auerbach stood outside in pressed cotton khakis, sunlight striking his face. "A little girl," my father had congratulated him. "There's nothing quite like having one of your own."

I remember my mother telling me not to get too close to the baby, but Mrs. Auerbach had only raised her hand and laughed. "If Maggie's washed her hands, it's okay for her to peer in and see the little bug," she told me as she nestled into a large comfortable chair, her body still full beneath her dress. I felt so happy at that moment as I leaned in and my finger grazed Ellie's cheek. Her eyelids lifted open, and I saw the soft haze of her newborn gaze, her little fist now unclenching. As Ellie's small finger reached out to touch my own, she became the baby sister I never had.

EIGHT years between us, I was always ahead in my milestones, but Ellie was never far from my family's house. She loved to putter in my mother's garden, where she wore my old rubber boots and used my little watering can with the painted daisy on the side. So that summer, when the pain in her legs first appeared, we held our breath as Mrs. Auerbach took Ellie from doctor to doctor, until a specialist in New York City finally told the Auerbachs that Ellie had a rare form of cancer.

She didn't get to go to kindergarten that year as planned. Those first few days of school, the yellow school bus still slowed outside her house, as though it was waiting for the little girl to hop outside.

"They told me to cut her hair short," Mrs. Auerbach confided to my mother, her voice low in a whisper. "So when it falls out, it's not too upsetting," she explained as the tears rolled down her face. The next time I saw Ellie and her mom, neither of them had their braids. Mrs. Auerbach had also cut her hair short, the moment the hairdresser had finished cutting Ellie's.

Their house transformed from a home where the planters were always filled with bright red geranium flowers and the windows were wide open to one that was suddenly shuttered and impenetrable. The curtains all drawn closed. Flowerpots filled with shriveled stalks and leaves.

My mother and I would still visit, but Mrs. Auerbach was no longer the mother with a carefree spirit and hopeful gaze. She looked gaunt and tired, her eyes rimmed in dark circles, her smile erased to a thin, drawn line. The air in the house was stale; orange medicine vials lined the counter. And most painful was little Ellie on the sofa, her scalp fuzzy like a newborn's, but her eyes far older than her five years.

ELLIE remained in the back of my mind for most of my adult life. I might hear wind chimes sounding in the breeze, and the image of a pregnant Mrs. Auerbach on her porch would flash through my mind. And every time I heard the sharp, metallic sound of a bicycle bell ringing in the air, it didn't make me feel cheerful but had the opposite effect. A painful reminder of the unfairness of life, and the incomprehensibility that a child could be taken from this world far too soon.

So much of Ellie's death remained unprocessed for me, buried underneath layers of suppressed grief. The Auerbachs moved away less than a year after Ellie died. Their house was now occupied by an older couple from Boston, who had moved to be closer to their son in New York City. Yet there were times I would see a little girl who looked like Ellie, the moon-shaped face and hazel eyes, the golden braids tied with white ribbon, and thoughts of her would come flooding back to me. After all this time, Ellie remained six years old in my mind, even though I was now a grown woman teaching students of my own.

ON Sunday, Bill and I went to visit friends in Westchester for a barbecue, and we spent the day on lawn chairs, eating hot dogs and wedges of watermelon, savoring the last weekend in summer. On Monday, the day before school began, Bill went to play golf with a college buddy, so I took a drive out to visit my parents.

My family lived even farther east on Long Island than I did, two towns over in a remote area called Strong's Neck. This was a place where people enjoyed their solitude. In the spring, the air was laced with the smell of honeysuckle and hyacinth. In the autumn, it was the rich scent of sugar maple and oak. Long stretches of land with tall grass and ancient trees bordered the winding roads, and many of the old houses dated back to the early settlers of Long Island. My own family's house was far from historic. It was a modest ranch with cedarwood shingles and shutters that my father had purposefully painted hunter green to match the pine trees surrounding the house.

My father had the veneer of a sturdy Irishman, but the soul of an old Italian craftsman. He had taken up making violins for his post-retirement hobby, a strange and exotic passion for a man who had been in sales his entire adult life. My childhood basement, where my friends and I used to play Twister or conduct séances during sleepovers, was now a workshop with wood shavings on the floor and glass jars filled with glue and varnish. Even the smells of my family home had changed. It used to have the unmistakable scent of simmering garlic and tomatoes. Now, the fragrance of freshly planed spruce filled the air.

When I rang the doorbell, my father answered. It always still amazed me to see him so transformed. My schoolgirl memories were of him wearing a navy blue suit and striped tie, gripping a saddle-colored briefcase. Now, my eyes had to readjust. Dad was wearing a vinyl smock, a pencil tucked behind his silver-flecked hair, and when he hugged me, I could feel the calluses on his fingertips.

"Hey, Mags!" His cheeks lifted with a smile as he kissed me hello.

"To what do we owe this surprise visit? You must've missed your old man, right?"

"I missed Mom's lasagna."

"I'll happily take second place to that." He grinned.

My father had won the prize when he married my mother, a first-generation Italian American. There was no greater cook in the world than she, as she could take anything and make it into something delicious. But my father always insisted it wasn't Mom's cooking that had made him fall in love with her, but rather her beautiful singing voice, which he believed to be more perfect than any instrument he could ever craft by hand.

"And you're in luck . . . she made manicotti last night. Help yourself to whatever leftovers are in the fridge."

"How are your hands today?" My father's arthritis had become especially painful over the past year and a half.

He lifted his hands up, the knobby knuckles and sunspotted skin betraying his sixty-three years.

"Nothing a little ibuprofen and an ice bath can't fix." He came over to me and hugged me. "Your dad's no wimp."

I rolled my eyes. "But are those violins really worth all the agony?"

"Well, to me they are."

I smiled. I knew that after a life in pharmaceutical sales, my father finally had the chance to devote himself to what he had always wanted to do, and no amount of pain or discomfort was going to stop him.

I slid my bag down and went to wash up.

BY the time I got out of the bathroom, my mom had come in from the garden. Her green clogs were by the side door, and she was standing barefoot by the kitchen sink, washing sprigs of freshly cut arugula that she had just collected in a straw basket. My mother looked artful even when she had been on her knees in dirt all day. Her chestnut brown hair was threaded in silver and pulled back in a loose chignon, and around her neck she had tied a red kerchief. Her old-world elegance never escaped her.

"Maggie!" Her eyes lit up when she saw me. She shook her wet hands in the air, and little raindrops of moisture fell onto the linoleum floor. "What a nice surprise. Are you hungry, honey?"

"Have I ever not been?"

You could see her perk up immediately at the thought of feeding me. She gestured toward the kitchen table. I followed without protest as she began to heat up the food.

MY parents had one of those classic love affairs. The Irish boy from the Bronx fell in love with the dark-haired Italian girl down the street whom his parents had warned him about. My father always told my brother and me that like the Sirens of ancient Greece, our mother had entranced him with her voice even before he saw her beauty. One day, when he was onstage rehearsing with his high school orchestra, he heard a girl singing behind the curtain. Notes floated toward him that sounded so perfect and clear. Family legend has it that he put down his violin and went off to search for her. And when he realized the tall girl with the long hair and dark eyes was the one with the voice of an angel, he fell head over heels in love.

And although my father's family initially resisted my mother, she eventually won over her future mother-in-law, not through her angelic voice or her cooking but rather through what the Irish call the gift of story.

My favorite was about my grandmother Valentina. Her American cousins had received a photograph of a petite Sicilian girl who looked malnourished and in need of a good home. When she finally arrived at Ellis Island, no one could make sense of the rotund girl who claimed to be their cousin. All the relatives whispered as they took the girl, who seemed to be bursting out of her clothes, back home to the tenement apartment near Arthur Avenue. They showed Valentina a room with a large metal tub where she could take a bath and change her clothes. The other women were rendered speechless as the fat little girl began to take off her coat, then her dress, then another dress, and then another. One by one all her layers of clothing were removed, and there stood the skinny child they now recognized from the photograph. They realized that instead of packing most of her clothes in Valentina's suitcase, her mother had made her daughter wear all of them for the entire journey over. She could then fill her suitcase with all the other necessities, like shoes, underwear, and sweaters.

My mother had gifted her love of story to me. Showing me that storytelling had the power to connect us to others, that a good tale could even bridge the space between children and adults. Whenever a child needed soothing, she had an arsenal of tales ready to tame even the crankiest toddler. She would offer a saffron-colored cookie and then tell a colorful anecdote about her friend from Sweden who had shared the recipe with her, so that the story was yet another ingredient folded into the layers of flour and butter.

"DID you paint your new bedroom yet, Maggie?" She placed a warm plate of oozing mozzarella-and-ricotta goodness in front of me. "Do you want me to come over and help you?"

"The color's actually growing on me, Mom, so I'm not sure I will need to paint it. I tell myself it's not off-white but buttermilk, and somehow it doesn't seem so boring anymore."

"Aah, the soothing color of buttermilk," she teased and sat down next to me. "You were always so good with words, Maggie. And you can always find the positive and the beautiful . . ."

I laughed. "I got that from you, Mom. If only I had inherited your gift with food, too." I lifted my fork to my mouth and savored the warmth and melding flavors. In truth, I thought it was my mother who could discover beauty where one was least expecting it. Many times, I felt she had that effect on me. I had grown up always feeling awkward about my height, strawberry-colored hair, and freckles. But somehow my mother had the magical capacity to make me feel better about myself whenever she smoothed down the stray tangles of my hair or cupped my face in her soft hands.

"So, school starts tomorrow. You must be excited, Maggie." I didn't answer her for a second, and she picked up on it right away. I could feel her eyes on me as I drew my fork through the puddles of runny ricotta.

"I actually came here to talk to you about something," I said, placing my fork down.

"Yes? What is it, honey?"

"Well . . ." I hesitated for a moment, trying to gather the right words. "On Friday, I went to drop off some of my supplies at school and get the classroom ready, and there was a note from the principal asking me to go down to his office . . ."

My mother's face looked puzzled.

"No, it wasn't like I was in trouble or anything. It was the opposite, actually . . . Principal Nelson wanted to offer me an extra assignment because he was so pleased with my work last year."

"Isn't that good news, Maggie?"

"Well, it's not that black and white, Mom. He asked me if I'd consider tutoring a child at home in English language arts who isn't healthy enough to be in the classroom this year. He was born with a heart defect, and he's too weak right now to go to class with the other kids. The district is sending two teachers to his house to keep him up to grade level."

My mother's hand reached toward me and she covered mine with hers. "Oh, honey, this child needs you."

I could feel my body stiffen. I blinked back tears. "I know, Mom. But I keep thinking about Ellie. I don't know if I'm strong enough to go into a home with a sick child each week." I sucked in my breath. "What if I can't handle it?"

My mother shook her head and looked away from me. I knew talking about Ellie was difficult for her, too.

"What happened with Ellie was so terrible, Maggie," she said gently. "And you were so brave with Ellie. You visited her all those times when she was sick even when it was hard to see her that way. You read to her. You did coloring books with her. Do you remember you even sometimes played school with her? Mrs. Auerbach told me you were the one person Ellie looked forward to seeing more than anyone." My mother sighed. "I know now your father and I didn't do you any favors by not telling you right away."

I felt my expression tighten. This had long been a sore spot between my parents and me. I was away at camp the summer Ellie
died. None of us could have predicted it would happen, of course,
but she passed away while I was gone. My parents didn't tell me
until after I got home, nearly a week after the funeral.

"I never got to say good-bye," I said, my voice breaking.

"We made a mistake. Your dad and I were young parents, and
we didn't want to ruin your summer. Whenever we told you, it
wasn't going to be easy."

"It's just one minute she was here, and then she was gone. Those
first few months after she died, I kept on thinking I was going to
hear her on her bicycle or see her on the porch with Mrs. Auerbach,
waving to me as I got off the school bus." The pain resurfaced, fresh
and raw.

"And you're afraid to get attached to this student?" My mother's
voice lowered. "That's understandable, Maggie. But we can't be so
afraid of experiencing pain that it interferes with the things we love.
Think about your dad, how much he suffers with his arthritis. I see
him every morning putting his hands in a basin filled with ice before
he starts his day's work on the violins. But he doesn't stop doing it,
even when things are difficult. He can't. And neither should you."

She leaned in closer to me and rubbed my back.

"Do you know the child's name yet?"

"Yuri," I said softly.

"I think you owe it to yourself to at least make an effort for Yuri,"
my mother counseled. "He's cooped up in that house and not able to
go to school like the rest of the kids his age. Think about what you
could bring to his life," she said gently. "And imagine what he might
bring to yours."

2

THE following Tuesday morning, as promised, I went to see Principal Nelson before classes started and gave him my answer.

"I'm thrilled, Maggie. You're going to do a great job with Yuri."

My face grew warm. I hoped he was right, but I felt plagued by uncertainty. I knew I had switched careers because I wanted to make a difference in the world and thought there was no better way to do that than by helping to shape a child's life. But, suddenly, the stakes seemed so much higher than they had before. I couldn't fail this sick little boy.

"I'll let the family know you'll be stopping by tomorrow to introduce yourself."

"Sounds good," I said and then hurried down the hall to get to my classroom before my first set of students arrived.

EVERY teacher, no matter the grade or how long they've been teaching, struggles these first few weeks of school. We have only a small window to connect with each child, and we need to form a good impression from the get-go.

Their muscles still cling to the memory of summer vacation—the sports at camp or lazy days at the beach. Most of them, particularly the boys, strain to sit still for the full period.

As one of the newer teachers, I still had great reserves of energy. In the morning, I transformed myself from bleary-eyed, coffee-deprived Maggie Topper in her petal pink cotton flannel pajamas into a caffeine-fueled teacher extraordinaire. I blow-dried my hair to a clean sheet of copper and wore clothes that I thought were professional but still had a bit of flair.

The unexpected revelation, I scrawled on the blackboard the first day I met with my sixth-grade English class. "We will learn when we're least expecting to."

"Cool," Oscar said. "No homework, then?"

"Not so fast. We'll be doing a lot of writing this year. There will be things you never thought of before you took your pencil to your paper." I gave my desk a little tap. "Now, how cool is that?"

The classroom rustled. I saw Jack shift in his seat. Rachel tore a sheet of loose-leaf paper from her binder and crumpled it in a tight ball. A pencil rolled to the front of the class.

"In a few days we'll begin making our writer's notebooks. Each of you will be writing your own personal narratives in these books. They're going to be reflective of all your thoughts. Your likes and dislikes. You're even going to decorate the cover with images or words you think best define you."

Some of the boys rolled their eyes. A few of the girls in the front were needlessly writing down every word I said.

"For those of you who are already half-asleep," I joked, "wake up. Because this year is going to be fun."

. . .

IT had been my mother who encouraged me to leave my job in PR and pursue a job in teaching. She took one look at me that spring after I'd been working nearly a year at Mellancamps Strategies and said, "Your eyes are looking dim, sweetheart. What happened to that sparkle I know so well?"

"It's just not how I imagined it would be," I complained. "I thought I'd like the frenetic speed of things in the office. The excitement of trying to help package the latest account. But everyone is angry half the time and yelling at each other . . . I feel sick to my stomach every day, nervous my boss is going to scream at me because I didn't order enough bagels for the directors' meeting, and I'm getting an ulcer over a job where I'm not even using my brain."

My mother was quiet for a moment.

"You're twenty-three, honey. You know you're young enough to make a career change. One thing you never get back is your time . . ."

"But to what?"

She knew the answer before I even asked the question. She had seen me dress up since I was a little girl and put my father's reading glasses on top of my head and use the easel in my basement as a makeshift blackboard. From the moment I first walked into kindergarten class, the classroom felt like my natural arena. I instinctively gravitated toward the desks closest to the teacher. I relished the proximity to this person who knew the answer to every one of my questions and, when they were talented, exuded an energy that radiated from every pore. Every day, I put my books on the classroom windowsill and pretended it was my own bookshelf. When I was in elementary school, I imagined I was the teacher. I sat with my back straight and my eyes alert, and I could transport myself into her seat or see myself standing in front of the blackboard.

"You can go back to school for your master's. Apply now and see if you get in. It can't hurt, Maggie. You're a person who thrives on a real sense of purpose. That's why you're unhappy at your job." She gave a little tap on my forehead. "Your brain is being wasted," she said. "And so is your heart."

I knew my mother was right. During my last year of college at Michigan, my friends were looking forward to their first jobs at banks or large corporations. Bill had accepted a job at a big insurance company that he had landed through one of his fraternity connections, and he couldn't wait to start. But I loathed the thought of leaving school. I lived for it. I loved its various cycles. There was always a chance to do something new and learn something different the following year with another set of professors.

I didn't look back once I started teaching. I loved the energy it gave me, the electricity that began as soon as I entered the classroom. It was so much more rewarding than marketing a new brand of marshmallows or a toothpaste that whitened your smile. Teaching was about opening children's minds to infinite possibilities, to make them think and question the world around them. There were certainly some days that left me exhausted or irritated, but how many jobs could actually give you the opportunity to make an impact on a life? With teaching, I had finally found a sense of purpose.

THE following afternoon, after my last class was over, I prepared to meet Yuri. I opened up my big floppy bag and placed my notepad and folder in it. I had written up a handout for all my students that described much of what we would be doing that year. I couldn't wait to get the children working on their individual writer's notebooks. I was happy that, in less than half an hour, I'd have a better sense of Yuri and what our time together would be like. I had willed myself not to imagine how sick he might appear. I didn't want to impress my memories of Ellie onto Yuri. I glanced at the address Mr. Nelson had given me and took a deep breath.

THE Krasny residence was only a fifteen-minute drive from the school, just past Moriches Road and not too far from the local farm where Bill and I had bought corn all summer.

The house was small, nearly the same size as our rental, but the exterior paint was peeling and it seemed to sag in a sigh of neglect. Outside there was a brick pathway that followed from the curb to the door. Dandelions poked out from the spaces in the cement joints, and the grass was covered in patches of clover.

I parked on the street and checked my face in the rearview mirror. I had been up since six a.m. that day, and my face clearly showed it. My fair complexion, with its smattering of freckles, looked sallow. The edges of my eyes were rimmed in pink like a tired rabbit. I wanted to make a good first impression, and a weary face surely wasn't the way to get a new student enthused about schoolwork. I fumbled in my bag for my mascara and lipstick and reapplied my makeup quickly.

I reached over for my handbag, locked the car, and made my way toward the house, dandelions folding beneath my feet.

SHE didn't introduce herself at first, the slender woman who answered the door. Her skin and bone structure were clearly Eastern

European. I had never seen such pronounced cheekbones. Her wheat-colored hair was coiled in a tight bun.

"Hello," I said, extending my hand. "I'm Maggie Topper, Yuri's English tutor."

Her fingers were slender and cold; her eyes were shadowed in dark circles. She forced a brief smile. "I'm Katya, his mother." She wore no mascara or lipstick, and I now wished I could tissue off the shade of Raspberry Glacé I had just applied.

"Please come in." She ushered me inside, her speech revealing a distinct accent. It wasn't that the words weren't clear. It was more her cadence, which made her sentences come out in a halting, staccato-like rhythm.

Inside, the house was dimly lit. The scent of simmering onions floated in from the kitchen. The house had that same stifled air and heavy quiet that I had remembered when I visited Ellie, as though illness had made itself a permanent guest.

"Yuri is on the couch." She gestured me toward the living room. "He's a bit tired today. The math tutor came yesterday." She walked toward the room's threshold and then stopped. "Can I get you some tea?"

"I'm good, thanks. Just had my third cup of coffee." I looked at her wrapped in her sweater. We were having an Indian summer, so outside it was close to 70 degrees, but Katya looked like one of those women who always seemed as if they were freezing.

"I think today Yuri and I can just get to know each other a bit," I reassured her. "And don't worry, I won't give him any homework, so he can get his rest tonight."

She forced another smile. "Good. He'll like that." Katya hesitated for a moment. "I guess I should mention, Yuri's had a hard time lately. He really liked going to his old school, even though he missed a lot of days being sick. With the new move and being home all day, he's been really down."

"I bet," I said. "Don't worry, I'll do my best to make our time together as fun for him as possible."

Katya nodded and lifted her hand toward the hallway.

"Anyway, the washroom is on the left. We all must be vigilant about hand washing. His heart condition can sometimes make breathing difficult for him." She inhaled deeply. "So even a little cold can be dangerous for Yuri."

"Of course," I said. "No need to explain. It makes sense why you'd have to be so careful."

I dipped into the bathroom, turned on the faucet, and rolled up my sleeves.

WHEN I walked into the living room, I found Yuri bundled under a down comforter, his face peeking out from a mountain of puffy layers. My first reaction was relief when I saw him, because he did not look sickly the way I remembered Ellie. Instead, he reminded me of a little bird. His blond hair was sticking up in feathered peaks. He had the same pale white skin and sharp cheekbones as his mother. Staring at me were two large marble blue eyes.

"You must be Yuri," I said. I was the one who now appeared like a bird. I could hear the sound of my voice, which was almost freakishly chirpish.

He pushed the covers down toward his waist, and I could see he was still in his pajamas. They were the old-fashioned button-down kind, blue and red checked like the kind my father wore.

"I'm Ms. Topper and I'm going to be tutoring you in English language arts."

He lifted his hand from the comforter and offered me a weak, half-hearted wave.

I smiled at him. "Yuri, we're going to have fun together this year." I sat down and placed my bag next to my feet and pulled out my folder. "We'll be reading lots of great books . . ." I lifted my eyes to him. "Do you like to read?"

I saw two textbooks already stacked on the coffee table next to him. Math and science. I also noticed a pocket Game Boy, but there were no clues about any recreational reading.

My question went unanswered. Instead, Yuri's eyes drifted toward the bird feeder by the window. Two starlings were pecking at a mound of seed, their feathered tails bobbing up and down. Spattered against the cedar decking was a spray of fallen seeds and wet leaves.

"Hmmm," I said, trying to refocus the conversation. "Did you read any books over the summer?" I knew Franklin had sent out a list of suggested summer reading to all the sixth-grade students.

Again, Yuri didn't answer. His gaze remained fixed on the window and on the birds outside, as though he envied that they were on the opposite side of the paned glass.

"So if reading's not your thing . . . I'm going to take that as a personal challenge for this year . . . to change that." I forced a laugh. "But in the meantime, how about telling me about something you do like?"

"I'd like not to be stuck inside all day," Yuri answered flatly.

I felt a chill run through me. All my hopes of dazzling Yuri with my boundless energy and creativity were quickly fading.

"I can imagine it's very frustrating not being able to go to school like everyone else," I said, choosing my words carefully.

"You can't imagine," he said, staring at me. "Nobody can."

For several seconds, the silence between us felt awkward and oppressive. I didn't have the buffer of other children in front of me, like I did in my classroom. I couldn't call on another student to fill the air. I didn't have a blackboard to turn to and start writing different prompts. It was just the two of us, and I felt like I was drowning in quicksand right there in front of him.

Luckily, Katya's voice soon floated into the room like a welcome life raft.

"Yuri? Ms. Topper?" She stood at the threshold of the living room, holding a tray of cookies and two glasses of milk. "You said you didn't want tea, but maybe I can tempt you with some cookies?"

"Now you know my secret weakness." I laughed. "In my family, food is our first language."

Katya smiled and placed the plate of cookies on the table between us.

"I hope Yuri is being a good boy for you." She looked over to him and gave him a knowing look, as though she had been listening to our brief exchange.

"As you can see, he is not so happy to be home all day."

Yuri reached over and took a cookie. A thin veil of powdered sugar settled on his lips.

"I think you'll find Yuri to be a very smart boy once you get to know him," she said, lifting the tray into the air. There was a gracefulness to Katya that seemed second nature to her and made her appear different than most of the other mothers I had encountered.

Yuri took another cookie and looked out the window. He made no attempt to counter anything his mother had said, as some children who are unhappy often do.

After she had left, I once again tried to whet Yuri's appetite for what we'd be doing together this year.

"So like I said, we'll be reading lots of great books . . . and doing some really fun things like making our own writing notebooks. All the students love decorating them. You'll see . . ."

But it was obvious Yuri wasn't listening to me. His eyes had returned to the window. The one remaining starling perched on the deck flapped its wings and flew off. As I reached into my bag to find my notepad, I could feel Yuri retreating from me, without his uttering a single word.

3

OVER the next few weeks, I visited the Krasny house six times, and each visit was less productive than the one before. Yuri failed to complete the homework I assigned him. I had left him a copy of *Where the Red Fern Grows* that my midlevel reading group at Franklin was using for discussion. When I tried to engage in a discussion with him about the book, it was obvious he hadn't even bothered to open it. I contemplated approaching Principal Nelson and telling him he might need to consider replacing me because I was failing to connect with Yuri. My frustration was taking its toll.

"The great irony of it all," I complained to Suzie over coffee, "is that I have command of twenty-four students in my classroom, but I'm unable to reach the one child who is sitting right across from me. How is that even possible?"

"I think you're being way too hard on yourself," she counseled.

"I'm not so sure. Maybe I'm just not cut out for this. Maybe I'm not as good a teacher as I thought I was."

"Don't be ridiculous." Suzie cut me off. "He's having a hard time. The kid's cooped up in his living room all day and not able to go to school like other children. Why would he be so quick to bond with you? You need to stop expecting him to be a normal kid, when he's not. His situation is unique . . . and so is he."

I made a face. I knew she was right, but it was so hard to have clarity when I was failing so miserably.

"The thing about kids, Maggie, is that they can tell right away when you're trying too hard. It's like they can smell it on you. He probably hates how everyone strives to put a happy face on when they see him."

I knew she was right. I had been trying too hard.

"Children need to feel that they can trust you. And maybe it takes longer with some kids than with others to earn that trust."

IT was far more challenging than I had anticipated to appear laid-back with Yuri and not push so hard. But then something unexpected happened between us. Something I could never have anticipated would help me connect with Yuri. It was baseball.

That afternoon, I was twenty minutes late to Yuri's house. An accident had shut down much of Route 25A, and I had to take two detours to get to him. When I arrived, Katya looked concerned.

"We weren't sure you were coming today. You're always so punctual."

"There was a bad accident on 25A," I apologized.

"He's in the living room watching TV. I told him he could watch a game since I assumed you weren't coming."

"No problem," I said, sliding my bag off my shoulder. "I'll wash my hands and go say hello."

I found Yuri with his feet up on the ottoman, his body bent forward and his eyes fixated on the television screen.

I walked deeper into the living room, and Yuri's head turned to me. A look of alarm crossed his face. He didn't want to have to stop watching the game.

"Hey, who's winning?"

"The Yankees are losing to the Orioles. It's five nothing, bottom of the ninth." His voice was tense. "They pulled Clemens, and now Grimsley's pitching. Too bad they can't put Rivera in."

I smiled and sat down next to him and started watching the game. "You're right. They're too far behind to bring in their closer."

I could feel Yuri glance at me sideways and smile.

It was strange. Even with silence between us, I felt the energy shift in the room.

I spent the next half an hour with Yuri watching the final inning of the game. It was a study in itself to observe him interacting with the players on the TV screen. The listless, disinterested child I had encountered in my previous visits had now transformed into an incredibly impassioned and informed fan. Seeing him in this new role made me realize that nothing was more alive for Yuri than baseball.

I was not a complete stranger to the game. I actually considered myself a pretty decent fan, enough to know what a "closer" was, anyway. My older brother was a die-hard Mets fan growing up and so was Bill. I loved going to the games and getting caught up in the feel-good energy of America's favorite pastime. I even had my own Al Leiter jersey that Bill had recently given me to wear to the occasional game at Shea Stadium.

But I was clearly out of my league with Yuri, who started quoting batters' statistics when they came up to the plate. He spoke of his four favorite players—Pettitte, Posada, Rivera, and Jeter—and why they made the Yankees so great.

When the game ended, Yuri picked up the remote control and shut off the television.

"Thank you, Ms. Topper, for letting me finish the game. I appreciate it."

"It was a pleasure watching you get so into it. You really know a lot about baseball, don't you?"

He smiled. "My dad and I really love the Yankees."

"Well, you're in for a treat, then, because guess what? I like the Mets." I couldn't resist teasing him.

"You're clearly rooting for the wrong team, Ms. Topper!"

"Am I?" I played along.

"They haven't won a World Series in thirteen years."

"I guess I have a special spot in my heart for the underdog," I said.

"Well, you've come to the right place, then, Ms. Topper."

"Have I?"

"Yep."

He lifted his hand and placed it on his chest.

"Meet Yuri Krasny. Underdog number one."

"You don't strike me as an underdog," I said, feigning that I didn't see the bevy of orange plastic pill containers next to the lamp, and the large dehumidifier by the couch.

"No?"

"Nope. And even if you did, the one thing I know about baseball is that it's the player you're least expecting to do anything who then hits the ball out of the park." All those late-night conversations I'd had with Bill and his fraternity brothers over the years swirled inside my head for a second, and I reached deep into my memory to pull out the right comparison to impress him.

"You know, like Bucky Dent hit that home run that time."

"Did you just say Bucky Dent?" An expression of disbelief washed over him. "You know who he is?"

Miraculously, a random reference that Bill had made over the summer to a friend of ours visiting from Boston about Bucky Dent's famous home run against the Red Sox had stayed with me.

"Of course I do. He was a little guy, not a particularly good hitter. But he still had one of the most important hits in Yankee history."

I saw Yuri's face change when I said that. Again, I suddenly felt something shift between us, and my spirit lifted now that I knew we had a shared interest.

I now had the hook with him I had been looking for. Who knew that listening to Bill and his buddies drone on about baseball for all those years would finally come in handy?

But it clearly had.

Yuri lifted his chin and looked back at me. And that's when I saw the sparkle of light behind his eyes.

It glimmered so brightly, it was blinding.

4

"WHY do you love baseball so much?" Now I had Yuri's interest, and I wasn't about to lose it.

"The thing with baseball, Ms. Topper, is that everything about it is unpredictable. You never know what's going to happen . . . You can either make the right play or the wrong play. You don't know if it's the right decision, but you have to go with your instinct," Yuri explained.

It was interesting to listen to him. So much of what he said made me think about my own decisions in teaching. I never knew who would be in my class or what impact their personalities would have on my teaching. There were so many varied outcomes when I began my lesson plan each day. Every student could bring about a small ripple of change.

I couldn't wait to tell Suzie that I had made a breakthrough with Yuri.

"Good for you," Suzie said over coffee. "Just as I expected, these things have a way of working themselves out naturally if you don't push too hard."

"What would I do without you?" I teased her.

Suzie touched one of her metallic autumn earrings and flashed me a smile. "I'm not so sure. You'd be second-guessing yourself a whole lot more."

"At least now I have a plan of action. I'm going to use baseball as a way to get Yuri more interested in our lessons."

Suzie smiled. "Now, that's the Maggie I know and love. I can't wait to see what unfolds next with the two of you."

I was energized knowing I had Yuri's love of baseball to work with. Before I went to his house again, I needed to find a novel we could use for "literacy circles," the informal book discussions I did with all my classes.

That night, I was on my knees with a box of books I had picked up at last year's Scholastic Book Fair when Bill came home.

"Hey," he said as he placed his briefcase on the chair and pulled off his coat. "How was school?" From beneath the starched white cotton, I could make out the contours of Bill's strong back. A gold-and-navy-striped silk tie, its knot already loosened, dangled from his neck.

"Sorry, I haven't gotten around to making dinner yet. Maybe we can order in Chinese?" I suggested, peeling myself away from the box of books.

I heard him walk into the kitchen and open the refrigerator, followed seconds later by the familiar sound of the snap and fizzle of a beer can being opened. Then the unmistakable sigh that followed the initial gulp.

He walked back into the living room, pulling his tie off from around his collar. "Yeah, sure. Golden Wok sounds good."

"You know, you saved me today . . . That student I told you

about . . . the one I was having so much difficulty reaching? Well, I finally broke through to him, and it was with something so unexpected."

Bill gave me a puzzled look.

I went over to him and kissed him. "Listening to you all these years really helped me with this particular student. And you know, I was almost ready to give up on the tutoring thing."

"So stop burying the lede, Maggie. How did I help?" He took another swig of his beer.

"With baseball. It seems we have a little Mets-Yankees rivalry going on now."

"Really? Glad to be of service."

"Yeah, he's a die-hard Yankees fan. I somehow pulled out a Bucky Dent reference I picked up from you. It must have been divine inspiration at that moment."

He smiled, faintly amused.

"I've got complete confidence in you. You'll have him loving the Mets by the end of the year."

Bill went to the large chair and reached for the TV remote.

"Are you going to call Golden Wok, or should I?"

He was already flipping through the channels.

"I owe you for today," I joked. "Let me do it."

5

I looked for clues in every one of my students' work. A single sentence could illuminate whether something was going on in their families or shed light on a hidden anxiety. The best, however, was when it revealed a passion for something. I didn't care if it was music or baseball. What I believed more than anything was that having something in your life that you loved deeply sustained you.

I would not forget that my first clue into Yuri's heart was baseball, but I still hadn't found the right book for us to read together. After Bill couldn't remember what his favorite book was when he was twelve, I thought I might have a better chance with my brother, Charlie, up in Boston.

"That's easy, Mags. *Shoeless Joe*. It was the inspiration for *Field of Dreams*, and what baseball-loving twelve-year-old doesn't love that movie? Hold on a sec and I'll check who the author is. I think I still have my copy."

I laughed to myself. Charlie had apparently also inherited my affinity for dragging along his old books wherever he moved.

A few seconds later he was huffing and puffing into the receiver. "Got it right here. W. P. Kinsella. The kid's going to love it. It's got everything . . . baseball . . . magic. A legend coming back to life." He was getting excited just remembering the book. "The opportunity to right old wrongs . . ."

"You're amazing. I owe you one."

"More like ten," he kidded with me.

"Are you and Annie coming down for Thanksgiving?"

"Do you think Mom would ever let me off the hook?" I could see him grinning behind the phone. "Yeah, we'll be there. Is Dad going to serenade us with one of his new violins?"

"You bet your life . . . Expect Paganini in between courses."

"Can't wait, Mags. And let me know how the kid likes the book."

A few days later, I found myself standing in front of the door to the Krasnys' house with two copies of *Shoeless Joe* from the school library tucked inside my bag.

I had had a tiring day at Franklin. One of my students had inadvertently hit a girl in the back of her head with his backpack when he swung himself around. It was clearly an accident, but the girl who was hit complained about feeling nauseated, and the nurse had to call her parents and warn them to watch out for a concussion.

Needing a little fortitude before I tutored Yuri that afternoon, I searched through every corner of my handbag for a piece of chocolate or candy. I found a half-melted green-apple Jolly Rancher and popped it into my mouth.

. . .

KATYA answered the door. Today, her hair was pulled back in a ponytail, and she was wearing a long, nubby turtleneck sweater and jeans. Her eyes revealed a lack of sleep. And she again was clutching her elbows as if she were perpetually cold, even though the house felt warm and cozy to me.

"Thank you for coming, Ms. Topper." She stepped back into the vestibule.

"Oh, just call me Maggie. We'll be seeing a lot of each other."

As I stood next to Katya, I couldn't help but feel like a mammoth compared to her. I was five foot ten in socks, and today I was wearing boots. I seemed a foot taller than Katya. She was so slight and fragile looking, it was hard to squash the sound of my mother's voice in my head, insisting that Katya sit down and eat something. I wasn't ever going to be slender. My build was a bit more on the athletic side, despite the fact that I was never good at sports. Katya was too thin. Underneath her porcelain white skin, you could see the fine webbing of blue veins.

I knew it had to be enormously stressful taking care of a sick child. I still had my own memories of seeing Mrs. Auerbach transform from a robust maternal figure to a wiry and gaunt one, consumed by Ellie's illness. Knowing there was little I could do to put some more meat on Katya's bones, I offered her what I could, a sympathetic smile.

Katya didn't return the smile but chose instead to inch a little closer to me.

"You must have done something right with my Yuri the last time you were here . . ." She nibbled slightly on her bottom lip. Its skin was dry and ragged. "His spirits were so much better after you visited."

"I'm so happy we hit it off, but I think we are going to have a little Yankees-Mets rivalry going on." I laughed.

"Yes, he loves baseball above everything else," she said softly. "He's never had the stamina to be able to play it himself . . . His heart is not strong enough . . . But when he's watching it on TV, I can see he likes to pretend he's part of the team."

I soaked in her words. Underneath her charming Ukrainian accent, there was a doleful gravity. Katya looked away from me. A single ray of sunlight streamed in from one of the windows, illuminating only the right side of her face. For a moment, the sight of her took me back to my one art history class in college and the faces of the saints with their golden halos.

"It has not been easy for him . . . for us." I could see a faint film of tears forming on her wide blue eyes.

She shifted to her left side, and I saw her long white fingers clutch harder against the wool sleeves of her sweater.

"He was born with a heart defect called Ebstein's anomaly. I was lucky my husband and I had already emigrated from Ukraine before I became pregnant and that I gave birth to him here. If we were still in Kiev, he would probably no longer be with us . . ." Her voice cracked. "But we were fortunate that the head of the molecular biology department at Stony Brook University had chosen to sponsor my husband, Sasha."

"That *was* fortunate," I agreed.

"Yes," she said softly. "But Yuri's heart defect obviously was not."

TODAY, when I walked into the living room, Yuri was propped up in a reclining chair with a blanket over his lap. His blond hair was combed neatly, and he was wearing a striped rugby shirt that made him look a lot more cheerful than during our first meeting.

"Hey, champ." The nickname just came out. It's what my dad used to call my brother when we were growing up, and Charlie always seemed to like it. I forced my voice to be an octave higher than it normally was, in order to sound upbeat. "How are you feeling today?"

His eyes followed me as I pulled a chair closer to him and sat down.

"I'm okay." He brushed his bangs away with the back of his hand.

Yuri's eyes seem to flicker at me as I fumbled to retrieve my folder and the book from my bag.

"You look good. I like your shirt."

He patted his chest and smiled.

"Did you catch the Mets game last night?" He was eager to redirect the conversation immediately toward baseball.

I stammered for a second. I hadn't even known there was one. I had gone to bed while Bill was downstairs, probably watching the very game Yuri was speaking about.

"Piazza hit another home run. I think the Mets might actually have a chance at the playoffs this year . . . It's about time."

I laughed. "They just might, right?" I felt a jolt of fear rush through me. I liked baseball, but it was clear I wasn't on the same level of knowledge as Yuri.

"I'll give you a pass this time for not being on top of yesterday's game," he teased.

"I'll be better prepared next time," I promised. I pulled out the schoolwork that we had to cover and the copies of *Shoeless Joe*, and put them on the coffee table between us.

"So . . . I've got a few more things with me today for you. An outline of what we'll be doing in class over the next four weeks and, also, a little surprise."

His two blond eyebrows lifted in curiosity. "What kind of surprise?"

I pointed at the book to show him. "This year we're going to be having book clubs in class. So you and I are going to have our own right here."

I handed him the book and let him soak in the cover. On the front was a black-and-white photograph of Shoeless Joe Jackson in his old-fashioned White Sox uniform. The image was set against a colorful background of a cornfield.

"Have you ever seen *Field of Dreams?*"

"Are you kidding? That's one of my favorite movies! I saw it with my dad."

"Well, this is the novel that inspired that film."

Yuri made a puzzled face. "You mean it was based on a book?"

"Yep, I was surprised myself when I heard that."

"There were a lot of crazy things that happened in that movie . . . hard to believe they could happen in real life. Like all those ghosts of the original White Sox appearing out of nowhere . . ."

I laughed. "That's the magic of writing. Anything is possible."

He turned the paperback over and studied the excerpted praise from the reviews.

"So here's your copy, Yuri," I instructed. "You read the first two chapters by Thursday, and I will, too. Then we can start discussing it . . . We'll have our own literacy circle, just like I do with my other students at Franklin." I pushed myself back into my chair. "And I want you to read the book this time, not avoid it like you did with *Where the Red Fern Grows.*"

Yuri laughed drily. "It's about baseball, Ms. Topper, how could I not?"

"Do you remember that line in the movie when Kevin Costner hears, 'If you build it, he will come . . .'?"

"Yeah, of course . . ."

I tapped the book. The melancholy I had felt when I first entered the Krasny home was now fading.

"It's all in there." I smiled. "You'll see."

6

THERE is no dance class today, Sunday, so Katya rises late. Sasha's mug of black tea is still on the kitchen table; his coat is on the couch. Another unusually warm day, she says to herself as she opens the window and lets the morning light filter through their apartment. Outside, the garden seems eerily quiet. Not a single bird. Not a glimpse of a squirrel or a chipmunk.

As she changes into her clothes, she catches herself in the mirror. The muscles of her legs look like tightly pulled ropes. Across her back are the thin, angry red lines from Madame Vaskaya's nails scratching into her flesh. In her ears, she can still hear her teacher reprimanding her. "Shoulders back! Shoulders back!"

Satisfaction is an impossible emotion for Madame Vaskaya. When the girls do not lift their legs high enough, she inches closer to them and hisses into their ears, "Higher! Your arabesque should pierce the sky."

In the ribbon waist of her skirt, she keeps a lighter. If the dancer's foot is still not to her liking, she pulls out her lighter and flips the switch underneath their leg. Katya can still see her friend Olga's leg wavering as she struggled to keep it away from the flame.

In her drawer, Katya finds her bra and underpants and pulls them on. Then her tights. And, finally, a dress her mother gave her for her birthday, with flowers printed on the fabric.

She has promised her mother she will come over later that day and start making Easter bread with her. Her mother strove to keep God in their home, even though the Soviet government and its schools aspired to have a population of atheists. She could easily recall the afternoons of her youth when Katya and her sister were dragged along to church, where the pews were filled with little old ladies and hardly another child in sight.

But now the traditions warm Katya. She looks forward to seeing her sister, and the two of them will braid the dough into decorative shapes. Roses and crosses. Then, later on, they will boil eggs in onion skin to deepen their color before arranging them in a straw basket with the kielbasa, horseradish, butter, and cheese. She will stay until dinnertime, and then they will all go to liturgy together, carrying the ceremonial basket to be blessed by the priest. Sasha will stay at home with his books. Her mother was so upset when she learned Katya was marrying a Jew. She couldn't break her mother's heart and let her know the real truth, that Sasha considered himself only a man of science and did not share their belief in God.

"IT'S still so hot today, Katya!" her mother complains as she opens the door. A note of bewilderment tinges her voice. She has a scarf tied around her head and her hair tucked beneath it. Her large blue eyes welcome Katya like a prescient owl. Her apron, tied around her thick waist, is dusted with flour. "Such strange weather for April." She ushers her daughter inside. "It feels like July."

Katya walks into the kitchen. On the stove, there is a pot filled with warm milk and sugar. Another loaf is already in the oven, filling the house with its sweet, yeasty scent.

"Have you already started making the Paska?" Katya asks, naming the Easter bread.

On the counter, a large metal bowl is filled with flour, butter, and eggs.

"Yes. Yulia is in the garden, already braiding some of the dough."

Katya washes her hands and then reaches for a glass, filling it with water from the faucet.

"I'm so thirsty from the walk over," she remarks as she quickly refills her glass. She ties a spare apron around her, doubling the sash around her narrow waist. "I'll go help Yulia."

The garden glimmers in the sunlight. Yulia sits at the wooden table with a tray and a bowl full of dough. She is making long ropes and then arranging them into rosettes and crosses.

Katya sits down beside her and begins to help.

"Just like old times," Katya muses as she pinches her younger sister.

"The garden is so quiet today," Yulia murmurs. "I haven't seen a single bird. And not a sound from the beehive, either."

It was the same as Katya's garden, as if all of Mother Nature were asleep.

7

WHEN she returns from her mother's house, Sasha convinces Katya to go down to the river before sunset. The second day of such unusual warm weather has put everyone in a good mood.

"My friend Vadim told me the water feels as warm as it does in August," he tells her as he rifles through their dresser drawer to find his swim trunks.

"How can that be?" Katya asks skeptically. "It should still be ice cold from the winter!"

He shakes his head. "Maybe we didn't have as much snow this year?" He laughs and pulls her close.

He inhales the scent of her shampoo, the smell of chamomile and honey that he now considers to be Katya's distinct perfume.

"Go get your bathing suit and take a swim with me. Think of how lucky we are to be able to do this when it's not even May yet!"

She goes and retrieves her black one-piece from the bedroom and changes in front of him. He watches as she wiggles into the nylon maillot, and he feels the desire to kiss her, to unfasten the ties of the halter top and let it all come down again to the floor. He almost wants to tell her to forget about the swimming, that he'd rather she wrap her sinewy legs around him so they can spend the afternoon drowning in each other's embrace. But then she turns around, and he can see in her eyes that he has whetted her appetite to go take a dip in the water.

"Are you ready?" She pulls two towels down from where they were drying over the shower door.

They put on T-shirts and jeans over their suits and head outside.

"I've never seen such a beautiful sky." Katya beams as the horizon is lit with deep orange and gold. The sun resembles a fireball. The clouds are apricot-colored plumes.

"Yes," Sasha agrees. "It almost seems unreal."

THE Dnieper River flows through the center of Kiev, its pearly gray waters the same color as the inside of a mussel shell. Katya and Sasha hurry down the steps of the embankment, anxious to swim before the sun sets.

The river is full of fellow bathers. Old women, with their hair tied back behind babushkas, revealing saggy arms and dimpled thighs, wade knee-deep into the water. Young men flirt with their girlfriends by playfully splashing water at them. A lone man floats on his back, soaking in the last rays of the late afternoon light.

"Come!" Sasha yells as he barrels into the water. "They're right! It's so warm!"

Katya pulls off her T-shirt and jeans and wades into the river.

Sasha is already waist-deep. He extends his arms to her, beckoning Katya to come closer.

"Isn't this wonderful?" he says in a burst of uncontrolled happiness. Everything about today seems like magic to him. She is in his arms now, and their skin is slippery as they twist into each other.

The water is warmer than Katya had expected, and she delights in the sheer weightlessness of her limbs. Her leg glides effortlessly behind her in an arabesque, and the contrast between doing that movement in the water and silt instead of on the hard wooden dance floor is elating.

She arches her back and extends her arms onto the glimmering surface of the river, allowing the ends of her long hair to dip into the water.

"My little white swan," he whispers to her as he reaches to grasp her around the waist.

Her eyelids are closed and fluttering, and Sasha watches them with wonder before kissing her, a perfect smile curled at her lips.

AUTUMN had arrived. The trees were ablaze in scarlet and amber. A rain of acorns fell on the roof of the cottage in the mornings, so much that Bill wondered aloud whether there was a sniper in the trees with a pellet gun. We would always drink our coffee in a hurry and leave the newspaper in an ever-growing pile to be read later. We would kiss each other absently as we headed out to our cars.

At school, I had five different book clubs going within each of my three classes, one for each level of reading. I had one boy, Finn, a natural athlete who was also a very strong reader, and I also assigned him *Shoeless Joe*. I had spotted him early on as a Yankees fan, because he often wore a Yankees jersey to school and I sometimes had to remind him to take off his baseball cap in class. If Yuri ever became strong enough to join the class, it would be good for him to have a peer who not only was a good student but also loved sports as much as he did.

As we got deeper into our writers' workshop, I would start assigning roles to each student so they could lead the discussion. Each student would get a title like "Literary Luminary" or "the Word

Wizard" and would be responsible for finding a passage with beautiful or descriptive writing, or for picking out the new vocabulary. The children would soon become more active participants in the classroom, beginning to take charge.

In the meantime, the landscape outside had begun to shift from the last days of Indian summer into full-blown autumn. Wicks Farm on Route 25A was already in full decorative mode for Halloween. A huge black papier-mâché witch that had been in existence since I was a child towered over the pumpkin tent, and fake cobwebs were strewn over the storage sheds. I had stopped by to pick up a small pumpkin for Yuri. During the night, I had the idea that I would paint Yankee pinstripes on a pumpkin and write in Magic Marker the number of his favorite player. At the checkout, I saw they were selling apple cider, and I picked up a gallon jug to bring as a gift for Katya.

Pulling up to the Krasny house, I noticed a wreath made of corn husks and cranberries had been placed on the front door. It added a bit of well-needed cheer to the facade.

When I rang the doorbell, it wasn't Katya who answered but a tall, sandy-haired man who I assumed was Yuri's father.

"Hi," I said, extending my hand as he pulled open the door. "I'm Maggie Topper, Yuri's English language arts tutor."

"Yes, my wife told me you'd be coming for his lesson. I'm Sasha." He shook my hand and gestured for me to come in.

As soon as I entered the hallway, I was taken in by a toasty smell wafting in from the kitchen.

"Something smells delicious," I said as I inhaled the comforting yet unfamiliar aroma. "What are you cooking?"

He laughed. "Something from the old country. Kasha and onions."

I slid off my coat. "In my house, I only know pasta. Sorry to sound so ignorant, but what's 'kasha'?"

"Buckwheat groats. It's our comfort food." A soft smile formed at his lips, and I instantly recognized Yuri in him. "It's rich in vitamins. Good for the boy, you know?"

Sasha lifted his chin in the direction of the living room, where I knew Yuri was waiting for me.

"I brought something for you and Katya," I said, handing over the cider. "And a pumpkin with Yankee stripes for Yuri," I leaned closer and whispered. "But don't tell him yet. I want it to be a surprise."

"Well, if you brought us something, I have to return the favor . . ." Sasha lifted his hand as if stopping me in my tracks. "Let me get you a bowl of kasha," he insisted, clearly touched by my gesture. "In Ukraine, we believe we warm our souls from the inside out."

He lifted the jug of cider. "And kasha with a glass of cider is much healthier than with vodka!"

"DAD took the day off," Yuri told me as I settled into the chair next to him. The paperback copy of *Shoeless Joe* was bent at the cover, and several of the pages were dog-eared. My pulse quickened.

"Looks like you've been reading, Yuri."

He smiled, and the mirror image of his father was now reversed before me. "It's a good book, Ms. Topper."

Seeing that I had succeeded in finding a book he enjoyed made my heart leap inside my chest.

"How far did you get?"

"I got to the part when his wife's parents come to town. But they don't have any faith he can build his own baseball field, even though his wife and daughter do."

"And what did you think about the way the author wove the story of Joe Jackson into it?"

Yuri was quiet for a moment. "Well, the first thing I thought of was that Shoeless Joe's childhood sort of reminded me of Mariano Rivera's. My dad told me Mariano Rivera had no money when he was growing up and he loved baseball so much, he made a glove for himself out of strips of cardboard."

"I didn't know that." I loved that I was learning from Yuri.

"Yeah. My dad said when Mariano showed up for spring training, he was the only player without a glove or a pair of cleats."

"But he wore his talent," I added proudly.

Yuri beamed. "Yeah! Exactly! My dad loves all the backstories of the Yankees' 'Core Four.' Jorge Posada comes from Puerto Rico, Andy Pettitte from Baton Rouge, Mariano Rivera from Panama, and Derek Jeter from Kalamazoo, Michigan. Even though they're from different places and backgrounds, they all learned to work together and make each other shine."

"That's such a great way of looking at the team, Yuri."

"Yes, and my dad loves their histories because it shows anything is possible in America if you work hard enough. He said it wasn't like that back in Ukraine."

"I think that's why so many immigrants came to the United States for the opportunity for a better life," I agreed.

"But part of the book upsets me, Ms. Topper. I keep wondering if it's true. Did Joe really throw the series?"

I had read a bit about the 1919 World Series and the so-called Black Sox Scandal. Several of the White Sox players had been accused of accepting bribes from gamblers to lose the series, and once news of the scandal broke out, those players, including the great Shoeless Joe Jackson, were banned from baseball for life.

"I just don't want to believe he's bad," Yuri said with such innocence.

"You know, Shoeless Joe was almost illiterate," I explained. "The thing he loved most in the world was baseball. Probably if he had really understood what the gamblers were asking of him, he would never have willingly agreed to throw a game. Plus, he had a fantastic World Series."

Yuri looked toward the window. The bird feeder was without seed. Only a lone squirrel scampered on the deck. Wet leaves were plastered to the wood, like large brown footprints.

"I just hate to believe he did anything bad on purpose. Maybe if he did do something wrong, it was only a misunderstanding?" Yuri's earnestness was touching. "Makes you realize you need to be smart, even in baseball."

"Absolutely," I laughed. "And, in the spirit of baseball, let me present you with a very special pumpkin to usher in the autumn season." I lifted it from my bag with great ceremony.

"He has Yankee pinstripes, but no number," I pointed out. "Which one should we give him?"

Yuri's face beamed. I could hear his dad's footsteps coming closer, and when I looked behind me, Sasha was standing there carrying a steaming bowl of kasha.

"I like Jeter. But my dad loves Mariano Rivera."

"The pumpkin's for you, Yuri. So you choose."

He decided on Mariano Rivera. "Put number forty-two on it. He's great under pressure, doesn't even break a sweat, and always closes the game. Maybe it will bring me good luck."

I took out a Sharpie from my handbag and drew a 42 on the pumpkin.

"Anything for a bit of good luck, right?"

I lifted the bowl of kasha and inhaled its nutty perfume. The first spoonful filled me with a warmth that reminded me of my mother's cooking. The hearth of a loving home.

·   ·   ·

IN addition to bringing along the pumpkin for Yuri that afternoon, I also brought the writer's notebook I had made when I was at Teachers College. My students at Franklin had already been given a composition notebook, and I instructed them to decorate the cover with images that were important to them. It was a way to get a better understanding of the student's inner self.

The images they selected would be "artifacts" about themselves. They could be anything. A student could tear out pictures from newspapers or magazines. They could cut out letters and form words that described themselves, like "artist" or "athlete." They could use old family photographs or postcards they had collected from past vacations. After they were done, I'd cover their books with contact paper to keep them protected.

I had covered mine with a postcard from Capri, an old childhood photograph of my brother and me, and another of my parents on their wedding day. I added foreign stamps and stickers that I had collected when I was little. And since I love food, I also cut out a triangle of pizza and pasted on the letters that formed the word "tiramisu." I took images from Richard Scarry's *What Do People Do All Day* because it was my favorite book when I was three. Lowly Worm and Huckle Cat were like old friends of mine. I finished it with an excerpt from *The Velveteen Rabbit* about how only love can make us real.

I had just spent the morning and afternoon showing the notebook to all my classes so they could see what a finished one looked like. They had only glanced at it from afar on the first day of school when I mentioned it would be part of the writing curriculum for the year. Now, with those early days behind us, they perked up at the thought of doing a craft, particularly one they could tailor to their own specific interests. I passed around my notebook.

"Cool. So we can glue on it anything we want?" Finn asked. He was wearing a Derek Jeter jersey, and I couldn't help but be reminded of Yuri.

"Yes, Finn. Anything that sums you up."

"Can we use photographs?" Oscar asked.

"Yes, you can."

Rachel raised her hand. "Can we make it three-dimensional?" I could see she was going to be the artist of the classroom. Like Suzie, she had a certain way with her clothes, using them as a means of self-expression. Rachel wore bangles up to her elbow in different colors and came to school with mismatched socks poking out from her Doc Martens. Today she had clipped a purple feather into her hair.

"Well," I laughed. "You have to be able to open and close the book. So don't go crazy. But, yes, creativity is encouraged."

When he saw my notebook later that day, Yuri asked if he could hold it. Immediately, I saw how his mind was racing to connect all the assorted images that I had assembled to define me.

"You like pizza?"

"I love it, Yuri."

"And you've actually been to Italy?"

"Sure have . . . spent my junior year abroad in Rome. I was also able to travel a bit after my program ended."

"So you saw the Colosseum?"

"I did, Yuri." I smiled. "It was amazing."

"I'd like to go there one day. My dad got me a book on ancient Rome."

I nodded, impressed. Not many parents introduced Roman history to their twelve-year-old boys.

I could see his imagination taking over. "This is the kind of homework that I like."

I laughed. "Later on in the year, we're going to be writing an essay about each artifact and why you picked it. But for now, your assignment is just to start working on covering your notebook. Got it, champ?"

"Got it!"

Yuri's face always brightened when I called him "champ." I gave him a playful punch on his arm and handed him a blank composition book.

"But you should keep on reading *Shoeless Joe*, too, because I want you to also write a one-page description on which character you most relate to."

It was part of the curriculum to ask the students to write about something that they particularly connected with, and as we moved along in the year, they'd be responsible for writing in their notebooks every day. Some days it would be independent writing, and other days, it would be specific assignments. But the goal was to have them writing as much as possible.

"I can't wait to see what you're going to write about, Yuri," I said with unabashed enthusiasm. "And one of the things I tell my students is if you ever want one of your entries to remain private, all you need to do is fold over the page."

Yuri made a face. "Okay. That's good to know. But in the meantime, I can't wait for you to see my cover," he added cheerfully. "We both love baseball and pizza."

9

THE images on Yuri's writer's notebook cover were still sticky with glue. A photo of a ballet dancer. An image of a glass laboratory beaker. A Russian Orthodox saint. A Jewish star and an evil eye. Unsurprisingly, there were quite a few Yankees baseball cards. Derek Jeter. Mariano Rivera. But there was also a pizza slice, a sticker of a broken heart, and a picture from a magazine of a smattering of puffy white clouds against a pale blue sky.

"I'm not finished yet," he said as he handed it over.

"This is great, Yuri. So much interesting stuff here. We'll wait to put contact paper on it until you're completely done." His cover was full of clues. My heart quickened. I felt as though I had been given a broken glass with all the intricate and jagged pieces. Over time, I would witness the glass being made whole.

"Thanks. I had a lot of fun doing it." Today, his face looked fuller, and I felt happy that he seemed to be getting stronger. "I did the written assignment, too."

"Great." I picked it up and opened the notebook, eager to read his work.

The character I love the most in Shoeless Joe *is the wife, Annie. She never gives up believing in her husband, even though he is a real underdog. Everyone except her and their daughter think he's crazy and believe he can't make his baseball field. But Annie believes.*

She reminds me of my mother, who believes I will get better. She doesn't listen to anyone who tells her anything else. My mother believes in me just like Annie believes in Ray.

10

APRIL 28, 1986
KIEV, UKRAINE

FOR three days the sky burns brightly. By now, the men and women are all sunburned, even though it's only April.

But then a dark cloud hovers over the city and the sky turns black. The color of ash. People begin to whisper a rumor about a terrible fire at the Chernobyl nuclear reactor. That night, as Katya comes back from the dance studio, Sasha is sitting inches away from the television.

The news channel is reporting that three days ago, an accident occurred in the town of Pripyat, where the Chernobyl nuclear power plant is located. But the information is sparse and the images are limited.

"There is no need to be alarmed," the broadcaster recites on the air. "The government is taking all necessary precautions."

Katya walks closer to the television screen and sits down on the couch next to Sasha. She peels off her tights. Her feet are red and blistered from her toe shoes. They look like painful gnarled fists, and she begins to massage them.

The television flashes images of a helicopter dropping sand, clay, and lead on the fire burning from the nuclear reactor. Boron, a radiation-absorbing material, is also dropped.

"Comrades, the men and women of Pripyat have been evacuated. The people of Ukraine are safe," the broadcaster emphasizes.

Sasha is staring at the screen; his face is white.

"The accident is under control. Firefighters have been on-site since it occurred on Saturday," the reporter continues.

Katya curls her naked legs beneath her skirt and nestles her head against Sasha's shoulder.

"They tell us not to worry, my love." She reaches for his fingers and pulls them to her lips.

He wiggles his fingers from her grip. His eyes are still focused on the television screen. The flames of the reactor burn a hundred different shades. Red. Orange. Blue. White.

"The reactor is only one hundred kilometers north of us, Katya." Sasha is already doing calculations in his head. She can see the scientist in him. He is suspicious of the calming words the government uses so freely. He wonders what the fire from the reactor has already burned into the atmosphere.

She shakes her head. "The government says they have everything under control."

He is quiet before he says another word.

Then, underneath his breath, she hears him whisper, "But even they can't control the wind."

11

"THERE'S a new substitute teacher for the orchestra," Suzie whispered in my ear over lunch. She was wearing a hot pink silk tunic with little crystal beads at the collar and palazzo pants. She had even matched her lipstick with it.

"Mr. Barton had to go back to Iowa to take care of his sick mother."

We were sitting in the faculty room together, and I was looking at my limp tuna-salad sandwich. I had a hard time eating things that were cold when the weather began to change. My body had its own barometer. Once the air pressure dipped and the leaves started to fall, I wanted a thermos of warm minestrone soup and a piping hot grilled cheese.

"He's a fox," Suzie whispered, her face beaming. "Have you seen him yet?"

"Who?" I was thinking about what passages of *Shoeless Joe* I wanted to focus on when I saw Yuri later that day, so I was not concentrating on what Suzie was saying.

"The new orchestra teacher! Are you even listening to me, Maggie?"

I looked up at her and immediately noticed she had lipstick on her teeth.

"You've got a little, um . . ." I tapped my finger to my tooth.

"Oh, thanks." She ran her tongue over her teeth, erasing the smear of hot pink.

She was about to begin describing the new substitute when I suddenly saw her face freeze. "That's him," she whispered, leaning in closer.

I felt like we were two sixth-grade girls rather than the teachers. But in truth, immaturity has no age limit. I surreptitiously nudged my pencil to the ground and then turned my head as I was retrieving it.

Suzie was right. He was handsome. Dark brown curly hair and green eyes. Tall with broad shoulders, he was wearing a navy roll-neck sweater and pressed khaki pants. I wouldn't have called him a fox, but he was boyishly handsome. When I looked at his face more closely, I noticed a small red scar near his temple in the shape of a horseshoe.

"Ask him to sit down, Maggie." Her eyes were popping. Her voice was urgent. "Ask him, I beg you."

Out of the corner of my eye, I saw him walk toward the Mr. Coffee machine and pull out a cup from the dispenser. He tore open two sugar packets with his teeth and added them to his coffee.

I wrinkled up my face. "Why don't you do it, if you're so eager? I've got some classwork to do." I crumpled up the aluminum foil over what remained of my tuna fish sandwich.

I pushed my chair out and was just about to get up when I heard a soft, almost melodic voice behind me.

"Hi, I'm Daniel. The new music teacher. May I sit down?"

. . .

HIS voice was as smooth as custard, and the politeness of his request hit me in the gut. I had fifteen minutes before my next period. So I did what I thought anyone would do in my position. I went up and got Suzie and myself two cups of the worst coffee on earth and joined him.

"So you're replacing Mr. Barton, is that right?"

"Yes, I've been told he had to take time off for family reasons."

We both nodded. But I was now only half listening. My eyes focused on the tiny scar. It made me instantly curious; it suggested a story.

"All those students and all those varied instruments in the orchestra . . . That's a heck of a job. You must be very talented in order to know how to play all of them." Suzie shot me a look and I nodded again in agreement.

"Patient more than talented." He took a sip of his coffee and winced. "Hmm. Not the best, huh?"

"No. Probably better to fill up at Dunkin' Donuts before you come to class."

We all pushed ours away.

"So what do each of you teach?"

"I teach art, and Maggie teaches English language arts."

"Let me guess, you always liked to draw, and you always liked to read when you were kids."

I laughed. "Yep, that basically sums us up in a nutshell. And did you always love music?"

"Actually, yeah . . . I guess I did." When he smiled, he had a dimple on his left cheek. The reverse shape of his scar.

"You and my father both." The words tumbled out of my mouth before I could stop them.

Daniel arched an eyebrow.

I felt strangely invigorated, knowing I had something unusual to contribute to the conversation.

"Yeah, my dad played the violin for years, but now he's taken it one step further. He's become a luthier in his retirement."

"He makes violins?" Daniel's voice perked up. "I've never met a luthier before."

I watched as an amused expression appeared on his face.

"I mean, how often do you even get to say the word 'luthier'? Makes me feel like I should be raising a goblet of mead, instead of this crummy disposable cup."

I laughed; his sense of humor was a welcome relief in the stale and often depressing faculty room.

"Does he have his own workshop?"

"As a matter of fact he does." I couldn't believe my father's eccentric hobby would ever come in handy in impressing someone.

"That's so cool. Where?"

I leaned in close. "It's in my childhood basement."

"Well, some of the best art has been done in basements over the years . . . We all know that."

"True," Suzie chimed in. "I'll never forget the Jackson Pollock project I did that went awry. My mother was not very pleased with the splattered walls."

Fifth period was about to begin, and I reached for my bag. "In all seriousness, if you're ever interested in seeing a violin made, let me know. My dad loves to share his knowledge with those who can appreciate it."

"I just might," Daniel answered, gathering his things. He said it like he meant it.

12

IT is the day before May Day. The weather is still unseasonably hot. And even though the nuclear reactor continues to burn in Pripyat, the government has not called off the big celebratory parade. Everyone will be lining the streets to celebrate. Katya and her fellow dancers from the school will be performing in traditional dress.

The local children have been making paper flowers to glue onto twigs that they have been instructed to shake as they promenade toward Kiev's main square.

Madame Vaskaya has made the girls rehearse daily from morning until late afternoon. The costumes are heavy, the skirts and the crinoline. The bodices with metal buttons.

But the girls are still happy for the rare opportunity to wear a costume. Typically, they are allowed to wear only a black leotard and flesh-colored tights. One leotard is given to them each year by the school canteen, and they must wash it out every night and then dry it on the radiator. Their toe shoes are not pink satin, but are instead made from pulverized wood and paper and are a murky dark blue.

Katya is now a full member of the ballet corps. She dreams of one day becoming a principal and being able to travel to Budapest or Prague as, given the strict Communist regulations, it is all but impossible to travel to the West.

She began her studies at the age of nine, her body analyzed by a Communist committee of dance experts. Her head was measured, as were the length of her torso and the distance from her leg to her hip. The arches of her feet were scrutinized. One of the women on the enrollment panel asked her to mimic clapping rhythms to see if she could maintain a beat.

As a young girl, she had watched Anna Pavlova dance *The Dying Swan* on television. The performance, from the Kirov stage in Moscow, had been broadcast on the national station. Although she had been only eight years old, Katya could still remember being enamored of Pavlova's beauty and elegance, her impossibly long limbs that floated out from the stiffness of her corset and tutu. Katya had walked over to the screen and begun to mimic the movements of the ballet.

"Incredible!" her father announced as he sat in his armchair, smoking a cigarette. "We have our very own swan!"

Her aunts were sitting at the kitchen table, drinking cups of black tea. "Look, Oksana," they told her mother. "Ivan is right."

"She's naturally graceful," her mother's eldest sister observed. "You should take her down for auditions this September. The Kiev theater has its own ballet school, and they choose the dancers when they're no older than Katya is."

Her mother did not answer either her aunts or her father. She simply untied her apron and sat down at the table. On the television, as Pavlova extended her leg in a perfect arabesque, Katya saw the reflection of her mother's face captured in the screen. It wasn't a look of amazement at the sight of Pavlova, nor one of disinterest. It was the unmistakable expression of longing.

13

THE news broadcaster announced that the fire in Chernobyl had been brought under control by the brave firemen who risked their lives to extinguish the flames. But in Kiev, they are told to keep their windows shut and that people should not spend too many hours outdoors. At the ballet studio, one of the dancers tells Katya that her little brother and his entire class have been bused to a camp in southern Ukraine for the remainder of the year so they do not have to worry about the radiation in the air.

This word "radiation," Katya doesn't know what it means. You cannot see it or smell it, yet the windows of the apartment buildings remain shut even as the weather becomes increasingly warmer. The government sends pamphlets in the mail issuing precautions. Everyone should have two sets of shoes. One for outside and one for inside the house. Water for cooking should be boiled, the skins of fruits and vegetables peeled.

It used to be that Katya looked forward to waking every morning hearing the birds outside their ground-floor apartment. When they moved in, she was excited they were some of the few tenants who had a little garden of their own. But since the Chernobyl accident, she no longer awakened to the sound of sparrows singing, but rather the blare of the watering trucks that came every morning with their long hoses to spray water on the perimeter of the building to wash away the radiation.

She and Sasha would lie awake in bed, listening to the hissing sound. She would sense his disgust as he pulled the sheets off his body and went to the stove to put the kettle on.

"They can't wash it away," he spat one morning as the water truck left for its next destination. He pressed a palm to the window and shook his head. "And for how long do we keep the windows shut, when every day we go out to work and breathe in the air?" He turned to her. "They have no idea what they've done to us, Katya."

She hated when he talked like this. The government had assured them they had taken every necessary precaution to keep them all safe. But still it nagged at her that they had moved most of the children south for an early summer break. How safe could it be for the rest of them if it wasn't safe for the children?

Then one afternoon in late July, when the air was thick with summer, she noticed that someone on the higher floor of the apartment building had opened their window. A few older women sitting on some benches pointed it out to each other, too.

The next day, she noticed two more windows open.

"Do you think it means it's finally safe to let the outside air into the apartment?" Katya asked Sasha that evening. The last few weeks it had been unbearably hot, and although they had two fans, the air that circulated was heavy and warm.

"I'd rather we didn't," he said. "Though, logically speaking, if we're outside every day going to work and the shops, it's not going to really matter."

By the following week, nearly everyone in the building had opened their windows.

"What do you think it means?" Katya asked.

"I think it means everyone has surrendered." He took a deep breath and walked toward the windowsill. "And that life must go on."

That evening, they slept better than they had in weeks. They made love with the sheets pulled back and the window wide open. The lace curtains of the apartment undulated gently, a white flag fluttering in the breeze.

14

YURI filled his writer's notebook with stories and poems. And yet, his remained the only notebook I had yet to cover with contact paper.

"I still might want to add to it. It doesn't feel finished yet. Can we wait a bit?"

I saw no reason to say no. In the meantime, I asked him to write about the baseball he had glued on the cover, and that night, with Bill snoring beside me, I stretched out in bed under the covers and read his words.

I like baseball because it requires a lot of smarts. Tons of kids play soccer because it's easy. You run around and then kick the ball into the goal. But in baseball, you have to keep track of every player on the bases, so the math of baseball is always changing. My dad said he likes the statistics too, and I agree. Baseball is like live math. It's much more interesting than a textbook. I also like that you can always change the stakes every time you're up at bat. Each player has the power to change the game. Although my doctor told my mom it wouldn't be a good idea for me to play on a team, I collect base-

ball cards just like a lot of other kids. Sometimes I put the baseball cards around the edge of my wall and try and create the perfect team. It's fun to imagine who I might draft if I were General Manager. One day maybe I will be one of the guys who pick the players. I won't be able to play the game on the field, but I'd still be able to do something with baseball.

I looked down at his handwriting, which was so much neater than that of most of the boys in my sixth-grade classes. All of them were always in a rush to get out of the classroom, constantly looking at the clock and calculating how many more minutes until lunch or recess. They wanted to be outside or in the gym shooting baskets. My brother was like that, too, at that age, with the endless sound of him throwing a ball into the well of his mitt and the thwack of our neighbor's bat as they played in the backyard.

But Yuri's journal entry echoed what he had first told me when I discovered that he loved baseball: he relished the mental gymnastics involved, all the possible outcomes every time a new batter came up to the plate. Of course, Yuri and his scientist father would enjoy doing all the calculations together. For a little boy who couldn't play the game, it was a way for father and son to actively participate together.

I flipped over to the next page of Yuri's journal, where I had asked him to find a descriptive passage in *Shoeless Joe* that he liked and illuminate why he had picked it.

My favorite descriptive passage in Shoeless Joe *is when Ray Kinsella is sitting next to the author J. D. Salinger in Fenway Park watching a game, and he is telling him about his magical baseball field back in Iowa.*

"I'd like to take you there. We could sit in the bleachers I built behind left field. The hot dogs are like they were in the old days, long and plump and fried on a grill with onions, and you can smear the mustard on with a Popsicle stick, and there are jars of green relish."

I enjoyed this passage first because it describes food and I love to eat. I could imagine the plump hot dogs and the squirt of mustard. I don't normally like green relish, but even that sounded tempting. This passage was so good I asked my mom to make us kielbasa sausages for dinner that night. I wrapped the sausage in a piece of bread and added on extra mustard. I also liked the passage because when I closed my eyes, it made me feel like I was there sitting in the stands watching the players. I felt like I was at a live baseball game.

I closed the notebook for a moment and ran my fingers over its cover, with its pasted images of the baseball and the food. And the mathematical numbers and the laboratory beaker, which were references to his father. But the ballet shoe remained a mystery. And the image of the broken heart was painful as a wound.

15

I had been looking forward to the Thanksgiving break. My brother and his wife, Annie, were coming down from Boston, and Bill had agreed to spend the holiday with my family. I had hoped that the long weekend would give us more time together. Despite our moving in together, Bill had over the past few weeks seemed strangely remote and preoccupied. He had just landed two new corporate accounts, and the additional hours at the office made him seem almost brain-dead when he finally came home at night. In the city, if one of us was too tired, we would simply avoid going over to each other's place that night, rather than expose our crankiness to the other. But now, with each of us under the same roof, it was impossible to hide our bad moods.

"Do you really need to work until midnight on those lessons plans, Maggie?" Bill complained one night as I spread out my papers on the floor. I had thought working in the same room as he would be vaguely romantic, but he seemed distracted by my array of papers and folders on the ground.

It was true that I was bringing my work home with me, but how could I not? Mine was not the sort of job that I could surreptitiously do on a BlackBerry, like he could. Lugging home twenty-five composition notebooks each night was hardly subtle. And I realized that my conversations with Bill had been lagging lately. If I were being honest with myself, though, what little extra energy I had went not into asking him about the two new tech companies he had managed to secure insurance for but into my classes and working with Yuri. Yet, even as I noticed the distance between Bill and me expanding, my heart did not suffer from loneliness. It still seemed strangely full.

I knew I had Yuri to thank for that. As much as I wanted to simulate a comparable classroom experience for him, I had to admit there was something refreshing for me about tutoring him one-on-one. He was so bright and articulate, and there weren't any distractions when I spent time with him. In my classes at Franklin, there was always some child arriving late or leaving early, or that group of kids who were kicking someone's chair or passing notes. And now, as some of the students were approaching adolescence, a few had started to physically develop, and the rush of new hormones caused a whole other layer of distraction. There wasn't a middle school teacher around who didn't feel they were sometimes teaching to a circus. But Yuri was completely focused when he was with me. All my best ideas and enthusiasm poured out of me, and I'd be lying if I said I didn't start imagining myself to be his Annie Sullivan, my lessons opening a whole new world to him.

Even Katya was starting to warm up to me. During my last visit, she touched my arm and told me that Yuri had given his copy of *Shoeless Joe* to his father to read.

"Those two really love their baseball," she remarked, clearly amused. "Me, not so much." That was the first time I heard her laugh.

"After the break, I'll ask him to write about something other than baseball, so don't worry," I promised. "You'll see."

She thanked me and opened the door. Outside, the autumn air smelled of maple leaves. "Have a happy Thanksgiving," I said as I stepped off the porch.

"You too. We don't have such a holiday for gratitude back home. It's a nice tradition."

I nodded in agreement on my way out. When I reached my car, I looked back at the small shingled house, and the blinds were still open in the living room. Through the window, I saw Katya walk over to Yuri and put a comforter over him and kiss him on the forehead.

AT my parents' house, the scent of roasting turkey and stuffing laced with sage from my mother's garden filled the air. My brother and Annie were already sitting in the living room, drinking spiced cider, and my mom was busy in the kitchen, her holiday table sparkling with polished silver and glimmering porcelain.

Dad offered Bill and me cups of the cider, but Bill asked if there was any beer instead.

I bit my lip. It's not that my family was all that sophisticated, but we had our rituals. Spiced cider on Thanksgiving. Mulled wine on Christmas Eve. Was asking for a Coors on Thanksgiving really that necessary?

My dad gave Bill an affectionate squeeze. "There might be some beer in the fridge in the garage. Why don't you go out and see what you can scavenge?"

I lowered my head as Bill went toward the mudroom and into the garage. I felt a pang of guilt run through me. Was I being unnecessarily harsh on Bill? I would never have been bothered by any of this when we were in college, yet now I found myself increasingly irritated.

"You can take the boy out of the frat house, but not the frat house out of the boy," my dad teased. "I guess he's not going to be up for hearing me play some Mozart on my new violin."

I took a sip of the warm mug of cider. "I wouldn't count on it, Dad. But I can't wait."

He wrapped an arm around me and kissed me on my head. "That's my girl," he said. "Can I convince you to come downstairs and see my latest masterpiece?"

Bill hadn't emerged from the garage yet. "Sure, I'd love to," I told him. I put my mug on the kitchen table and followed him downstairs.

WHEN I was growing up, my father spent a lot of his time on the road, traveling to places that felt far away and cold. Minnesota. Wisconsin. North Dakota. "Now, if it was Italy," my mother would tell us over the dinner table when my father's chair seemed glaringly unoccupied, "I'd make him take all of us!" Still, you could see how much she missed him when he was gone. When the phone rang after nine p.m., she'd leap from her chair to answer it. Her voice changed when she spoke to him. It was a softer, gentler voice than she used with my brother and me. She'd pull the cord, stretching out its rubber coils as far as it could reach, trying to find some privacy from our prying ears. All we could ever make out of their conversation was her asking whether he was okay, and her concern if the midwestern weather delayed his return. But as children, we rarely spoke to him on the phone. "I'm calling long-distance," Dad would remind us if either Charlie or I picked up the receiver. When we'd ask our mother how he was faring, she'd always tell us the same thing: he missed us and the food in his hotel was downright awful.

But now, with his retirement, my father finally had pockets of spare time. Nothing would stop him from doing what he loved, not even his chronic arthritis, which I knew caused him great discomfort. He had worked his whole life to be able to pursue his dreams of carving violins, and he wasn't going to give that up.

He relished creating his workspace. A large farmhouse table he had found at a garage sale was placed in the center of the basement, surrounded by large metal shelves where he kept his many supplies, chisels, and saws. The box of metal files and the menagerie of glass jars that stored his brushes and solvents were kept within reach.

On the walls he had put up posters from classical music festivals from around the world and one from the violin-making workshop he'd taken at Oberlin College. There was also one of an enlarged Stradivarius violin and another of an Amati. During the course of my childhood, I had seen my own share of basements. Some had pictures of Ferraris taped to the walls. And I had seen far too many posters of Farrah Fawcett in her red bathing suit. But no one I knew had images of rare stringed instruments pinned to the painted Sheetrock like my dad did.

"Look at this," he said as he lifted a freshly planed sheet of spruce. He brought it up to his nose and inhaled. "I can almost smell the juniper berries."

I leaned over and brought my face closer. He was right. The scent was intoxicating. The wood was as smooth as marble. It was hard to believe my father's hands could make something so beautiful.

On the shelf rested a violin he had nearly completed. "The varnish is almost dry on this one," he appraised, holding it gently by the scrolled neck. The back side, made from flaming maple, filled the surface with elegant, rippling lines.

"I wish you played, honey. How I'd love to make you a violin."

I laughed. "Sadly, I didn't inherit any of your or Mom's musical talent, nor did Charlie. Don't forget, I had one year of lessons and I was awful!"

"I know." He shook his head playfully. "One of life's cruel jokes on me."

I patted my dad on the back. "What I find amazing is that I have an Irish American father making violins in the basement. If only mom's ancestors came from Cremona instead of Sicily, they'd be so proud."

"The irony is almost poetic." A smile crossed his lips. "I'm still waiting for your mother to perfect her corned beef and hash."

WE went upstairs and found my brother and Bill sitting by the television, watching football.

"Come sit down, Mags." Bill patted an empty space on the couch. "It might be good research for you and Yuri. You can show him you know about sports other than just baseball. Broaden the kid's horizons a bit . . ."

"I don't think Yuri likes football," I said. There was already an empty can of Coors on my parents' end table. Another one was now in Bill's left hand.

"Don't be so sensitive, Mags. I was only kidding. Come sit down."

I didn't want to sit down.

"You need to stop thinking about that kid twenty-four-seven," he muttered as he pulled the can away from his lips. "It's really not healthy."

My eyes grew wide. "What did you say?"

"Nothing, Mags. I just don't think it's normal how much you're fixating on that kid. It's not like he's our son. He's one student you're tutoring, for God's sake. You don't have to talk about him every second."

I could feel my blood pressure rising. I wanted to scream at him, and the only thing holding me back was that I didn't want to make a scene in front of my parents.

Bill tried to backpedal. "C'mon, you know I was just joking."

"My mom needs some help in the kitchen," I said as I excused myself. "And you're hardly funny."

An hour later, we were seated around the dining room table with mounds of food on our plates, watching my father carve the turkey, but my appetite had all but left me. Instead, my mind wandered to what the Krasnys' Thanksgiving table would be like. I doubted they'd have baked ziti alongside their roasted yams, but I knew their sense of gratitude would put ours to shame.

16

SEPTEMBER 1984
KIEV, UKRAINE

SHE had met Sasha when she was nineteen. She and her friends had just finished their examinations and were waiting to hear whether they'd be invited to dance in the Kiev ballet corps. They had all agreed to go out to a disco that night and celebrate.

He told her later that he had noticed her as soon as she walked in, with her black-market jeans, ribbed turtleneck sweater, and silver hoop earrings. Her blond hair was pulled into a high ponytail, her blue eyes lined in kohl. From the side, her chiseled profile resembled a Russian Nefertiti.

He was smoking Kosmos cigarettes with his friend Andrei, the two of them huddled in a corner enveloped in a cloud of fumes. Modern Talking, a rock band from West Germany, was blaring from the speakers. When the song ended, he approached her at the bar and offered to buy her a drink.

She said she drank only water. He ordered a finger of vodka and joked with her, as she sipped from her glass, that others might think she was outdrinking him.

They danced afterward, their bodies bumping against each other, his hands encircling her tiny waist. Above them, the glitter ball sprinkled white dewdrops of light, and as the music pulsed through the room, she twirled and danced with a freedom that was so foreign to her long days of strict ballet.

"You must be a dancer," Sasha whispered into her ear. He thought of silvery fish that glided through the water so effortlessly. Katya was like that. She didn't need to think about how her body moved to the music; it was innate.

That night, after her friends piled into a taxi, she let him press her against the cement wall outside the disco and kiss her good night. After they departed, he couldn't stop thinking about her. He could still feel the weight of her body against his chest, the sensation of her warm hand in his. The scientific part of him thought of the connection between the moon and the tide. This was how Sasha felt when Katya left him, as though there was an invisible pull between them.

He couldn't wait for Katya to call him, even though he had written his number down and slipped it into her jeans pocket. He remembered her mentioning that the theater was in the midst of casting their next ballet performance. So the following Monday, after she and her friends lined up in the hallway to see who had made the first cuts of the tryouts, she exited the studio of the state ballet academy and discovered that Sasha was waiting outside, flowers in hand, hopeful she'd have good news to share.

His eyes lit up as he saw her, and he took large strides to meet her. When their fingers grazed each other's, he felt a spark traveling down the length of his body. It ricocheted across her eyes, like a flash of brilliant white lightning.

17

OCTOBER 1984
KIEV, UKRAINE

SHE learns that he is finishing up his doctorate in cellular biology and that he is five years older than she. Their first year dating, he will take her to the river and tell her about the importance of the current, and its impact on the fish spawning cycles. He will speak about the rhythms of life and the secrets of nature. As much as he is used to being clinical in his research, he realizes he is no longer objective when he is in Katya's company. When he sees her approaching, her gait is so light, she seems like she is floating, with no weight at all.

And yet, she communicates in layers. He learns quickly that her words don't always reveal what she is really thinking. He must watch her body language instead. When she is frightened, she pulls her arms close around herself. When she is distracted, her fingers pull at the stray hairs behind her ear. When she wants to be loved, her doe-like eyes lift to meet his gaze. Water to water, he thinks as their eyes lock. The first time he makes love to her, he feels the echo of her heartbeat against his. And when he leaves her the next morning to go to the university, he can still hear its pulse against his like a phantom memory. It is then he realizes that the rhythms of love mimic those in life. Like a song one can't shake from one's head, carried wherever we go.

ONE Sunday, when Katya is not dancing, Sasha brings her to the city's municipal gardens. He packs a picnic lunch of kielbasa and a loaf of black bread. He spreads a blanket down and watches how nimbly she tucks her legs underneath her skirt. Her lips are the color of beetroot, her face pale as the moon. He leans over to kiss her and feels she has the capacity to alter time for him. When he is in her company, it is as if he is moving in perpetual slow motion.

After they eat, they stretch out on the blanket and feel the sunlight on their faces. He reaches for her hand and tells her about the butterfly effect.

"The flapping of a butterfly's wings in the rain forest can alter a hurricane hundreds of miles in the distance. Isn't it amazing that something so small can change the outcome of another thing so far away?"

She turns toward him, her hip resting against the blanket, and smiles. He kisses her again, but this time he takes his hand and holds it behind her head, smoothing the tangles of her hair with his palm.

She thinks of all the small things that had happened weeks earlier that led her to go to that disco that night. Normally, she was not as social as the other girls in the school. She hardly ever went out dancing, as her feet were tired and sore at the end of the day. She had just finished her exams, and had she not been standing next to Elsa at the bus stop that afternoon, she would never have been invited to go.

And yet, here she now was, with Sasha's hand threading through her own. The warmth of his fingers penetrated her whole body.

"I had no idea butterflies held that much power in their wings."

"They do," he whispered back. And when he closed his eyes again, he envisioned Katya onstage at the national theater, her arms stretched out and her body leaping from the ground. Weightless, as if she had harnessed the wind.

18

WE drove home from Thanksgiving without talking to each other. Bill turned the knobs of the radio to WFAN and listened to the commentary on the Cowboys game. I gripped the steering wheel, wondering if he even cared that I was upset.

Although the sports talk coming from the speakers filled the air, the silence between Bill and me was painful. I didn't expect him to apologize for drinking beer and isolating himself in the TV room all night, but I at least thought he'd apologize for his callous comments about Yuri on the ride home. But he made no effort at small talk. I heard only Steve Somers talking about how great the Cowboys had played.

When we pulled into the gravel driveway, the house was pitch dark. We had left without turning the outside lights on, and now we fumbled over the uneven path to the front door.

Once inside, I switched on the hall light and hung up my coat. "I'll be up in a minute," Bill muttered as he draped his coat on the couch. "I want to check on the game." His striped tie was loose around his neck, his shirt half-untucked. An image of Bill at our senior-year formal flashed through my mind. He had made my heart swoon that night when he arrived at my dorm in his tux, a bouquet of roses in his hand. The person before me now seemed as if he were from another planet.

"It's ten o'clock, Bill." Even I knew the last football game that day had been over for several hours.

"Not in California," he said as he sank into one of the upholstered chairs. "I'll come upstairs soon."

I turned my back and headed up to our bedroom. The night air had seeped inside, making the house as cold as an icebox. I had grown up with a father who insisted we not turn on the heat until after Thanksgiving. "A sweater is the best insulation," he'd tell my brother and me before handing us woolly cardigans from the closet.

Now, as if performing a familial Thanksgiving ritual, I went over to the thermostat and raised the heat to 70 degrees for the first time that season. I changed into my pajamas and pulled the covers down, sliding into the bed before turning on my reading lamp.

The week before, I had bought the paperback of Toni Morrison's latest novel, *Paradise*, and had placed it on top of my copy of *Shoeless Joe*. Bill's side of the bed was a fluffy mound of pillows. I pulled one over to my side and propped myself up like a princess. As much as I wanted to begin Morrison's new book, I reached over for *Shoeless Joe* instead.

I wanted to end the day with something that would lift my spirits, and I knew there was more magic in those pages than just a baseball field constructed in the middle of a farm in Iowa. There was the magic of a little boy reading with his night-light turned on and his mind ablaze with possibility. I wanted to believe that even if Yuri's weak heart prevented him from ever playing baseball, his mind had no limits. It could still be filled with dreams.

. . .

I returned to school the Monday after Thanksgiving, curious to see how my students had enjoyed their mini-vacation. I had given them one assignment over the break to write a short essay on one of their family's traditions. I told them about my father's refusal to turn the heat on until Thanksgiving and about my mother's ritual of sun-drying her tomato harvest every September.

"So it doesn't have to be a Thanksgiving tradition?" Jennifer asked.

"No. It just has to be one that is unique to your family," I clarified.

They all had their writing journals on their desks. The covers colored the room from afar.

Just as I was about to ask Finn to read from his journal, Oscar got up to sharpen his pencil.

"Really, Oscar?" I strained to put humor into my words. "Do you really need to sharpen your pencil right when we're about to start reading from our notebooks?"

The class giggled.

"No, Ms. Topper. It's just . . ."

"It's just that it seemed like a good idea at the moment?" I gave a playful roll of my eyes. "Let's save the sharpening until we need our pencils, okay?"

"Yes, Ms. Topper." He sat back down at his desk and slumped a little in his chair.

I smiled to myself. I was improving. Last year, I would have lost my cool with Oscar and probably disciplined him too harshly. I was slowly learning and getting better at using a little humor to get kids to correct their mistakes.

I turned back to the class. "Who wants to read first? How about you, Finn?"

Finn blushed slightly and opened up his notebook, then lowered his head. After a few seconds of hesitation, he began to read:

My family has a tradition of eating Mallomars the first week in September. That's when they first hit the shelves at Waldbaum's. Most people don't realize that Mallomars are not sold in summer. They're a cold-weather treat and are only available September through March because the chocolate melts easily. My mom buys my sister and me our own box every September 1st. And when I unwrap the yellow foil of the box, it almost feels like Christmas.

Who didn't love a good Mallomar to initiate the winter months? There was something very special about the thin coating of chocolate that encapsuled the soft, pillow-like marshmallow. It had the slightest bit of saltiness that made it difficult to eat just one. Finn's journal entry made me want to get in my car and get a box or two for myself right away.

"You've made me downright hungry," I told him. I walked closer to his desk and smiled. "Well done."

"My mom packed some in my lunch box. Do you want one?"

I smiled. I loved how kids took everything so literally.

He reached down to get his backpack from under the desk.

"No, you should save it for yourself, Finn."

He suddenly reminded me of Yuri. It was more than their mutual love of baseball or their intelligence. It was that they had each retained their own sense of boyish sweetness at a time when it was vanishing from so many of their peers.

"This in-between state of boyhood at the cusp of young manhood . . . it's such a beautiful but fleeting time. I don't know. I wish I could capture it in words," I told Suzie that afternoon.

"It's just . . . we're at our wit's end with so many of these kids," I said. "But there's still a kind of translucence to them now. They're like these eggshells, and if you look closely, you can see the young adult emerging beneath the skin."

Suzie nodded. "I know . . . I see it in their bodies and faces. They're becoming more chiseled; the baby fat is falling away."

"Even their voices. Some of them are already a little deeper, right?"

"I was a mess as a teenager. I wish my skin looked as translucent as an eggshell," Suzie said. "You make it sound so pretty, Mags."

I laughed. "That's what my mother always says about me. I'm always trying to find a sliver of light when everyone else sees shadows. It's the romantic in me." I smiled ruefully.

19

THAT afternoon I drove up to Yuri's house and rang the doorbell, excited to see him after the five-day break.

The Krasnys' front door still had a corn husk and cranberry wreath outside, and as I waited, I could hear the sound of classical music coming from inside.

"Come in," Katya said, waving me into the hallway.

"I should turn down the stereo," she apologized. "Sometimes when I'm restless, I put on a little Tchaikovsky and it soothes me. Back in the Soviet Union, I trained as a dancer."

"Why does that not surprise me," I said as I placed down my handbag. "You have a dancer's build."

Katya forced a smile. "So I've been told. But it was a long time ago, and a world away."

By the time I walked into the living room and sat next to Yuri in his large, plush chair, the music had come to a halt. Katya's mood, however, still lingered in the air.

.   .   .

YURI had finished *Shoeless Joe* and now pushed his most recent journal entry in front of me.

"You said to write about family traditions. I wrote about making pierogi with my mother."

I laughed. "How did you know the way to my heart is through my stomach, Yuri?"

"I didn't know that." His eyes widened. "Does that mean I automatically get a good grade?"

"It depends on the writing, not on the food," I teased him. "And you're the second student of mine today to write about something they love to eat."

"It's more than just enjoying the pierogi. I like to make them with my mom." He reached over and handed me his journal.

In my family, food is a very important tradition. My Mom celebrates Christmas and Easter, and my Dad is Jewish. So one thing that we love to do as a family is make pierogi every New Year's Eve because it's one holiday when we can create our own tradition. I help peel the potatoes for the stuffing while my mom rolls out the dough. Knowing how much work goes into making them, my Dad says he can feel our hearts in his stomach. He says he can taste the love with every bite.

"My mom and I used to make tomato sauce together every Sunday," I confided. "I'd skin the cloves of garlic and chop it very fine. She'd sauté it in olive oil and ask me to go downstairs to get one of her jars of canned tomatoes. When she poured the tomatoes into the pan, it was like she was releasing summer into our kitchen."

I looked at Yuri in the big recliner. He was so much smaller than Finn, his frailty made more pronounced by his oversize chair.

"Food connects us to our past, doesn't it?"

"Yes, I think so . . . that's why the hot dogs and mustard bring back memories of baseball for Ray."

"That's right, champ." A memory of my father and me sharing a hot dog at a Mets game flashed in front of my eyes. "Did you finish the book over the break?"

"Yeah, I did." He looked over to the paperback on the coffee table, its brown surface strewn with marble composition books and pencils. "I told my dad it was a book I wished didn't have to end."

20

KATYA had been surprised when Sasha confided to her that he was Jewish, but even more taken aback when he said he did not believe in God. She heard her mother's voice in her head, telling her that even though religion was technically forbidden in the Soviet Union, you still must believe in God, you just couldn't talk about it. But Sasha's lack of belief was due not to his devotion to Communism or the motherland, but to his family's history.

"My father spent the first three years of his life in a cave in Western Belarus. The Germans came to their town and sent half the Jews to a concentration camp and the others to the ghetto."

Katya's face tightened. "How horrible," she uttered, trying to be sympathetic. "I know my family had their own suffering during the war."

Sasha tapped a spoon against the wooden table. "Don't tell me another sob story about your grandfather who got trench foot and had to have three toes cut off," he half joked.

"Four," she informed him. "The flesh closed off like a club."

"Everyone from here to Siberia has a similar story."

"Don't talk like that," Katya whispered as she leaned closer to him. She couldn't help but be afraid someone would hear them and report them for being anti-Communist.

His face twisted. "Those stories are different, Katya. My grandfather's neighbors, all full-blooded Ukrainians, were more than happy to point out every Jew's address to the Nazis."

"I'm sorry," she apologized. Katya now avoided his eyes. She suddenly felt ashamed. "I can't begin to imagine."

"You don't have to be sorry. You weren't even alive then." He forced a laugh.

She managed a meek smile, but secretly she had heard her grandmother say derogatory things about Jews in the past. But, then again, her grandmother was distrustful of almost everyone, she thought as she tried to appease her sense of guilt.

He looked at Katya, with her delicate hands wrapped around the ceramic mug, and wondered if he should tell her the rest of his family's story.

"Maybe I should stop. I don't want to upset you."

She shook her head. "No, Sasha. Tell me the rest. I want to know."

He pushed his mug toward the center of the table and settled himself back in his chair. Then he began:

"My grandfather had scouted out the caves days before the roundup and instructed my grandmother to run there with the children if she ever heard gunshots. He had already left some provisions. Bags of grain. Jugs to collect rainwater. And most importantly, a millstone to grind the grain for bread."

He ran his fingers through his hair, then cleared his throat before continuing.

"They lived there for three years. And as horrible as it was, my father and his family had a better chance of surviving in that freezing cave than any other place in Ukraine."

She felt nauseated picturing his family's ordeal, but she forced herself to focus on each word.

"When they finally returned to their village after the end of the war, they were the only Jews left."

"Too much suffering, Sasha . . ." She didn't know what else she could say. She had heard vague stories about how the Communist government had ordered many of the Jews to settle in far-off Uzbekistan and Kazakhstan after the war. She was glad that Sasha's family had been spared that fate, at least.

"Indeed," he said, lifting his mug and finishing the last sip of his tea, "And now you have my family's sad, dark story." He had in fact edited out much of it—refrained from telling her the stories his grandfather had told him about the earlier pogroms and the torching of the family's house by angry mobs. Instead, he tried to steady himself by falling back into the beauty of Katya's eyes.

"Is that why you don't believe in God?"

"I don't believe in God for many reasons, Katya. For one, I consider myself a man of science. But even deeper than that, I can't believe a god would stand by and let so many perish so senselessly, so violently. Not just Jews, but how many millions of Russians died in the last fifty years?" he challenged her. "And I believe nearly every one of those souls died praying to a god that didn't listen."

"I understand why you say this, but I still believe . . . Do you think I'm ridiculously naïve?"

"No." He smiled. "Of course I don't."

She looked at him with soft eyes.

"The same way you said you can't imagine a god that doesn't listen, I can't imagine a world this beautiful that could be created without God's help."

He folded his arms and studied her as though he were examining a rare species. Sasha was someone who was sensitive to all changes. The slightest alteration in temperature or sound level would not go unnoticed by him. With Katya, he noticed that the light in the room changed along with her. Some women can enter a room and be lost in a sea of other people. But Katya illuminated the space she occupied. Her internal light burned as bright as a candle.

"You're something special, Katya," he told her. "Can you still date a heathen like me?"

She blushed. "I think I can. But tell me, do you at least believe in heaven?"

"How could I not?" He smiled at her. "It would be painful for me to imagine that I could only enjoy your beauty in this life. I must believe it waits for me in the afterlife, too."

She laughed and reached for the warmth of his hand.

THE first time he saw her dance, he felt something stir. Even though she wasn't center stage, his eye was drawn to her. A magnetic energy that pulled him with each of her movements.

"Never in my life have I seen anything more beautiful than you up on that stage," he gushed to her after the performance.

Her cheeks flushed red. "I was just one of many dancers up there, my love. It was Alexandra who had the principal role."

"My eyes were only on you," he said, leaning in to kiss her over the bouquet of wildflowers he had brought.

He wanted to tell her more, but he felt that he didn't have the right vocabulary to express himself. The language of dance was so different than that of science, and Sasha's inability to adequately articulate himself frustrated him terribly. He sensed one could never capture in words the ethereal, for it was the opposite of holding something concrete in your hands. And perhaps that was yet another one of the mysteries that made Katya so alluring to him. Her magic could not be quantified nor contained.

A few months later, over a late dinner in the square, he proposed. The ring was a simple gold band in a red velvet box, and she slipped it on crying, "Yes! Yes!" over and over again. That night, as he made love to her and her hand reached out to touch him in the moonlight, he felt perhaps he had been wrong all these years. There was something that was equally as inexplicable as all the senseless pain and death in the world. There was the beauty. And there was love. He didn't utter those words into Katya's ears, but he thought them to himself anyway. There just might actually be a god.

KATYA'S family is not pleased when she tells them that she and Sasha plan to marry.

"But he'll be one of the youngest doctoral candidates in his department," she says, hoping to win their approval.

"Suffering," her mother whispers to her as they wash the Sunday dinner dishes together. "His people attract it in their bones."

21

THE weather after Thanksgiving became positively glacial. The mornings were so dark, it was hard to force myself out of bed. As Bill showered, I found myself hitting the snooze bar of my alarm clock for just a few more minutes of sleep. At least the holiday spirit was already in the air. During my drive down Moriches Road, many of the homes were swathed in Christmas lights, and the store windows on Route 25A were bedecked in artificial snow and colorful ribbons. It always gave me a slight energy boost as I pulled into the school parking lot.

Suzie was standing in the main entrance that morning. She had already begun to wear her most outrageous sweaters to beckon in the holidays. Today's outfit was a cardigan with little silver paillettes attached to the fuzzy wool. Her hair was tied in a topknot, and her lipstick was cherry red.

"Good morning, sunshine," she teased when I walked in. I was clutching a cup of Dunkin' Donuts coffee, and I felt like I still had pillows under my eyes.

"I need whatever you're having," I groaned as I lifted my paper cup in her direction. "The coffee isn't doing it for me, even with two extra sugars in it."

"I had some tofu scrambled eggs this morning. Can I bring you some tomorrow?"

"Maybe not." I laughed. "But you might be onto something . . ."

She gave me a little nudge with her staple gun and lowered her voice. "Daniel was chatting about you the other day. Seems he's in the market for a new violin."

I looked at her, puzzled. "What does that have to do with me?"

"Your father, silly. He asked me to check if your dad might talk to him about it."

I laughed again. "Ah, my father, the luthier . . . who knew it would make me so popular."

"Unless it's just a ruse to spend more time with you." Her eyes twinkled. "You should tell that Bill of yours that someone else might have eyes for you. A little jealousy might reignite the flames of passion." She giggled again.

"You're a nutcase, you know. But thanks for making me feel at least better than roadkill today. You're a good friend."

OVER the summer, my mother had handed me a clipping from a Dear Abby column, in which a teacher described how, for the past twenty years, she had assigned her sixth-grade students to write letters to their future eighteen-year-old selves. She asked them to consider who they might become at that age and what their dreams of the future were. Once the children finished their letters, she asked them to self-address the envelopes and promised to mail them back on the afternoon of their high school graduation. "You can't imagine how much joy this brings them," the teacher had written in the column. "And for me as well, to make a connection with them one more time before they enter the adult world."

"Isn't that a fabulous idea?" my mother had gushed over coffee and biscotti. "I think you should make this one of your classroom traditions, too."

I lifted the small newspaper clipping in between my fingers and reread the teacher's description in the fine print. "It does sound like something that could end up being quite meaningful."

"For *you* and the students." She clasped her hands in front of her, and I noticed she was wearing my grandmother's vintage gold ring with the oval amethyst in the center. "I mean, can you just imagine their surprise when it arrives in the mail all those years later, right when they're about to leave for college?" She made a small clucking noise with her tongue. "They'll think it's amazing getting a letter they wrote when they were only twelve."

"No kidding." I was tickled by her overflowing enthusiasm. "You're amazing to clip this out for me." And I didn't say no when she offered me the last biscotti.

THE letter-writing assignment was such a great idea, I couldn't wait to mention it to my colleagues. There were two other English language arts teachers at Franklin Intermediate besides me: Angela Tizzo and Florence Konig.

Both Angela and Florence had been at the school for over twenty years. They reminded me of Laverne and Shirley. One was tall with frosted blond tips on her feathered locks, and the other was short and round with cropped gray hair. They were close friends, with grown children of their own, and seemed to have an opinion on everything. But since they had both shared their favorite projects with me when I arrived at the school, I thought it would be the right thing to ask whether they wanted to do the letters with their students, too.

"It's a great idea in theory, Maggie. But do you really think you could keep three classes' worth of letters every year for the next six years? Just think of all that paper!" Angela said dismissingly. They were a Greek chorus of naysayers.

"And what if the child moves? You'll be so disheartened if the letters don't reach them," added Florence. "Imagine getting all those envelopes returned to you."

"I just wanted to give you the option," I said, trying to ignore their pessimism.

"Why don't you do the book cover project?" Angela suggested. "The kids love designing their own cover art."

"Or a diorama of their favorite interior scene from a book? That's also a winner with the kids every year," Florence said.

"But they've already decorated their writer's notebook covers," I answered. I was going to stand firmly behind the letter assignment. "This project encourages them to imagine their future."

"When you've been teaching for nearly twenty-two years, Maggie, come back and tell me if you still want two hundred letters in a filing cabinet in your basement."

I rolled my eyes. I hadn't known Florence for very long, but I did notice that while all the other teachers changed the decorations within their classroom each year, and even went so far as to pick a motif for every season, Florence had maintained her theme of "butterflies" since last September, when I first started at Franklin. Who even knew whether she'd kept it every year since she first began teaching twenty years before? Regardless, what I did know was that Florence didn't seem like she had any intention of cycling in anything new and fresh in her classroom.

I gathered up my folders and made a gesture that I was excusing myself. "No worries," I said to Florence and Angela. "I never did mind a crowded basement. I've learned from my father, it's a sign one has a creative life."

22

"FOR today's class, we're going to be doing something a little outside the box," I told my sixth graders as I handed them each some ruled paper and an envelope.

"I want you to write a letter to your eighteen-year-old self."

The children all looked at me, slightly perplexed. On the back of each envelope, I had written in bold letters, *A Letter from the Past with a Message for the Future.*

Finn raised his hand. "Is this kind of like a time capsule?"

I smiled. "In a way, Finn. It's a time capsule of your current thoughts and aspirations."

The students started murmuring among themselves, and a few of them exchanged curious glances. It sounded like a beehive was starting to hum.

"I want you to write to yourself where you think you will be when you're eighteen. What you hope you're doing then. What you think will be important to you." I gave them a big smile. "Be creative. And think deeply on this one. When you're finished, I want you to put your home address on the envelope."

After a few initial grunts from a couple of students who said they weren't sure what to write down, the kids got to work. Lisa asked me twice if I was sure it was okay if what she wrote actually didn't happen by the time she graduated. "Part of the beauty of this exercise is that you're documenting what your dreams are now, at this very moment," I reassured her. "Whatever happens, happens. But I know you'll appreciate then looking back and seeing what you had once hoped for."

Eventually all the kids lowered their heads toward their papers, and the sound of their pencils filled the room. I heard Zach lean over to Finn and whisper that he thought he'd get drafted by an NBA team.

"Oh, I almost forgot," I interrupted. "Don't lick your envelopes. When you're done, I want to be able to savor your letters both now and again in six years before I mail them back to you. I'm going to hold on to them, and I promise you, you'll see them again the year you all graduate high school."

A wave of smiles passed over the classroom, and the children's reaction to the assignment had rejuvenated me. Florence and Angela might not love my letter-writing idea, but the kids did, which felt like a victory to me.

AS I went to my car that afternoon to drive out to Yuri's house, the first snow of the season began to fall. Tiny snowflakes hit my windshield as I turned my wipers on and headed in the direction of the Krasnys'. By the time I pulled next to the curb of their house, the snow was close to an inch thick. As I walked toward the door, my feet appeared to be making footprints in a dusting of confectioners' sugar.

Katya offered to make us all cups of cocoa to celebrate what felt like the first day of winter. Inside, she had the heat on high, and Yuri was dressed in a pair of baseball pajamas.

"He's feeling a bit weak today . . . He had a bad night. Sometimes his heart is racing so much, it's hard for him to sleep."

Her fatigue weighed down the air.

"Please let me know if there is ever a time he doesn't seem up to seeing me. We can always take a break and I'll come back again when he is feeling better."

"I know," she answered softly. "I nearly canceled today, but he always seems more full of life after you leave."

I smiled at the compliment. "I think he's a boy who enjoys conversation. There's so much in that head of his and so much wisdom that seems far beyond a boy his age."

I could sense immediately that my comment had struck a nerve with Katya. Her eyes looked sadly out the window. "I wish more than anything that he could be around more children. And you know in this country . . . friendships begin with the children. The parents start bonding at the playground while their children are in the sandbox. But for Yuri and me, it's always been just us."

She pulled at her sweater, the sleeves lengthening like long knitted tubes over her fingers.

"There was never going to be a playground for him or for me. And even when he was well enough to be in school, Yuri had few friends. He has always seemed older than the other kids." Katya let out a sigh. "We really did try to keep him in school, but it was too much for him. He was constantly getting sick and he just didn't have the stamina for it. So when we moved to this district last year, the doctor really pushed for him to be tutored at home because of his condition."

I nodded, but then an idea occurred to me.

"I realize that attending school every day is too much for him, but I wonder if I might be able to bring him in to class, even for one visit? It might make him feel more connected if he met some of my other students."

"You're always so kind, thinking of his best interests." She twisted her sleeve's cuff in her fingers. "I really do appreciate it. But let's see what the doctor says. I made another appointment for Yuri today. I can't say anything without asking him first."

I understood her need to be cautious. Yuri's immunity was low due to his limited exposure to other children and all their germs. The last thing I wanted to do was compromise his system. But I knew there was more to a child's development than what could be found in books or scripted from pen to paper. A child also needed friends.

23

KATYA'S father sells fur hats at the outdoor market every Sunday afternoon, while her mother collects the money and socializes with the customers.

For her wedding day, her father takes one of his prized white fox pelts and makes a small neck scarf for her.

"A little bit of glamour for my ballerina," he tells her as he kisses her outside the town hall. Her sister, Yulia, brings a small nosegay of flowers for Katya to hold.

The two families do not mix well. They stand rigid as the young couple signs their marriage certificate, Katya dressed in a simple white dress and Sasha in a suit that had once been his father's. In the bureaucratic room, the only adornments for the celebration are the Soviet and Ukrainian flags hanging from a small metal pole in the corner.

Later that afternoon, the garden of Katya's childhood home is lit with small lanterns. Outside, they drink sparkling wine from plastic cups as the guests blow clouds of smoke into the cold air. She still wears the white fox scarf her father made for her, her long neck wrapped in a layer of the softest fur. Her aunt has baked a special casserole made from wild mushrooms, and Katya eats it heartily, for it's her favorite dish.

When the frigid temperatures become too much for even the hardiest guests, they pile into Katya's family's living room and put a bootleg Beatles album on the record player.

Two of Katya's classmates have been invited to the festivities. Their long hair has been braided and coiled on top of their heads, so they resemble elegant giraffes. They pull the men off their chairs and get Sasha's friends from the university science department to dance. The men's faces already red from the vodka, they blush even more as they attempt in vain to keep to the rhythm of the music.

After midnight, when all the guests have left, the newlyweds return to Sasha's apartment on the other side of town. Once inside, he cups her cheeks in his hands and kisses her passionately on the mouth.

"My beautiful bride," he says as he lifts her onto the bed.

As the radiator hisses in the background and the windows fog with steam, her legs wrap around him, and he can swear he senses the merging of their heartbeats. A union that pulses through his veins.

24

JANUARY 1987
KIEV, UKRAINE

THAT first year they were married now seemed like a distant memory to Katya. Their whole apartment in Kiev was no bigger than her living room in her new home on Long Island, the one they had enough money to put a down payment on. The tiny stove with the flickering pilot light that she used to cook Sasha's favorite meals on seemed prehistoric compared to her General Electric range, which turned on without her needing to strike a match. And she was still amazed by her American refrigerator. It seemed as big as the old wooden wardrobe in her grandfather's house in the country. It could make ice or offer water just at the tap of a button.

She bought groceries now in the Grand Union. Five different types of milk, pyramids of pasta, even an entire aisle just for cookies. Katya's mother had spent nearly every afternoon standing in line with her ration coupons just to get the most minimal ingredients. The government back in the Soviet Union controlled even their stomachs: the amount of milk, meat, and cheese allowed per person in each family. But here, she could push her cart through the gleaming store and get everything she needed in one efficient sweep. In the beginning, she felt as though what she saw around her couldn't last. How could one have fresh blueberries or bananas in the middle of winter? Even the department stores enthralled her with their endless sales. She could hardly believe her good fortune nearly every day she ventured outside.

And yet she had been so unsure when Sasha first told her that he wanted to apply to leave Ukraine after Gorbachev announced those with Jewish ancestry could emigrate.

But after her dance injury, she was of no use to her ballet company until her ankle healed. And after that, she had no idea if she would ever regain her strength or the ability to dance professionally. What other options did she have if she could no longer perform? With no college degree, she would probably end up working in a shop, the very kind her mother waited outside of all day just to buy kielbasa.

DESPITE moving halfway around the world, Katya still kept a pair of her old toe shoes in her bedroom drawer. They were the only ones she ever wore that were made of pink satin, the pair intended for her debut solo performance. In her third year in the corps, she had finally been given a short solo, and she knew that if the ballet master was pleased with it, she would be closer to becoming a principal in the company.

She had vigorously practiced her solo for weeks. The choreography for the role was intense, with much of the dancing *en pointe*. Then, the morning before opening night, when she was rehearsing in one of the studios by herself, she heard the most horrific crack in her ankle as she turned in her pirouette. She let out a scream of agony. But the rest was a blur to her. It was Lana who rushed into the studio and discovered her wailing on the floor.

The X-rays revealed a devastating Weber B fracture to her left ankle. The morphine had numbed the pain, but the doctor did not soften his words.

"We can set the bone with a metal plate and pins, but you will be on crutches for several months. The plate and pins will have to remain in place for a full year."

Sasha arrived at the hospital shortly after Lana had notified him, and now he held Katya's hand.

"Are you saying I can't dance for a full year?" Her voice cracked as she tried to spit out the words.

The doctor looked grave. "Yes, I'm afraid. The ankle is shattered, and the surrounding soft tissue is severely damaged. I hate to be the bearer of bad news, but you will have to stay off this foot for that long."

Sasha was about to say something comforting, but Katya held up her free hand and stopped him.

"My career is over," she said. "Even if I can regain my strength in a year, I'll lose my place in the company. There are at least a dozen dancers vying for every spot."

"You could recover faster than the doctor believes." Sasha tried to be hopeful. But Katya couldn't bear it. Sasha, the man who proclaimed to look at things only through a scientific lens, was now trying to ignore the facts to spare her pain. It made her feel even more hopeless to think that he'd resort to such implausibilities because he was so desperate to soothe her.

"Sasha, there are girls who find crushed glass in their toe shoes because other dancers are trying to sabotage them. Do you think they're going to wait for me to get better and return?" She willed herself to force back her tears.

She lifted her eyes toward the X-ray lit against the white screen. "Look at that," she insisted. The film showed the shattered bone. "What more do you need to see? It's medical science. The facts are indisputable."

25

THE kids were eager to hand their letters back to me. When I collected them, their eyes were full of life, as if they had just written down a secret they couldn't wait to share.

That night, I hunkered down early with the letters and a cup of peppermint tea. Bill had called to say he was working late, and I was excited to read them without any distraction.

I smiled as I went through them. Most of the students wrote about how they hoped they had gotten into a good college or had made the varsity team in high school. Lisa Yamamoto had filled her envelope with three paper cranes for good luck. Another student mentioned wanting to live in Australia. Jack, who was short for his age, hoped he had grown to be six feet tall.

Finn's letter was especially poignant. He described his little sister, who had already had several operations on her left leg. He said he hoped that by the time he was eighteen, she would finally be able to run with him outside, and that one day he might go to medical school and discover a way to help others like her.

I held on to his letter a little longer than the others. I've realized that there are many things you can teach a student. You can teach them math or grammar, and you can encourage them to be more patient or careful with their homework. But there are other things that are more difficult to teach in a classroom, such as compassion and kindness. These were qualities Finn had clearly taken to heart, by witnessing his sister's struggles at home.

I had often seen Finn's mother waiting outside for him in the school parking lot when I was leaving to head over to Yuri's. Finn never failed to wave to me before he ducked into their white Volvo station wagon. He'd always raise his chin a bit and swing his backpack a little higher over his shoulder before he pulled open the door. "Bye, Ms. Topper," he'd holler in my direction as he slipped inside.

On a few occasions, I had taken a peek at Finn's mother sitting behind the steering wheel. She always wore her blond hair in a pony-tail, and a pair of fashionable tortoiseshell glasses framed her gaze. In the backseat, I had noticed a little girl who looked like a miniature version of Finn's mother. I had imagined his family as the preppy sort who all had matching canvas beach bags with their initials mono-grammed in the middle. But after reading Finn's letter and learning that his little sister had a physical handicap that limited her activities, my perception of him and his family changed. Now, when Finn talked with such passion about playing sports, I realized he wasn't just play-ing for himself; he was playing for his sister, too.

WHEN Yuri handed me his letter at his house the next afternoon, I realized in the flurry of describing the assignment during my last visit that I had overlooked one essential detail: I had forgotten to tell him not to seal it.

Now, as I held his letter, I saw that he had not only sealed the envelope but had also taken great steps to decorate it. Knowing all the extra work he had done, I didn't have the heart to ask him to put the letter in a new, open envelope.

"Did you enjoy writing it?" I asked as I slipped the envelope into my bag.

The other children had all seemed so excited when they handed over their envelopes to me. But Yuri seemed more pensive now.

"I think it was a good assignment," he said after a lengthy pause. "It made me think hard about what I really hope for in life. And it was helpful to put it down on paper."

"I'm glad you got something out of it." I smiled at him. I could see he had caught sight of a red cardinal on the snow-dusted deck.

"I wonder when you mail it back, where I'll actually be," he said softly, again his eyes focusing on the little red bird.

I immediately pictured him in his graduation gown and mortarboard. A diploma grasped in his hand. I imagined him several inches taller. His voice deeper. Maybe even having a girlfriend.

"You'll be savoring your last day of high school, champ," I answered confidently.

He nodded, and I saw his gaze lift as the bird flew off into the distance.

"Cardinals, Blue Jays, Orioles," he listed, changing the subject. "So many baseball teams take their names from birds. Did you ever wonder why?"

"Actually, Yuri, I never thought about that before."

"It must be amazing to have the ability to fly. To be so much closer to the clouds. To see everything from above."

"Yes. It must." I reached over and squeezed his arm. "Should I try to arrange to have your letter delivered by carrier pigeon?" I teased him.

He turned his head now and faced me. His pale blue eyes again struck me with their sparkle. "Oh, Ms. Topper, wouldn't that be something!"

LATER that afternoon when I returned home, I studied his envelope more carefully. Yuri had written his address in meticulous block letters on the front side. And on the back, underneath where I had inscribed *A Letter from the Past with a Message for the Future*, he had taken the sealed flap of the envelope and used it as inspiration for a baseball diamond. With an array of colored pencils, Yuri had created the most beautiful drawing of a baseball field with ears of corn growing in the distance. His own field of dreams.

To be honest, I thought about holding his letter over a pot of boiling water and steaming it open. That was how curious I was to read it. But I stopped myself before going that far. The weekend before, I had purchased a metal filing cabinet for the express purpose of storing all the kids' letters. I had written on a large manila folder *High School Class of 2006* with a thick black Sharpie. I put all the envelopes from my classes at Franklin in the folder before filing them away in the cabinet. I went downstairs and slipped Yuri's letter in with the other envelopes.

When I got upstairs, I shut off the light. I had completed my end of the assignment for now. There was nothing more to do than wait until the following year, when I would give my new students the same assignment. And by that time, the high school class of 2006 would be one year closer to their graduation.

26

THERE were two images from Soviet television that Katya still carried in her head. The first was of the helicopter dropping sand over the burning reactor in Chernobyl, and the other was of the Jews in Moscow chanting, "Let us go! Let us go!" On each occasion, she remembered that she sensed the world was changing. Not just because of what was being broadcast on the television but because of Sasha's reaction to it.

Both times, she had noticed that his body language changed as he sat on the sofa watching. His shoulders grew higher, his torso pitched forward, and he knotted his hands in front of him. In the reflection of the glass, she saw his eyes fixate on the television screen.

She had never realized before marrying Sasha how much anti-Semitism there was in Ukraine. But in the short time they had been married, she already felt that it had become an oppressive part of their lives. Sasha's experiments were often sabotaged in the laboratory. Their second spring together, he was passed up for yet another promotion, even though she knew he was far more qualified than his colleague who was offered the job.

Some days he would come home and could barely talk to her because he feared that if he unleashed his rage, he wouldn't be able to stop himself from breaking everything in their apartment.

So it came as no surprise to her that when Gorbachev announced that anyone with Jewish heritage would be allowed to leave the Soviet Union, Sasha started making plans to leave even before he expressed them to her.

When he finally brought up the subject to her over dinner one night, she looked up from her plate and saw his eyes determined to convince her that they should leave.

"If you were dancing this year, Katya, I might not pressure you. But this may be our only chance for a better life."

"But at what cost, Sasha?" She raised her arms. "What will happen to our families when we leave? They'll be labeled the relatives of traitors! They will suffer the consequences for our selfishness. I couldn't bear that."

"An opportunity like this might never happen again, Katya. Gorbachev can ban the emigration as quickly as he approved it."

Her mind was racing, and she could barely concentrate on what Sasha said afterward to convince her it was the right decision. It was easier for him to leave, as both of his parents had passed away and he was an only child. But she still had her parents and sister to think about.

"We can start thinking about building our own family when we get there. In a place where our child will have every opportunity." She felt his hand on top of hers and his eyes fixed on her own. "Not one where there are quotas on how many Jews can apply for university. Not one where the name Krasny has people labeling him a Yid."

He came closer to her and pulled her into his arms. "Look at me, Katya."

She lifted her head to him.

"You have to trust me, my love. This is the right thing for us."

Her silence was her confirmation. He read her answer in her eyes. The next afternoon he went to get an application.

27

OCTOBER 1987

KIEV, UKRAINE

KATYA'S mother said three words to her when she learned they
were applying to leave.

"You're not Jewish," she muttered. The inflection of her voice was
cold as steel.

"No, but Sasha is . . ." Katya stood in the threshold of her parents'
kitchen. Her mother, sitting at the table, refused to look at her.

"Mama . . ."

Her silence was deafening. And Katya found herself imagining
what was traveling through her mother's mind at that moment. *You
failed us as a ballerina. You failed us when you married that Yid. And now
you're failing us by leaving us here alone in our old age.*

When her father came home an hour later, Katya was loath to
tell him.

"Papa, I have some news," she said tentatively. She was fully aware her voice sounded different whenever she spoke to her father. She instinctively regressed to a little girl when she was near him.

"Sasha wants to emigrate to America."

He flinched. "I thought we were born in this shithole and we'll all die here. I didn't know you could just pick up your stuff and go."

"It's not a joke, Papa. Gorbachev is allowing the Jews to leave."

Her father went to the refrigerator, pulled out a bottle of vodka from the freezer, and poured himself a glass.

After the first few swallows, he lumbered into the living room and lowered himself into his chair.

His face softened now as he finished his drink.

"That poor ankle of yours robbed you of the life you were meant to have." He waved for his daughter to come closer to him and then pulled her into one of his strong hugs. He smelled of alcohol and cigarettes.

"I'll get the pins out in the United States, and maybe the physical therapy there is so good that I'll be able to dance again in an American dance company."

"My little *lapushka* already has her American optimism."

"Not completely, Papa." Her eyes welled up with tears. "I'm afraid they might do something to you and Mama if we leave."

"We're old. What more can they do to us?" He shook his head. "Do you think they can crush me?" He lifted his glass and took another swallow of his drink. "If they call me the father of a traitor, I'll survive. And so will your mother."

But in the kitchen, Katya could hear her mother smashing pans.

28

SOMETIMES when Katya looked around her home, it struck her how little trace there was of the woman she had left behind in Kiev. It wasn't just because of all the comforts of American suburbia that now surrounded her: the stocked refrigerator, the Pontiac in the driveway, or the living room with its nice wooden furniture. Instead, because her life now focused on caring for Yuri, it was as if she had been transformed into an entirely different person from who she had been back home, where nearly every moment had revolved around her ballet.

When she first learned that she would have to stop dancing for at least a year, she felt as though she had lost all sense of self. Before, she had always trained her body like an athlete. But now, for the first time since she was nine years old, she no longer spent her entire day rehearsing in the studio or in the company of her fellow dancers. In secret, Katya felt as if she would never make a full recovery, that her body had betrayed her. Already she could see she had lost the once predominant muscles in her thighs and calves. She had certainly not grown heavy, but her body was no longer as hard and tight as it once had been. With every day that passed, she began to let go of her dreams of ever returning to dancing.

So when Sasha proposed the idea of emigration, Katya agreed because she felt that her homeland had nothing left to offer her. She told herself she had to believe in Sasha and his instinct that they would be better off in New York than staying in Kiev.

But immigrating to America was not an easy thing to do. Sasha had to prepare a statement for the United States government detailing his troubled life as a Jew under Soviet persecution. He spent hours at their dining room table working on an old typewriter, describing all the incidents of anti-Semitism he had endured, first at university and later at his workplace. He detailed all the obstacles that management had put in his way to prevent him from advancing in his career. And even after all that, the papers for immigration required multiple signatures, including from Sasha's boss and even from the power company saying they had paid all their bills. Even the local library was required to sign the application, stating that neither Katya nor Yuri had any overdue books. God forbid he left the country with a bound edition belonging to the motherland.

Sasha also had to endure meetings with his boss and colleagues, where they denounced him for being a traitor, and Katya's mother was so hurt, she could now barely utter two words to her. Most painful was her sister, who also begged her to reconsider. At night, Katya would stare at the ceiling and count the days until they could leave for a place that would grant them a clean slate to start their new life.

WHEN they finally left for the transport city of Chyop, they were not allowed to bring more than one hundred dollars out of the country. But they carried with them a tin of caviar and a bottle of Armenian cognac, because they had heard that in order to cross the border, they would need luxury items to offer as bribes.

In their two suitcases, they packed only a few items of clothing, some photographs of their family, and their wedding portrait. At the last minute, Sasha insisted that Katya also pack the pair of toe shoes she had worn to rehearsal on the day of her accident.

"Take them," he urged, noticing that she had placed them in the box of belongings they intended to give to their friends and family.

"I won't be dancing again." Her voice now had a practiced tone of stoicism and steely reserve.

"You don't know that, Katya. And, look, they still have a lot of life in them."

He took them out of the box and handed them to her to pack. He was right: the toe box was only slightly scuffed, and the ribbons were still pristine. How she had marveled at them the first time she placed her feet in them and laced the ribbons up her ankles. Now, they seemed like relics from another life.

She muttered another protest but finally acquiesced. When they arrived in the States, Katya hid the shoes in her underwear drawer, wrapped in a silk scarf. She placed stockings and socks over them, a small pushpin and sewing kit by their side. There, they remained untouched, a secret she shared with no one.

EVEN if Katya were healthy enough to resume her dancing career, she knew there would still be a number of other obstacles. The major ballet companies were all in Manhattan, but Sasha's work required them to live close to Stony Brook University, in the eastern part of Long Island, nearly two hours' drive from the city. So instead, she spent her days refining her English at the local community college and adjusting to her new life.

Sasha went off to work every day to a world she knew little about. He dressed carefully in the morning, buttoning his collared shirt and always wearing a tie, despite the fact that very few of his co-workers wore one. She remembered with a sweet fondness that afternoon he came home and withdrew a piece of paper from his briefcase that had the words "Yankees" and "Mets" on it with a question mark next to each one.

"The men at the office love baseball," he informed her. "They told me that if I'm to become a true American, I should pick a team."

"Really?" Katya was incredulous. "They said that?"

"Well, I think they were joking, *lapushka*, but it would be a nice way for me to bond with them. I tried to talk to them about soccer, but they had no interest.

"I've been doing a bit of research. The obvious choice is the Mets," he told her. "They're on a winning streak this year, despite the bad press of Darryl Strawberry's drug problem.

"But, as you know," he told Katya, "I've never been one to pursue the obvious."

She laughed and sat down beside him at the kitchen table, the piece of paper with the two baseball teams in front of them.

"Most of the men at work are Mets fans. All of them are, actually . . . except for one guy named Carl." Sasha took a pencil and tapped it against the table. "Carl told me you can't get more American than the Yankees . . . Joe DiMaggio, Babe Ruth, Lou Gehrig, and Mickey Mantle. They're all national heroes."

Sasha bent over to his briefcase again and withdrew two heavy books wrapped in protective cellophane he had gotten from the library. Both were on the history of baseball.

"I started reading about it during my lunch break. I think I'm going with the Yanks," he said.

Over the next few weeks, Katya witnessed Sasha transform into an expert on a sport that was wholly new to him. He studied each game. He marveled at the mental strategy that success in the sport required. He memorized the names of the players and their numbers, and showed a gift for keeping the records of each team in his head. She knew that this was part of her husband's personality. He thrived on the ability to make a decision and then immerse himself in the research so deeply that he became more knowledgeable than his peers. But secretly Katya envied his ability to claim something as his own. While he embraced America's oldest pastime, she longed to find something in this new country that she could claim with an equal passion.

AS Sasha settled into his routine at work and started to make friends with his coworkers over his new love of baseball, Katya struggled to find fulfillment in her small excursions to the grocery store or in her English classes. She could call herself neither a workingwoman nor a stay-at-home mother. Rather, she was an isolated immigrant who had no real friends except the few other women who went to the library every Tuesday night to learn English. So she was thrilled when she discovered, six months after they arrived in New York, that she was pregnant. For now, she had a new sense of purpose. She began to drive by playgrounds and imagine herself sitting on a bench with the other mothers watching their children playing in the sandbox. She envisioned colorful birthday parties with ice cream cake, a delicacy she had never heard of before she arrived in the States, and the idea of a cake made purely of ice cream thrilled her. Infinite scenarios of maternal happiness flooded her mind.

Sasha and she became even closer knowing they were bringing a life into the world together. She no longer felt fragile from the shadow of her old injury but rather felt heartier than ever. Sasha helped by preparing old-world dishes for her that were nourishing and that he believed would make their child strong. He made goulashes and lots of kasha. He kept a bowl of boiled eggs in the refrigerator and started a garden in their backyard so he could grow his own tomatoes, carrots, and onions. He joked that if he had a son, they would watch baseball together, perhaps spend their weekends playing catch.

At night, the more romantic side of him would return, and he would place his hand on her growing belly, telling her there was nothing in the world as beautiful to him as the sight of her with their growing child. "A love within my love," he whispered as he held her close. He would read to her, aiming his voice in the direction of her womb. He read them novels in English, telling Katya that the three of them would master the new language from the words of a good book.

Although Katya's pregnancy was uneventful, the birth itself had been painfully difficult, and Yuri had presented blue. The pediatrician initially thought he might have a blockage in his lungs. But when Yuri's color returned, another doctor in residence thought he heard a heart murmur. After three exhausting days of meeting with specialists and undergoing countless tests, including an angiogram, they were told it was a far more severe condition. Yuri had been born with a rare heart defect called Ebstein's anomaly.

"Basically, Yuri's heart is different than most children's, because his tricuspid valve sits lower than normal in the right ventricle." Dr. Rosenblum took out a pencil and drew a diagram on a piece of paper for them. "This means that as the child's heart develops, part of the right ventricle merges with the right atrium, and that portion of the heart becomes enlarged and impacts its ability to work properly."

Katya sat there in the doctor's office while Yuri, only a few days old, slept in her arms. At that time, her English was only good enough for her to make out a few of the words that the doctor said. But Sasha, whose English was much better, appeared to be taking in each sentence. Every few minutes, Sasha would ask the doctor if he could translate for Katya, because he knew the darkness of not knowing what was happening caused her great distress.

The pediatric cardiologist told them that it was hard to predict what sort of life Yuri would have. Ebstein's anomaly had a myriad of potential outcomes. Some children could live years without having any problems, while others struggled quite profoundly with breathing, irregular heartbeats, and other complications. Some children may never require surgery, while still others might need intervention as early as three or four years old.

"The best thing I can tell you," the doctor said as he stood up and shook Sasha's hand, "is to keep a careful eye on him. Any changes in color or breathing, you call me immediately."

As they drove back home that afternoon, Sasha looked into the rearview mirror to check on his wife and child every time the car slowed down for a red light. He could see Yuri strapped into his car seat, sucking on his fist as he slept, and Katya with her hand resting gently on the blanket that covered Yuri's knees. Sasha had never driven so slowly and carefully in his life. Through every bend in the road, he maneuvered the car as though he were carrying the most precious and fragile cargo.

From the moment they brought him home from the hospital, all of the focus Katya had once channeled into dancing, she now poured into Yuri. They brought the crib from the nursery into their bedroom, and Katya slept only in fifteen-minute intervals. She maintained a constant vigil, her body incapable of surrendering completely to rest. Most of the time she lay on her side, her eyes carefully monitoring his breathing. She watched his little chest rising and falling though the fabric of his cotton onesie. She listened for every gurgle, every groan.

When morning came and Sasha went off to work, Katya held Yuri to her breast and stroked his cheek with her finger, believing that her mother's milk would somehow make him stronger. But even she knew it could not cure what really ailed him.

She still wasn't sure she understood completely what the prognosis would be for Yuri, even after Sasha had explained countless times what the doctor had said.

"We must always watch him," Sasha said over and over to her, but she was already doing that every day and every night. The lack of sleep had made her tense and irritable. Sasha could leave for work every day and have some distraction there, but she lived with a continual sense of panic that something might go wrong at home. That Yuri might find himself gasping for breath and she wouldn't be able to help him.

Finally, one Saturday when Yuri was nearly three months old, Sasha sat her down and was firm with her.

"We cannot live in constant fear, Katya. You must accept what Dr. Rosenblum says. There are many grays to his condition. We can only wait and see how he develops. But we also have to learn to live in the present."

He took her into his arms, and he felt the lightness of her entire being falling into him. He tightened his arms around her as she began to cry.

"He will get stronger," he told her. "I promise you that little baby will grow into a perfect little boy."

She was now sobbing into his chest. All the emotions she had bravely pushed deep inside her over the past three months, in order to ensure she was giving every ounce of her strength to her baby, now dissolved as Sasha held her.

When she finally finished, Katya felt the sunlight on her back streaming in from the window, and it restored her. Over the next few months, she saw Sasha's words come true. Yuri somehow managed to grow stronger with each passing day.

29

SASHA had held on to each word the doctor had said about Yuri's condition. He needed to understand every ounce of knowledge Dr. Rosenblum was willing to share with him. He wanted to dissect the information and put it back together again, slowly and methodically, so he could tell Katya without hesitation that he comprehended their son's diagnosis and that he would do everything in his power to make sure Yuri received the best care.

He remembered how the doctor had told him that an infant's heart was the same size as its little fist, those five little fingers rolled tight. "Yuri's heart, although now no bigger than a walnut, will grow as the child grows, always maintaining the size of his closed hand." The doctor had lifted his own hand, letting it hover slightly over his desk, before making a fist. Now, as Sasha stood over the crib, with Yuri's fingers shut tight and pulled close to his tiny mouth, he tried to imagine his son's heart beating inside. He had read in a scientific journal about how patients with positive energy—who refused to succumb to despair—often had better outcomes than those with negative attitudes. Hadn't he even heard on a radio show how one listener had called in and said he tried to visualize his cancer remission and that he could improve his prognosis by imagining a future that included good health?

Sasha had always considered himself a man of science, but as he looked at his sleeping child, he found himself desperate for anything that would help improve Yuri's prognosis. He took deep breaths and thought of the air reaching into his lungs and his heart pumping blood into his veins. He closed his eyes and began to imagine his own heart synchronized with his son's. He would *will* it to grow stronger. The damaged ventricle wall would not deteriorate further, Yuri's tricuspid valve would not leak, and the right side of his heart would not enlarge. Sasha realized that he had always taken the stance that he did not believe in a god. But secretly, he now knew that he would believe in anything if it could help save his son. If there was even the slightest possibility that his imagining an invisible thread repairing his son's heart defect would help, he would seize the opportunity. If Katya asked him to go to church with her and pray on his knees for Yuri to secure him a clean bill of health, he would do it without protest.

He opened his eyes and stared again at the little baby sleeping in his crib. Katya had dressed Yuri in footed pajamas with blue and white stars printed on the cotton. The mobile above dangled with a myriad of stars, a large white moon, and a yellow sun. The constellations of love, he thought as his eyes focused again on his child's curled fist. When Yuri's fingers loosened and a thumb found its way into his tiny mouth, Sasha took another breath. His body wrestled between fear and hope. He inhaled the sweet smell of a sleeping baby—the perfume of talcum powder and diaper cream—and placed his hand on the top of Yuri's chest. He could feel his son's beating heart through the cotton fabric, and its rhythm gave him comfort. And at that moment, Sasha knew his son was strong.

30

AFTER Yuri's birth, Sasha struggled to feel useful and relevant, as there was so much that he now felt helpless about. He fumbled with changing Yuri's diaper, and unlike Katya, he didn't always hear his son's crying. His wife always seemed to sense it, even before the noise pierced the air.

During feedings, as Katya sat propped up on pillows in their bed, he watched her hold Yuri to her chest, observing her milk flowing from her breast into the baby's pursed lips. Sasha was both humbled and awed by how nature bonded an infant to its mother so tightly. He longed to also be able to give something to his son that was unique to him.

He soon learned that Yuri loved it when his father read to him. He would watch as Yuri's pupils dilated with wonder at the sound of Sasha's voice. He felt his own heart race with happiness each time Yuri offered him a smile. Over the years, Sasha tried a variety of new projects with Yuri to try to replicate those early sensations of pure joy. When Yuri was still a toddler, Sasha brought home Legos and a wooden castle with a full set of knights. He also gave Yuri a children's microscope and attached a mobile of floating planets over his bed. But it wasn't until he eventually introduced his son to baseball that Sasha found the one thing that would connect the two of them forever.

YURI was five years old the first time he watched baseball on television. Sasha had been elated to explain it to his son, even though he was still relatively new to the game himself.

He remembered that sometime around the fourth inning, Yuri had pulled out a sheet of drawing paper and crayons and begun sketching a television set with the image of a baseball field and players depicted on it. Just when he thought his son had finished the drawing, Yuri added two stick figures sitting on a couch in front of the TV screen, each with its own horseshoe-shaped smile.

"It's me and you, Daddy." He beamed, handing the finished picture to Sasha.

All these years later, Sasha still had that sketch taped to the wall next to his desk at the lab. Five-year-old Yuri's signature on the bottom was big and lopsided, but every part of the drawing still made Sasha happy. The drawing documented when the bond between them was first sealed.

YURI took to the game immediately. By six years old, he had a full understanding of the rules of baseball and how much quick thinking was involved in each play.

Like his father's, his mind could retain facts and figures easily, and soon he had memorized the names of all the Yankees and the numbers on their jerseys. By the time Yuri was seven, he could recite every batter on the team's average, home runs, and RBI total.

Sasha bought them matching Yankees jerseys and caps so they could dress in full pinstripe regalia every time they sat on the couch watching a game together. Katya, who had no interest in sports, served them snacks like cut-up kielbasa on mini rolls and chocolate babka for dessert, always trying to hide her smile and playfully chastising them for roaring too loudly.

As Yuri got older and his heart condition prevented him from joining Little League or playing with children his own age at school, Sasha saw how baseball nonetheless saved his son, for Yuri could still be a passionate and dedicated fan. Sasha would take him to the Tri-Village flea market on weekends and buy him three or four packs of baseball cards. Yuri would then spend countless hours organizing his burgeoning card collection into special albums with see-through flaps. He started to vary the way he would organize the cards. Sometimes he placed them in alphabetical order, while other times he decided to arrange them by team or by position. Sasha would bring home special Lucite protectors for Yuri's most prized cards, which allowed him to display them proudly on his bookshelf.

During baseball season, Sasha would often come home and see Yuri standing in front of the TV, imitating the nuances of each player's batting stance or the way they prepared for their pitching windup.

Sasha marveled at Yuri's attention to detail. He would choke up his hands on an imaginary bat to imitate Derek Jeter and then slowly circle the bat behind him while waiting for the pitch. And for the diminutive second baseman Chuck Knoblauch, he would crouch virtually down to the ground with his bat placed almost horizontally and far behind the rest of his body. But Sasha was always the most amazed when he watched him imitate Andy Pettitte on the pitching mound.

Yuri would take his Yankees hat and pull it way down over his brow and then raise his glove like a shield just below his eyes. Staring intensely ahead, he'd simulate Pettitte's movements, first raising his hands over his head and then lifting his left leg into the air, so slowly and purposefully that, as he moved, Sasha was reminded of watching Katya, years before, display the strength and gracefulness of her ballet.

He's playing the game in his mind, Sasha thought every time he saw his son carrying out the ritual. Yuri's eyes fixated on the screen, his focus so all-consuming that he probably didn't even notice his father silently watching him. And it warmed Sasha to know about the wondrous gift he had given to his son, a love of something that defied his illness. When Yuri watched baseball, he was like any other boy. He was joyous and he was free.

31

WHEN I reached Yuri's house later that week, the snowfall that had blanketed their driveway just days before was now a mixture of dark puddles and sand. But inside the house, I found Katya looking sunny and happy. Her honey-colored hair fell softly over her shoulders, and she wore a red sweater dress that showed off her dancer's physique. I noticed she was even wearing a pretty matching shade of lipstick. She looked like an entirely different person with the added color.

I was happy to see Katya looking so well, as I knew it meant that Yuri must be feeling stronger. It was funny how little it took for me to be so optimistic. A red outfit and some lipstick, and I already had Yuri fully cured.

Even the fragrances in the house were different. I was a bloodhound when it came to scents wafting in from a kitchen. Typically, the Krasnys' home smelled like simmering onions or was filled with the toasty aroma of kasha. But this afternoon, the rooms were rich with the perfume of butter and shortbread.

"Smells like you've been baking," I observed cheerfully as I pulled off my coat.

"Yes, I made cookies." She gestured toward the kitchen. "Yuri's been feeling much better over the past three days. No complaints of a racing heart or being short of breath. So I wanted to celebrate a little." She extended her hand toward the living room. "Here, let me bring you to him. I've left some cookies on the table for both of you."

We walked into the living room, and I was shocked to find him not bundled in his comfy chair but instead sitting cross-legged on the couch. He was dressed in sweatpants and an oversize Yankees jersey. This was the first time I hadn't seen him in his pajamas. On the coffee table, I noticed a plate with three cookies and a scattering of crumbs.

"Hey, Jeter," I teased when I saw him wearing the shortstop's number, 2.

"Hi, Ms. Topper." His eyelashes fluttered open as I walked into the room. Next to him, I could see the cover of his writing notebook.

"Good thing I see your notebook out. I'm collecting them from all the kids this week to make sure everyone's been doing their daily entries."

Yuri glanced over at his notebook and seemed to fidget slightly.

"Don't tell me you haven't been keeping up on your writing?" I chided playfully.

"No, I have."

I sat down in the chair beside him and studied him again. I sensed something I couldn't quite place that was suddenly making him feel uncomfortable, perhaps even anxious.

Yuri must have realized I was picking up on something, so he deftly redirected his gaze to the plate of cookies.

"You should try one. They're really good."

"I was hoping you'd offer," I said, lifting one off the plate.

"My mom used my grandmother's recipe from back in Ukraine. They're one of my favorites."

"I can taste the butter. I just might have to steal another," I confessed as I contemplated eating a second one.

"You really should." He pushed the plate toward me.

"No, you need them more than I do, champ," I said, pleased that a sense of ease had returned between us. "Finish them off."

He lifted the last few and popped them into his mouth one at a time. Finally, I saw a smile cross over his lips.

"Okay, now that we're done with our snack, let me ask you. Did you have fun with the latest writing assignment?"

Hoping to ignite my students' curiosity, I had instructed them to write about something they experienced in their life that had made them "wonder." I was excited to hear what Yuri had written.

He wrinkled his brow. "Actually, I did. It took me a while to decide what I was going to write about. But then after I let my mind wander a bit, it came to me."

"So you managed to get over your writer's block. That's great, Yuri."

"Yeah, the strange thing is, Ms. Topper, I never liked writing before. But now I notice I feel a lot better after I do it."

"Well, that's really good news. You know what to say to make your teacher happy."

"I said it because it's true, not to make you happy," he answered flatly.

I felt my face warm at his words. I heard Suzie's voice in my head. *The thing about kids, Maggie, is that they can tell right away when you're trying too hard.* Yuri didn't want me to always be chirpy and full of positivity. I was sensing he wanted someone he could be real with and not have to censor his thoughts or emotions around.

I took a few seconds to find my composure and give Yuri what he wanted. He wanted me to be honest with him.

"Well, truth is important in writing," I said slowly. "Pursuing it is the essence of why writers write and artists create. Michelangelo used his chisels to release a figure he believed was buried inside a block of marble. Monet used impressionistic brushstrokes to evoke atmosphere and light. Both of them were searching for ways to reveal something you didn't see clearly at first glance."

Yuri's eyes flickered. He was listening to everything I was saying, and I could feel it.

"Writers use words in that same way. They are searching to find meaning in a world that's often difficult and confusing. They pursue truth by questioning what's around them." I paused for a moment before continuing. "Am I making any sense?"

Yuri smiled. "Yeah, a lot."

"Good. I'm relieved." It was strange how quickly a teacher could sense when they were floundering with a student. It felt good to know that I was getting through to him now.

"Sometimes the blank page is scary, Ms. Topper, and I don't know how I'm going to fill it. But then I just close my eyes and write what I feel."

"That's the beauty of it, Yuri. When you surrender yourself to the process and just start putting the truth down on paper."

Yuri nodded.

"So let's get back to *your* writing. Why don't you read me what you wrote for your 'wonder' essay?"

"Okay, if you insist."

"I do." I smiled.

Yuri reached for his notebook and searched for a few seconds to find the right page. He took a deep breath, lowered his eyes, and then began to read:

"My Mother's Shoes" by Yuri Krasny

In my mother's dresser drawer are a pair of pink ballet toe shoes. I found them one afternoon when I was looking for a safety pin and she was out at the grocery store.

The shoes have long ribbons like the kind you find on a fancy present or on a little girl's bow. I don't know much about these shoes. But I do know that my dad said my mother used to be a really good ballerina back in Ukraine. My parents came over in 1987 and my dad now works in the lab at Stony Brook University, but my mother doesn't dance anymore.

Sometimes I wonder what my mother's life was like before she got here. I like to imagine her on a big stage, the music playing as she does her leaps and twirls. I know it sounds bad, but I wonder if she would still be dancing now if she didn't have to worry about me.

I didn't tell my mother I found her shoes. I looked at them for a few minutes and put them back in the drawer. They are her secret. But I wish I knew more about them and her life before she and Dad came to America.

I listened to Yuri reading, savoring every one of his words. There are those rare, exquisite moments in teaching when you can almost feel your student's thoughts, as though they were fingers reaching out to grab your hand. I would never know if Yuri had heard his mother and me speaking in the kitchen earlier about her dreams of dancing again. But in his one-page essay, his writing captured perfectly the mysteries of his mother's past.

"You're right," I said. "Those shoes do make you wonder about what other things people choose to keep secret."

"Yeah . . . but she probably doesn't even realize I know about them. So don't say anything to her, okay? I hate to have her worry about anything else."

I raised my hand. "I give you my word. I promise I'll never betray anything you say . . . or write to me in confidence."

Yuri's smile faded into a serious expression. "My dad is always saying, 'You take care of the people you love.'" He looked at me. "I guess he doesn't want me to worry that he and my mom are always having to take care of me."

A flash of translucence appeared in his face at that moment, the boy morphing into a young man.

At his words, I felt my heart melt.

Yuri put his notebook on the table.

"So, can I have it now?" I asked. "I'll read the rest of your entries when I get home tonight."

"Oh, yeah, sure," he said, but that strange sense of discomfort seemed to wash over him again.

He closed the notebook and gave it to me. I slipped it into my bag.

Yuri sat back in his chair.

"Is everything okay?"

"Uh-huh." He stretched the word out.

"Well, then let's get started on discussing *Bridge to Terabithia*. I'm curious what you thought of Jess and Leslie's unlikely friendship."

Yuri again seemed distracted. I was having such a hard time reading what was causing him to be so anxious. We had seemed to be bonding so nicely over the writing exercise, but now I sensed I was losing him again.

I took another deep breath and waited several seconds for him to regain his focus.

"I thought it helped them both survive difficult circumstances."

"Yes, that's true."

"I also liked how Jess set goals for himself with his running. How he wants to earn his father's respect through sports."

I nodded. "That's right. And Jess doesn't have an easy life, does he?"

"No," Yuri answered. "He's got it rough. His friendship with Leslie helps him, though. She shows him so many things that he wouldn't know about if they weren't friends."

"That's right! She introduces him to a whole other magical world."

Yuri shifted in his seat. "That's the great thing about friends, I guess."

"Yes. You learn so much from them, right? You can gain a new perspective from all their experiences and even just by listening to them. Just like I'm learning from you right now, Yuri."

He forced a smile. I could tell he was still preoccupied by something, though.

"Ms. Topper, would you mind if I have my notebook back for a second?"

I looked at him quizzically. "Sure, Yuri. Is there something wrong?"

"No, I just need to fix something."

I retrieved his notebook from my bag and handed it back to him. He opened it up and riffled through the pages until he found one that had been folded over to ensure it would remain private.

But now he was smoothing the page back, so it became flattened.

He closed the notebook and handed it back to me.

"Thank you, Ms. Topper," he said softly. "I guess with writing, sometimes you write things just for yourself. And then later, you realize if you *really* trust the person who's reading it, it's okay to share."

.   .   .

THAT night as I left Bill in the living room watching an episode of *Law and Order*, I went upstairs to read my students' notebooks. I saved Yuri's for last, knowing there was something in it that required my full attention. When I got to the page he had initially folded over only to later change his mind, it seemed to signify how far Yuri and I had come over these past few months. The flattened page was a symbol of trust.

> *Sometimes I really hate being me. I love my mom and dad, and I know Dr. Rosenblum thought it was the right decision for me not to go to school this year after I got sick so much last year, but it seems to me like you only get to be a kid once in your life and I'm not getting that chance. I wish I could have even one friend my age. Someone I could really talk to about things I love, like baseball and even birds. I know I have my dad to talk to about baseball and Ms. Topper sort of likes baseball too, but it's not like she's a super-fan. She thought Mariano pitched a perfect game last season, but it really was David Wells. She's a lady and can make mistakes like that I guess, but sometimes I just wish I could fly over to Ms. Topper's classroom and be a bird, like a pigeon or something, peering outside her window, just to be close to other kids.*

As I read the words, I could feel Yuri's pain lifting off the page. Knowing I was powerless to soothe a child's suffering gripped me in the same way it had years before, when I saw little Ellie watching as the yellow school bus passed by her house. I so wanted to help him. *But how?*

.   .   .

FOR the next few days I struggled over what to do with the information Yuri had chosen to share with me. I realized it would be a betrayal of his trust to show his notebook to Suzie or even my mother, as deeply as I craved their counsel. But I still wished I had someone to brainstorm with me about what I might be able to do to make him feel less isolated.

It wasn't until I was standing in front of my third-period class and my eyes fell upon Finn that inspiration struck. It was the Yankees hat on his head, which he had forgotten yet again to take off after recess, that sparked the idea.

THAT afternoon as I left for Yuri's house, I felt the fog of not knowing how to make his situation better lifting. I realized I might have found a way to soften his isolation.

I waited until I finished my lesson with Yuri. Katya was standing over the sink, wiping up the counter.

"We had a great session today. It's wonderful to see how he's completing all of his reading assignments and doing his daily writing entries."

Katya looked up and smiled. "He's a good boy. He wants to do well. But of course, it is hard to be cooped up here all day."

It felt like a window of opportunity was opening for me, so I seized it.

"It's true. It's hard that he doesn't get to have any interaction with the other children," I agreed sympathetically.

"Even when he was at the other school, it was hard for him to connect. He is an old soul in some ways. Because of his condition, he has experienced a different kind of childhood, and he is more mature than some kids his age. I know he considers Dr. Rosenblum a friend."

I lowered my eyes and then lifted them to meet hers. "Well, truthfully, a doctor, as much as he is a part of Yuri's life, can't be the same as having a friend his own age."

Katya gave me a hard look. The room suddenly felt cold.

"I'm saying this because I care about Yuri," I continued, determined to help Yuri, "but would you ever consider having him visit the class, even if it's just for one day? I know you and I discussed it a while back, and it would be such a treat for him."

Katya's gaze softened. "I did ask the doctor about that recently, but he thinks it's still too much of a risk to have him be near so many children at this point." She took a deep breath. "It's bad enough knowing there's nothing we can do about the Ebstein's anomaly and irregular heartbeat. But, in the eleven years we've had Yuri, we've always been vigilant about his immune system . . . protecting it is something we can actually control. His breathing has always been an issue, and even a little cold could have him running to the ER. And during the winter, there's an even greater risk for colds or, even worse, the flu . . ."

I had anticipated her answer. It was understandable, but I had also been thinking of a more creative solution, an alternative option.

"Well, I certainly understand your concern. I do have another idea that might work, though. A compromise of sorts.

"I wonder if I might be able to bring one of my other students . . . another really special boy, to one of my two sessions here each week, so Yuri can have a little more interaction and our book discussions can be more involved. A third party would really help."

"You mean, bring him here?"

"Yes, perhaps it wouldn't overwhelm Yuri's immune system if it was just one other child, and he took precautions to wash his hands like I do when I visit."

Katya was listening. I could see her pondering the possibility.

"Let me think about it and discuss it with my husband and Yuri's doctor."

"Of course," I said.

"It does seem like a good compromise."

"I wouldn't have brought it up if I didn't think it would help Yuri, and I really have the perfect boy to invite."

I didn't say his name aloud. But I knew right away the other child would have to be Finn.

32

AFTER her injury, Katya had recurring dreams where she was still dancing. In her subconscious, she was still a girl who could lift her ankle above her head, and could leap and pirouette. How she missed that weightlessness as she jumped, feet pointed and arms out stretched. In her mind, her body tapered like an arrow, so compact and precise, she could pierce the air.

There were dreams where she was onstage and the strong beams of light focused solely on her, where she danced the roles of Stravinsky's Firebird or Tchaikovsky's swan. She wore feathers on her head and crowns with sparkling center jewels. She danced in a frenzy, her body morphing from woman to bird.

When Katya awoke, there was always a moment of disorientation, a confusion between two worlds—one where she was still a dancer in Kiev, and one where she was an isolated immigrant in the United States.

After Yuri's diagnosis, she stopped dreaming of dancing. She didn't sleep long enough to have dreams. She still slept, but only in fits and bursts. And even though Yuri was no longer an infant sleeping in a crib, but rather a middle-school-age boy, her impulse to check on him never went away.

Sasha slept like a bear, his body curled toward the nightstand, his worry stopping the moment he shut his eyes. Katya envied his ability to turn off his mind and surrender to sleep. But her body woke every hour. Even after all these years, there wasn't a night that she didn't carefully peel away the covers and walk silently down the hallway toward Yuri's door.

Some nights, she even brought Yuri into bed with her and Sasha. After all, it was her husband who once told her he had met a scientist who told him that hearts had their own language. "Two hearts in close proximity can synchronize themselves," Sasha explained. "Some even believe the closeness of another heart can heal a broken one," he whispered to her long before they even had Yuri. So on those nights when Yuri slept beside her—her heart pressed against his back—Katya wondered if Yuri could feel her love pushing through his skin, willing her son to be healed.

33

IT was funny that such a small bit of news could make me so happy. Just knowing Katya was open to my bringing another student over to meet Yuri put a little spring into my step.

As I drove down the winding country roads toward home, I was already thinking about the project I would assign the two of them. They were both sports lovers, so I thought about a newspaper project where I would ask them each to write a column about a specific event when an athlete had changed history. Jesse Owens running in the 1936 Olympics and Jackie Robinson's experiences as the first black baseball player were possibilities. Any story about an athlete overcoming adversity was something I thought both boys would enjoy.

By the time I pulled into our gravel driveway, it was dark outside. Bill wasn't home yet, so I turned on the light and began making dinner.

On the radio, Ricky Martin's "Livin' la Vida Loca" played, and I found myself doing a little salsa as I padded through the kitchen, searching for pots and pans.

Half an hour later, after I simmered some garlic and onions, poured one of my mother's jars of summer tomatoes into the pan, and boiled some pasta, I saw the lights of Bill's car pull up to the house.

"Hi, honey!" I hollered as I heard him come through the door and put his keys on the table. "Spaghetti and Mom's sauce for dinner! I'll be right there!" I was so excited to share with him the good news.

I turned the flame down on the stove to let the sauce simmer and went over to kiss him hello.

"Hey," I said as I walked into the hallway to greet him. But the other words that were about to follow, the "how was your day" or "are you hungry for dinner," immediately fell to the wayside. Bill was standing there with bloodshot eyes and his collar half-open. His typical crisp navy Brooks Brothers suit was crumpled and, strangely, he was wearing an old University of Michigan baseball cap. Even worse, he was wearing it backward.

I walked closer to him, and I could smell the yeasty scent of beer coming out of his pores. I hadn't seen him look that disheveled since his fraternity rushing days.

Suddenly all the good feelings that had gone into preparing dinner, all the love from my mother's home-grown tomatoes, had evaporated. Now, all I could see was my boyfriend of six years, who looked like a combination of a barfly and the crumpled, half-shaven detective Lieutenant Columbo.

"Sorry I'm late. My buddy Ben came out to the Island for business, and then he surprised me at work."

"I made us dinner," I muttered. "I had some good news I wanted to share, but maybe now's not such a good time."

I watched as he pulled off his coat and draped it over the couch. "I'm all ears, Maggie. What's the good news?"

I was about to tell him, when I stopped. I didn't want to sully my happiness with his pub breath.

"Nothing. Just forget it," I said as I turned my back on him and went to plate the dinner. He didn't even seem upset that I was so annoyed at him. If anything, it felt as if he wasn't listening to me at all.

I heard him switch the television on, and I poured the pasta into the colander. But it had boiled for too long. It was soggy and lifeless, and I couldn't bear to serve my mother's tomatoes over it. So I refilled the pot with water and started over.

34

"HE was just decompressing a little after work," Suzie said in Bill's defense the next day at lunch. We were three weeks away from Christmas break, and I noticed she was already ushering in the holiday by wearing a bright red chenille sweater, black velvet leggings, and a very colorful snowman pin.

"Don't let it get you down, Mags. Men like a beer every now and then with the guys to blow off steam. It's like women with chocolate cake."

"I wish we had some cake right now," I said wistfully. Suzie and I hardly ever ate in the faculty room. The place perpetually smelled like microwaved leftovers and burned coffee. It was really disconcerting to open the refrigerator and see ancient cartons of milk or foam take-out containers with Post-its on them blaring *Do Not Touch!* You'd think that from all the Rubbermaid containers with teachers' names blazing in red Sharpie marker, every teacher at Franklin was a kleptomaniac.

One thing was undeniable. The faculty room was incredibly depressing and only worsened my mood. But it was too cold to eat outside, and my classroom was being used for student testing, so I tried to focus on my conversation with Suzie.

"The thing is, Suze, I've been with Bill since sophomore year of college, but this is the first time we've actually lived together. I guess I just didn't notice all the drinking and the endless television watching before. It used to be I'd show up at his dorm room or even his old apartment, and he'd always be ready to go out and grab dinner or see a movie . . . But now, I feel like the only thing that connects us is that we're sharing a home together."

"Are you saying you now realize after six years of dating that you have nothing in common?"

"Well, we both still like the Mets." I shrugged, trying to make a joke out of it. "There always used to be some intelligence imbuing our conversations. He was this funny, witty guy who had an amazing knowledge of trivia and pop culture. But now when he comes home he just seems like a tired, old ex-frat guy. He's twenty-eight going on seventy-eight."

"Yuck." Suzie made a face. "I didn't even like those guys when they were *in* college." She lifted a forkful of casserole to her mouth. "I guess I always preferred the more bohemian types. You know . . . the kind that listened to the Grateful Dead and wore a rainbow macramé belt," she chuckled. "God, Mags, the jocks always thought if they just put some James Taylor or Cat Stevens on a mixtape, they could have you on the spot."

"I guess I was an easy target. I lost my virginity to Bill listening to 'Fire and Rain.' I think Bill might still have that copy of James Taylor's *Greatest Hits* sitting around just for that purpose."

"You did not!" she shrieked. "I'm never going to get that song out of my head now."

"I did. In fact, if he had lasted for a few seconds longer, we could have added 'Sweet Baby James' to that glorious memory."

Suzie groaned.

"I'm glad I've now become unforgettable for you," I said, clearly pleased with myself. Just then the bell rang.

"Jesus, we're going to be late for our classes."

We dumped our now-empty containers on the shelf in the kitchen before we rushed to our classrooms. Neither of us had written our names on the lids. Time would tell whether they would still be there when we got back or whether they would fall victim to the dreaded Franklin canister thief.

"Slow down, Ms. Topper," I heard a voice call out in a warm melody of concern.

It was Daniel, who was standing outside the music room.

He gestured toward my boot. My shoelace was untied.

"Wouldn't want you to trip and fall . . ."

"Thanks." I bent down to tie the laces, and when I looked up, his hand was extended, offering to help me up.

"And here I was thinking chivalry was dead," I joked as I let my fingers thread into his.

"Never," he added quickly. "I assure you, Ms. Topper, there are still one or two knights to be found at Franklin Intermediate."

"Well, that's the best news I heard all day." I beamed. We were now only inches apart from each other, and the scent lifting off his skin was strangely familiar. It must have been his soap. He smelled clean and woodsy, the fragrance of freshly cut pine.

35

CHRISTMAS was coming soon, and if maintaining my students' concentration was challenging right after summer break, it was even harder in the days leading up to winter vacation. The kids were dreaming of presents and vacations in Florida. I had to admit, even I was a bit distracted; there was no holiday I enjoyed more. For the past three years, Bill and I had split Christmas Eve and Christmas Day between our respective parents' houses. As I started to think of all the family presents I still had to buy, I also began to arrange for Finn to come to Yuri's house. The first step was seeing whether Finn himself would be up to it.

I announced to the class that in the last two weeks before break, we would be discussing different examples of men and women who had overcome adversity. Their final assignment before Christmas would be to write a newspaper column about a moment in history where someone had stood up to injustice. I gave examples of Gandhi and Rosa Parks. I knew most of the boys in the class would want to cover an athlete, so I suggested Jesse Owens or Jackie Robinson as other possibilities, too.

After school was over, I caught Finn on his way out to meet his mother. I motioned to him that I had a quick question for him.

"What's up, Ms. Topper?" He tossed his L.L.Bean knapsack over his shoulder, the straps already a bit tattered and frayed. He looked like a puppy as he stood there with his wide eyes and shaggy blond hair. I had to fight back the urge to move his bangs away from his eyes.

"Got a favor to ask you, Finn." I jumped right to it. "I have a student the same age as you, he'll be twelve in June. I tutor him twice a week in his home because he's too weak to go to school."

"Really?" Finn interrupted. "What's wrong with him?"

I'd been hoping to be a bit vague about Yuri's condition, but Finn was clearly too curious a kid to let me off the hook.

"Well, how can I explain it?" I struggled for a second to find the right words. "He was born with a rare heart condition and has a weak immune system, so he doesn't really have the stamina right now to be in the classroom with so many other kids around. I was hoping you might want to come with me to visit him one afternoon. I think a little interaction with a kid his age would be good for him." I smiled. "And he's a huge baseball fan, like you. I think you'll have a lot in common."

"Sure," he said as his voice perked up. "Why not?"

My heart felt like it leapt an extra beat in my chest. "Really, Finn? That's fantastic!" I leaned over and gave him a little squeeze on his shoulder. "I'll call your mom to make sure it's okay."

"Yeah, no problem, Ms. Topper. I'm sure she'll be fine with it."

"I'm sure, too. It's probably best if she drives you, though, just because the district might not want me taking you in my car."

"She's out there now waiting." He motioned toward the parking lot. "Gotta run."

I waved at him to go.

"One more thing." He stopped just before exiting the front entrance. "Is he a Mets or a Yankees fan?" he shouted.

"Yankees!" I hollered.

He threw his head back and laughed. "Cool. Then I really do want to meet him!"

36

I met Bill my sophomore year at the University of Michigan. It had taken me a full two semesters to get acclimated to life at a big university. Growing up in Strong's Neck, I was used to rambling country roads and houses that echoed a quiet New England sensibility. For the prom, my friends and I all bought our dresses from the Laura Ashley shop in Stony Brook Village and dabbed the backs of our necks and wrists with Anaïs Anaïs to feel feminine and pretty. Our high school dance was filled with awkward boys and a gym full of streamers. John McMannis, my date, ditched me halfway through the night for a girl named Gina Lorenzo, who wore a black spandex Betsey Johnson dress and a pair of fishnets. I remember standing in a corner, rapping along with some friends to "Ice Ice Baby" blaring on the gym's speakers, when I noticed Gina reemerge in the gym with my date, her fishnets torn above her thigh.

By the time I met Bill, I was no longer wearing my flower-printed dresses, and thankfully, my corduroy pantaloon jumpsuit had been given away, too. It didn't take me longer than my first freshman party to realize that the boys in college were not all that enticed by the feminine tea dresses I thought made me look like a character out of a Jane Austen novel.

I ditched the fabric bows that had kept my hair back in a ponytail for most of high school, and started wearing my hair curly and free. When *Pretty Woman* came out that year, I learned how to scrunch my tresses with L'Oréal Pumping Curls, and I supplemented my wardrobe with jeans and fuzzy sweaters from Urban Outfitters. But despite my more contemporary appearance, there was still that shy girl from Long Island who saw herself as big-boned and awkward, nothing like the blond midwestern ponytailed girls who seemed to be born with a homecoming king by their sides.

The evening I first met Bill, I was hanging out at the counter of the Brown Jug, eating French fries and gravy with my best friend, Katie, when he came in and sat down with some of his friends. At one point, I reached over to pull out a few napkins from the metal dispenser, and I accidentally knocked over his drink.

"Oh my God," I apologized, my face burning with embarrassment. "Please let me buy you another one."

He refused my offer and asked if, instead, he could buy a round for Katie and me. His manner was boyish and sweet, and when the drinks came, I was impressed that he had also ordered another plate of fries and gravy for us all to share. I loved that he dug into the fries as heartily as Katie and I did. He was also incredibly tall. Six foot three with a strong build and the familiar features of my father's Irish family, there was something about him that made me feel immediately comfortable. When we walked out next to each other, I didn't dwarf him with my five-ten frame, and he also laughed at every one of my jokes, even when no else did.

A group of us stayed up almost all night. We ended up back at the South Quad, playing drinking games. I remember thinking how chivalrous he was for drinking the rancid beer for me whenever I lost at quarters so I wouldn't have to.

In the days that followed, he pursued me with an impressive amount of effort. I found out he had asked my roommate for my class schedule so he could miraculously appear exactly when I was exiting Angell Hall. He invited me to watch basketball games with him, at a time when the school's team was at its apex and everyone was reveling in the exploits of the Fab Five. It was then that he started telling me stories about why he loved sports so much. And when he spoke about them, his entire voice changed. It sounded so alive, like the way ice changes when it hits a glass of sparkling lemonade. Everything began to pop and crackle. He knew the history of basketball so well, about all the great players and their records. And when baseball season started, the names changed, but his enthusiasm stayed the same.

But nowadays, Bill seemed like a glass of lukewarm water. Nothing seemed to excite him except his work buddies and the new BMW catalog that had come in the mail. He kept that on his nightstand, flipping through its glossy pages whenever I brought my own work up to bed.

The fireplace, which I had been so excited to snuggle in front of during our winter weekends, remained untouched. The house, despite my constantly raising the thermostat to an ever-higher temperature, always felt cold.

I couldn't help but think of that light that drew me to my special students. I had never thought that a person's light could change. But whatever spark had initially drawn me to Bill had shifted over the past few months. It was a terrible thing to say, but I knew it was true. His eyes had grown dim.

37

I called Finn's mother the following day, and she said it would be her pleasure to drop Finn off at the Krasnys' one day after school. The few extra hours she would have free that afternoon meant she could devote more time to her daughter.

"He's got basketball practice on Thursdays, but any other day would work." I could hear her shuffling some papers in the background. "What's their address? Let me get a pen."

"Thirty-five Moriches Road. Not far from the St. James General Store."

"That's close to us," she said. "I really think it's a lovely idea."

"You have a great son, Mrs. Laffrey." I felt the need to tell her just how much I enjoyed having Finn as a student. "Not only is he smart and a pleasure to teach, but he's incredibly compassionate as well. He's always helping the other kids when they're struggling, and he never seems preoccupied with acting cool." I felt a true sense of teacher's pride as I spoke.

"Thank you, Ms. Topper. That's so nice of you to say." I suddenly heard a girl's voice holler in the background. "I gotta run, but let's say I drop Finn off at four thirty next Monday. Would that work?"

"I'll check with Yuri's mother, but if you don't hear from me otherwise, consider it done."

THE following Monday, I called Katya during my lunch period just to make sure that Yuri was feeling up to having a visitor that afternoon. During school, I confirmed that Finn had no signs of a cold or cough. The last thing I wanted to do was bring someone contagious into the Krasnys' home. Yuri's health had seemed stable to me over the past couple of weeks, and I knew if there was any reason to postpone the visit, Katya would be the first to tell me.

When I arrived, I noticed there was a small Christmas tree in the living room with a garland of delicate lights wrapped around its branches. The smell of fresh pine was invigorating, and I immediately thought of my own family's tradition of buying a tree from one of the local farm stands, and my mother making hot cocoa and cinnamon-dusted cookies for my brother and me as we trimmed the tree.

"The place smells so good," I told Katya as she hung up my coat. "I see you got your tree up. It looks great."

She looked in the direction of the living room and smiled. "Yes, we did it this weekend. My husband's Jewish . . . but doesn't believe in God." She let out a nervous laugh. "Still, he knows how much I like these American traditions. We would have never been allowed something like this back in Ukraine."

"I love the festivities, too," I admitted. "We always need a little bit of added cheer when it's freezing outside."

"Yes, and Yuri also loves it. He sat with me yesterday at the counter and helped me make the cookies. I really think he's excited to meet this other boy . . ." She hesitated for a moment, as if embarrassed she'd forgotten his name.

"Finn," I added, helping her out. "Finn Laffrey. You'll see. I think he and Yuri will hit it off."

MRS. Laffrey's Volvo pulled up at exactly four thirty. I was sitting in the living room with Yuri. Katya had brought in a second plate of cinnamon-sugar cookies because Yuri and I had already finished off the first one. I held a cup of steaming tea between my hands and had been telling Yuri that I felt like a bit of a matchmaker, like in the musical *Fiddler on the Roof.* "But instead of marriages, I work in the business of friendship," I joked with him.

"What's your criteria for making a match?" he asked as he brushed his bangs out of his eyes. "I'm just curious why you chose him."

"Both of you are good students who like to read. Both are kind and interesting to talk to. And, oh yes, a mutual love of sports!"

Yuri grinned.

"And before you even ask me," I added, "I've already checked. He's a Yankees fan, like you."

KATYA walked Finn to the living room, and I got to my feet, anxious to make a proper introduction.

"Finn, meet Yuri." I made a grand gesture with my hand. "And Yuri, meet Finn."

"Hey!" Finn lifted his hand to greet him. "Cool jersey." He noticed right away that Yuri was wearing a Mariano Rivera jersey as he sat in his comfy chair. Finn, on the other hand, was wearing Andy Pettitte's number.

Yuri smiled and made a small wave back. "You like Pettitte, huh?"

"Yeah, he's my favorite," Finn said, and suddenly an ease flowed between them.

"He's a good guy." Yuri's face brightened. "Hard year for him last year with his dad being sick, but he kept his playing strong."

This sort of exchange was exactly what I'd hoped for in bringing the two boys together.

"Yeah." Finn nodded. "I heard during practice for the World Series, he wrote 'Dad' in silver on the inside flap of his hat to keep him close to him when he was on the field and couldn't be at the hospital with him."

"That's really cool. I didn't know that." Yuri appeared impressed. "Guess 'cause my dad likes Mariano Rivera."

"Yeah, he's awesome, too," Finn agreed. I looked at them both, and the whole room seemed to brighten with their smiles.

"So let's get started, then, why don't we?" I motioned for Finn to join me on the sofa. "And make sure you try one of these cookies before we begin, Finn. Yuri and I ate an entire plate of them just before you got here."

Finn reached over and took one. A smile crossed his face after the first bite.

WE spent the next hour discussing Lois Lowry's *Number the Stars*, the book we had just started reading in the writers' workshop at school. At the end of the hour, I mentioned that Yuri might want to do a mock sports column on a famous athlete who had overcome adversity in sports, as Finn and many of the other boys in my class were doing for their next writing assignment. The next time we met, we could talk about what obstacles the athlete they had each chosen had overcome.

"Sound good?"

The boys nodded their heads in agreement. "But, Ms. Topper." Yuri smirked. "Does being on the Mets count as an athlete having to overcome adversity?"

"Very funny," I answered, though I could see that Finn was also amused.

As we were wrapping things up, Yuri looked over to Finn and asked if he was on any sports teams.

"I'm playing on a travel basketball team now with my friend Charlie." He leaned over and tied his shoelace, flipping his hair to the side so he could see the laces better. "And I hope to make the school baseball team in the spring."

Yuri's face fell, but I could see he was still trying to force a smile for Finn. "You're lucky," he said in a quiet voice. "Maybe one day in the warmer weather I can come and watch you play."

38

THE boys saw each other one more time before we all broke for Christmas vacation. By the end of their second meeting, a lively dialogue ensued between them about their research for the mock sports column. We talked about Jackie Robinson and Jim Thorpe, two athletes who demonstrated talent with great fortitude in spite of all the hurdles they had to navigate in order to compete. We also touched upon the civil rights movement in the United States.

Even in just two visits, I could see how much Yuri brightened at the sight of Finn entering the house. I still met with Yuri once a week by myself, but those solo sessions seemed far more subdued compared to the times when Finn was also there.

I had visited my parents' house in the interim, and my mother, always prescient, noticed that I evaded any conversation about Bill. "Are things okay at home, honey?" She treaded carefully. I could see her searching my face for clues. In front of me was a bowl of Italian wedding soup. Instead of inhaling it like I usually would, I just moved one of the meatballs around in the broth, while a wilted leaf of escarole wrapped around the neck of my spoon.

"You're not eating." Her eyes drifted from my face and rested on the steaming bowl of soup. "So I guess I've found out my answer."

I felt her hand reach over to mine, and her warm fingers instantly enveloped me with maternal kindness. "Maggie, tell me what's the matter."

I felt my stomach seize up. I didn't want to tell my mother that the man I had just moved in with, whom I had dated for six years now and the one I assumed I would marry one day, was becoming like a stranger to me. Our once common ground seemed to be disappearing, and the move to the cottage—which was meant to cement our relationship—had instead exposed cracks in it that I hadn't noticed before. As hard as it was for me to accept, I was beginning to suspect that our hearts might be very different.

"It's nothing. Really," I lied. I swallowed hard, but there was still a lump in my throat. "Just growing pains, I think. We're both adjusting to the fact that we're also roommates now, not just boyfriend and girlfriend."

She smiled. "Yes, that's a big adjustment. After your dad and I were married, I didn't know how long I'd make it after I learned he couldn't fall asleep without listening to WQXR on the clock radio. I wasn't a big fan of classical music back then."

"Are you even one now?"

"I can appreciate a string quartet far better than I could when I was twenty-two," she laughed. "Back then, I just wanted to listen to the Beatles or Sam Cooke.

"Sometimes people get a little distracted during the holidays," she added in Bill's defense. "But I know how much Bill enjoys all the seafood we make for our Italian Christmas. Seven courses of happiness," she said, and I could hear in her voice how much joy it brought her to cook for all of us. "So if he likes that, then he can't be all bad . . ."

I loved how she always channeled my grandmother and great-grandmother Valentina when she cooked at Christmastime. It was as though the memories of them were pressed into the flour and egg mixture as she rolled out the sheets for the ravioli. She hummed her mother's favorite songs as she dusted powdered sugar over her cannoli. *Food is love.* I heard her favorite words echoing in my ears.

And yet, I knew that so many languages of love existed. Some forms, however, were more obvious than others. But if you took a step back sometimes, you could find it in the most unlikely places. And the discovery of it was often the greatest reward.

39

SASHA never told Katya that he had recently discovered an article in a scientific journal that mentioned how mushrooms absorbed radiation from both the atmosphere and the soil in which they grow. Katya had always loved mushrooms. She added them to eggs, mixed them with barley, and sautéed them with bits of chicken and ate them with rice.

Back in Kiev, he loved the sight of her returning from the market holding a basket of produce just harvested from the forest: wild oniongrass, fiddlehead ferns, and berries when they were in season. He remembered how that autumn, several months after the nuclear reactor accident, she remarked that the man at the market said the mushroom crop had been more plentiful than ever that year.

Katya knew enough to stay away from the strawberries that were as large as chicken eggs and the apples that grew in unusual gourd-like shapes. But mushrooms and blackberries, she couldn't eat enough of them.

A few years after Yuri had been diagnosed, and after perestroika had begun in the USSR when information about the children affected by the nuclear fallout was finally released, Sasha made a list.

The water she had bathed in. All the mushrooms she had eaten. The sunburn she had in the early days before we knew a nuclear accident had occurred. Sasha looked at the list and convinced himself that these were all elements of a tragic scientific equation that had ultimately produced Yuri's heart defect.

Katya's sister, Yulia, was now grown up and worked as a nurse in a hospital near the Belarusian and Ukrainian border. "There's so much cancer here," she told him. "All these strange tumors . . . and so many babies are being born with a hole between the two lower chambers of their heart. I've seen so many cases of Ebstein's anomaly just like Yuri, even though it's been over ten years since the nuclear accident. And, Sasha, there's nothing we can do to help them." Through the telephone, he could hear her clicking her tongue thousands of miles away.

"The doctors say they never saw this amount of problems before Chernobyl," Yulia whispered. "Even though the government officially denies the connection." She never told any of this to Katya when they spoke on the telephone, and Sasha also kept the troubling information from his wife.

"She already blames herself," he told his sister-in-law. "But she did nothing wrong. The government told us we were all safe."

"The women of childbearing age must have been the most vulnerable," Yulia confided in him. "I see the consequences of it every day. A whole new generation born with so many problems."

He always tried to convince himself that they were lucky they had gotten out of the Soviet Union when they did. That he was now employed at a prestigious university lab and that their health insurance provided them and Yuri with the best health care around.

But at night, whenever a sense of restlessness took over him, Sasha would tiptoe into Yuri's bedroom and just stare at his sleeping boy. He remembered that, when Yuri was an infant, his crib was placed within arm's reach from their bed, and Katya slept with one eye open, afraid that he might stop breathing during the night. After they had moved him to his own room and into a big-boy bed, Sasha would often wake to find her sleeping on the carpet next to Yuri. His perpetual guardian of safekeeping.

Even now, they often eclipsed each other in the night, two ships making their rounds to Yuri's bedroom just to make sure he was breathing soundly in his bed.

But time had transformed Yuri from a delicate little infant into a handsome young man. It was undeniable that his health was fragile, but he still was like the other boys his age in many ways. His bedroom was decorated with posters of his favorite Yankees players. A mobile of the solar system hung from the ceiling. On his nightstand, he proudly displayed the signed baseball that Sasha's boss had gotten for him.

The moonlight streamed into the room, and Sasha marveled at his son. He was a miracle to him. His beautiful skin, his perfect features. His bubbling curiosity and warm sense of humor.

Sasha loved him with so much ferocity that it sometimes felt like a sharp, shooting pain in his heart.

From the moment Yuri was born, Sasha had promised his Katya that their son would triumph over his diagnosis.

But he never once let his wife know his deepest secret, that he was no different than she was. Sasha, too, worried every day that something might happen to their beautiful boy.

40

TWO days before Christmas break, my desk was littered with presents from my students. I had never realized how badly I must have needed a bath before I received this treasure trove. Brightly packaged boxes of soap, bottles from Bath & Body Works, and neon-colored loofahs enveloped me in a cloud of conflicting perfumes.

There were a few sparkling exceptions. Lisa Yamamoto had given me a gorgeous bento box with lacquered chopsticks, with a note that said she thought I'd think this could be a nifty new lunch box to bring to school each day. Roland McKenna gave me a box of chocolates. And from Finn, I received a ceramic coffee mug with "World's Best Teacher" emblazoned on the front.

I had bought a box of chocolate lollipops in the shape of snowflakes to give out to all my students. While they were at recess, I attached a little note to each of them that read *Happy Holidays* in bright red marker.

The kids were still in the gym for recess when Suzie came into my room for a quick chat. I looked up from one of my notecards and smiled at her.

"Hey, just thought I'd check up on you. The other day you seemed a bit down."

There were small bells attached to her sweater, and she sounded like a wind chime when she walked.

"You're Jingle Bells today?" I teased her. "When are you going to be Rudolph? Tomorrow, on the last day of school?"

"Gotta have a sense of humor, Mags," she said, pulling at the pockets of her cardigan. "All the kids' eyes were on me today when I showed them how to make plaster of Paris. The bells are taking full credit, of course."

"You crack me up."

She came closer and picked up the wrapped presents from my desk. "Looks like the art teacher gets hosed on Christmas presents, that's for sure." She picked up a bottle of rose lotion with a bow around its neck. "I'm impressed."

"I guess they think you smell awesome already. Feel free to take something."

Suzie grabbed a bar of soap and brought it to her nose, inhaling the strong, synthetic fragrance.

"The truth is, the handmade notes are what I love the best. Forget the ones in perfect script that so eloquently express their gratitude. I know their mothers wrote those." I shook my head. "No, I love the ones like this . . ." I lifted Lisa's card, which had her signature origami crane pasted to the outside.

Dear Ms. Topper,

You make school fun. It doesn't even feel like school in your class. I hope you enjoy bringing your lunch in this bento box and maybe even learn to use chopsticks! Thank you and Merry Christmas.

Love,
Lisa

"Or this one." I showed her Robert's.

Dear Ms. Topper.

Merry X-mas. You've been super nice this year, so I hope you get lots of presents. Here's one from me. You don't have to share the chocolate with your family, if you don't want to. It's all for you.

From,
Robert

Lastly, I showed her the one from Finn.

Dear Ms. Topper,

Thanks for asking me to do writer's workshops with Yuri. He's cool and I'm happy to help out. I'm hoping he gets stronger so we can hit some balls outside together this spring.

Your student,
Finn

Suzie looked amused. "From the mouths of babes."

"Right? I want to save each one. Maybe I'll put them in the file with those letters I had them all write to themselves. That cabinet in my basement can become my own personal time capsule."

She laughed.

"What are you going to get Bill this year? Anything good?"

I made a face. "I've been stressing out over it. I have no idea."

Suzie's hand floated over the sea of presents on my desk. She paused on one of the handmade cards that was taped to a bath caddy.

"Why don't you make him something homemade? Screw expensive presents. Write him something from your heart. You said it yourself, the notes from your kids are the presents you like the best."

"I'm not sure he'd appreciate the sentiment," I told her as I taped my final holiday card on its chocolate lollipop. "I think he'd prefer some Mets tickets or a Beer of the Month Club . . ."

"How about a James Taylor mixtape?" She burst out laughing.

"Seriously, what about you, my dear? What's on your Christmas list this year?" she queried. "Something with a little sparkle?"

"You know, Suze, honestly . . . if I could have anything, it would be what Finn wrote in his note." I sighed. "I'd love the chance to see Yuri play some baseball."

41

SOMEONE had left one of the doors to the auditorium open, and the sound of the school orchestra playing "Ode to Joy" floated through the hallway. I knew the melody from the days when I had butchered the notes so terribly on my first—and last—violin, when my father quickly realized I had not come close to inheriting an ounce of his musical talent.

The music was strong and lifting. I had fifteen minutes before my next period, and I found myself being pulled into the back of the room, strangely comforted by the mixture of the different stringed instruments.

The children's heads were bowed toward their sheet music, their arms gliding the horsehair over the strings. Even if I could never master playing the violin, I still felt my body responding to the music, as though triggered by something warm and familiar.

At the front of the stage, on a little wooden podium with his back to the empty seats, stood Daniel. His baton dancing in arabesques.

He moved like he was in a trance. One hand held the baton while the other gesticulated freely, its fingers coaxing melodies into the air.

I watched as he turned to the different sections of instruments, signaling one group to soften their playing and another to increase theirs. His shoulders hunched over the music stand, his dark curly hair bobbing with each note.

I could have watched him for hours, with the intimacy of observing something beautiful and private. He had transformed from the funny, sweet new substitute teacher into something more abstract, more interesting. An artist, lost in his craft. I couldn't help myself. I felt that I had witnessed magic.

42

I had lingered in the auditorium until the last minute before the bell rang, savoring the music and the sight of seeing another side of Daniel. As the sounds changed from a performance to the rustle of sheet music being shuffled into folders and feet tapping the back of metal chairs, I rushed to my classroom to teach my last class before the winter break.

The students were restless. Conversations about who was going where for the vacation were intermingled with media-fueled paranoia about Y2K. I heard Oscar mention how his father was stockpiling cash out of fear that his bank account would be wiped out in a cyber-attack. Lisa said her parents had filled their basement with gallon jugs of Poland Spring water, flashlights, batteries, and a suitcase full of dried ramen. It occurred to me that Bill and I had done nothing to prepare for any possible calamity. I looked over at my desk filled with more gifts of cellophane-wrapped body wash and moisturizers, and knew that no matter what happened on January 1, I would be clean and smelling pretty.

Fully aware that my job as a teacher was to create a classroom free of fear or anxiety, I knew I had to put an end to all these apocalyptic Y2K scenarios the kids were sharing and try to focus their energy on something more positive.

I attempted to regain their attention by asking them to write a list of their New Year's goals. "I've got quite a few of my own," I said as I walked through the maze of desks, watching as they pulled out their notebooks. "I'm going to put on the top of my list that I'm going to listen to my inner voice more. You know what that means?"

"Your conscience?" Lisa answered.

"In a way. But more like my inner compass. I want it to keep me focused on my best path.

"I'm also going to try to stop eating so many cookies." I patted my stomach.

The class laughed. "Okay, now all of you have fifteen minutes to write up your list."

They hunched over their desks and began writing. I looked over at Zach's list and it made me laugh. *Be neater*, it read. He was the student who always came to school with his shoelaces untied, his hair uncombed. He never threw a single paper out from his Trapper Keeper, and his desk always felt sticky even after the janitor came the night before. I tapped on his shoulder and he turned around.

"Good one," I said, and I gave him a thumbs-up.

AFTER the final bell of the year rang, I watched as the students rushed outside, their peals of excitement ricocheting through the halls. I wasn't supposed to have a lesson with Yuri the day before we all broke for vacation, but I wanted to stop by anyway to give him his chocolate lollipop and my holiday note. I didn't want him to miss out on anything I did for the other children if I could help it.

I had spoken to Katya briefly on the telephone, and she said he was having a lazy morning. He'd had an EKG the day before, and he was tired from the day out.

"He'd love to see you, though, so come anyway. We have a little something to give you."

I drove down the familiar back roads from Franklin to the Krasnys' home. The ancient elm trees with their heavy, twisting boughs were padded with the most recent snowfall. Somehow, my commute to Yuri's house seemed less harried underneath this downy white canopy than it typically did. A squirrel scampered across the road, and I slowed down to make sure it got safely across.

There was a warm glow of candles in the front window of Yuri's house, and I realized as I walked closer to the front door that it was a Hanukkah menorah. The plastic white candles even had fake melted wax in the mold.

"Happy holidays," Katya said as she opened the door for me. She looked festive in a red sweater dress and black tights. I was dressed like a Wookiee from *Star Wars*, with a big hat with fur trim and an oversize parka. I stomped the snow off my boots and walked inside.

"I see you've embraced the complete holiday experience," I said, now feeling ten pounds lighter after peeling off my outerwear. I pointed to the tree and the menorah.

She laughed. "Yuri likes to celebrate both holidays so he can get extra presents. Typical kid. The more gifts to open, the better." Katya feigned disapproval, but you could tell she was charmed by Yuri's abundant enthusiasm.

"And I like it because, as I told you last week, we could never have had any religious festivities like this back in Ukraine." She lifted her hand and smoothed back her ponytail. "I've made some progress with my Jewish atheist husband . . . At least he's now an agnostic."

I chuckled.

"Ms. Topper?" Yuri's voice emerged. I looked over and saw him standing next to the Christmas tree. He was wearing soft fleece pants and a long T-shirt. "Come look at this!"

I walked down the two carpeted steps that led to the small living room. I had seen their tree on my last visit with Finn, but this time there were several presents arranged underneath it.

Yuri reached down and picked up a small rectangular one that was wrapped in shiny red and gold foil.

"This is for you. Merry Christmas." He was beaming.

The present felt heavy, like it might be a book. I immediately thanked him and walked with him over to the sofa. I carefully tried to peel off the tape so I could keep the wrapping paper pristine. It felt like good manners not to tear it open like a savage.

I looked down and saw he had given me a beautiful leather journal. It was chestnut brown, elegant and stately. The edges of the paper were even trimmed in gold. "I thought you might want a grown-up writer's journal of your own," he said sweetly.

"This is the most beautiful journal I've ever seen," I insisted, bringing it to my chest. "I've never had anything like it. Thanks so much, champ."

His cheeks flushed a soft pink. "There's a note inside, too."

I opened up the journal and saw the small envelope. "Should I read it now?"

"Nah, read it later," Yuri answered. "I just wanted you to know it's there."

I smiled at him and then leaned over and gave him a hug. I had never hugged Yuri before, and in my arms, I could feel his sparrow-thin bones. He was so fragile, I worried I could have broken him in two.

"I remember your family's tradition of making pierogi for New Year's Eve," I told him. "Mine has a tradition of always giving chocolate."

I reached into my purse and handed him the chocolate snowflake lollipop that I had also given to all my other students. Somehow my gift and the note that just read, *Happy Holidays to a great student!* seemed paltry next to Yuri's thoughtful gift to me.

When I left his house that afternoon, I didn't wait until I got home to read his note. I opened it in the car instead. And this time, I had no one to impress with my good manners, so I tore open the envelope. The soft off-white paper was reduced to a ragged edge.

Dear Ms. Topper,

I wanted to get you something special for Christmas, because you're so kind to come to my house each week. I never enjoyed reading or writing before I had you as a teacher. You made me see that books can be fun, almost as much fun as baseball. And so I wanted you to have a nice writer's journal. I hope you enjoy filling it up like I now enjoy writing in mine.

From your student,
Yuri

P.S. Let's go Yankees!!!!

I placed the note back in the ripped envelope and then inside the journal. For now, my frustration at home was eased by the purity of Yuri's gesture. I wondered for a moment what my life would be like without teaching, and I thought about how Katya had once described the size of a person's heart as mirroring the size of a clenched fist. I loosened my grip on the journal and placed it on the car seat next to me. My heart opened, like a hand releasing a balloon up into the air.

43

LEAVING Yuri's house, I felt the way Suzie had often described as "walking the line." She said it meant when a person experienced two intense emotions at once. One could feel extremely happy and also horribly sad at the same moment.

It was terrible to admit, but as full as my heart was after receiving Yuri's beautiful note, I started to dread returning home. Perhaps it was because Bill and I had yet to trim our tree. Or maybe it was because every time I suggested we read together or snuggle by the fire, or I tried to share something amusing that Yuri had said, he had no interest. Maybe because it had been six months since we had begun renting the cottage, and we had yet to cook a single meal together.

So instead of driving straight home after Yuri's, I decided to go to my parents' house first. My sadness over my current home life made me nostalgic for my own childhood traditions. I loved helping my mother prepare the dough for the ravioli using Grandma Valentina's old rolling pin, or watching her as she dipped her pastry brush in olive oil and confidently glided it over sheets of pasta.

I drove slowly to make sure I didn't skid. The twenty-minute drive out to Strong's Neck was scenic but often icy in the winter. Still, the ride was cathartic for me. I loved seeing the old farms of my childhood, their pitched roofs dusted in snow and set against an oyster blue sky. I felt my body soften as I drove over the narrow Strong's Bridge, frosted over with ice.

So much of my youth was connected to this landscape. How I loved when my mother told me bedtime stories about the heroic Revolutionary War spy Anna Strong, who had lived a stone's jump from my own house two hundred years before. "She communicated her information for the American soldiers via the color of the clothes on her laundry line," my mother told me as she sat on the edge of my bed, her face illuminated by a beam of white moonlight. I would fall asleep thinking about Anna standing outside her clapboard home, her cotton dress fluttering in the breeze, her hands pulling colorful clothes out of her laundry basket and pinning them on a string to form a secret code.

Even decades later, the memory of my mother bringing Anna to life stirred something inside me.

I pulled into their driveway and clutched my coat around me as I rang the doorbell. It was getting colder by the minute, so I turned the handle and pushed my way indoors.

Once inside, I was greeted by the sound of the stereo on full volume, with one of my father's favorite violin concertos permeating the house. I could also sense that my mother was home by the scent of her biscotti wafting in from the kitchen.

"Mom?" I hollered over the music and walked toward the kitchen to find my mother. She had her back turned to me and was sprinkling powdered sugar over a tray of biscotti. Somehow she still managed to look elegant. Her hair was in a loose chignon, and a few stray strands dangled close to her cheeks.

"Maggie!" She turned around. Her voice was flush with surprise. "What are you doing here? We weren't expecting you until tomorrow."

"Just feeling a little homesick." I walked over and hugged her. "I missed seeing you in action."

My mother's face softened as she wiped her hands clean on her apron. "I'm just finishing up my baking now."

I smiled. I knew full well all her rituals of preparation. She would do the Feast of the Seven Fishes, just as her mother and grandmother before her always had. It was one of the few things in my life that remained a constant. The freezer was filled with trays of ravioli and the stock for the shrimp risotto. When I was little, I'd count the seven fishes she intended to prepare, the calamari, the grilled scampi, the Dover sole stuffed with crabmeat, the lobster tails, the prawns for the risotto, and the baked clams. We never ate as well as we did on Christmas Eve.

"Dad's in the basement, working on a new violin." She smiled. "He's saying this one is going to be his masterpiece. Ever since he went to that workshop at Oberlin, he's been working like a madman."

"Who knew you'd be married to a modern-day Stradivari?" I teased.

I snuck one of the cookies and licked the crumbs from my fingers.

"I'm not sure if they're any good," my mother said, watching my reaction.

"They're the best, Mom. If I stand here any longer, I'll devour the whole tray." I kissed her on the top of her head. "So I better go see Dad instead."

. . .

THE basement door was open, and I followed the steps down to find my father. I discovered him hovering over a violin, painstakingly applying the varnish in long careful strokes. I hated to interrupt him while he was this engrossed in his work, so I stood on the stairs for a few minutes, taking in a bird's-eye view as he glossed the instrument in deep orange-amber hues.

My midtwenties had brought a softening in my behavior toward my father. I was no longer as impatient or irritated with him as I had been as a teenager. The sight of him moving a little slower, his posture bending ever so slightly forward, his hands a bit more knobby, caused me to pause and realize I needed to slow down and appreciate the man in front of me before it was too late. I started to see him with adult eyes and could now appreciate his complexity: he was capable of being both a man dedicated to his family and one who could maintain his artistic soul. That was no easy feat in a world with so many pressures and demands.

He had worked his whole life to support his family, and only after his retirement had he finally learned how to craft something that he had always loved. My father adored everything about the violin. The sound, the sensual shape, and the elegant F-hole designs carved into the frame. The flame-like pattern of the maple wood. He had started to play it when he was eight years old and had even been good enough to be asked to audition for Juilliard. But when he wasn't accepted, he found himself at a local college, studying economics and accounting, while playing his violin only at night.

"The best thing my violin ever got me was your mother," he used to joke to my brother and me. Neither of us had taken to the instrument when he tried to give us lessons, and so for much of our childhood, my father's passion came out in other ways. While we wanted to listen to the local pop station in the car when we were younger, the radio dial was permanently tuned to the main classical music station, WQXR. If a violin concerto came over the radio, he'd start emulating the soloist at traffic lights. And on long family trips, he would try in vain to rally my brother and me to play a game of "guess the composer" after hearing only the first bars of the score.

Charlie and I had always found his classical music obsession slightly annoying as children—we wanted to listen to our own music, which we could share with our friends—while our mother yearned for music she could sing along to. My father would end up compromising with all of us by putting an "oldies" channel on the radio, his face transforming as my mother's voice floated through the car. It was a scenario that always caused Charlie and me to huff and puff and roll our eyes. But years later, everything that had once annoyed me about my father now had the opposite effect; his quirkiness and his unequivocal love for my mother charmed me.

"DADDY?" He had just put his brush down to rest and turned around, wiping his hands on his smock.

"Hey, beautiful!" His whole face lit up when he saw me, and his voice lifted. "You're a surprise to see. Did you decide to start Christmas a day early?"

"I just missed seeing Mom making all the preparations. For some reason, I was feeling really nostalgic today."

"Well, if nostalgia inspires you to come for an extra visit, I'm good with that," he laughed, and his eyes crinkled. "Come and give your old man a hug."

I stepped down and walked into his arms. He smelled of varnish and turpentine, and I felt my eyes begin to water as my cheek settled against his flannel shirt.

"What's the matter, baby girl?" I felt his large palm on the back of my head, and then he began to smooth my hair.

I wanted to tell him that I was merely playing house with Bill and everything just felt wrong, but I couldn't find the words. So I just let him hug me for a little longer.

I left my parents' house after dinner, not saying a word to them about Bill. I knew tomorrow we'd arrive together, and I didn't want to spoil everyone's Christmas Eve. I rode back in silence, not even listening to the radio, as I did almost every other day. The sky was silky and black. The stars were radiant, and I drove home bathed in the light of a full moon.

44

I arrived home close to ten p.m., and when I walked in, Bill was sitting in the comfy chair by the TV, watching a basketball game.

"I was about to send out a search crew to look for you," he joked, without getting up from the couch.

I pulled off my coat and dropped my bag on the chair. "I stopped off to see my parents after work."

"Aren't we seeing them tomorrow? Why the need for repeat visits?"

I shrugged and flopped down on a chair to pull off my boots. "I was feeling strange today. I guess I just wanted to see them."

It was clear he had already eaten. The tall pot we used to boil water for pasta was in the sink, and there was an empty jar of sauce on the counter. In the colander the spaghetti had stuck together in a big, gloppy mound. I was glad I had eaten earlier with my parents.

"Mags," he hollered from the living room. "My mom wants us at their house by noon on Christmas Day. Does that work for you?"

I left the pots and spaghetti where they were. I wasn't in the mood to clean up after his mess. I walked back into the living room and leaned against one of the plaster walls.

"We should leave by ten, then. There'll be traffic on the expressway."

"Sure. Whatever you say . . ." His eyes were still focused on the game.

Looking at him, I finally knew why I was so incensed by his laziness. I knew Yuri would have done anything to get out of his chair and go outside to take advantage of all that life had to offer. And even with all his physical limitations, his curiosity couldn't be stifled. But here I was with a man who seemed to have no curiosity, no desire to do anything other than flop down in front of the television during his free time, despite being perfectly healthy. I felt a rage swell inside me.

"You know what I'd really like?" I said, my voice rising. "It's for you to pick up those logs of cherrywood that have been sitting in the corner of the living room since June and make me a damn fire!" I pulled the remote from his hand and shut off the TV.

"I want to wrap my Christmas presents tonight with that fireplace going in full blaze. That's what I want for Christmas!" I was nearly hyperventilating from my rage. "Can you do that for me, Bill? Can you?"

He looked at me like I had been snatched up by Martians. I had never exploded at him like this before. He just sat there, stunned.

I watched as he got up, his eyes searching to find the old me somewhere behind the angry red face and glare. He reached the corner of the room where the logs were piled in a basket, and began to transfer them to the hearth. Bill had been an Eagle Scout in his younger days and knew quite well how to build a fire. He layered the logs into a makeshift pyramid. Then he went to the kitchen and took yesterday's newspaper and tore it into large strips, which he then crumpled into balls and placed underneath the rack. He worked swiftly, his body bent over the hearth. When he was finished, he went back to the kitchen and retrieved a box of matches, then lit each of his balls of paper to ignite the fire.

I watched as the flames began to rise. Bill closed the screen, brushed off his knees, and stood up.

The smell of burning cherrywood permeated the room. Finally, I could feel myself softening, the rage dissipating from my body.

I sat down on the couch and curled my feet underneath me. Bill sat down next to me and admired his own handiwork.

"Merry Christmas, Mags," he said quietly. I pulled the wool throw over my legs and searched underneath the folds of the blanket to find his hand.

45

BILL and I arrived at my parents' early the next evening, carrying boxes of presents and a nice bottle of Chianti Riserva. Their house was draped with twinkling lights, and my father had wrapped the front door with a large red satin ribbon.

It had begun to snow that morning, and as Bill and I teetered up the front steps, I felt like a child again, giddy with anticipation of my mother's food and the house full of good cheer. My brother had arrived earlier that afternoon with his wife, and I was eager for him to unwrap the grilling tools I had gotten him from Brookstone. I was sure he was going to love them. I had also thrown in a new cookbook from Bobby Flay to make it extra festive.

My dad answered the door and gave Bill and me huge, hearty hugs. I had been home only twenty-four hours earlier, but the house had since been completely transformed. Bing Crosby was singing Christmas carols on the stereo. Dad had draped garlands of holly over the banister and had even gone so far as to dangle mistletoe above the threshold to the living room.

Charlie came over with his wife, Annie, and slapped Bill on the back. "Good to see you, bro," he said before coming over and planting a kiss on my cheek.

"Are you ready to dive into the seven fishes? Annie's been counting the minutes until Mom serves her calamari."

I laughed. Mom always infused her cornmeal with lots of dried oregano and pepper before she flash fried it. Charlie and I used to fight over who got to finish the last pieces.

"Watch out," I warned Annie. "The calamari wars are intense in the Topper house."

"Consider yourself forewarned," Bill added. "Maggie was honing her feisty skills last night with me."

"Really? I would have liked to see that." Charlie raised an eyebrow at me.

"I just wanted a fire," I defended myself. I gestured toward the roaring one my father had made. "I don't think there's anything wrong with that."

Dad came over and threw an arm over my shoulder, squeezing me toward him. "Nothing's wrong with that. Bill should cherish a girl who knows what she wants."

I forced a smile. "You have to see our little house, Annie. It's all New England charm, right here on Long Island!"

"The way your mom described the place, it sounds like it's lifted straight from the pages of a Jane Austen novel."

I laughed. "It's far more modest than that, but you know I'm a sucker for old-world charm. I think the real estate agent had never seen someone become so starry-eyed at the sight of low ceilings, no closets, and uneven floorboards." I threw a glance at Bill. "But reading by a fire or taking a soak in an old claw-foot tub goes a long way with me."

"You like the place, too, Bill?" Charlie looked over at him.

Bill shrugged. "My needs are simple. What can I say? My comfy chair fits in the living room. My TV works. And my commute is now fifteen minutes shorter, and I'm making more money. So yeah, I'm good with it."

I could see my brother was about to make a joke when my mom suddenly appeared in her bright red apron, carrying a tray of calamari.

"Let the festivities begin," my father cheered. We all fell upon the food like a swarm of buzzing bees.

46

I drove home with Bill nodding off against the car's windowpane. We fell asleep that night like tired children, not brushing our teeth or taking off our clothes. The next morning, I turned the shower on extra-hot, running the water over my face and body as I tried to wake up. When I was finished, I wrapped the towel around me and twisted my hair into a turban.

"Bill," I said as I sat at the corner of the bed. "We should leave in an hour if we want to be on time for your folks."

He raised a groggy hand to his eyes and rubbed his lids. "Geez. What did your dad put in that spiced wine? I can hardly move."

I ignored him. It wasn't the wine that had given him the hangover, but all the other alcohol he had consumed along with it.

I leaned over to kiss him. "Merry Christmas. May your year be merry and bright."

He kissed me back with dry lips. His breath was heavy. "Merry Christmas, Maggie Ann."

He always called me Maggie Ann when he was trying to be affectionate. As if the addition of my middle name could evoke some bygone era of early Americana or Southern Gothic or something or other that he thought I'd interpret as charm. He was right. It always made me smile.

"Give me ten more minutes," he muttered as he rolled over on his stomach. "A man needs all of his fortitude before he sees his mother."

BILL'S mother was indeed formidable. The kind you never would call beautiful, but rather belonging to that strange sphere of females who when you called them "handsome," everyone knew right away what you meant. No one ever described a petite blond woman as "handsome." It was reserved solely for tall, big-boned brunettes who didn't take nonsense from anyone. And that, indisputably, was Bill's mother.

I liked Eleanor, even though she was as different from my own mother as one could be. She didn't cook and she hated to garden, but she had been one of the first women in her neighborhood to go back to work full-time after giving birth. Even at sixty, she worked five days a week at the local bank, handling residential mortgages. Bill's father, Jerry, a retired engineer, was proud to relinquish control to his extremely capable wife. "She runs everything like clockwork" was his favorite phrase to describe Eleanor. I could already hear him saying it as I took the hair dryer and began to blow out my hair.

WE drove north to Mamaroneck, taking turns listening to each other's favorite radio stations. I had eaten so much the night before at my parents' house that I was almost relieved that Eleanor's Christmas Day lunch would consist solely of a rotisserie chicken and coleslaw from the local grocery store. Bill was an only child, and Eleanor loved to say how she hated any leftovers. She prided herself on having nothing but empty containers at the end. If there was even one leftover pickle, she was visibly annoyed.

We pulled into their driveway a little after noon. The pale yellow house with its gutters draped with sharp, long icicles seemed to sag from the weight of the snow. There were no traces of Christmas lights anywhere on the exterior. The smells of their house were also so different from my childhood home during the holidays; the most obvious reason was that their synthetic tree had no fragrance. I had grown up with a father who waxed on about the beauty of a balsam fir or Canadian spruce if he could find one. But it all went back to efficiency with Eleanor. She wanted something she could simply pack and unpack again in a box she stored in the basement. The tree achieved its purpose—it commemorated the holiday—but there was no art or beauty to be found with it. It was meant to be practical and efficient without any fuss.

ELEANOR greeted us, wearing a navy knit pantsuit and pearls. Her dark brown hair was in a neat French twist.

"You two made good time, didn't you," she said, kissing us both on the cheek.

"We did," Bill agreed, proud that his mother noticed just how punctual we were.

"Your dad is downstairs getting some paper plates from the storeroom. I have some crackers and cheese laid out in the den. Go help yourselves."

She took our coats and we made our way into the next room. The fake tree glimmered with a few twinkling lights and ornaments. Bill took our shopping bag and put our gifts underneath the tree while I sat down on the sofa.

"So how is school this year?" Eleanor asked as she sat down across from me. "Any diamonds in the bunch?"

Something about her phrasing made me feel immediately uncomfortable.

"Well, they're all wonderful children. But yes—I have a few very special ones this year."

"Tell her about Yuri," Bill urged as he made a cheese-and-cracker sandwich from a Ritz cracker and slice of Port Salut. From afar it looked like a psychedelic Oreo. I was surprised that Bill, who never asked me about Yuri, was now all of a sudden prodding me to tell his mother about him.

"Yuri?" Eleanor's voice rose slightly with interest. "Do you have a Russian in your class?"

I laughed, slightly uncomfortable. "No, Eleanor. I'm tutoring a little boy whose parents are originally from the Ukraine. Hence, the unusual name."

"Tutoring?" Her voice sounded surprised. She took a moment to gather the information before her long arm reached for a slice of cheese. Her nails were polished brick red. "Have you taken that on for some extra pocket money?" She took a bite of her cheese. "Good for you, Maggie. I'm impressed. You've really always had a great work ethic."

"Oh no, he's a student in my district who has a heart condition. I tutor him at home so he can keep up with his grade level."

"My Maggie's going to be an all-star mother someday," Bill said, squeezing my knee. "All this practice teaching is going to pay off the moment we have kids."

I stiffened at his words. We had never discussed having children in the way so many young couples often do as a way to peer into the future. The thought of becoming parents had seemed so far in the distance, yet now, as Bill referenced the possibility of it, I was incensed that he saw my job in teaching only as a practice run.

"Teaching is not practice, Bill. It's a real job and an incredibly important one," I corrected him.

"Of course it is, dear," Eleanor said as she whisked away the light dusting of crumbs that had settled on her pantsuit. "Bill had a mother who worked, he knows that."

But it occurred to me that perhaps Bill didn't want what he had had in his own childhood. He wanted the opposite. He didn't want my energy or affections diverted.

I felt my body pull away from him. Even my knee didn't want to touch his. I knew I wanted to have my own children someday, but I certainly didn't think of my job as "practice" for that.

Eleanor was now leaning over and trying to pull more information out of Bill on his own job. "So are you getting a bonus this year, honey? How much?" In her voice I heard the pull of a magnet, its fingers searching for the confirmation of numbers and figures.

I was just about to excuse myself to go to the bathroom when I heard the sound of Jerry's voice entering the room.

"Merry Christmas," he announced brightly. Clutching a stack of paper plates and napkins, his gray hair combed back, he looked like a dead ringer for the way I imagined Bill would look in forty years' time. The ruddy face, the water blue eyes. And the Giants jersey he had put on over his crew neck sweater.

"Very funny, Jerry." Eleanor's voice was dry as dust. "Now take it off."

He laughed. "Nothing like upsetting the old lady for some holiday fun." He peeled off the jersey and flopped down on one of the chairs next to us.

"So what's going on with my favorite young couple?" Jerry leaned over to the crystal swan dish and popped some M&M's in his mouth. "Sorry, you know I'm not much of a cheese fan, El," he mumbled as he scooped up another handful and brought it to his lips.

Eleanor feigned a smile and looked toward the tree. "Perhaps we should exchange our presents now. It's always nice to do that before we sit down to eat."

Bill reached over and made one final cheese-and-cracker sandwich before heading over to the tree. I felt a slight wave of nausea flooding over me. I no longer wanted to be there. Even worse, I was seized by a sudden insecurity that everyone was going to hate the gifts I had brought. For Eleanor, I had picked out a Talbots scarf and a costume gold-link necklace that I thought she could wear to work.

Bill had suggested a flannel shirt and fleece as a gift for his father. Everything was wrapped in sparkly silver paper and tied with red satin bows.

In my house, when gifts were exchanged, there was a multilayered ritual for how you were to receive them. You first acknowledged the beauty of the paper, then you carefully unwrapped it and always made sure to show your gratitude for the thoughtfulness of the present. By the time you actually got to the gift, you had already complimented the person who gave it to you, maybe five times. I realized this was excessive and over the top, and Bill had actually made jokes about this when we first started dating. The first time he'd given me a birthday present, he'd become so impatient to see my reaction, he'd reached over and started tearing off the paper himself.

This year, his family had made things easy for me. The Lord & Taylor gift box just had an elastic string over it to keep the lid closed.

"For you, Maggie," Eleanor said as she handed it to me. "We asked Bill, and he said you're always saying you're cold all the time."

I smiled and slid the elastic off the box. I could tell it was too light to have a space heater inside. I was right. Inside was a hot pink chenille robe.

"That'll sure keep you warm," Bill chirped.

"It certainly will," I agreed. "Thank you so much."

"And it will go well with my gift, too." Bill handed me two boxes.

I opened the first and discovered a pair of deerskin slippers. In the second was a red cable-knit sweater.

"You do say you're always so cold, Mags," Bill said meekly.

I could feel my eyes beginning to water. I knew I was being ridiculously oversensitive. Perhaps I had made a few too many comments that I found the cottage a bit drafty, but I was just hinting then that I wanted Bill to make a romantic fire.

"That's my boy," Jerry said as he held up his new flannel shirt and admired it.

Bill opened my gift. I had splurged and gotten him a sports watch, the TAG Heuer model he'd been admiring. "We've both been working so much," I said softly. "I thought it would be sweet to give you the gift of time."

"You're sure original, Maggie." He laughed. I knew he was trying to give me a compliment, but it fell flat. "Guess that's why you were an English major, not me."

THE Christmas break passed uneventfully. Quiet swept through the cottage, and the icicles on the edge of the windows made me feel as if part of me was frozen and not ready for the thaw. Still, I found warmth and comfort in my various rituals around the house. I used the time off to organize my things and finally unpack the few stray boxes that I had left stored away since June. I slept in and took long baths. We had been invited to Suzie's place for New Year's Eve, and I was looking forward to having the chance to get dressed up and drink a little champagne with friends.

I had even bought a sparkly new dress for the evening. "Wear something outside your comfort zone," Suzie had instructed me, giving a little pinch on my rear. "You have a great figure, but you're always hiding it."

I gave her an affectionate smack on her arm. "Cut it out," I teased back. "I wouldn't want to distract my students with all the greatness I have tucked underneath these baggy chinos."

"I'm serious, Mags. You're only young once; don't waste it." She slid her hands down the curves of her own body. "I love you. You know that. You're the only one I'd ever share my art supplies with, that's how deep a friend I consider you . . . so listen to me. Wear something hot on New Year's Eve."

I let out a huge laugh. The art-supply comment cracked me up. Suzie guarded her materials like they were the jewels of the Vatican. All the other teachers were scared to even ask to borrow a pair of her scissors or a few sheets of construction paper. But I knew Suzie would offer me her last pot of glitter.

"You just want me to wake Bill up, don't you?"

Suzie made a face. "It's you I'm aiming to wake up, honey. I actually wasn't thinking about Bill at all."

IT might have been wrong of me, but I decided to return the chenille robe that Eleanor had gifted me. I would use the credit at Lord & Taylor to buy something I actually liked. If everyone thought I was complaining of being too cold, what better way to warm me up than purchasing a stretchy black velvet dress with a deep plunging neckline.

It certainly was outside my typical comfort zone, but when I looked in the department store mirror, I felt transformed. The dress hugged me in all the right places. "Now that's a dress!" the salesgirl said with enthusiastic approval.

I appraised myself one more time in the mirror. With the store credit, it would set me back only an additional eighty dollars. I stood on my tiptoes, imagining myself in my black patent heels.

"I'll take it," I told the salesgirl. And when I emerged from the dressing room, I triumphantly handed over my credit card.

BILL was sitting in the den when I came downstairs in my new black dress. Also gone were the pumped-up curls of my college days. I blew my hair smooth and then rolled it into soft, sensual waves, using an old photograph of Lauren Bacall as my inspiration. My strawberry hair looked vibrant against the dark velvet, and I made a special effort to put mascara on my blond eyelashes for a dramatic effect. I was going all out this time. Bill hated perfume, but I put some Turkish rose water in my bath so my skin would have the lightest scent of floral.

"Are you ready yet?" he hollered just as I was descending the stairs.

I took two steps down and saw him sitting on the big comfy chair. He was wearing jeans and a half-zip pullover.

"You're sure all dressed up," he said cheerily, putting down the remote.

"It's New Year's Eve, Bill," I murmured so quietly I'm not even sure whether he could hear me. I felt like a roller coaster that was crashing down, my heart plummeting into my stomach. All afternoon I had been imagining how Bill would react to the sight of me transformed. I wanted to believe his eyes would open wide and he would leap from the comfy chair and not be able to resist me. But I was wrong. He didn't even bother to get up.

Don't let yourself cry when you have mascara on. I heard my mother's voice in my mind. I was two seconds away from looking like a melting black crayon.

"I thought it was just a casual party at your friend's house," he proffered. He stood up and looked down at what he was wearing. "Should I go change, Mags?"

It was already dark outside, and when I came into the den, I caught myself in the reflection of one of the windows. My hair, the dress, the sad look of disappointment on my face.

"It doesn't really matter," I mumbled. My feet were already starting to pinch in my shoes. Bill opened the front door and reached for his car keys. "I'll drive there and you can drive back," he said.

I nodded. I was glad at least one of us seemed to have a plan.

BILL drove to Suzie's blithely. He turned the radio to WFAN and smiled at me as we navigated toward her house.

When we arrived, it was Suzie who instantly made me feel better. "Hey, pretty woman," she said when she opened the door. "Vavavavoom!"

She was looking pretty seductive herself. Gone were the oversize sweaters with paillettes or jingle bells. Suzie was wearing a floor-length red velvet dress with fake white fur at the breast and hem. Her ample cleavage looked as though it were peeking out from a nesting rabbit.

Suzie took the bottle of champagne from Bill and waved a finger at him. "You better watch out for her, or she'll be swept up by all the cuties here tonight."

Bill made a face. "I'll proceed with caution, Suzie."

She looked over to me. "Just wanted him to consider himself forewarned. It is, after all, the last night of the millennium. Anything could happen."

"Don't tell me you have a bunker stored with a year's worth of ramen and Poland Spring," I said, shaking my head.

"Do Ring Dings and Mountain Dew count?" She pinched my arm.

"That really might be the end of the world," I laughed over the music. "Now where's that champagne?"

SUZIE lived in a basement apartment, but she had outdone herself in making it appear festive. There were glimmers of sparkle everywhere. Tiny white Christmas lights were draped on the walls. Votive candles swamped her bookshelves, and long tapers flickered on the dining room table. The entire room glowed.

"Do you want a drink?" Bill asked as soon as we had both shed our coats. I shook my head no and began surveying the room for a familiar face. "I'll have something in a few minutes. I need to pace myself."

In the corner, I did see someone I recognized. Daniel was standing by himself drinking a glass of red wine. He was wearing a moss green velvet blazer and jeans. Suzie had just changed the CD in the stereo. "This one is for all of you out there," she hollered over the music. R.E.M.'s "It's the End of the World as We Know It" now blasted through the room. Everyone at the party cheered.

Maybe Suzie was right. I needed to embrace the fact that we were stepping into a new century. I didn't think we'd wake up tomorrow and our checking accounts would be wiped out or that the power grid would be shorted, but this was the only time in my life I'd be alive to witness a change in the millennium.

Feeling emboldened, I walked over to Daniel and pulled at his sleeve. "Guess we both had velvet on the brain."

His eyes lit up, and the white of his smile was intensified by the lavender fluorescent light bulbs Suzie had put in to mark the occasion.

"I was trying to think what they might have worn in 1899." His lips turned up wryly. He looked at my dress. "But I gotta be honest, you wear it a lot better than I do."

I laughed.

"You look great," he said again. "I mean it."

"Thanks, you made my night." I nestled my back against the wall. "I'll be glad to put all this Y2K stuff to rest. It's getting kind of old already."

"Yeah, I know, but it did make me take a look at my life and force myself to stop waiting to do things I'm passionate about."

"Like what?"

"Well, to start, I haven't gotten out of my head the fact that your father makes violins." His voice rose above the music. "I'm in the market for a new one. And I'd still love to see what he does."

The image of my father exuberantly showing Daniel his work floated through my mind. I knew how much my father would enjoy it.

"You want to visit his workshop?" I was tickled by the thought of it.

"Yeah, I do. Am I stepping out of line?"

"God, not at all. My dad would love that, but you'll need to put aside a couple hours. When he gets started on the art of violin making, it's hard to cut him off."

From the corner of my eye, I could see Suzie giving me a thumbs-up and moving sensually toward the dance floor as Sugar Ray's latest song replaced R.E.M. In her red velvet and faux-fur-trimmed dress, she looked like a sexy Mrs. Claus.

"I love the idea of making a day of it."

I know it sounds corny, but I felt as though I were in a scene in a movie. My skin tingled and my heart beat a little faster. I suddenly felt incredibly alive. That is until Suzie came over and pulled me onto the dance floor.

"I'm not letting you leave tonight without seeing you dance first," she hollered into my ear.

With her arm thrust through mine, Suzie led me to a small square of flooring where she started spiraling me around to Britney Spears.

"Now that's my girl," she yelled over the music. Suzie was mouthing *Hit me, baby, one more time* when she gave me one more exuberant swirl.

But this time my lower and upper body seemed to go in opposite directions. I felt my knee give way, and suddenly I was sliding to the ground.

"Oh my God, I'm so sorry, honey." She bent down and tried to help me up. But I sat there on the ground like fallen fruit, my ankle throbbing. I pulled off my shoes, silently cursing myself for wearing such impractical heels, and hobbled over to a chair.

I looked around for Bill but couldn't find him in the crowd. When I raised my head again, Daniel was standing in front of me, pouring ice from a red plastic cup into a paper towel.

"You need some ice," he said as he lowered himself to the ground and held it to my ankle.

It was funny that I would hear Yuri's voice in my head when I felt the cold relief of the ice pressed into my skin. *You take care of the people you love.* As I was recalling those words, Bill was nowhere in sight.

HOW strange it all was. As my ankle throbbed, the rest of me felt numb. I was vaguely aware of Daniel and Suzie buzzing around me, but they seemed very far away. I made the appropriate responses. Told Suzie not to worry before she went in search of Bill. Thanked Daniel. When Bill finally arrived on the scene, I admitted to him that I had kind of lost the New Year's spirit. And as I threw an arm over his shoulder, I asked if he'd take me home.

We made it into his car, and I pressed my face to the chill of the frosty window as Bill turned on the ignition.

"I've got a surprise to share. I wasn't going to say anything until tomorrow. But now seems like a good time to tell you . . ."

"Sounds mysterious." I forced myself to sound intrigued, despite the pain.

"I'm going to get a new car with my bonus. I'm thinking a BMW roadster. Maybe even red."

I closed my eyes. "Really?" I forced my voice to sound excited for him, but truthfully, the excitement in his voice, something that I hadn't heard in a long time, only made me feel sad.

47

MY leg propped up on pillows the next morning, I realized I was about to witness the execution of my six-year relationship. For weeks now, I had felt trapped. But my physical immobility now had triggered another sensation. I needed to acknowledge the truth: that Bill and I were not going to grow closer within the four walls of this cottage. Not even the most idyllic setting could mask the fissures of our relationship. Bill looked outward to find happiness; I looked inward. Suddenly everything that had seemed murky before now appeared crystal clear.

BILL walked toward the bathroom and turned on the shower. I heard the rush of the water, then the familiar sound of him closing the glass door. When he emerged, I was sitting up straight. My eyes focused on him wrapped in his towel.

"What's wrong?" Bill asked. "You still upset about last night?"

"It's a new year," I said slowly.

"We were great in college," I continued, the words falling flatly from my mouth. "But in real life, we're . . . we're just not working."

He was quiet. The winter glare penetrated our bedroom. He looked painfully bare, standing half-naked.

"Mags . . . is this about last night? I didn't even see you fall."

"I realize that," I said. "Suzie had to find you afterward. She said you were chatting up a storm with Vicki Di Piazzo."

"You're not being fair. She cornered me all evening." He turned his back to me and pulled out a shirt from the dresser, rolling it over his chest quickly.

I didn't answer him. The truth was I was actually relieved that he'd spent the entire night talking with Vicki Di Piazzo, the gym teacher. It made me feel less guilty that all I wanted to do was to cozy up to Daniel and talk about teaching, his love for the violin, and how he believed music could change a student's soul.

"Come on," he insisted and sat down on the bed.

I forced myself to continue. "I thought this cottage would be perfect practice for our setting up house together." I looked around the bedroom, noticing all the touches I had brought in to make it seem charming. The floral bedspread, the framed photographs of us at a Michigan basketball game. But none of it had brought us closer. The simple fact was we no longer had college and campus life in common. We didn't have the distractions of Manhattan, either. Real life happened, and we were each going in different directions.

"Maggie," he said. "You're not being fair. You've been in a rut ever since you started tutoring that kid Yuri. You and I both know that. This has nothing to do with us."

I looked at him, incredulous. It had everything to do with us.

"The thing about my job, Bill . . . it forces you to change the way you see things. And with a student like Yuri . . . I see life differently *because* of him, and that's a good thing. It's not a rut." I took a deep breath. "If anything, it's an epiphany."

"Maggie."

"Please don't," I said, lifting my hand. "It's a new year, a new millennium. It's time for a fresh start for both of us."

"And how are you going to pay for this place on just one salary?" His voice suddenly sounded steely.

"I have enough saved up to pay the rent by myself till the end of the year. Then I'll look for another place if I need to . . ." I refused to let him think I had to rely on him to pay the bills.

"This is bullshit, Maggie." He got off the bed and went to his sock drawer. He pulled out a Tiffany catalog that had been buried underneath his socks. He flung it on the bed.

"To think I was going to propose to you on your birthday!"

I looked at the robin's-egg blue box on the cover, the satin white ribbon tied in a perfect bow, and none of it moved me. How many times had I imagined a perfect proposal? A velvet box offered on a bended knee. And yet, now all I wanted to do was fling the catalog back at him.

"I'm sorry," I said, trying to hold back my tears. "I know it isn't you who's changed. It's me . . . I'm the one who's different."

"You're damn right!" he said, the palm of his hand slamming down on the top of the dresser.

HE had packed up all his things by the end of the week. The television was gone, too, as was the comfy chair. But there were still some dry logs in the corner basket. I poured myself a glass of wine, propped up my still-healing ankle on a tower of pillows, and did what I'd been wanting to do for some time. I made myself one hell of a fire.

48

AFTER Bill left, I went into overdrive paring down my budget, trying to live as simply as possible. I canceled the cable. I stopped ordering in delivery for dinner and stayed as far away as I could from the mall. At the same time, with Bill gone, I was throwing myself into my work even more. We were still reading *Number the Stars* in my class, a novel that takes place in Denmark during the German occupation. For most of my students, this was the first time they would be reading about the turbulence and horrors of World War II. Aside from discussing the touching friendship between the two young girls at the center of the story, Ellen and Annemarie, I wanted to explore the theme of heroism.

I thought that Yuri and Finn would have a particularly interesting discussion about it. The two of them had really taken to each other. They fed off each other's enthusiasm, not only because of their mutual affection for the Yankees but because they also seemed to thrive on the personal and philosophical conversations we often had regarding the books we were reading. I noticed a difference in how Finn acted in my classroom compared to when he was with Yuri. In class, he seemed a little more self-conscious about how much he participated. It was as if he was keeping track of how many comments he made or how often he raised his hand, not wanting to come across as too bookish to the other kids. When he came to visit Yuri, though, he seemed to let his guard down, and I saw how much he enjoyed having free rein to contribute as much as he wanted to the discussion.

As I adjusted to the solitude of living in my storybook cottage by myself, one of the highlights of the New Year for me was seeing the two boys form a friendship of their own. When I reread the novel to prepare my class notes, I couldn't help but think of Yuri and Finn replacing the characters of Annemarie and Ellen. Two friends, one more vulnerable than the other, whose friendship deepens in the face of adversity.

"Who do you think is the hero in the novel?" I asked the boys. The two of them had settled down after discussing the latest news about the Yankees.

"Well, there are a lot of heroes in the book," Finn said.

"Annemarie's parents are . . . They take Ellen in and hide her," Yuri added.

"And don't forget Peter, who's in the Resistance."

"The fisherman who takes Annemarie and her family to safer shores is a hero, too . . ." Yuri's eyes perked up. I could tell the difference for him in having Finn joining the discussion. It added a bit of boyish competition to the mix.

For homework, I asked them to further ponder what it meant to be a hero. Did it mean only that you always acted bravely, or was the definition more complex?

Two days later, as I read Yuri's notebook, I was overwhelmed by his response.

I don't think you can be a hero unless you have something to lose. A lot of people in Denmark wished their King Christian was in charge instead of the Nazis, but being a hero is more than saying you don't agree with something. To be a hero, you have to risk something. You have to feel danger. Annemarie and her family are risking their lives to hide Ellen. Annemarie also risks her life when she sneaks out in the night to get the false papers to the fisherman who is taking Ellen and her family to Sweden. Peter is shot in the end of the book because of his efforts to help others. All of these people are heroes in my opinion.

It was approaching the end of February. Nearly two months had passed since Bill moved out, and I had made myself into an expert at building a fire. I may not have been an Eagle Scout like Bill, but I was resourceful and determined to do it even more so now that I was single.

It had become a nightly tradition for me, so I carved out the time to do it. Every Saturday afternoon, I went to one of the local farms that sold firewood and loaded up my trunk with logs. Learning how to build something that could keep me warm and cast a beautiful light in the room made up for my lack of companionship.

And although the house was quieter than I liked, I managed to find company by hearing the voices of my students come alive in their writing.

Annemarie's father is a hero when he pretends Ellen is his daughter. He came up with the idea so quickly when that Nazi asked him, he became an instant hero when he did that, Lisa Yamamoto wrote in her perfect script. She drew a picture of the interior of an apartment with Annemarie and Ellen hiding in their beds as Ellen's father stood in the doorway, arguing with the German officer.

I thought Peter was the real hero in the book, Roland McKenna wrote.

He actually died risking his life, so he was the biggest hero of all of the characters in the story.

Finn's was the last notebook in the stack. I pulled it over and placed it on my lap. The decorations on the cover were mostly glued cutouts of athletes from *Sports Illustrated* and the sports section of *Newsday.* Derek Jeter at home plate. A team photo of the 1999 Yankees. Pictures of Wayne Gretzky skating and Michael Jordan dunking a basketball. But then I spotted a photo on the lower right corner that must have been a few years old of Finn with his baby sister on his lap—his arm draped protectively around her as she grasped a tattered stuffed animal.

I leafed through the pages from earlier in the school year before reading his response to this latest assignment.

> *I think in order to be a true hero you can't think of yourself as one. A hero does the right thing by instinct. Annemarie's family does not have a lot of time to think about whether to take Ellen into their home, but they do it because they know it's right. Peter helps find safe passage for Jewish families because he knows they need his help. I think people who are heroes know what's right and wrong. They won't go against what they know to be the right thing to do, even if it means risking their own life.*

I wasn't sure what it was about Finn's entry that touched me so deeply, but I found myself forcing back tears as I read it. He had drawn a medal of courage with red and black Magic Markers, and I had to put his notebook to the side, out of fear that one of my tears would fall and cause the edges of his drawing to run.

49

I had started to grow used to the sound of hearing only my own movements around the house, along with the banging of the old radiators and the wind whipping against the windowpanes. Although I found myself lonely at times, I didn't miss the blaring of the television on all night or having to clean the sink of Bill's stubble from his shaving. When I opened the coat closet, I was no longer greeted by a mass of down parkas and puffy vests, and I could find my trench coat with ease. But what I did miss—and I missed it a lot—was that easy and familiar conversation that pulls you out of the rut of a long day. As much as I loved lying in bed at night with a good book and the freedom to smear a face mask over my cheeks like war paint, there was the inescapable reality that I was spending all my nights alone.

Then, just after Presidents' Day weekend, I found myself somehow trapped in the faculty room with Suzie when Daniel sidled up to our table.

"Maggie Topper." He said my full name in such a soft, lulling voice that I noticed Suzie could hardly contain her Cheshire cat grin.

"People don't use full names often enough . . . There's a musicality to saying a complete name that I like," he mused.

"Anyway, I've been trying to find a moment to ask you something . . ." The color in his face suddenly deepened, and it was hard not to find him incredibly charming. He paused and now looked toward Suzie, as if she were going to help him find the right words to say. But she just pushed open her Tupperware of pasta primavera and gave him her biggest, brightest smile. As charmed as I was, Suzie was amused to see a grown man struggling to talk to me.

"So I know I mentioned this at Suzie's party, but I'm wondering if I could take you up on your offer to visit your father's workshop. I really want to replace my violin, and the more I think about it . . . the more intrigued I become about your father and his instruments."

I giggled. "You have no idea how excited he'll be if I bring him a potential customer. He hasn't quite mastered the art of self-marketing yet."

Daniel flashed another smile. Suddenly the deep red flush vanished from his face. He was beaming.

"So let's plan a time to go. Speak to him and let me know what works for you, too." He slapped the top of one of the empty chairs. "I'm excited about this, Maggie. I really am."

"I'm happy, too." I gave him a playful tap. "You're going to make me daughter of the year if you end up buying one of his violins."

Suzie grinned as he turned to head back to class. "Now what do you think the likelihood is that he actually buys one of your dad's instruments, Mags?"

"I don't know . . . twenty percent? My dad will be thrilled even just to have the chance to talk music and violin making with someone who's as interested in that stuff as he is."

"My guess is, it's a done deal, one hundred percent," she said as she replaced the cover on her lunch. "You amaze me, Maggie, if you don't realize that Daniel has a huge crush on you."

THE following Sunday, Daniel pulled up to my cottage in a red Honda Civic. I heard his footsteps treading on the gravel path before he even had a chance to ring the doorbell.

It was a bit pathetic, but I had spent much of the prior evening trying on different clothes for our outing. The logical and skeptical part of my brain kept telling me to stop imagining this as a romantic rendezvous. We were going to see my parents, after all, and no sane male would suggest a visit to a girl's family as a first date. Only someone who really wanted to purchase a violin and nothing else would suggest such a ludicrous plan. But I still couldn't help but want to look as fetching as possible. I tried on nearly a half dozen pairs of pants until I found the ones that flattered my hips the most.

I thought about how Katya always looked so effortlessly chic with her long tunic sweaters and pants, but I didn't have that ballerina body that looked good swaddled in so many layers. After trying on every blouse I had in my closet, I selected one in French blue cotton and tied a scarf jauntily around my neck like my mother did when she needed a bit of a boost. I wasn't quite sure the look worked for me. I looked either very French and chic or like a stewardess for Air France, but there was no going back now. He had already rung the doorbell.

When I opened the door, Daniel was standing at the threshold, holding a box of chocolates. "Thought I should bring your parents something," he said, lifting it up for me to see.

Suddenly my nervousness dissipated. He looked so earnest standing there with his box of chocolates, I knew that he wasn't going to notice if my black pants matched my blue blouse or not.

"How sweet of you." I waved a hand toward the living room. "I just made a pot of coffee. Do you want some before we leave?" He stepped inside, and his eyes glanced over the room. The house still smelled of the cherrywood I had burned the night before.

"You have a working fireplace?" Daniel asked, eyeing the mantel. "How did you find this place?"

I laughed. "The PennySaver. It was a real stroke of luck."

"I'll say," he said, impressed. "You'd probably vomit if you saw the hole I'm renting. It's normally a two-family house, but I'm the non-family-related tenant who's stuck in the basement."

"Sounds quite lovely . . . Milk or sugar in the coffee?"

"However you take yours is good for me."

"Light and sweet, then?"

"I'd like that . . . ," he said, and I watched as he carefully moved the pillows of the couch to sit down. "Yes, light and sweet sounds perfect."

WE drove out to my parents' with no music on the radio, just a bit of small talk. It was a treat to bring a fresh pair of eyes to see my beloved Strong's Neck. I rolled down the window an inch, and an icy breeze rushed into the car. I admired him in profile. His high cheekbones, the small sickle-shaped scar, and the head full of Byronian black curls.

"I feel like I'm traveling back in time with you," he laughed as we drove over the bridge. "Your cottage, your fireplace, and now this . . ." He pointed to a horse farm not far from the old Selah Strong homestead, a place where my dad had taken me to ride my first pony when I was no older than five.

"It's very special out here, and it's nice to show it to someone new. "Want to hear a cool story?"

"Absolutely," he said. "I'm all ears."

And just like my mother did, sitting at the edge of my bed all those years before, I began telling him about the spy Anna Smith Strong and her wicker basket full of colorful clothes.

"NOW, let me tell you a story," he said as I drove deeper into the Neck. He told me how he had grown up in Riverdale, that his father was a history professor and his mother had been a concert pianist until arthritis cut her career short. After her professional retirement, her career was spent teaching a few private students at their home.

"We always had music in our house, you know? My mom or her students practicing, or a record playing or the radio on . . . ," he shared as his eyes drifted out the window. The snow had mostly melted, except for a few frozen islands that would dissipate in the next rain.

"Don't tell me: WQXR."

"Yep, that's the one."

"*All classical, all the time,*" we said in unison.

"But I don't think my brother and I had the sophistication to embrace classical music like you did. I preferred my Olivia Newton-John and Duran Duran."

"All music stirs the soul in some way. Guess I can appreciate all kinds."

We were now in my parents' driveway. "Well, that's a huge relief . . . I don't have to worry that you're going to snub me the next time we run into each other in the faculty room."

"I hardly think you have anything to fear." He opened up the door of the car, hopped out, and gave a dramatic rolling gesture with his hand. "You're a Renaissance woman, Maggie Topper."

I laughed under my breath as we walked toward the front door. "I hope that's a good thing."

He raised one of his eyebrows and shot me a devilish look. "Now, I don't even think I need to answer that one, do I?"

ONCE inside, Daniel was greeted by the scent of eggplant parmigiana and the sound of a violin concerto.

My parents could hardly contain their excitement. I was the cat who had brought in the bright yellow canary. Daniel offered my mother the box of chocolates, and his broad shoulders cut a handsome figure as he leaned over and shook my dad's hand.

"Hear you're in the market for a new violin, son."

I could feel the energy of the room shift. My parents were completely taken with him within seconds of meeting him. "Yes, and when Maggie mentioned you have your own workshop, my curiosity was piqued. I knew I had to see it."

My dad was beaming, and I could see my mom sneaking glances toward me out of the corner of her eye. She was less impressed that I had brought home a music-loving violinist than by the fact that he was a single and handsome man. I looked at her apron and saw a fine dust of cocoa powder near the pocket. It appeared she had also made her tiramisu.

"After you're done downstairs, I've made a little lunch, Daniel, if you have time to stay . . ."

"It smells so good, Mrs. Topper, how could I say no?"

I watched my mother bloom in his presence. Happiness oozed out of her. He was so well mannered, he made Bill look like a convict from Alcatraz.

"Let's get down to the workshop before my wife tempts you with any more talk of her cooking."

Dad pulled open the door to the basement and waved at Daniel and me to follow him.

"Make sure he tries the one that looks like there's a bird in the pattern of the maple," my mother called out to my father. "That one's my favorite."

"Your mother is right," he said. "It really looks like it has wings."

DOWN in my father's lair, the smells of tomato, garlic, and ricotta were replaced by the scent of maple and spruce.

My father did not yet have that many violins in his inventory. The ones from his first few years of learning the craft after his sessions at Oberlin were not what he planned on showing to Daniel. I knew he had at least four more-recent pieces that he was especially proud of, which were the ones that I myself had heard him play. But as was par for the course, I knew that he'd first want to explain his process to Daniel in great detail. And Daniel might even get a kick out of hearing it.

The two of them took to each other immediately. My dad pulled out different examples of wood, the maple, the spruce, the oak . . . and brought them up first to his nose to inhale the scent before giving them to Daniel to also enjoy, like a wine enthusiast sniffing the bouquet before indulging in the first sip. Dad pointed out which wood was used for which part of the instrument and how the beautiful patterns of each piece could inspire the soul of the instrument. He brought out three examples, one in a rich red varnish and the other two more amber in hue, before placing a fourth one on the table. This was the one whose back looked like it had a pair of angel's wings.

My father reached for the last one and tucked it under his chin. He took his bow and began fiddling up and down, his body moving into the instrument like it was his partner in their own dance.

"Unbelievable, Mr. Topper! You can certainly play the fiddle . . . Did you ever play professionally? Maggie didn't mention it . . ."

My father laughed. "No, it didn't work out for me. I tried when I was a kid to get into Juilliard and a few other music schools, but they didn't take me. Guess I wasn't up to snuff." He patted his hands on his smock. "And when I met Maggie's mom, I had to find a job that put food on the table. But I never abandoned my love of music." He looked over to me and smiled. "Maggie can tell you, I tortured her and her brother with all my classical stuff for most of their childhood."

"Most of my childhood? How about all of it!"

"So music was your life, but it was not your livelihood? And it made you feel happy, and it made you feel so good . . ." Daniel's voice lilted. Deep and soulful, the lyrics were immediately familiar to me.

"Oh my God, did you just quote 'Mr. Tanner'?"

"I did, indeed. With a few minor adjustments,"

"I'm not kidding you, Daniel. I was obsessed with that song when I was a teenager."

"It's true. My girl's a huge fan of Harry Chapin." Dad's fingers gently touched the edge of one of his violins. "Such a tragedy . . . He died too young . . . and from Long Island, too."

"You don't need to tell me," Daniel insisted. "My college roommate was from Huntington. I know the lyrics to nearly every one of his songs. 'Cat's in the Cradle,' 'Taxi,' 'Mail Order Annie' . . ."

I had loved Harry Chapin ever since my best friend put on "Cat's in the Cradle" down in her basement during a sixth-grade sleepover. His songs always told a story, and they gave me the same sort of escape my favorite books did.

"I think I have his greatest hits in my car," I mumbled, still in a state of disbelief. "We'll have to pop in the CD on the ride back home."

My father tapped his bow on his worktable. "I don't mean to interrupt you kiddos, but your very own Mr. Tanner would be honored if you tried out one of his instruments. A little honest feedback from a fellow musician would be good for me."

Nearly an hour later, after Daniel had tried out each of the violins and my father gave a tutorial about all the details that went into crafting them—the chisels used for carving the scrolled neck, the saws, the jars of varnish—I could sense that Daniel had fallen in love with the one my mother had mentioned. The one whose pattern in the flaming maple resembled a pair of wings.

"You'll fly with that one." Dad went over and gently touched the rounded edges. "But it's special to me. I'd be sad to part with it."

Daniel pulled the instrument out from his neck and held it up to the light. "It's definitely a real beauty."

"Why don't you take it home with you?" Dad suggested. "Play it a bit and see if you really do love it. I don't want you to make a rushed decision, and there's absolutely no pressure either way. I've only sold a couple of my fiddles, to family friends, so it's not like the customers are beating down my front door."

"Well, not yet, Dad," I added in his defense. "Maybe in ten years you'll be known as the Stradivari of Strong's Neck."

Daniel smiled. "That's very kind of you, Mr. Topper, but I'm not sure I could afford it on my salary, even if I did end up wanting it." His eyes gazed at the strings. "It's a true work of art."

"The truth is, Daniel, I haven't given much thought to what price I should sell it for. I'm making these violins to give me something enjoyable to do in my retirement, right? Honestly, it's all a labor of love."

My dad withdrew a scrap of paper and a small pencil from the pocket of his smock. He tallied up a few numbers and then circled one at the end. "That's the cost of my materials and little bit extra for the time involved. Think about it, and let me know if you think it's fair."

Daniel's eyebrows raised. "Are you kidding me? This is more than fair. You'd practically be giving it away . . ."

"I'd be giving it to a fellow music lover, who also happens to be a friend of my daughter's . . ." He shot me a quick glance. "Think of it as a gift to me, too."

50

WE drove home listening to Harry Chapin's greatest hits, the music filling the air. In the reflection of the car window, I could see Daniel's hands resting on my father's violin case, his fingers gently tapping out the melody against the black handle.

I hadn't felt this happy in months. And now, as the lyrics floated between us, I felt reinvigorated. Our conversation had been so easy. We talked about everything from the smell of the Franklin cafeteria to the perils of teaching the clarinet to twelve-year-old boys with braces. I laughed harder than I had in months. And that laughter made me feel lighter, less lonely, and infinitely more joyous than I had for some time. I had a new friend in Daniel, and it felt good.

What I also realized was that I came alive being around someone who was as thirsty as I was to learn. I loved teaching because my students' curiosity fueled me. And that's why I preferred to spend my lunch hour with Suzie, who was a waterfall of artistic energy, rather than the other English teachers, Florence and Angela, who, with their one-dimensional pragmatism, were anything but inspired.

Daniel, however, was part of that special group—he had the same spark behind the eyes that I looked for in children.

I coasted into the driveway and turned off the ignition. Suddenly, with no more music around us, we seemed to grow more serious.

"I hope the violin lives up to your expectations," I said. "But really, there's no pressure. If you don't like it, we can always do another trip back to the maestro and see if there's another one you want to try out."

"A full-service family," Daniel joked. "I like it. Far better treatment than I'd get at Sam Ash."

He opened the door and popped out. "To say this has been one of the best afternoons I've had in a long time is an understatement, Maggie," he said as he walked backward toward his car, lifting the violin slightly in my direction.

"I'll be looking out for you in the faculty room tomorrow!"

The scent of microwaved plastic and stale coffee no longer seemed so off-putting to me. Instead, I was elated at the thought of it.

51

SUZIE didn't seem so thrilled that I forced her to eat lunch with me the next day in the faculty room. "But I brought a salad," she said. "I don't need the olfactory overload. Can't we just eat in your classroom, like usual?"

"I really want to hear how much he liked my dad's violin, but I don't want it to look like I'm stalking him, either."

"It's hard to imagine you as the woman from *Fatal Attraction*." She leaned in closer to me. "Does he have a little bunny you could cook if he crosses you?"

As much as she teased me, Suzie surrendered and had her lunch with me at the circular table, with its tomato-sauce-stained top and the stench of old Mr. Coffee floating in the air. In return, I had to fill her in about our adventures with my father and his workshop. Not to mention the rides with Daniel to and from my parents' house.

"I assume Josephine made a feast," Suzie mused as she stabbed a piece of lettuce with her fork.

"Eggplant parmigiana with fresh ricotta and basil. But she went all out with the tiramisu."

Suzie shook her head. "In my next life, I'm coming back as you."

I laughed. "I think she enjoyed having another man to feed. She misses my brother, and you should see her expression when a new person compliments her cooking." I made a funny face, sucking in my cheeks and batting my eyelashes, in my best imitation of her.

The clock on the wall continued to tick, and I kept sneaking glances toward the door to see whether Daniel would walk in. We had only fifteen more minutes before the bell rang and we would have to return to class. Suzie sensed my nerves.

She leaned in closer to me and whispered, "He's probably helping some student whose braces got stuck on her mouthpiece again."

I was just about to give her a little smack on the shoulder when Daniel entered and headed straight toward our table.

"So glad I caught you, Maggie Topper." He reached for one of the empty chairs and sat down. "I played your father's violin all last night. It's got a fantastic sound . . . so rich and velvety. It puts my old fiddle to shame."

"Slow down, fella," Suzie said, lifting a hand. "You're going to choke to death if you don't pause for a second and breathe."

"Sorry, it's just so damn exciting to play an instrument, knowing the hands who crafted it. Your dad is the real deal, Maggie."

I blushed. "I'll be sure to tell him." I looked down at my half-eaten container of the leftovers my mother had sent home with me. I loved my dad deeply and was so proud that he had dedicated his retirement to fulfilling a lifelong dream of making violins. But somehow I felt a strange sense of disappointment wash over me. I wanted Daniel to also at least mention something that didn't involve my parents, as childish as that seemed.

And then, just as the bell struck, he leaned over and looked me straight in the eyes and said, "And you know, I thought it was pretty cool you knew I was quoting 'Mr. Tanner' to your dad."

I wasn't sure if he actually said what I thought I heard him say next, because then the bell struck, its sound shrill and loud. But I was pretty sure he said, "Maggie, you're pretty cool, too."

52

THERE were days when Sasha was driving to work at the laboratory that he felt outside of his body, as if he had become suspended in the air and his actions were being observed through an analytical lens.

The dark plastic steering wheel of his Pontiac was clutched by two pale hands; the catch of his reflection in the rearview mirror seemed to belong to someone else. He had recently required the assistance of glasses, and his once full hairline had started to thin.

To make himself as efficient as possible, Sasha worked hard to keep his professional and private lives separate. He published papers on neutrino oscillation in scientific journals that had received critical praise. His colleagues had come to like him. He was now known to be able to talk about baseball as well as any native New Yorker. No one knew the game's statistics better than he did.

But he never shared the burden of Yuri's heart defect with his coworkers. He kept that anguish to himself, bottled tight and stored at a distance. He was grateful for the health insurance he had through his job, for it enabled Yuri to have the best care. But he kept all the fragile details between him and Katya. But his worst fears, he did not share with his wife. He refused to let her know that he dreaded every cold or chest pain that afflicted his son. Or that the second he got back into his car for the ride home, his mind was no longer filled with his latest scientific data, but rather brimming with thoughts of Yuri.

DESPITE his worries, Sasha was still amazed by how much he himself had changed. The thoughts that now swirled within him were so different than the ones he had in his youth. Before he met Katya, he thought that a home was only a structure with four walls and a roof over one's head. He never gave much significance to a stove that was always warm or a bed that was filled with heat from another's body. He was lucky he got into university, where he could bury himself in his books and enjoy the comfort of science, where almost anything could be clinically explained.

Back in those days, he had prided himself in his ability to see facts clearly. But now he realized that the truth wasn't always black and white, and instead could be discovered somewhere in the soft shades of gray. At age thirty-eight, Sasha had come to believe that the most beautiful things in life defied explanation. How could one honestly explain how a soul feels the pull of another before a single word is exchanged? How could one believe that a child will defy his doctor's grim diagnosis and grow to be not just a little boy but a bright and curious young man?

At some point, from the jaded young man that Katya had first dated back in Ukraine to the man he was now, he had become infinitely hopeful. Fatherhood had made his heart beat stronger. His emotions no longer frightened him. Instead, they fortified his need to fully protect his wife and son. At night when he pulled Katya to his hips, she would beg him to take off his newly acquired glasses and to dim the lights low. "No, I want to see you," he insisted. Despite over a decade of marriage, he still marveled at the sight of his wife hovering above him. He loved the sweet smell that lifted off her skin and the flash of her eyes. The twist of her body as it curled into his like a snail seeking shelter. After Yuri was born, he sensed Katya preferred the modesty of darkness, a forgiving cloak of shadows where she would not be judged. Katya saw flaws in herself where he saw perfection. And while he made love to her with his eyes wide open, hers were nearly always closed.

SASHA was forever curious about what floated behind shut eyelids. When he walked in the door each night and he saw his little boy sleeping in his chair, the television broadcasting men running around the bases to a stadium of applause, he couldn't help but wish he were privy to the dreams now floating through his son's head. He would have done anything in the world to exchange hearts with his son, just so Yuri could know the thrill of the dirt beneath his cleats and the wind whipping through his hair.

Still, the sight of a sleeping child never ceased to fill him with warmth. He scooped his son up in his arms and walked down the corridor, then laid him on the bed. As he pulled the blanket over Yuri, he studied the image of his son a little bit longer, just as he had when he slept in his crib as an infant. Adjusting his glasses, Sasha made sure the memory of him was pressed into his mind. He wanted to capture what he knew was transient and fleeting. Innocence and boyhood were not infinite stages in any life.

The only constant was a parent's love.

53

YURI seemed to grow stronger after the snow began to thaw. His body, which had appeared so frail and younger than his years when I first met him, was now filling out. At first, I had seen so much of Katya in his face. The large blue eyes, the high round forehead and sharp cheekbones. But now, I could see parts of his father, Sasha, also emerging. Even his laugh, which used to sound like a giggle, became throatier and more like that of a young man than that of a little boy.

But then a strange thing happened. Out of nowhere, Yuri became withdrawn and restless. For all the weeks that Finn had been visiting, Yuri always seemed hungry for Finn to talk about his activities, as though he was living vicariously through them. But now I saw how he seemed to almost resent it. He appeared particularly agitated when Finn mentioned tryouts for spring baseball. His schoolwork also seemed to suffer. When I collected his writing notebook, I saw he had skipped an entire week of writing assignments yet felt no need to explain why he had chosen not to do the work.

Every time I tried to gently prod Yuri about what was bothering him, I was rebuffed. I pulled Katya to the side and asked her if she had any idea, but she didn't have any explanation, either. Even Finn now seemed hesitant to come to his weekly sessions at Yuri's house. "I don't know, Ms. Topper," he said to me after class at Franklin one afternoon. "I'm starting to think Yuri may not want me there anymore."

"I don't think that's the case, Finn," I replied, trying to soothe his concern. "There's something going on with him that he doesn't want to share right now. But I don't think it has anything to do with you, honey. Even his mother is perplexed why he's suddenly so irritable."

Finn gave me a shrug. "My mom always says everyone's entitled to be in a bad mood every now and then."

"Yeah," I agreed. "I know I've sure had my share of bad moods."

"Me too," Finn laughed. "But if it's okay with you, my mom thought I should give Yuri some space this week. If he does still want me to come, I can visit next Thursday."

My heart sank a little after Finn left. I knew he was trying to put on a brave face. I, too, had picked up that Yuri seemed to be creating distance between them.

Yuri's change in demeanor weighed heavily on me. I was so distracted by it that one morning, I nearly walked into Florence Konig in the corridor as my third-period class went off to gym.

"You need to look up from your feet when you're walking," Florence chided me. "You nearly ran me over."

I raised my head. She was right. I hadn't even seen her walking straight in front of me. I saw her eyes study me for a second. "Everything okay with you, Maggie?"

"Fine, fine. Just got a lot on my mind."

"Are you sure?" she persisted. "I've got a second sense about these things, and it looks like you're having a rough time."

I paused for a moment. The hallway in Franklin was no longer crowded with children, and Suzie was nowhere to be found. It was just the two of us standing there alone, and suddenly, Florence, in her sensible pantsuit and with a rhinestone butterfly pin neatly secured on her blouse, didn't seem so hard and jaded as I had previously thought. She actually seemed kind.

"It's a long story," I muttered to myself.

She glanced at her thin gold watch, and her gray eyes met mine. "Looks like we both have forty minutes until our next class. I think that gives me plenty of time to hear all about it."

ON the door to Florence's classroom she had taped a banner that read in big purple letters, *Life Is About Learning.*

She saw me glance at the words and waved me inside. "It's true, isn't it?"

"Yes, very much so." I sighed. "I'm still trying to learn every day how to do this job. But some days, I feel like I'm utterly failing."

Florence gave me a surprisingly sympathetic look, one that was free of judgment. "Maggie, we all feel that way sometimes, and I've been doing it for a lot longer than you have, trust me."

But this time, Florence's reference to her tenure and seniority didn't bother me. At this point, I realized, if she had any wisdom to offer, who was I not to take it? I nodded and slid into one of the student chairs and looked around her classroom. The room appeared identical to the way it was last September. There were butterflies scattered across the four walls: paper butterflies cut out from construction paper, images of butterflies taken from magazines like *Scientific American* or *National Geographic*, and photos of butterflies emerging from their chrysalises. On her bulletin board, Florence had written the names of each of her students on neon-colored butterfly decals.

"You certainly like your butterflies," I remarked, looking around the room.

"Yes, I do." Florence turned around and admired her handiwork. "There's a long story behind why I like them so much." She paused and looked at me softly. "But why don't you tell me your story first."

IT felt almost like a confessional. Me sitting at one of the low student desks, Florence in her high-back chair, her helmet of silver curls framing her pink cheeks and her hands clasped in front. I found myself telling her about my whole journey with Yuri since September—the initial rocky start, the joy I found when I discovered his love of baseball, and then my introducing Finn to him.

"But suddenly I feel like I'm in the dark again," I said hopelessly. "It's like I'm back at the beginning, with a student who doesn't want me there. And I have no clue what to do about it."

Florence's face, which I had always thought looked upon me with an air of disdain, had transformed into a visage of kindness and understanding.

"This job is hard, Maggie. Every child has a story that is always unfolding." She cleared her throat. "And, as their teachers, we have one as well." She reached into one of the metal drawers in her desk and opened it, retrieving a slender paperback book.

"You probably don't know why I love butterflies so much or why I don't rotate my decorations every season like all the other teachers do. But there's a reason behind it. It's a large part of my story."

She walked over and put the book in front of me.

"Have you ever read this? It's called *I Never Saw Another Butterfly*."

I picked up the book and glanced at it quickly. On the cover, which looked like a child's collage, it read, *Children's Drawings and Poems from Terezin Concentration Camp*.

"My parents are Holocaust survivors," she said, her voice instinctively lowered. "My mother gave birth to me in a DP camp in Czechoslovakia after she was liberated from the concentration camp Terezín. She and my father had been deported there from a small village near Brno. Luckily, they were never transported farther east than that, because most of the people there were eventually sent on to death camps like Auschwitz."

I felt my body grow numb. "I had no idea, Florence."

"Few people do. Angela knows, of course." She took a deep breath. "My mother became a teacher nearly a decade after she got to America. She went back to school, learned English, and eventually taught in the Westbury school system for thirty years. She was a complete inspiration to me."

"I can imagine," I said.

"But the reason I'm sharing this book with you now is that my mother actually knew the woman at Terezín who encouraged these children to write their poetry and create their drawings, even on the smallest scraps of paper, even when they were starving or freezing and had only the rags on their back. She believed with all her heart that a teacher's job is to make children feel safe, to make them believe their ability is boundless." Florence steadied her voice. "Her name was Friedl Dicker-Brandeis. The poetry and drawings inside this book exist today because this teacher encouraged the children to use their minds—and their imaginations—in their darkest hour. And that, Maggie, was an extraordinary gift. Friedl was a fearless woman and she put her students above all else. She believed nothing was more important than to ask these children, even in the most horrific circumstances, 'What are you thinking? What's in your imagination and in your mind?' At the end of the war, they found over seven hundred drawings and poems by these children, most of whom had perished."

I shuddered and felt tears forming in my eyes, thinking about all of those children.

"The title, *I Never Saw Another Butterfly*, is taken from one of the poems." Florence said.

"I surround myself with butterflies each day, Maggie, to remember why I do this job. And to remember that there is nothing more important than opening up a child's mind to infinite possibility."

I nodded. I knew I needed to hear that reminder.

"Take the book home, Maggie. Read it, and maybe even share it with Yuri. I know something good will come of it. As I tell my kids each year, nothing can stop a butterfly from spreading its wings."

I read the book that evening from cover to cover. Absorbing the words of the children whose voices were silenced far too soon. The next day, when I visited Yuri, I asked Katya if we might be able to go outside on the deck and do our classwork there.

"Sure," she said. "Some sunshine would do him good."

I was pleased. I wanted to be around nature and not trapped inside with Yuri when I gave him the book.

Outside the birds were singing, and two frisky squirrels ran alongside the edge of the wooden banister.

Yuri and I sat on two of the teak chairs.

"I don't know what's in your mind lately, but I miss the ease of our old conversations," I said gently. "A friend of mine gave me this book the other day, and I thought you might find it interesting. Most of the poems in it were written by children, many who were close in age to you.

"I really want you to read it, Yuri. It shows how even with physical limitations, even with great suffering, the human mind and one's imagination cannot be contained."

Yuri studied the book, pausing over the reproductions of the children's artwork and reading some of the lines of poetry.

In the soft daylight, I saw his face change. "What happened to those kids?" he asked. "They were Jewish, right?"

"Yes," I said softly.

"So they died in the Holocaust?"

"Most of them did, Yuri. Yes."

"My dad lost a lot of family in World War II."

"Many people did. But it was particularly devastating for the Jewish people."

Yuri nodded. His eyes traveled to a small white butterfly on one of the geranium plants hanging by the sliding door.

"You know, my father has always loved butterflies. When I was a really little kid, he told me about this theory he believes in . . . It's called the butterfly effect. One single thing can change the destiny of everything. Something as small as a butterfly's wings flapping in South America can start a chain of events and alter the rest of the universe."

"That's so interesting," I said. Yuri had no idea how my heart leapt in my chest to have him opening up to me again and responding to the themes of the book.

"One small thing can change the course of an entire life," I said.

"Exactly." His eyes now flashed with that distinct light that had first drawn me to him all those months ago.

I wanted to tell him that being his teacher had changed my life, but before I could, he said something I wasn't expecting.

"I want to go back to school, Ms. Topper. Having Finn here has been great, but it only shows me what I've been missing. I want to be with other kids. I want to be like that butterfly." He took a deep breath. "I want to be free."

MY conversation with Yuri had left me more determined than ever. I needed to be his advocate, his champion rooting for him to spread his wings as much as he was physically able. The book Florence had loaned to me served as a reminder of why I had chosen to become a teacher. Even though I had not decorated my room with butterflies, I did see each of my students as those beautiful winged creatures, whom I wanted to see make the most of their wings and fly.

And so, on my next visit, I asked to speak to Katya in private about the possibility of Yuri returning to school. "He's been relatively healthy all year," she acknowledged. Katya draped her fingertips over the rim of her teacup and let the vapors of steam travel through her open hands. "As I told you, he was always sick in the fifth grade. The constant colds. And for Sasha and me it was hell . . . not knowing if Yuri's difficulty breathing was just related to his cold or whether it was from his heart condition . . ." She took her hands off the cup and wrung them in her lap. "You have no idea how it feels to constantly worry about the life of your child." She lowered her head. "I don't think I know what it's like *not* to worry anymore." Her voice broke on the last words, and she lifted the napkin from her lap to dry her tears.

"I want him to have a normal life. I do, more than anything." She looked out the kitchen window. A red cardinal was pecking at the bright yellow bird feeder on the wooden deck. "I see how his face lights up when Finn visits him. I can hear their chatter about baseball, all that innocent, boyish banter. And I want him to have that every day. I do . . . I'm just . . ." She stopped midsentence.

"You're just scared," I said, completing her thoughts. "Which is perfectly understandable." I reached for her hand. "I know you worry about Yuri and keeping him as healthy as you can, but he can't stay in this house forever and live in a bubble. Even as a teacher, I know there's only so much a child can learn from books."

She nodded her head. "I know you're right. My husband says the same things . . ."

I knew Sasha had taken Yuri out to a few baseball games in years past. "Why not bring him to one of the basketball games at Franklin?" I suggested. "And when it gets warmer, you can take him to some of the school's baseball games, too. He can see Finn play and cheer him on.

"Yuri's growing up," I said gently. "Even I can see the changes in him just over the past few months. You've had this whole year with him at home, but you don't want him to become completely cut off from the world. What sort of life would that be?"

Katya lifted her eyes, now glassy with tears. "I want to keep him safe, because I blame myself for his condition."

I squeezed her hand again. "Don't say that; there's nothing you did that caused it."

"Chernobyl. Do you know of it?" She bit her lip and her whole body seemed to shiver. "How could I not have known that something was wrong when it was as hot as summer that April? I baked in the sun that afternoon. I swam in the river that was as warm as bathwater." Her expression was pained. "And now I hear they're saying that the radiation was absorbed in the mushrooms. I ate so many mushrooms before I got pregnant." She let out a nervous laugh. "My body must have soaked up all that poison like a sponge. I'm surprised I'm even still here."

Katya pressed her face into her open palms and shook her head.

As I listened to her, I had a terrible feeling in the pit of my stomach. Her grief was contagious, and I thought I might start crying along with her. "Katya, you're not to blame. It was all a terrible accident."

"They waited three days before telling us anything had happened," she muttered, her words lost in her sobs. "Three days, can you imagine? That whole time, I burned myself like a lobster, sunbathing like a fool."

54

THAT night, I had difficulty sleeping. I had been excited to talk to Katya about the prospect of Yuri's coming to class a few times a week once the weather warmed up, but our conversation that afternoon revealed much more than I had expected. Katya was terrified that something might happen to Yuri when she wasn't around. Getting her to agree was not going to occur overnight.

As frustrated as I was that Katya hadn't yet agreed to let Yuri attend school once a week, I was bolstered by the fact that Yuri seemed to be channeling his frustrations into his writer's notebook. Now that he had been transparent with me about his restlessness, he knew he didn't have to put on a happy face for me. He even started speaking more frankly with Finn, saying how excited he was for him to have made the middle school baseball team but how much it stunk for him knowing he'd never get the chance to do it himself.

Then, to my surprise, I learned that Sasha had taken Yuri out to Franklin to sit on the bleachers and watch one of Finn's games.

"He came out in full Yankees regalia," Finn told me after class.

"It was really cool. I got the game ball and gave it to him after. You should have seen his whole face light up after that!"

I found myself getting emotional and wished I had witnessed the scene myself.

"Wow, that's really amazing, Finn," I gushed. "Fingers crossed, with each baby step, we get closer to having him come in one day a week for class."

"Yeah, I'm really hoping that happens, Ms. Topper. And I think so is he."

WHILE my professional life was consumed with trying to navigate the best options for Yuri, my personal life, on a good note, was improving. Daniel and I began to spend more time together, taking a few more trips to my father's workshop. He said he was even thinking of attending the summer program in the Midwest that had kickstarted my father's education in learning how to make violins. At first I worried that he was only feigning interest in me in order to spend more time with my father, which, as Suzie pointed out, sounded pretty crazy when you said it out loud.

As the weather changed from snow to spring rain, I still lit fires on the weekend. But now Daniel would arrive around four p.m. most Saturdays, and we'd make dinner together. He'd stop off beforehand at the local grocery store to pick up a few provisions, and we'd play a game in which we had to prepare something out of the random items he had purchased.

"I can make anything tasty with a little garlic and olive oil," I challenged him. He'd stand over me as I chopped the garlic and sautéed it in a pan, the aroma permeating the house and making me feel instantly like I was back at home.

After dinner, as the fire roared, he'd place his violin beneath his cheek and play whatever came into his mind. Some nights it was an Irish jig and other times it could be Stephen Foster. It was interesting that he sounded so different than my father did when he played. My dad always made the violin sound almost melancholy, but Daniel's playing was bright and cheerful. The notes sounded high and springy, as if life were bursting off his strings.

"Let me see if I can play 'Cat's in the Cradle,'" he teased. "Something a little more somber for a change." He picked up the violin and began plucking the strings, searching briefly to find the right notes. And then, above the music, I heard him begin to sing. *"Little Boy Blue and the Man in the Moon. When you coming home, Dad?"* I suddenly felt the urge to cry.

"Did I do something wrong?" He stopped and lifted his bow off the strings. "I thought you'd like that one."

"I do," I muttered. "I do." I wasn't sure why it had suddenly made me so emotional. It wasn't as if I had a father who never made time for my brother and me when we were growing up. We'd had the opposite, and I knew it.

Daniel put the violin down and sat next to me on the couch. He placed his arm around me and inched closer.

"I hope you're not going to be mad at me for doing this," he whispered into my ear.

Then he leaned over and kissed me.

55

THE kiss. I replayed it over and over in my mind. And not just the kiss. I replayed from the moment Daniel leaned in and surprised me with it to the minute he left my place later on that night.

That kiss had brought me all the way back to the seventh grade, when Timmy Mitchell, the boy I'd secretly had a crush on for three years, kissed me behind the cafeteria. I had the same rush of emotions, even though I was now twenty-seven instead of twelve. I was over the moon that our attraction to each other was mutual. But on the other hand, I was scared out of my mind that the other teachers might find out. It didn't take a rocket scientist to realize that having a relationship with a coworker in a small school wasn't necessarily the smartest idea.

"You can't think of ending this before it even begins," Suzie counseled. "Now tell me how it happened again." She was having fun with me. "I'm having a hard time imagining the sudden transition from a depressing song about a delinquent dad to a passionate kiss on the couch."

Suzie started humming the melody to "Cat's in the Cradle." Then she began singing it in a country-western voice, even though it wasn't that kind of song.

"And then, bam, kiss?" She burst into hysterics.

"It does sound kind of out of left field," I agreed. "But I can't stop thinking about him. I feel like I'm back in middle school again."

"Hate to break it to you, Mags, but you are."

I playfully hit her on her shoulder. "Stop it, you know what I mean."

"Listen, Daniel's got that poet's soul that you love. That was what was missing with Bill. And it's hard to find, trust me."

I didn't say a word, but I knew Suzie was right.

"Anyways"—Suzie took a jab at me—"I thought you preferred James Taylor when you were making out."

I didn't answer her. There was a reason that Daniel loved Harry Chapin's songs as much as I did. The best things in life came down to people sharing their stories. And that first kiss felt like a first chapter. It was filled with curiosity and an invitation for more.

SPRING had come. The crocuses had pushed forth. The enormous trees that bordered the winding roads from Franklin to my cottage had started to bud. Everything seemed to grow more positive and hopeful after the thaw of winter.

After much deliberation, Katya decided to allow Yuri to come to Franklin one day each week.

I could hardly contain my excitement that she had finally agreed to the one thing I had been hoping for all year. Knowing I would have to make my classroom as germ-free as possible, I rushed off to the grocery store and loaded my cart with paper towels, Fantastik, and lots and lots of Clorox wipes. The janitors were supposed to use disinfectants provided by the administration, but I worried the room might not be as clean as it needed to be. So with my new set of supplies in hand, I rolled up my sleeves and secretly started spraying every surface in the room with a vengeance. I cleaned desk after desk, scrubbing away all the pencil doodles and the stickiness, especially Zach's grimy desk, which I attacked as though it were a hothouse of germs. Then I scoured every surface I could reach, from the top of the bookshelves to the rim of the chalkboard. Next I focused on the doorknobs, both the one inside the classroom and the one that faced the hallway. Not leaving anything to chance, I even wiped down all the pens and pencils in the canister on my own desk.

THE next morning, my stomach was so tightly wound, I could barely eat any breakfast or drink a cup of coffee. How would my other students react to Yuri? Would they accept him, or would they think he was too much of a fragile outsider? I couldn't help but think of how chickens peck at the weakest in their group, or piglets force out the runt of the litter.

Still, as delicate as Yuri might appear when he first arrived, I comforted myself that his buoyant personality would ultimately prove to be infectious. Despite his physical limitations, no one could deny that he had a certain spark about him. After all, he had won over Finn immediately. So I had to tell myself that even though he wouldn't be coming in each day and I would not be able to control every interaction he had at Franklin, at the very least, Yuri would have a solid friend in Finn from the get-go.

Despite Suzie's efforts to reassure me that I'd always striven to maintain a classroom full of kindness and a safe learning environment for all my kids, I was still anxious to protect Yuri from any harm or discomfort. The administration had sent a letter out to the parents, letting them know that we would have a new student in the classroom with special concerns. But I knew that the other children would be immensely curious about anyone new joining the class midyear.

"I have exciting news," I told my third-period class the day before Yuri's arrival. "We'll be having a new student in our class. Yuri Krasny. He'll be coming in one day a week, and we'll need to give him a warm welcome."

"Why only one day a week?" Rachel asked.

"That's a very good question," I answered. I knew one of them was going to ask this, and I had rehearsed my response over and over in my head. I didn't want to alarm the children or make them afraid to interact with Yuri, but I also had to give them an answer that would satisfy their curiosity.

"Yuri was born with a special health condition. His parents have had to take very good care of him so he can maintain his strength. That's meant that, over the years, he hasn't always been able to come into a classroom and be around other kids." I gave the class a big smile to inspire them to be happy about this new addition, not nervous. "The good news is that I've gotten to know him, because I've been tutoring him at his home a few days a week this year."

Lisa appeared unsatisfied with my explanation, which I had purposely kept vague. "What sort of condition?" she persisted.

"Let's just say we need to keep things as safe and as clean as possible in here, as we discussed in the letter home to your parents. So I'm going to be passing out antibacterial wipes on the mornings he's with us. Everyone'll get one," I said, lifting a canister of Handi Wipes. "And everyone will use them. No exceptions. Understood?"

Oscar raised his hand. "Is he going to die?"

Before I could formulate an appropriate answer, Finn blurted out, "Of course not!"

I glanced over at Finn's desk. The determination on his face said it all. He wanted this to work out for Yuri as much as I did.

I spoke to Katya the night before Yuri's first day, informing her of all the safety measures I had implemented. "I've told the class they should make sure that if they felt sick or had a cough or sneeze, to let me know right away," I reassured her. If one of the students showed the first signs of having a cold on any of the days before Yuri was to come into class, I would call her that evening. We couldn't expect the parents of the other students to keep their children home for a cold, especially working parents, but we wanted to make sure Katya had all the facts she needed to ensure that Yuri was never at any undue risk.

"I'm still a nervous wreck," she said. I had to press my ear hard against the receiver to hear her, her voice sounded so faint.

I tried my best to reassure her. "If it ends up being too much for Yuri, we'll go back to the way things were. For his sake, let's see if he can have a little more interaction with the other students his age."

"Get some sleep," I urged her gently. "You know I'll look out for him as though he were my own. I promise you."

"Sasha tells me I need to let him live as full a life as he can, while still minimizing the risks," she said. "I just can't let anything happen to him. I know it sounds wrong to say, but he's not only my son . . . he's also my best friend."

56

I met Katya and Yuri at the front office the next day. He was dressed in clothes I knew were chosen by his mother, not him. The red-checkered button-down shirt. The navy knit vest. The khaki pants pressed with a pleat down the front. For Katya, this was how you dressed on the first day of school. Little did she know that for most of the other boys in Franklin, that just meant jeans and a T-shirt that wasn't stained.

"Don't you look handsome?" I complimented him. He was wearing his backpack, the straps on each shoulder. "Are you okay with your bag?" I asked. "It looks so heavy."

"Yep," he answered immediately. He was so eager, you could feel it lifting off his skin.

"He's so excited about today," Katya said. "He already met Principal Nelson, who introduced us to Ms. Stern, the school nurse. Yuri knows to go to her if he ever has a problem."

"Great. I'm glad we're all set." I glanced at Katya and gave her a confident nod. "So let's get you to the classroom, Yuri." I made a playful flourish with my hand. "Everyone's bursting at the seams to meet you."

. . .

THE room smelled like fake lemons. Between the Handi Wipes and the disinfectants I had used the day before, the air was laced with the message of "clean." One thing was certain: Yuri was walking into a pristine classroom.

As soon as he entered, I could sense the energy in the room change. The familiar became the unfamiliar. Except for Finn's, all eyes were on him, each child trying to immediately form their own opinion about this new addition to the class.

"Everyone, please, let's give a warm welcome to Yuri," I said brightly.

The students gave him a wide range of greetings, from a few half-hearted waves to some more enthusiastic hellos.

I saw Robert not greet Yuri at all. And this, despite it not surprising me about him, made my heart hurt.

Zach gave him a nice nod and a smile. He started to give Yuri a high five, but then realized quickly it was best to keep his hands to himself.

"There's a seat next to Finn." I gently ushered Yuri toward it. "Why don't you go sit down and we'll get started."

I watched as he slowly made his way toward his desk. I had cleaned it so many times, the metal legs and the beige top were sparkling. He slipped his backpack off his shoulders and settled in. I could tell how nervous he was, but when I looked up, I saw Finn reach over and give him an affectionate slap on the back. I noticed Oscar and even Robert take note. And I knew that Yuri was now going to be okay. Finn had his back.

YURI was much more tentative than when he was with me alone. But I also saw in his eyes how interested he was in hearing what the other students had to say during our class discussions.

Then, on his third visit, we were discussing metaphors, and I asked the class if they could give me an example of a metaphor they remembered from one of the books we had read in class and explain to me what it meant.

Lisa's hand shot up. "The wheel of life in *Tuck Everlasting*. In the book, Tuck says life is meant to turn and turn and never stop. That it has to keep moving like a wheel."

"Yeah," said Zach. "The Tuck family is stuck living forever, but Jesse knows it's not right. Everyone and everything is supposed to die at some point."

I felt a wave of concern surge through my body. I had chosen not to assign this book when I was tutoring Yuri because of the way the book touched upon the fragility of life and examined themes of mortality, and now those attempts to keep Yuri's emotions safe and protected began to unravel.

I quickly glanced over at Yuri to try to gauge how he was reacting to what the other kids had said, and saw his brow wrinkle, his eye dart to mine. But rather than appear sad, he looked angry.

"How about another example of a metaphor from a book we read?" I asked the class, trying to redirect the discussion to a different book.

"The stars in *Number the Stars* are not only the stars in the sky, but also the Jewish people of Denmark," Rachel answered.

I breathed a sigh of relief, thinking I had diverted attention from a book that might have upset Yuri, but I was wrong.

After class, Yuri came up to my desk and leaned in close.

"How come I didn't get to read *Tuck Everlasting*?"

I stammered for a second. "I . . . I thought . . ."

But Yuri finished my sentence for me. "You thought 'cause I'm a sick kid, it wasn't a good idea?"

"No, Yuri . . . I just thought . . ."

He shook his head and bit his lower lip. "It's bad enough I can't do all the stuff that other kids get to do, like baseball. But not letting me read the same books, that's just mean. You never treated me like a sick kid until this."

My face felt like it was hot and on fire. I forced back my tears. I knew telling him I wanted to protect him wasn't going to make him feel better. "I'm sorry," I said. "I made a mistake."

"Can I have the book?" he asked, and he held out his hand. "I want to read it."

I reached over to the wooden bookshelf behind my desk and pulled out my paperback copy. "Here," I said, giving it to him. "I hope you enjoy it. It's a very special book."

He took the book from me, not even making eye contact, and walked out the door.

"YOU need to forgive yourself," Suzie counseled when I told her what had happened in class.

She pushed a box of tissues in my direction so I could wipe away my tears.

"Your impulse is to keep him safe, and he just wants to be treated like a regular kid."

"Now I have greater empathy for his mom," I said, sniffling. "It's like I'm caught between a rock and a hard place, trying to open the world up to him but also struggling to protect him from getting hurt."

But there was a lot of truth in Suzie's words, and I would quickly realize during Yuri's weeks in school that I would never be able to control the words that came out of the other students' mouths. One afternoon, I heard Anna Ling lean over and ask him if he was still lucky enough to not have to do gym class.

Yuri's face flushed red. "I wouldn't exactly say 'lucky' . . ."

Anna hated gym. She tried everything to get out of it. Lately, she had been asking to go to the nurse after complaining of "girl cramps" a few minutes before gym class. So today, when she said she had stubbed her foot on the way to school and didn't think she could do scooter dodgeball, I felt a weak spot for her. I also thought it might be nice for her to stay behind in the classroom and keep Yuri company.

"The two of you can help me rearrange the bulletin board for next month." I pointed to the stack of colorful construction paper and the staple gun. I was happy to be on good footing again with Yuri and thought it was a good idea to give the job to someone other than Rachel, who was always the one I naturally assigned the crafty things for the classroom to. "We can make a checkerboard background."

Anna loved art, nearly as much as Lisa and Rachel did, so I knew she was going to leap at the chance to help decorate the board. Right away, she started making suggestions to Yuri about the different color patterns they could use in the background.

Yuri moved slowly and carefully as he worked, while Anna was a ball of energy. She buzzed and blabbered the whole time, but I sensed Yuri also was enjoying having the chance to do something creative.

Just before the other students returned to class, I saw Yuri walk over to one of the windows that overlooked the baseball field.

"It looks like it's not going to rain today, as they had predicted." A big smile crossed over his face. "That means Finn's team gets to play ball today."

I walked closer to him. "Those clouds do look like they're on their way out," I agreed. "It seems like a great day for a ball game."

"My mom said I could go," he said, beaming. "You know, the thing is, Ms. Topper, it's like what you told us in class today about how the imagination is one of the body's most powerful tools." He took a deep breath. "When I watch Finn play, I imagine it's me up there at the plate. Like my mind is traveling into his body, taking that first swing. And it feels so good."

57

THAT May, with things going smoothly, Katya agreed to let Yuri increase his time at Franklin to twice a week. She would always drive him to school and pick him up at the end of the day. Her car was often in back of Finn's mother's on the pickup line, their motors idling as they both waited for their sons.

From the outside, it appeared as though Katya was taking her own baby steps with Yuri. She was learning to let go a bit by giving him a little more freedom and time with his new friends. She also spoke about maybe teaching ballet at a local dance school but hadn't yet found the courage to introduce herself to the director. "You should do it," I said, trying to encourage her. "With your background, you would have so much to offer the children."

"It's been so long since I danced, though," Katya added. "And sometimes my mind plays tricks on me. After my injury, I still danced in my dreams when I slept. I'd wake up and be confused about whether my fracture really happened or whether that was part of the dream. But after Yuri's birth, I never slept long enough to have dreams." She looked down at her hands. "Yet, it's so strange . . . In the past year, I've started having dreams where I'm dancing again. The other night I had one where I was back in Kiev, performing on the stage of the National Theater." She closed her eyes. "The chore-ography runs through my head like the scenes of a film. I wake up and my body feels tired, my muscles even feel sore."

I tried to imagine what it must be like to have trained so hard for something you always wanted, only to have it suddenly vanish. I knew my own path in teaching had its struggles, but there was room for mistakes and the possibility to learn from them. But Katya had worked basically her entire youth to dance professionally, and that dream had been shattered in an instant. Motherhood had not given her a free ride, either. From the moment Yuri was born, she'd had to worry about what most mothers took for granted. That her child's lungs would take in air, that his heart would pump blood through his tiny body. I knew that Katya allowing Yuri to attend class twice a week was an enormous step for her and that she was subsequently relinquishing much of the control she had nurtured in order to keep him safe and healthy.

I promised Katya that, during recess, Yuri would sit in the bleach-ers and not engage in any activities that might put stress on his heart. Yuri had not protested, as he realized that these precautionary mea-sures put upon him by his parents and teachers were only meant to protect him.

During the two days he came to class, I came out to keep Yuri company on the bench during recess before making sure he felt well enough to do one more period. Most of the time, we'd chat about who had the fiercest dodgeball throw, which he surprisingly attrib-uted to Anna Ling. Some days, as the long fingers of sunlight warmed our faces, I'd try to playfully pry from him some class gossip—like if he knew who had a crush on whom. But one Thursday, I had a scheduling conflict. There was a mandatory department meeting that I knew would keep me from sitting outside on the bleachers with Yuri.

"You'll be okay without me, champ?" I asked, giving his shoulder an affectionate squeeze.

"Sure thing, Ms. Topper. Don't worry about me."

"Great. Tomorrow, I'll be there." I smiled at him, watching as he zipped up his sweatshirt, grabbed his brown paper lunch bag, and headed toward the cafeteria with Finn.

I eyed the clock all through the staff meeting. Mr. Nelson kicked his feet up on the table and started asking me and the other English language arts teachers to give feedback on one of the textbooks we were using in the classroom. Angela and Florence put in their two cents, and I agreed with them that I thought they were a good resource for the children. With eight minutes before recess ended, I headed outside to see how Yuri was doing.

But the bleachers were empty. He always sat on the first tier, but now there was no one sitting in his spot. I saw Oscar throw the pink rubber ball toward Zach.

"Hey, guys!" I hollered. "Where's Yuri? I don't see him."

Just as I said those words, my eyes scanned the school yard. I didn't see Finn, either.

"And where's Finn?"

The boys stopped in their tracks, the ball landing hard against the ground next to Oscar's sneakers.

"Uh," Zach muttered. "I think they went into the woods to look for something."

"The woods?" I knew Zach was a terrible liar. I turned around to see the two lunch aides who were supposed to be monitoring the students outside.

"Fabiola? Tina?" They had red shoelaces around their necks with whistles, their hair pulled back in high ponytails, but they were hardly holding up the yard like vigilant wardens. Instead, they were both hovering over a group of girls who were arguing about whose turn it was to bedazzle their matching denim jackets with fake gemstones.

"Where's Yuri?" I ran over to them, already out of breath. I pointed to the empty bleachers. "The boys say they saw him go off in the woods with Finn." My heartbeat was escalating. I knew these boys. They weren't rule breakers. Panic had already taken hold of me that something had happened to them.

Fabiola whipped around. "Yuri? Yeah, I saw him sitting there just ten minutes ago. I swear." You could see she was trying to remain calm but realized if something had happened to the boys, it was on her watch.

I glanced at the time. There were five minutes left until the kids had to be back inside. I didn't think twice. I started running toward the woods that separated the school from the main road.

But before I had run even five yards, I saw the two of them emerging from the break in the trees.

I was furious. Why on earth would they have gone to the woods?

You could see their happy faces vanish instantaneously when they saw me standing there in the middle of the field, my black tulip skirt whipping around my knees in the wind.

"Uh, Ms. Topper," Finn said quietly. "We thought you had a meeting."

"I did. It ended," I said firmly. "But where were the two of you?"

Their eyes fell to their sneakers, but it was obvious that they weren't looking at ladybugs in the forest.

For several long seconds, no one said a word. **The sil**ence was painful as I dreaded one of them further damaging the now-broken bond of trust between us with a lie.

But I was wrong.

"I'm sorry," Finn said before Yuri could get two words out. "It was all my fault. I convinced Yuri to go with me to the mini-mart. They always get a new shipment of baseball cards on Thursdays, and I wanted to make sure we got the first dibs."

"Geez, baseball cards?" I said as I ground down on my teeth. "You know you scared the living daylights out of me!"

Fabiola and Tina were blowing their whistles, sounding the alarm that everyone had to get inside to class.

"We both got Ken Griffey Jr., though." Yuri smiled, offering up his new stack of cards to me as a gesture of peace, with the Cincinnati Reds all-star on top. "What are the odds of that?"

"Pretty slim," I acknowledged, but gave them both a hard stare. I wanted them to know that what they had done was unacceptable and I was furious.

"You know I have to tell Principal Nelson about this . . . and I'll definitely have to call your parents."

The boys' faces fell.

"I know it's hard for you to understand it at your age, but your parents trust me to watch over you when you're here at Franklin and to keep you safe," I told them firmly. And although it broke my heart, I marched them both down to the front office.

AS the boys sat on the bench outside Principal Nelson's office, we called both of their mothers.

Finn looked visibly upset, his face pale. When his mother arrived, he lowered his eyes when she told him how disappointed she was in his behavior.

"We expect more of you," she said, shaking her head. "You should know better than to do something like this, especially with Yuri."

A look of shame washed over Finn's face, and it gutted me.

But when Katya stormed into the office, furious with Yuri—and, I suspected, also equally angry with me—I was surprised to see Yuri's reaction. He didn't look upset or ashamed, like Finn had. On the contrary, Yuri looked oddly defiant.

Katya was shaking her finger, her face as pink as a grapefruit. "Why are you smiling, Yuri? I'm so upset. Something terrible could have happened to you!"

Yuri looked at me, then at his mother, and sucked in his chest.

"'Life's got to be lived, no matter how long or short,'" he said, quoting one of the lines of *Tuck Everlasting*. "And I'm smiling because this is the first time I've felt like a real kid."

I called Katya that evening, dreading the conversation as I hit the buttons on the phone. She had summoned all her strength to entrust me with Yuri for those two days a week at Franklin, and I knew, at a minimum, I owed her an explanation.

When she answered the phone, I could hear in her voice she already knew why I was calling.

"I'm mad at him, don't get me wrong. But *you* promised me . . . you promised you'd always be watching him. What if he started having trouble breathing outside, and no one was there to help him?" I could hear her fear, made more desperate in the hypothetical world of what-ifs that she had lived in since Yuri's birth, crackling over the telephone wire.

I started to say Fabiola's name, but she interjected, her voice like a bullet through the air. "Miss Fabiola? Miss Tina? I don't know these women. I only know you. Not them."

"I'm sorry. I won't let it happen again, I promise you," I apologized. "I will tell Mr. Nelson I can't do any more meetings during recess when Yuri's there. Only after school."

"I know my Yuri broke the rules. He says it was his idea to go get the baseball cards . . . that he wanted to have a little adventure at school." She took a deep sigh. "But I'm still really upset, even if my husband says boys will be boys."

I closed my eyes on the other side of the receiver. This was a moment in the conversation when I knew better than to side with Sasha against her.

"But I told him, our Yuri isn't a typical boy."

"No," I agreed quietly. "He isn't that at all."

WHEN I saw Finn in class the next day, I pulled him aside. "Yesterday was unfortunate, but I hope you learned from your mistake and we can move on from it."

Finn shifted one foot in front of the other and looked down when he spoke.

"When I told him about this place with the best cards . . . he got so excited. We really thought we could just get them and get back quickly."

"You just can't leave school like that . . . As your teacher, I'm responsible for keeping you safe."

"I know and I'm really sorry, Ms. Topper. I guess at the moment I felt responsible for keeping Yuri happy at school, and it really backfired."

My hand squeezed his shoulder. "You make him happy, Finn. I know you do."

"He said those matching cards we now have were lucky. That his was going in his prized album."

Finn shoved his hand into his pocket. "I told him I didn't have an album, but I'd keep mine on me at all times."

KATYA kept Yuri home from Franklin the following week. "He needs rest," she told me on the telephone. "And who is this Ken Griffey Jr.?" she asked. "He told Sasha he would do the same thing just to get his card again."

I had trouble stifling my laugh. "He's a really great baseball player, now on the Cincinnati Reds. The fans love him because it's so obvious how much he loves to play the game."

That broke her iciness. She couldn't help but chuckle. "Okay. He'll be back at school next week."

I breathed out a sigh of relief and promised her that nothing like what had occurred last week would ever happen again.

The next time I saw her, I brought along some tiramisu my mother had made the night before. "It means 'pick me up' in Italian," I explained as I handed her the aluminum foil tray filled with clouds of mascarpone cheese dusted with cocoa powder.

"Sounds just like what we need." She smiled. I sensed she had forgiven me, and as I entered their familiar living room, I felt my body relax. The district would no longer pay me for a second session, since Yuri had started coming to class twice a week, but I sometimes felt the pull just to sit in the Krasnys' living room and be with him. The baseball season was now in full throttle, and I found it immensely entertaining to hear Yuri's take on the Yankees. He was hopeful Derek Jeter would lead the team to another World Series that fall.

"My dad told me that when he first arrived in America, the Yankees were in a terrible losing streak, and the Mets were on top. But he still rooted for them no matter what," he said, looking up from his big comfy chair. "And now look at them!" He beamed. "Another year of being champions, I think."

I tried to tease him about the possibility that the Mets might rise from the ashes and steal the thunder from the overconfident Yankees. But Yuri would hear nothing of it.

"The Mets will never beat the Yanks, Ms. Topper. No way!"

"I have supreme faith in the underdog, you must realize that by now, Yuri."

He shrugged. "The statistics tell another story. Two World Series in a row, three in the last four years. With Mariano Rivera, Bernie Williams, Derek Jeter . . . how's your team going to beat that?"

"If I didn't believe they could win, what kind of fan would I be?"

Yuri was sitting on his comfortable yellow lounge chair, his big eyes ignited by the topic of baseball. "You'd be a realistic one, Ms. Topper. That's what you'd be." He took one of the pillows and squeezed it to his chest. "Ask David Cone and Dwight Gooden. Now that they're Yankees, they're not missing the Mets so much anymore."

I laughed. "I'm going to hope we do get to duke it out in the fall. My sources are telling me this is going to be a great year with Mike Piazza catching and that dreamy Al Leiter pitching."

"Don't hold your breath." Yuri was having fun with all our baseball banter. "But if there's ever another Subway Series, we have to promise to watch it together. No matter what. And Finn, too." He adjusted himself in the chair and then extended his hand. "Let's shake on it, Ms. Topper. That way I know it's real."

ON Friday night, Daniel came over and made dinner. My mother had recently given me a mandoline slicer, and we practiced making waffle cuts of potatoes and baking them in the oven. On the radio,

Macy Gray was playing "I Try," and suddenly he and I were dancing in the kitchen.

I felt his breath on my neck, his hand traveling up my back, bringing me closer into him. He whispered "Maggie" into my ear, then said my name in full again: "Maggie Topper." His voice sounded like the most beautiful music in the world. As the song slowed down, he cradled my head in his large, strong hands and told me he was falling for me. "Like a star dropping from the sky" were his words. I held on to that sentence as if it were a jar of fireflies illuminating my heart.

58

THE school year was rapidly coming to an end. The wind was laced with cherry blossom petals. The students began counting down the final weeks on their fingers, and as I collected their writing assignments, the contact paper on their writing-workshop books was now starting to peel off. The blue-lined pages were full of their thoughts and ideas, with some of the pages coming loose from the binding.

For the next assignment, I asked the kids to write about something in particular they wished they knew more about. They could describe any person or event, as long as they could explain why it sparked their curiosity.

I gave them an example of a black-and-white photograph that my mother had on her dresser. It was of my grandmother Valentina, the one who had arrived in America wearing all her clothes and who appeared transformed when she later emerged from her bath. I told the class how I had always heard stories about her from my own mother but that I still yearned to know more about her. The class burst into hysterics when I shared the part about her coming out of the tub and the surprise on everyone's faces upon learning she had worn all her dresses and every blouse and skirt, covering up her tiny frame with clothes.

I shared with them how my mother still cooked using Valentina's recipes and how her memory was kept alive through the mix of flavors and textures in the food. I told them I wished I had gotten the chance to meet her and hear more stories about her life back in Sicily and how it felt to be married at sixteen to a man she had known only a short time. "The best stories begin with questions we don't know all the answers to," I advised. "So when you write your assignment, think about a question to which you seek an answer."

In Yuri's writer's notebook, I found the following response:

Ebstein and Me

When I was five years old, I didn't go to kindergarten like the other kids on my street. My parents told me I would go the following year, because not everyone has to go to kindergarten. When I was six, my parents did let me go to school, but I knew from the beginning I wasn't like everyone else in the class. I have an abnormality of the right ventricle. My dad said the walls of my right ventricle are thinner in my heart than in everyone else's, but it's also bigger, which I think is good, even if the doctors don't. Who doesn't want a bigger heart, right?

The hard thing is that I can't do things other kids my age do. Like baseball. I wish I could run around the bases like my friend Finn. I wish I knew what it felt like to hit a home run. My doctor says I can't play because I could make the leaking worse in my tricuspid valve. Now I only have a medium leak. But if it gets worse, I'll need surgery.

My dad told me about a doctor named Ebstein who put a name on what I have. I often wonder if Dr. Ebstein ever wondered what it was like to be a kid who had it. Did he just see it as something that is broken in the heart? Or did he think about all the stuff that kids with Ebstein's can't do? I wonder if Ebstein ever wondered what it was like to be a boy like me.

Yuri's notebook seemed like a living and breathing extension of him now, and I cherished knowing that he felt close enough to me to share his most private thoughts. I closed Yuri's journal and shut my eyes, but the tears still escaped. I didn't think anyone could imagine how hard it was to be a twelve-year-old boy who dreamed and breathed baseball yet had never been able to play it. But Yuri's words came pretty close to making me understand.

59

JUNE filled the school with restlessness and warm bodies itching to be outside for the summer. The smell of freshly cut grass on the recess fields hovered on the kids' clothes as they stumbled back to class. It took every ounce of my energy to get them to concentrate on the last few weeks of assignments. Their writing workbooks were bursting with a year's worth of work, and their backpacks were equally tattered. Some of them no longer even zipped shut. Still, there wasn't a parent in the world who would be rushing out to replace anything with so few days left of school. It became a running joke that many of the kids no longer had any pencils in their cases, so I became the dispenser of the necessary school supplies just to get through the final days' work. The irony that Suzie was in this position almost every other day of the year, with teachers like me begging her for a crayon or a few pieces of construction paper, was not lost on me. I now felt her pain.

Yuri, however, continued to increase in popularity with the other students. He had become the class mascot of sorts for the last two months of school. He kept score while Finn and the other boys played basketball at recess. He also shared a bond with Anna, making the most colorful bulletin boards or classroom decorations when the other students were at gym. There had been only one or two instances when he had to leave school early because he was feeling too fatigued. Otherwise, his endurance seemed fine, and he didn't suffer from any breathing problems or other issues related to his heart defect.

In the spring, my cottage had become even more beautiful than I had ever imagined. I had missed the short blooming season of the peony bushes when Bill and I first came to look at it the previous year. But now, the entire front side of the house was bursting with pale pink and candy-striped powder-puff-size flowers. I cut them by the fistful and decorated every corner of the house with them. When I ran out of vases, I used an old watering can and prided myself in my resourcefulness.

Daniel started coming over more than one night a week, and I had to pinch myself on those evenings when I could just recline lazily on the couch after a dinner of pasta and wine as he serenaded me on my father's violin. But there were other evenings when it was completely silent, our bodies nestled together underneath the protective cover of my Laura Ashley duvet, the only sound coming from our thumping hearts.

I was happy to have a friend in Suzie. Only an artist like her would immediately understand when I said it was the comfort of silence between Daniel and me that made me feel as though I could trust in what was beginning to feel like love. I loathed to say the word, as though merely uttering it would cause me to jinx everything and it all would suddenly go up in smoke. But my guard softened, and I found myself thinking of him during those moments of empty space at school.

"I always tell my students there are places you need to put a lot of color in your painting, but there are other places you need to leave blank," Suzie explained. "Love is a little like that, Mags. You need space in between the pockets of color. Otherwise, it's just too much. Everyone and everything needs room to breathe."

I sensed a lot of wisdom in what she said. That was one of the many reasons why I adored Suzie. And looking at the way she was dressed today—her hot pink blouse with a few embroidered butterflies contrasted with a pair of stretchy black trousers—it was clear she had applied the same philosophy to her outfit. If she'd also had a detailed pattern on her pants, it would have been too much. But by mixing it up, she had achieved an overall effect of fabulousness.

It had occurred to me that my lease would be up in the next few weeks, and I started to realize that it was too big an expense for me to keep paying the whole rent by myself out of my modest salary. It was far too early to ask Daniel to move in with me. I thought about asking Suzie to, but there was only one bedroom, and even if we could create another one for her in the living room, I winced thinking about all the sparkles and craft paraphernalia she would bring into the space that I had cultivated to be the image of old-world charm.

"You can't give it up," my mother insisted when I told her I might have to move. "Are you having trouble making the rent now?" She softened her question by adding another spoonful of ziti onto my plate.

"I can do it . . . It just makes it hard to save any money. Basically all my salary goes to paying the bills."

"Listen, Maggie, the home is the most important space a person can have. It's a refuge for the soul. I want you to renew the lease, and if you run into any difficulty, you know your dad and I will always help you out."

"But I don't want to have to ask for help, Mom," I said as I pushed my fork into her ziti.

"I know you don't," she whispered. "But one day you'll realize that parents are meant to throw out a lifeline if their child is in distress. No matter the age." She reached over and squeezed my hand. "That's just what we do."

60

KATYA and Sasha came to the moving-up ceremony at Franklin, an event held every year on the last day of school. The teachers all loved it, as there was a nice bit of pageantry and celebration involved. Principal Nelson always took a few minutes to reflect on the past year and mention those students who had distinguished themselves in some way. It ended with each of the students getting a certificate for completing either the sixth or seventh grade.

I had immediately noticed Yuri's parents walking into the auditorium. Compared to the other parents, who were dressed casually in jeans and cotton polos, the Krasnys looked formal and out of place. Sasha in a pale gray suit and thin red tie, and Katya in a long, pleated skirt and white blouse. Every part of her slender frame was cloaked by material. The two of them sat as close as they could to Yuri, who was in the third row, next to Finn.

It was hard to believe that the wan, delicate child—the boy who when I first met him was almost too lethargic to rise from the living room chair—was now laughing along with his friend and classmate, his face beaming with good health.

I felt a pang of satisfaction knowing I had pushed Katya to let him attend classes at Franklin. I knew it had taken every ounce of courage for her to send him at first. But as I looked over at her sitting beside Sasha in the auditorium, I saw that both of them were overjoyed to see Yuri so happy and vibrant. I remember how Katya had described the early weeks after Yuri had first been diagnosed with his heart condition, a time when every waking moment centered on whether he was breathing without difficulty and whether his heart was working as it should. Sasha had promised her then that their son would grow to be a healthy young boy, even though they both secretly feared it was impossible. But there Yuri now was, sitting next to his best friend, seemingly as healthy and as happy as every other twelve-year-old child in that room.

AFTER the ceremony, I greeted Sasha and Katya and thanked them for coming. I mentioned how brave I thought they were for letting Yuri be at the school nearly every day that last week.

"I know how much you worry about him, but look at how he's thriving," I said as I pointed to him standing with Finn and two other classmates. They were all laughing and having a good time.

"We wouldn't have felt comfortable if you weren't his homeroom and English teacher," said Katya. "Just knowing you were keeping an eye on him made it so much easier."

Sasha's eyes scanned the crowd. "If you had only seen my middle school graduation," he laughed. "We had to pledge our allegiance to the motherland, and our lives were already all planned out for us."

Katya gave Sasha's arm a playful swat. "We know how fortunate we are to be here . . . and we're just so happy to see Yuri finally doing so well . . ."

I agreed. It felt like we had all accomplished an important milestone having Yuri back at school. But I knew that it wasn't only me who had helped make the transition easier for him. Finn's efforts had also been essential. I searched the crowd to find him and saw he was now walking over to his parents and sister. The little girl, dressed in a yellow sundress with her hair in a matching ponytail like her mother's, was steadying her left side with a single metal crutch braced to her arm. When Finn approached, she lifted it slightly in his direction, like a toy soldier offering him a congratulatory salute.

Yuri suddenly appeared beside us. "Finn asked me if I could go to his Little League game tonight. It's the championship, so can I go? Dad can take me . . ."

Katya hesitated.

"I wanted to surprise you with something at home, to make this day festive for you. You know how proud we are of you, Yuri." She turned to Sasha. "We made pierogi for you late last night, and even ordered your favorite ice cream cake from Carvel."

"Yes, a chocolate and vanilla baseball bat cake." Sasha squeezed Yuri's arm.

"But it's the last game of the season," he pleaded. "And Finn wants me to come. He says I bring him good luck . . . Please, Mom."

This was a common exchange between any mother and son, certainly one that I had overheard countless times and which easily could have happened fifteen years ago with my own brother and my mom. But still it was strange to see Katya and Yuri engaged in this kind of negotiation. I could tell how frustrated Katya was as she tried to suppress any visual clues of her annoyance.

Truthfully, Yuri had always been so agreeable whenever I came to the Krasnys' house. I had never seen him have to ask for anything, because Katya always circled him like a mother hawk, making sure she met every one of his wishes or needs. But now I sensed that Katya just wanted her son to come home with her.

"Daddy took the day off, Yuri," she said in soft protest.

"Let him go, *lapushka*," Sasha answered, his voice emerging as a balm to soothe her irritation. He wrapped his arm around his wife. "The boy wants to celebrate with his friend at the game . . . I'd be happy to take him." Sasha's eyes searched mine for a little friendly support.

"It's the American way. Right, Ms. Topper?" He playfully looked over in my direction. "Good baseball equals a good time. It's simple math."

I laughed. "That's the kind of equation only boys can dream up. But who am I to say? Today's the last day of school." I folded my hands playfully in front of me. "So I'm officially on vacation."

61

THAT summer I kept myself busy and earned a little extra income by working as an administrator at a local day camp. I accepted a few dinner invitations from the Krasnys, happy for the excuse to see Yuri, but I spent most of my free time with Daniel. In mid-August, we went on a road trip from Long Island all the way down to Savannah, Georgia. The whole trip was ten days of songs blaring on the radio, road stops at greasy fried-chicken joints, and the rapture of some really exquisite donuts along the way. He told me every story he could remember from his childhood, including the one that revealed how he got the sickle-shaped scar below his temple.

"I fell three feet from a friend's tree house," he said, laughing at the memory. "A sharp oak branch sliced through the skin, luckily not my eye or ear." We continued to fill the air with stories, and we spent most nights in modest motels, saving up our money for three nights at a luxurious former plantation. The romance was high and the Georgia humidity even higher. I knew it was love when Daniel looked at my hair one morning and saw that my normally manageable locks had swollen to three times their normal size.

"You look five inches taller," he joked as he wrapped me in his arms. We laughed even more as we strolled through the town's old alleyways and dipped into its charming antiques stores. At night, I buried my nose in sprigs of fresh mint and bourbon mixed with simple syrup, my body relaxing into the comfort of a wicker chair and a ceiling fan on the porch of our hotel.

But the trip would not have the happy ending I imagined. In my version, the one that I had written in my mind, Daniel and I returned home, where he carried me over the threshold of the cottage and threw me on the couch, making mad and feverish love to me, our relationship sealed by the fact that we had just enjoyed ten days of harmonious bliss. But instead, when we arrived, there was a message on my answering machine from Katya. Her voice sounded shaky and worn out, as if she had just been crying for hours.

"Yuri's had a bad week. We're in the hospital now. He's asking to see you, Ms. Topper. Something about the Yankees and the Mets." She left her phone number at the hospital and urged me to call as soon as I could.

I arrived at Stony Brook Hospital the next day and was told by a woman at the main desk, who peered up from her computer screen, that Yuri was in the ICU. She pointed toward the long white corridor behind her and instructed me to take the elevator to the fourth floor.

Past the rows of open doors with only partial views of hospital beds, I discovered Sasha waiting in the corridor outside Yuri's room. He was nearly unrecognizable. Bleary-eyed and unshaven, his face was shadowed by grief and fatigue.

"Last week, he started complaining of a racing heart and had difficulty catching his breath. We took him to see Dr. Rosenblum, who had his concerns and told us to keep careful watch if things got any worse. Then all these stomach problems started appearing." Sasha took a deep breath. "He had stomach cramps, which he never complained of before, diarrhea . . . The doctor told us today that there's massive dilation on the right side of his heart." Sasha looked as though he was going to be sick.

"Katya's a mess. She's in there now with Yuri." His head moved in the direction of the door to Yuri's room. "He's been watching baseball all day, all night. The only thing that seems to distract him is that he thinks the Mets and Yankees might just make it a Subway Series."

I forced myself to smile. I had been thinking the same thing on our trip back from Savannah. Both of the New York teams appeared to have an excellent chance of making the playoffs.

"Isn't there something they can do?" I was desperate to hear how Yuri's doctors were planning to help him.

"Tricuspid valve repair—the surgery Yuri needs—brings with it a tremendous amount of risk," Sasha said, fighting back tears. "I've always been a man who was confident in science. But now I don't know where to put my faith."

Any words I had evaporated on my tongue. I had always prided myself in having an answer to almost every situation. But I found myself mute. All I could offer was a hand on his arm, a pathetic attempt to give some comfort.

"Go in and see him," Sasha said softly. "He's been asking for you since he got here. My wife can't talk to him about sports, and I've been focused on what the doctors are saying. Not on how well the Yankees or Mets are doing."

"Yes, of course." I walked over to the door to peer inside his room. Yuri wasn't visible from the door's small glass window. All I could make out was Katya bent over his hospital bed, her hair piled into a messy bun, one arm resting on Yuri's blanket.

When I entered Yuri's hospital room, I was instantly overcome with emotion. The happy and vibrant student from the Franklin moving-up ceremony months before had transformed into a very sick-looking boy, and my painful childhood memories of Ellie came flooding back to me. His face was gaunt and had a faint yellowish hue. An IV was taped onto his forearm, the long cord draped over his bed. The rest of his body was enveloped in a mound of white sheeting and covers.

"Ms. Topper!" Yuri's voice emerged from the din of hospital machinery. The sound was scratchy and urgent.

As shocked as I was to see Yuri looking so weak, I steeled my nerves, refusing to let him see how concerned I was.

"I've missed you, champ," I said as I came closer to him. My eyes caught a glimmer of something I wasn't expecting within the cocoon of Yuri's sheets and blanket. Peeking out from Yuri's bedding, I saw the glint of a golden-figured baseball player.

"What you got there, Yuri?"

He gently adjusted the sea of wires and cables that emerged from his hospital gown and pulled back the side of his covers to reveal a gleaming gilt trophy with a blue marble base.

"Finn's team won the Little League championship that night after graduation. He gave me his trophy."

Katya turned to me; her eyes flashed.

"He's slept with it every night since he got it." Her voice broke off. "Finn told him it would bring him good luck."

62

THERE are certain places one always associates with children. Playgrounds and classrooms, or suburban cul-de-sacs filled with bicycles and street hockey nets. Stretches of shell-strewn beaches with plastic pails and shovels abandoned for chilly waves, and hot baking asphalt parking lots where chubby little hands grasp folded dollar bills hopeful for a Popsicle from the ice cream truck.

But there are other places that our minds never connect with children. Because they are simply incongruous with youth. There isn't a single soul who wants to associate the sterile white of a hospital with children. A childhood should instead be saturated with color: as golden as the sun and as vibrant as a rainbow. I wanted to weep when I saw Yuri's face drained of its typical pink color, his blue eyes so sunken. For as much as Yuri struggled to appear happy and excited to see me, I couldn't escape where he now was. The sight of him in a hospital bed with long cables draped over his torso, the electronic drone of beeping monitors in the background, was far crueler than I could have imagined.

Katya looked at least ten years older than the last time I had seen her. Her large eyes were rimmed in dark shadows, and wisps of hair had come out of her bun. She was dressed in a simple linen sundress, and her body appeared shrunken. Yuri's hospitalization had clearly consumed her.

Yuri, however, tried to be in good spirits despite his weakened state, and the contrast in his and Katya's expressions made me wonder if he even knew how grave his condition was.

"I'm glad you're here, Ms. Topper," he piped up. "My mom is getting sick of watching so much baseball with me."

Katya let out a weak laugh. "Yes, it's true. I don't understand this sport at all."

On the television, in the far corner of the wall, a midafternoon game was on the screen, though the sound was muted.

"Don't tell me you've been reduced to watching a Royals game?"

Yuri shrugged listlessly. "I know, but it helps pass the time." His voice sounded different to me, as if there was a gurgle caught in his chest. From underneath his white hospital blanket, I saw his chest rise and fall, his face twitching slightly.

"Well, how about we forget about the Royals and talk about my amazing team . . . They're enjoying quite a streak, aren't they?"

"Are you kidding, Ms. Topper?" He started to laugh. "We still have Mariano Rivera and Andy Pettitte. They're unbeatable. Keep dreaming."

I playfully waved my finger at him. "Never underestimate the underdog. I've always told you that."

"It looks like I'm the underdog again," he said, lifting his arm with the IV. "So maybe I should switch teams." He was having fun with me. "Nah, I could never do that!"

I enjoyed engaging with Yuri about a sport he took so much pleasure in. "I brought you a little something." I reached into my bag and pulled out a paperback copy of *The Glory of Their Times: The Story of the Early Days of Baseball Told by the Men Who Played It.*

"I think you're going to love it. It's written from the perspective of twenty-five major leaguers."

"Cool. Maybe we can discuss it with Finn here at the hospital?" Yuri tried to force a note of optimism in his voice. "You don't want my mind to go to mush, do you?"

"I don't think that could ever happen, Yuri. You've got such an impressive brain in there."

An enormous grin appeared on his face, and I felt my heart twinge.

"I'm serious, Yuri. There are a lot of things you could teach me, you're so smart."

"It just stinks that my heart hasn't caught up to my brain," he said as he tried to stifle a cough. "I hate that I always feel so tired."

I found his hand and squeezed it. Even though he was twelve, his hand still felt small in my own. "Are you tired now? Should I leave?"

"No, please don't. I like having you here. "

"I like being here, too, champ." I worried he could hear my voice cracking.

"I'm just going to close my eyes for two seconds."

Yuri shut his eyes, his fingers still clasped in mine, softening in sleep. Katya had left to get me a cup of coffee. When she returned, she told me I could leave.

"I'll stay," she said softly. "I know he was so happy you came to see him today."

"No, I *want* to stay," I insisted.

I wanted him to know that I hadn't left him. When he woke up, I wanted him to see I was still there waiting, ready and able if he wanted to talk baseball.

63

YURI'S operation was planned for the following Monday. Hoping to distract Yuri and his family from the dread of his tricuspid valve surgery, Daniel offered to come and play a little violin for him.

Yuri was certainly no classical music aficionado, but the chance to hear the school music teacher play live in his hospital room was enticing enough for Yuri to agree to Daniel's offer. Knowing that he was going to play on a violin that my father had actually made was an added bonus.

The two of them had met only in passing, at the moving-up ceremony, and Yuri had no idea that we were dating. Truthfully, I hoped no one at the school did, other than Suzie. Daniel and I had agreed to keep our relationship under wraps for as long as we could. School gossip was the scourge of any budding teacher romance, and we wanted to avoid it at all costs, impossible as that seemed. There wasn't a teacher alive who didn't enjoy speculating about a school love affair.

·   ·   ·

THE morning Daniel and I were to go to the hospital, he arrived at my front door and tenderly handed me a brown paper bag with two jelly donuts and a carrier holding two cups of coffee. The rosebushes were in full bloom in my garden, and under the canopy of trees, we drank our coffee, our backs against the tall throne of Adirondack chairs, and licked our fingers clean after eating our donuts.

"I love it here," he said. "You're so lucky to have all these birds."

Daniel always heard music everywhere he went.

"I know I am." I smiled. "I feel like I'm in my own time capsule whenever I come home." The cottage had no air-conditioning, but I had gotten used to sleeping with the windows open and waking to the sound of sparrows.

Daniel finished his last sip of coffee and placed his cup on the grass. "I know this must sound a little crazy, but I'm nervous about seeing Yuri today."

"Why on earth would you be nervous?" I made a face. "He's the one having surgery tomorrow."

Daniel lowered his voice. "I know, Maggie. And I know how much he means to you."

"That's why I was so happy you asked if you could come with me today." I watched his face soften, and I wanted to caress his cheek.

"It's just that I was up all night, wondering what I should play for him."

I put my empty coffee cup on the arm of the wooden chair and went over and sat on his lap. I took my fingers and ran them through his thick curly hair. His forehead gleamed a soft honey color, his skin tan from spending so much time outdoors over the past few months.

"Why don't you wait till you get there to choose? Maybe you'll be inspired," I whispered as I leaned over and kissed him.

.   .   .

THAT afternoon we spent several hours in the waiting room before we were finally able to see Yuri. Katya and Sasha took turns coming out to see us, apologizing that we couldn't yet go in.

"So many tests before tomorrow," she said, wringing her hands.

"Maybe we shouldn't have come. It's all so hectic for you now."

"No, no," she insisted. "Finn's mother brought him by yesterday and it did wonders for Yuri's spirit. He'll be just as happy to see you." She squeezed my arm. "It will help distract him, you know that."

Katya looked over at Daniel. His black violin case was resting against his shins. "And your idea to play him some music . . . it's the perfect thing to do."

Daniel smiled. "I hope next year he can take orchestra with me. We'll make sure he gets a great violin."

"My dad would probably leap at the chance to make him one," I said enthusiastically.

"Oh, he'd like that," Katya said. "Or at least I would . . ." Her voice faded off. "I always loved classical music. The Americans, they don't listen to it enough. It's a balm for the soul."

AT four p.m., Daniel and I finally were allowed to see Yuri. Finn's trophy was no longer tucked inside his bedsheets, but instead now rested on the faux wood side table along with an orange pitcher of water and plastic cups. A dog-eared copy of *The Glory of Their Times*, the book I had given him, was there, too. I was happy to see that Yuri had found some time to read it.

Yuri looked dramatically worse. The light blue circles that had rimmed his eyes during the school year were now so black, he looked like a raccoon. And his face looked puffy and swollen.

"Hey, Ms. Topper." His voice was barely audible. "Thanks for coming. Hope it's not too much of a drag to keep visiting the hospital."

I went over and sat by his bed. White surgical tape was stretched between his fingers, and a long plastic tube snaked between us as I held his hand.

"Are you kidding, champ? I'd drive a thousand miles to see you. And guess what? Today I've even brought along my own maestro. He's going to play you some tunes."

Yuri peered up at Daniel and tried to force a smile.

"Hey, buddy, is there anything in particular you'd like to hear?" Daniel lifted the black violin case in Yuri's direction.

Yuri thought for a moment. "Can you play something my mom might like? Maybe something from a ballet . . . preferably Russian, of course."

"Let me see what I can do," Daniel said as he unhinged the case on one of the hospital chairs. "Tchaikovsky's *Romeo and Juliet* might do the trick." He pulled out my father's violin, the amber hue sparkling in the late afternoon sun. Daniel tucked it underneath his chin and raised his bow. "It's called the 'Love Theme.'" He winked at me.

The horsehair slid over the strings, and the sound of the first notes filled the air. Daniel's eyes shut as the music lifted through the room.

I looked over to Yuri, who had also closed his eyes, his face softening as he listened to the music. For a brief moment, Katya, too, seemed transported to someplace other than the hospital room.

Love filled my heart at that moment, as pure as the music that emerged from Daniel's violin.

64

YURI made it through the four-hour surgery and spent the next week recuperating in the hospital before finally being allowed to go home. During those last few days in August, I would often visit the Krasnys. Sometimes Daniel would accompany me and other times I would go myself, but Yuri and I always had our own stadium seats right next to the TV. He would have to recline on his back for several weeks more so the wound in his chest could properly heal. Sasha and Katya had placed a bed in the living room, meaning his comfy chair was now relegated to the far corner of the room. Finn must have let the other kids know about Yuri's surgery, because several cards from them were propped up on the side table next to his bed, along with a collection of orange plastic medicine containers and boxes of surgical gauze and tape.

Katya moved silently through the house as the Yankees game roared from the television. Sasha now also never missed any of the night games, but for the afternoon ones, it was just Yuri and me. As weakened as he was by the operation, baseball seemed to at least partially restore him.

"The Mets are playing like they're a shoo-in for the World Series."

"Not so fast, Ms. Topper," Yuri said between taking sips of lemonade through a bendy straw. "There's still over six weeks left until then."

"I'm in a betting mood," I teased.

By September, as school started up again, my adrenaline was high and I was excited for a new year of teaching. On top of that, the Mets were challenging for first place in their division, and the Yankees had a strong lead in the American League East. Many of the sixth-grade boys in my English language arts class that year had decorated their writer's notebooks with the insignia of whichever team they were rooting for. But many other students had no idea what was going on in the world of baseball. Just like last year, some of the girls maintained a slightly cringe-worthy obsession with Britney Spears and continued to challenge the boundaries of appropriate school dress by wearing skirts that barely covered their bottoms, paired with knee-high socks and loafers. Some of the students in math club couldn't believe there hadn't been any fallout from Y2K and began talking about all the bad things that could still happen with their computers by the end of the year, claiming it didn't have to happen only on New Year's Eve.

"Thank God for some sunshine," Suzie said as she extended her arms to embrace the crisp autumn day. We were sitting outside having our lunch while the kids were at recess, warm fingers of light ricocheting over the grassy field. Over the summer, she had gone to healthy-cooking classes at the YMCA and started taking late afternoon walks, so she had slimmed down considerably. She was still crunching on her cruciferous salad of shredded Brussels sprouts, carrots, and jicama when Finn shouted over from the soccer field a hearty hello in our direction.

"Do you know he gave Yuri his baseball trophy? Yuri brought it along to the hospital for good luck."

Suzie put her fork into the empty container. She closed the lid and was quiet for a moment. I could see her looking at Finn as he navigated the field, the swirling black-and-white soccer ball moving deftly with every one of his dribbles.

"You know I'm always complaining about how bad some of the kids are, how they don't clean up their messes at the end of art class, how they talk half the time I'm trying to explain the difference between tempera paint and acrylic. But when you see a kid like that, you know how damn lucky we are." She let out a long sigh. "Sometimes that gold just rubs off on you."

65

DURING each of my visits that autumn, Yuri expressed increasing concerns about his favorite team, as the Yankees almost had a late-season collapse. Still, they managed to hold on and eke into the playoffs. The Mets, however, finished strong and easily won the National League wild card.

Both teams won their first two playoff series, finally ensuring that the Subway Series would happen. Finn and I went to Yuri's house to watch the first game, and the boys relished—at my expense—seeing the Yankees win it in extra innings.

"It's not over, not by a long shot," I warned, shaking my finger like an old schoolmarm. "Don't underestimate my Mets."

Although I didn't make it to the Krasnys' for the second game, I couldn't wait to see Yuri the next day. Everyone was talking about the crazy drama that had happened at the game, when Roger Clemens threw a piece of a broken bat at Mike Piazza in an incredible display of poor sportsmanship.

"Yuri, what was up with Clemens? There isn't a teacher alive who would have allowed that sort of behavior in their kindergarten class!"

Yuri was propped up on several pillows. His hair was just as I remembered it when I had first met him, blond feathers askew like a baby bird. A plastic cup with a straw was within arm's length of his chair.

"I couldn't believe it myself," he answered weakly. "But maybe it was an accident, like he confused the bat with the ball."

I shook my head. "You can't fool me, Yuri. You know what a hothead he is. If he was on the Mets, you'd be having a field day mocking me right now."

Yuri squirmed and smiled mischievously. "He's a great pitcher, though . . ."

I was happy to have something to distract him with. Katya said he had spent most of his days since his discharge from the hospital sleeping downstairs and that he had little interest in anything except when the Yankees were on TV. Katya had thought it best to wait to arrange any further tutoring for him until he had regained his strength, so I suspected Yuri's days were passing more slowly than usual.

"I would have given Clemens a lot more than just a time-out . . ."

"I bet you would, Ms. Topper." He forced another smile, but I could see he was feeling low.

"Have you seen Finn lately?"

"His mom dropped him off for a bit the day before yesterday, and we relived the highlights of the first World Series game. But it's getting more difficult to see him now because of all his basketball commitments. He's the point guard this year. I imagine he's got a lot of pressure on him."

Yuri slowly adjusted himself in his chair and stifled a cough. "I hate that I can't go to school this year. I'm so mad that just when I was making all those friends, this had to happen." He pointed to his chest.

My heart broke for Yuri. Part of me wondered whether I had made things worse for him—and his health—by urging Katya and Sasha to send him back to school last year.

"You just need to get stronger, champ. In a few months you might be able to return. And anyway, if you were in school right now, you'd have missed all those midafternoon playoff games."

"That's the good part," he said, faking a bit of optimism. "And maybe I'm going to end up stronger than I was before the operation. That's what my dad keeps telling me."

"Your father's a smart man," I said with great confidence. "So I'll place my bets on him."

"Well, in that case you'd better switch baseball teams," Yuri chuckled. "Because the man who first got me to be a Yankees fan was my dad. And he started rooting for them in 1987, when your team was on top of the world." He lifted his hand and started to gleefully count on his fingers. "Since then, the Yanks have won three World Series and the Mets have barely made the playoffs."

"Another bit of proof that he's a genius, Yuri. So I'm going to listen to whatever your dad says about your recovery. And after you're back to a hundred percent, we can talk about me switching teams."

ON the way out, I saw Katya hunched over the kitchen table reading a magazine, a cup of steaming tea at her fingertips. When she heard me rustle in my bag to find my car keys, she looked up and our eyes met through the doorway.

"I'm so happy he's out of the hospital," I said as I walked closer to her. "And that he's back home."

I pulled one of the small kitchen chairs over and sat down.

Katya pointed to her cup of tea. "Can I make you some?"

"Thanks, but I had some coffee before I came . . ."

She nodded and brought her mug up to her lips.

"He seems like he's getting stronger every time I see him," I said. "It looks like the surgery was a real success."

"Yes, we're just so glad it's over," Katya murmured.

She reached into her blouse and took out a necklace with a small crucifix dangling from the chain. "Sasha hates that I've started wearing this again. But I can't tell you how many times I prayed when we were in the hospital." Her voice cracked. "The doctor wouldn't tell us about Yuri's chances of surviving the surgery. Can you believe that?" She was wringing her hands so tightly that her knuckles had turned white.

"But Sasha always demanded statistics. He wanted to know if it was worth cutting open Yuri's chest for such a risky operation. He kept pushing the doctor for answers . . . Was Yuri more likely to die from the surgery than from his failing heart?"

She fidgeted in her seat and put the crucifix back inside her blouse. "I told Sasha, 'I'm a mother. I just want to take care of my son.' I don't question the doctors, I can't think about statistics or survival rates. Every day I just wake up thankful he's still sleeping in that bed." She paused and sucked in her breath. "He sleeps most of the day, but I can hardly shut my eyes. I feel like I'm back to that time when he was a few weeks old. I'm constantly afraid something could happen to him if I let myself fall asleep for even a second."

"You're exhausted, Katya," I interrupted. "Why don't you let me sit in the living room while he naps, and you go upstairs and rest."

"No, no . . . you were just leaving . . . and I'm sure you have other things to do."

"I don't have anywhere to be but here," I said as I reached over and touched her shoulder.

"Go upstairs and I promise I will watch over him."

. . .

YURI sleeping. His eyes closed, the lids a pale shade of blue, almost lavender. I sit staring at him as he slumbers, wondering what it must be like for Katya to watch him like this. For me, he is an image of boyish sweetness; his relaxed features soften as he rests. His mind is far away, lost in dreams that I am not privy to. I wonder whether in his dreams he is playing sports, whether he has another life where he is active and his heart is strong.

I don't find myself worrying as Katya described herself doing. Perhaps it's because I'm not a mother. I hear his measured breathing, see his small chest rising and falling from underneath the cotton coverlet, and I trust his body to work as it should.

Instead, I savor the quiet calm of just seeing Yuri resting. I imagine only good things. His return to Franklin, joking with friends. Playing ball with Finn.

I watch the maple leaves falling from the branches in their back yard and the squirrels gathering acorns on the wooden deck, and I feel lucky to be guarding over Katya and Sasha's precious little boy.

I didn't see Yuri again until the fifth game of the World Series. I brought Daniel along despite the fact that he was a Yankees fan, having grown up in the Riverdale section of the Bronx, where if you were caught rooting for the Mets, you'd risk being hung up by your toenails. When he picked me up that afternoon, he couldn't help but make an off-color remark about the Mets jersey I was wearing.

"Now, if my jock brother saw me escorting a girl who has her own Al Leiter jersey to a World Series game, I think he'd advocate disowning me from the family."

I laughed. "You mean, despite the fact that I'm cute and good with kids?"

"He wouldn't see past those annoying orange and blue colors."

"I tell you what," I said as I handed him the eggplant rollatini my mom had made for me to bring to the Krasnys. "I promise not to wear this when I meet your brother. I'll let him fall in love with me first before I break the news about the Mets. Deal?"

Daniel opened up the car door with one hand and I slipped inside. "You're too smart for your own good, Maggie." He handed me back the eggplant to put on my lap.

"That's right, brains over beauty," I teased back. "You wouldn't want it any other way."

He turned on the ignition. "Luckily with you, I got both."

KATYA had made a feast for dinner, so my mother's eggplant was in good company on the dining room table. The food was all set out in a generous buffet: potato and meat pierogi, stuffed cabbage, a tray of grilled kielbasas, and bowls of brightly colored borscht.

Everyone but Yuri ate all the delicacies she had prepared. Katya, who had the least amount of baseball knowledge and interest, was far more preoccupied with whether Yuri was getting anything down than with who was winning the game.

His white paper plate, with a sampling of glistening pierogi, rested on his lap and remained untouched. But what he lacked in appetite, he made up for in enthusiasm for the game.

"It's too bad Finn couldn't be here," he said, turning to me. "But his uncle is in town, so his parents are having their own party."

I looked over to the fireplace, where I saw that Yuri had placed Finn's baseball trophy on top of the mantel for good luck, just like he had done at the hospital.

"But you're wearing your favorite Jeter jersey, and you have Finn's trophy on display over there. So I think you have your superstitious armor all set."

Yuri grinned and pointed to my Mets jersey. "And I see you do, too, Ms. Topper."

"Yep," I said as I settled down into the sofa. I took my fork and ate my first bite of one of Katya's pierogi. The warm potato filling reminded me a little of my mother's gnocchi, though I could detect onion and black pepper on the inside.

Sasha lifted the TV remote and increased the volume.

The Yankees had won three of the first four games, needing just one more victory to clinch the series.

"If the Yankees win tonight, we're all toasting with some ice-cold vodka that's in the freezer," Sasha announced.

"Even you, Yuri," he kidded.

"Most certainly not." Katya cut him off. "We'll have the fresh gingerbread and whipped cream I made to celebrate."

BERNIE Williams started off the scoring with a solo home run in the second inning, and Yuri and his dad were hooting and clapping like madmen.

The Mets pulled out two runs off of Andy Pettitte, the Yankees' pitcher, but then Yuri's favorite player, Derek Jeter, hit a home run to tie the game at 2–2.

"Woo-hoo!" Yuri yelped. His hand landed on one of the cushions in his makeshift bed.

Daniel, it seemed, did not share his brother's love for baseball. Instead, he looked amused by the fact that the score made both sets of fans squirm. He helped himself to another kielbasa, and I was sure I saw Katya smile as he filled his plate.

. . .

IN the top of the ninth, the Yankees scored twice, when a throw by the Mets' center fielder hit Jorge Posada as he slid into home plate. The ball rolled into the dugout, and Scott Brosius was able to score, making it 4–2 Yankees. Their superstar reliever, Mariano Rivera, would then try to close out the game in the bottom of the inning. Even I had to admit that, at this point, it was unlikely my team was going to win.

"It's not over till the last out," Daniel chimed in, hoping to give me some support. His hand rested comfortably on my leg, and I returned the gesture by placing my own hand over his.

What Daniel didn't realize was that I didn't ultimately care whether the Mets won the World Series. Or rather, I would have cared a lot more had I never met Yuri. Either way, there was a win in it for me.

In the bottom of the ninth, with a runner on and two outs, Mike Piazza hit what looked like a sure game-tying home run off the great Mariano. But Bernie Williams caught it in the deepest part of the ballpark, and the Yanks won the game and the series.

That evening there were fireworks lifting off of Yuri's eyes. And I secretly was joyous, despite the fact that my team had lost. Nothing could have rivaled seeing the sheer happiness on Yuri's face as the Yankees ran onto the field and lifted Mariano onto their shoulders, tearing off their baseball caps in ecstasy. I had always told Yuri that I loved the Mets because they were New York's underdog team. But the Yanks had made Yuri feel like a champion, and for that, I silently thanked them as I lifted my fork and happily dug into Katya's fluffy square of gingerbread and cloud of whipped cream.

66

I had last seen Yuri just after Thanksgiving, and although he was still recuperating, everyone in the Krasny household seemed in good spirits. Katya's holiday wreath of corn husks and dried cranberries signaled a bit of warmth and festivity. I had stopped by with a plate of my mother's lasagna to share with them. "More food?" Katya said as she took the tray from me. "I can hardly move, I've eaten so much over the past few days."

"That's America," I joked. "The land of plenty and then some."

Katya smiled and pointed toward Yuri.

"He misses school, and all the friends he made last year." She shook her head. "But the doctor doesn't want him to return yet."

Katya placed the lasagna in the refrigerator and then moved effortlessly toward the stove.

"Tea?"

I nodded yes.

"Finn still visits him," she said, trying to sound positive. She turned on the burner on the stove. "But I have to be honest, he seems to spend a lot of time looking out the window since the operation, just staring at the clouds."

I was glad Finn had continued to come see Yuri even though we were no longer having our weekly reading-group sessions together. At the beginning of the school year, I had seen Finn in the hallway at Franklin and had been amazed by how much he had grown over the summer. He was now nearly the same height as me, and his shoulders had broadened and his face had become more angular. There was less and less of that translucent stage that Suzie and I had found so fascinating, as now a young man had nearly fully emerged.

I missed having Finn in my class, as I did Yuri. I found myself filled with a bittersweetness when I saw my former students move through the corridors. I knew I would never have them in my classroom again, but I also realized they would go on to accomplish a myriad of other things when they left Franklin. This part of the cycle of teaching never ceased to pull at my heartstrings.

BUT the upside, the part that always restored me, was my new batch of students. I had just assigned my latest class the task of writing their own personal narratives in their writer's notebooks, and I knew their passages would bring me closer to their inner thoughts.

The days slipped by quicker than I would have liked as I tried to squeeze in time with Daniel and my parents among all my responsibilities at school. I was going to get in touch with Katya and schedule another visit with Yuri before Christmas, but Sasha's call came before I had the chance.

The phone was ringing when I pulled into the driveway at the cottage. I have a thing about ringing phones. While other people have no problem letting the answering machine pick it up, I will do anything in my power to reach it before it starts recording.

After quickly unlocking the front door and flinging my bag onto the ground, I managed to get to the phone just before the machine clicked on.

"Ms. Topper?" The voice was barely audible. I will never forget the sound, because it didn't resemble Sasha's voice at all. It was the quietest whimper.

"Mr. Krasny?"

There was a horrible silence that followed. And in that silence, I knew almost intuitively that something terrible had happened. It was the lack of words, the inability to say what would make it concrete. I heard it all on the other end of the receiver, though I didn't want to believe it.

"Mr. Krasny? Sasha?" I asked again, my heart racing.

"Yes, it's Sasha." Again, the words were so faint it sounded as though they were uttered by someone struggling to breathe.

I pushed my ear closer to the receiver. "Is everything okay?" My own voice emerged with a palpable panic.

"It's Yuri," he said, his voice cracking. Again, I heard silence and then what sounded like a chest heaving. "It was a sudden arrhythmia."

"What?" My voice ricocheted out of my chest. "But he's okay now, right?" I could already find myself willing another reality, one where Yuri was in front of me, smiling and happy.

"No," Sasha managed to say before his words were lost to the sound of his sobbing. After that, everything just crumbled.

I dropped the phone and fell to my knees.

THE details all came later, the horrible scene described to me when I met them in their home, their faces crumpled and red. Katya sat on the sofa, her body sagging, her eyes rimmed in pink. She couldn't speak, and she had clearly stopped eating. The two of them looked like empty chrysalises, hollowed by their grief.

We sat there in the living room, where every trace of Yuri remained intact. His books were still on the coffee table, next to his half-nibbled pencil and the orange plastic containers for all his medications. On top of the fireplace sat the baseball trophy Finn had given him. The room seemed to be a purgatory, every object remaining in place despite the absence of its owner. I felt that my mind was playing tricks on me. How could Yuri not be sitting in that big fluffy chair? How could it be that I'd never hear his voice again or see his wide blue eyes come alive when we spoke about baseball or books? And how did the birds outside dare to sing, when the boy who always sat by the window—watching them take flight—was gone?

Every time Katya tried to speak, her voice failed her. It was Sasha who, after summoning all his strength, informed me of the painful details. Yuri had been complaining of a bad headache that day, and Katya had thought it was just due to the rain and change in air pressure. Yuri fainted on his way to the bathroom, and Katya held him in her arms as she waited for the ambulance to arrive.

"It was all so quick," Sasha said softly. He sucked in his breath. "By the time I got to the hospital, Yuri was already gone."

DAYS later, on the morning of the memorial service, I could barely get myself out of bed. I simply could not comprehend that Yuri was no longer here. I still heard his voice, his laugh. I saw his face everywhere—his blue-jay-colored eyes, vital and alive. But the image of Katya and Sasha sitting like two ghosts in their living room provided stark contrast to those memories. I told Daniel I didn't think I would make it through the service; my grief would be too much.

They had asked me to speak at the funeral. I stayed up all night trying to write something, but now, as the paper fluttered in my hand, I worried my voice would escape me.

I remember so little of that afternoon. There are things I still wish to block out. The sight of Sasha and Katya in the front seats, their bodies lost in their black mourning clothes. Their faces so pale and drawn, they looked as though they had to be propped up, like two puppets that would soon collapse without their strings.

Katya did not just move through a room, but always glided. Her limbs weightless, her body effortlessly beautiful. Now, she could hardly stand. When I reached out to embrace her, she sagged in my arms.

In the center of the room, Yuri's small coffin was set out. A wreath of white flowers lay on top with a piece of paper attached that simply read, *Love.*

I could hardly look at it. I did not want to think of his body inside that lacquered box, knowing the boy I loved so much would soon be lowered forever into the earth.

"Daniel." I could barely say his name, so instead I squeezed his fingers. "I won't be able to read this." I handed him my eulogy, hoping he'd offer to read it for me. But Daniel gently pushed it back.

"Maggie," he whispered. "You loved him, and he was always so brave for you. You must be brave for him."

IN a room with pale gray walls, a wooden podium cast to the side, many familiar faces appeared. Lisa Yamamoto arrived with her mother, as did Rachel Mendelsohn and Roland McKenna. I saw Principal Nelson quietly dip in and take one of the chairs in the last row.

Florence came, her small rhinestone butterfly attached to the lapel of her dark suit, her face drawn and serious. Even Angela came later, sitting quietly in the rear.

Then I saw Suzie. In her somber clothes, she was nearly unrecognizable, her long hair pulled back into a respectful bun. When she approached me, she did not speak. Instead, her arms enveloped me, and I felt the warmth of her skin soaking up my sorrow like a sponge.

Lastly, Finn arrived with his parents and his little sister. While most of the mourners gravitated toward the seats closest to the back, I saw Finn walk up to the row of empty seats closest to the Krasnys. Dressed in a navy blazer and khakis, he looked five years older than he normally did in his school clothes. As he helped his mother get his sister in her chair, holding her crutch as she sat down, our eyes caught each other's, and I saw how stoically he was trying to fight back his tears.

Later on, I stood at the podium, my fingers clenching the sides of the pitched surface. I closed my eyes and inhaled, praying that my voice would hold out until I had spoken my last word. I refused to look at the casket but instead focused on the wooden doors as the rest of the voices faded away. I took a deep breath and felt something shift inside me, as though Yuri were suddenly there in front of me. I began as if I were speaking solely to him.

Yuri,

All night I've been staring at this paper, thinking about how I could capture you adequately. During the entirety of our friendship, I sought to teach you the power of words. How many times did we discuss passages in books that moved us? We both learned together how words have the power to inspire us, to unify us, to fill in those spaces of the unknown. But today, I feel like I'll never have the words to fully describe you.

Yuri, many people say a smile can light up an entire room, but for me it was your eyes that were the brightest lanterns. I have never seen eyes so crystal clear and radiating with so much light. I never told you that I used to see your eyes in my head, long after I'd left you for the afternoon. They'd float inside my mind like beacons in a dark storm. I saw so much in those eyes. Intelligence, humor, curiosity, and a yearning to do more in life than your heart would ever physically allow you to.

Yuri, a teacher is supposed to teach her pupils, but I know I learned more from you than you ever learned from me. You taught me to cherish the world around me. You pushed me to think harder, to challenge myself and my students in the classroom. You taught me about bravery. When I visited you in the hospital, you looked like a warrior strapped to all those machines. You taught me to do what so many of us take for granted. To breathe unhindered, to savor each baseball game, and to dream of one day being strong enough to play.

I will never understand how a life budding with so much possibility, brimming with so much curiosity, could be taken so early from this earth. I will never understand how a boy with the most generous heart I know could have his own heart stop beating before its time. But what I do know is that you have left a mark that is unforgettable not only on me but also on everyone else whose life you touched. I will always remember that afternoon that you said the words from a book you fought me to read: "Life's got to be lived, no matter how long or short," you quoted from Tuck Everlasting. *And, Yuri, you will never know how much you taught me the meaning of these words.*

You once said that Derek Jeter was your hero because he never

gave up, because he brought his best to each and every game. Yuri,
you are, and will always remain, my hero, my champ.

I closed my eyes and felt my strength slip away again. I had been like one of those women who, when their children are suddenly trapped beneath a car, are momentarily blessed with Hulk-like strength. But now after I had finished speaking, I felt like I was about to collapse.

My face must have blanched, because I remember little else except Daniel lifting me back to my chair.

And then the blurry memory of leaving the church later and seeing Finn a few steps ahead of me, pulling his Yankees cap out of his side pocket. I noticed the flash of Yuri's name written in silver Sharpie under the brim before he tugged it down over his forehead, the visor obscuring his falling tears.

YURI was buried under the shade of a huge maple tree. His headstone was painfully simple: *Yuri Alexander Krasny. Beloved son and friend.*

After the interment, Daniel drove us back without saying a word. The silence enveloped us. The notes of grief are impossible to share.

67

THE time following Yuri's death was not easy for me. I spent the first few months afterward in a fog, unable to process how a child so bright and full of curiosity could be gone. There were days it took every bit of my strength just to get up from my bed and drive to school, because all I wanted to do was curl myself into a ball and cry for hours on end.

I slept fitfully. I couldn't close my eyes unless I had the sound of the radio or the television to distract me, because I couldn't get the memory of Yuri's memorial service out of my head. I saw the image of Katya rigid in her chair. Her wide blue eyes staring at Yuri's little white coffin with tears streaming down her face. And I knew if my pain was great, hers must have been unfathomable.

Sometimes I awakened in the middle of the night and heard Yuri's voice in my head. I had dreams that were so intense, where I imagined him sitting there in his big, comfy living room chair, his bright blue eyes staring at me with great lucidity. I heard his boyish voice chirping about the Yankees. I saw his pale fingers reaching to flip the pages of one of the books we were reading. I felt the atmosphere between us as a cross between excitement and melancholy, a boy eager to do more but thwarted by his physical fragility.

And then I would awaken and realize that it was only a dream, and my entire body would begin to tremble. I was soothed only by Daniel, who told me he believed that the soul flows on like music. That it fills spaces that are open and wide. Like breath and air, it travels where the heart is most open, during grief, during love. He would take my hand and bring it to his chest, pulling me back to sleep with the rhythm of his heart.

I had called the Krasnys several times after the funeral to check on Katya and Sasha, but I only reached their answering machine. But now it had been nearly three weeks since the funeral, and after leaving several messages, I decided to bring a tray of my mother's lasagna to their house as a gesture of love. Knowing they did not have family around them, I wanted them to know they were not alone in their grief.

I drove out to the Krasnys' on a cold, brittle afternoon. Winter was nearly upon us, and the trees that lined the roads were stripped bare. And yet, the ride out to their house was so familiar that if I closed my eyes, I could recall myself driving out with my bag full of schoolwork only a year ago, eager to spend time with Yuri.

I had a plan. If they didn't answer the doorbell, I'd leave the food on the front stoop with a little note. This way they would know, even if we didn't have a chance to speak, that I continued to hold them and Yuri in my heart.

It was clear, however, that they were home when I arrived. Both Sasha's and Katya's cars were parked outside, and I could see the pale glow of a lamp through the windows.

So with great trepidation, I turned off the car, reached for the glass dish covered in foil, and started walking toward the front door.

IT was Sasha who answered the doorbell, his face unshaven, his white hands shaking as he took the tray.

He could barely say my name as he gestured for me to come inside. Grief has its own color and scent. The house was dark and stale.

"I'm sorry I came without notice," I apologized. "I'll only stay a moment. I just wanted to check on you both."

He nodded. His pale eyes were rimmed in pink.

"I've left a few messages for Katya on the phone," I said softly.

"Yes," he mumbled absently, as if that was the only word he could manage. He was spiraling around with the lasagna, as if he wasn't sure where to put it.

The house looked as if it were collapsing inside. A coat lay on the floor. A single blue moccasin was marooned by the door. There were piles of newspapers on the sofa, and a mug and several plates cluttered the coffee table.

Eventually, Sasha placed the tray of food on the kitchen table. "Please," he said, gesturing me toward the sofa.

I walked toward the living room. It had remained eerily untouched. The chair. Finn's trophy. The orange medicine containers. Nothing had been changed or thrown out.

"We haven't really had the chance to . . ." He gestured toward the relics of what remained of Yuri. He looked down at his shoes, and I saw his glassy eyes pool with water.

"I understand," I said awkwardly. "I only wanted to stop in briefly and bring you something. I know it must be hard to eat . . . but the Italian in me needed to show that I was thinking of you and Katya."

"You have always been so kind." Sasha shifted in his seat, then leaned over and cradled his head in his hands.

"You should probably take it back with you. It will go uneaten . . ."

"You can always freeze it," I offered. "Or even throw it out. I just wanted you both to know . . ."

"We know, Maggie," he said. "We know . . ." And his voice splintered, painful as broken glass. Even hearing him use my name made everything feel awkward and raw.

I was just about to say something when I caught sight of Katya in her bathrobe. Her hair, straggly and unpinned, flowed over her tightly cinched robe.

She looked at me, her eyes hollow, her face sunken and concave. The same vacant expression I had seen in Mrs. Auerbach's gaze years before was now staring back at me.

Before I had a chance to say something, her voice sliced into the air. She spoke loudly, in Russian, words that were incomprehensible to me.

Sasha's face blanched, and he turned away from me, responding in Russian in a voice that was low and measured.

The air in the room changed. "I shouldn't have come." My voice broke off. I was trembling.

He rose and walked toward her, moving her hair away from her face. Then, without any more words between them, he started to lead her back to bed.

I sat there for a moment, stunned. Several minutes passed and Sasha had not reemerged.

I stood up and slung my bag over my shoulder. I let myself out, shutting the door behind me.

I could barely drive myself back home after I visited the Krasnys. The encounter with Katya loomed in my mind. Of course, I didn't understand what she had actually said. But from her tone and the way she had looked at me, all I could think about was that she blamed me for Yuri's death.

When I pulled into my driveway, it took all my energy to get inside the house and up to my bedroom. Daniel would not be at his home yet, so I reached for the phone and called Suzie.

"She's in the deepest black hole imaginable, Maggie. She's mourning her son. This has nothing to do with you."

"I think it does," I said, sobbing. "I think she blames me for Yuri's death . . ."

"Honey," she said gently. "How could she ever think such a thing?"

"Maybe she thinks he should never have returned to school . . . Maybe she thinks the increased activity weakened Yuri's heart somehow . . . like that time he and Finn snuck off together . . ." I could hardly catch my breath in between my words.

"I think it has to do with missing Yuri so damn much, Maggie, you'd be losing your mind, too, if you lost your child."

I covered my mouth to try to stifle my sobs. "I should never have gone over there unexpected like that."

Suzie was silent for a moment. "Maybe that's right. Maybe you shouldn't have, but there's nothing you can do about it right now. In a few days, call them again and apologize. Tell them you came over because you loved Yuri and you care about them." She took a deep breath. "Broken hearts don't heal overnight."

I hung up the phone. Tears streaked down my cheeks. I wasn't sure broken hearts could ever heal; they beat differently, forever altered.

68

AFTER that afternoon, I called the Krasnys once. Twice. A third time, all within a month. Each time the message I left on their answering machine went unanswered.

The next month I tried again. The third month, I called one last time.

Daniel held me at night. He smoothed back my hair and whispered in my ear that he loved me. "They just need their space." He tried to console me. "It has nothing to do with you." But I was still haunted by the memory of Katya's eyes and the words that I didn't understand. During my lunch hour, when I continued to worry out loud, Suzie finally silenced me.

"You might never know what Katya said. And I know how hard that is."

I looked up at her. My beautiful friend with her hard, shining eyes. Her chenille sweater with a smattering of sequined stars.

"But you need to live your life and honor that boy in a way that does justice to his memory." Her voice was strong and firm. "Don't replay his parents' private grief in your mind over and over like a record. Maggie, it's not yours to play."

HER words pierced through me, and as difficult as they were to hear, they also awakened something inside me. I began to think of life differently, trying to readjust my sense of timing. I strove to live more in the present and appreciate all that was around me. I tried to honor Yuri's spirit by throwing myself even more into my classes and my students. I thought of him every time I pointed out the images of the Colosseum or the pizza slice on my writing workbook cover. And I thought of him every year I assigned *Shoeless Joe* to a boy who loved sports, and I could almost hear his voice in my ear as we discussed which passages were the most moving.

And there were other smaller gestures that I made to connect me with Yuri's memory, ones that made my life a little sweeter, a little slower, and inspired me to savor the world around me. I bought a bird feeder and put it outside my kitchen window. It was simple and unpainted, a classic wooden house with a perch and a round open door. And when a beautiful red cardinal or a dazzling blue jay came to feed, I thought of Yuri every time. The birds' visits felt like a reassurance—that his spirit continued to exist around me—just as their majestic wings spread open and they flew confidently back into the sky.

LIFE, as it does, continued forward. Daniel moved into the cottage after Christmas, and the months that followed were nothing like my earlier experiences there with Bill. The house came to life with the sound of his instruments. Not only my father's violin but also the old banjo he had played in college and the ukulele he was trying to learn how to play. We bought extra shelves for our bedroom and lined them with our favorite books and CDs. The house, which had always seemed quaint, now felt full and more complete; it had begun to feel like a true home.

One afternoon that spring, I sat in one of the white painted Adirondack chairs in the garden, reading a book under the shade of the linden tree. The air smelled of lilacs and freshly cut grass. I put my book down when I saw Daniel walking toward me.

"Maggie Topper." He said my full name and gave me a smile that could have melted a glacier. He was holding something in his clenched fist. Before I had a chance to speak, he got down on bended knee and asked me to marry him.

I will always associate the scent of lilacs with Daniel's proposal and his warm kiss afterward. When he slid the ring onto my finger, I looked down at the slender platinum band, the circular stone flanked by a perimeter of pavé diamonds. A small circle of perfectly cut white stars.

"I had been planning to propose last winter, but it seemed wrong to not let you mourn Yuri properly."

I kissed him again, my eyes glistening with emotion. How did I get so lucky to find this man with a beautiful heart and a musician's soul?

"Yes, I will marry you, Daniel O'Reilly," I whispered into his ear as he wrapped his arms around me. That afternoon, as the wind blew the lilac blossoms into the air and the robins jumped across the grass, I felt the cycle of life swirling around me, intoxicating and invigorating. That same blending of nervousness and anticipation I'd felt as a young girl on the first day of school.

69

OUR wedding took place on a warm sunny day in early July. My mother cut fresh flowers from her garden and made me a garland of baby pink roses, lavender delphiniums, and white snowdrops. She opened up her own wedding dress and lengthened the skirt with edges of antique lace so I could wear something with family history, her nimble fingers wanting to press love into everything that ushered me into my new life, including all the food for the reception, which she served on my grandmother's hand-painted dishes on a long table lit with candles in the backyard of our cottage.

We drank from flutes of champagne and danced to Van Morrison, Daniel pulling me close and singing *"She's as sweet as tupelo honey"* in my ear. We made love the next night in a small inn in Vermont with the French doors of the balcony wide open, our bodies illuminated by a bath of pure white stars.

AFTER four years of marriage, Daniel and I were ready to start our family. I had never thought about having children when I was with

Bill, but now it was something I wanted badly. I had spent my twenties surrounded by other people's children, as had Daniel, and once we entered our thirties, baby fever hit us both hard. We started to imagine the extra bedroom as a nursery. I paid a visit to my gynecologist and left feeling healthy and strong. I took folic acid supplements every morning and even started purchasing my favorite children's picture books whenever I was at the bookstore.

At night, Daniel would indulge me, and we'd play a game of trying to come up with names for our unborn progeny. Juliet if it was a girl and George if it was a boy, because that was the English version of Yuri. We imagined our combined features. His wavy locks, my dark eyes, his musical talent, and my family's height and appetite.

The first few months we started trying for a baby were like a second honeymoon. We couldn't wait for school to be over each day. The garden was abloom with the flowers I so loved. The fireplace was finally getting to enjoy some time off, after having served us well over the winter. We made wonderful dinners of pasta and grilled vegetables and avoided drinking too much wine. We ate alfresco and watched the fireflies light up the lawn. We didn't know exactly when we'd hit the jackpot and see the pink sign on the pregnancy test, but we vowed to have fun until it appeared.

But then after Christmas, after nearly eight months of trying, I began to suspect something was wrong. I was now thirty-three and certainly not on what I considered to be the older spectrum for having a child. A second visit to my gynecologist turned into a more elaborate discussion of having blood work done to see whether I had any hormonal imbalances. A sonogram was also suggested, to see whether my ovaries might be polycystic or whether endometriosis could be to blame.

However, the doctors could not determine any medical reason that prevented me from conceiving. Daniel was then tested, and nothing could be found on his end, either.

Still, month after month, my period arrived and my heart sank with every cycle. The constant roller coaster of thinking that this was finally going to be the month for the egg and the baby we were waiting for made me an emotional wreck. As soon as I felt a pulling pain in my abdomen, I immediately went from thinking the embryo was implanting itself to fearing I was going to miscarry before I even had a positive pregnancy test.

IF you have one friend in your life who will come running to your house at a moment's notice, a friend who can hear the pain in your voice or even in your breathing when you try to reach them on the phone, if you have a friend who knows you that well and loves you that much, then consider yourself one of the luckiest people on earth. That person for me was Suzie. More than a friend, she was a lifeline and beacon of positivity and hope when all I wanted to do was crawl back into bed with a hot-water bottle and a half-empty box of Kleenex.

"It came," I would say, and she knew that that little bit of blood would once again usher in a new flood of tears for me. Another failure. Another cycle without a baby. There were days she found me behind the school parking lot, near one of the large trees that bordered Franklin's property, and she would withdraw tissues from her sleeve and blot away my tears. She also provided my alibi for the other teachers when I found myself having to call in sick after the ovulation drug Clomid left me feeling nauseated and faint.

Daniel did not know the words to comfort me, but he tried in his own way. My frustration welled inside me, silencing me in a way that I had never before experienced. We had exhausted our savings on two rounds of in vitro, and I began to fear that we would never make it out of this dark hole. The worst-case scenario suddenly seemed real: Daniel and I might not ever have children of our own. That reality, so awful and gut wrenching, swallowed me up whole. Whereas I used to rejoice at the news of a fellow teacher announcing her pregnancy, I now loathed every woman who seemed healthier and fitter than I was. I envied everything about them. I felt like I had been consumed by an ugly green monster, one with a hideous, jealous soul.

I took Suzie's advice and tried acupuncture. I ate spinach and other greens rich in folate and vitamins B and D. There was no longer pretty lingerie from Nordstrom or home-cooked meals of silky pasta in butter and sage before we slid between the sheets. I didn't have the energy for seduction, and foreplay between Daniel and me was reduced to wielding a digital basal thermometer and me demanding he perform on command. But nothing worked. There once was a time, when my cycle began anew each month, I felt anything was possible, but now all I felt was despair.

MY mother, desperate to help, suggested something so ridiculous that I wasn't sure whether to be angry at the sheer ludicrousness of her proposal or to hug her for being willing to try just about anything to help Daniel and me conceive. She had read about an island off the southwestern coast of Italy called Ischia, a place of sacred waters where—legend has it—the Sirens used to bathe when they couldn't conceive. In her voice, the island emerged as a beacon of hope. And then she pressed two plane tickets to Italy into our hands.

At the end of August, with Daniel's fingers grasped in mine, we flew over the Atlantic, and I tried to let go of my hopes of having a family. I knew my mother's wish was to somehow encourage us to heal as a couple. So I surrendered to the fact that this trip would at least be the first step to restoring us. We traveled first to Rome and then on to Naples. We ate pizza crafted by wiry men who pulled out beautiful, charcoal-dusted discs on their wooden paddles, with runny mozzarella made from buffalo milk and tomatoes warmed in the sun. From there we took a ferry to Ischia, where the water of the legendary gulf was as warm as bathwater, and the scent of lemons lifted off the air.

I fell in love with Daniel for the second time on that trip. I saw his face transform when he heard Vivaldi's music wafting in from the small stone church in Trastevere. I marveled at his passion for all the craftsmanship by the local artisans and his insistence we buy a small wooden Pinocchio to take home as a souvenir for my father. Suddenly, the possibility that we would be a white-haired, wrinkly old couple without any children of our own did not seem like such a death sentence. I now saw myself as lucky to have met someone to share the world with, and with whom I could still experience a life full of love.

But on the way back home, Daniel told me I looked different to him. I didn't want to say anything, but secretly I felt something inside me had changed. My whole body seemed warm and content. And most strange, I had an unfamiliar sensation, as though I had swallowed a butterfly.

THE following spring, I was close to being full term. I had a big, round belly and breasts, and all I wanted to do all day was lounge in bed and eat mozzarella with my feet kicked up on a stack of pillows and a hand-held fan blowing on my face. I had long since passed those first few months of nausea, and my mother had taken to feeding me and her unborn grandchild with even more unbridled enthusiasm. Every craving I had she indulged. Daniel had already put on ten pounds from sharing her extra trays of lasagna and manicotti with me.

Quietly, I rejoiced that all the pieces of my life that I had been hoping for had finally fallen into place. Daniel had taken a job at a new school and had even received an unexpected raise in salary. But more importantly, we were both excited that after trying for so long to have a baby, we would soon have the summer off to savor the first months of parenthood.

We had already finished the last touches of the nursery, converting the spare bedroom by filling it with white pine bookshelves and a rocking chair with a blue-and-white-gingham seat. My dad had come over and helped Daniel assemble the crib, the two of them humming softly to themselves as they fitted all the pieces together.

When they were finished, my mother and I pulled the cotton sheets over the small mattress and tied the bumper around the edges. Both of us found it hard to believe that soon there would be a baby sleeping in this perfect little nest.

The pregnancy had made me more emotional than ever. It wasn't just the influx of hormones flowing through my body. It was also that I felt something surging in my heart from the love I felt for this child swimming inside me, kicking at night and pushing with his little fist or foot against my middle. "The weight of love" is how I described it to Daniel. I was nervous. I was excited. I was worried. I was elated. Every day, I felt my connection to our baby grow stronger.

That June, I still had less than three weeks left before the baby was due, and with the nursery completed and the drawers to the wicker dresser filled with clothes from my baby shower, I was able to finish up the school year at Franklin without too much stress. It was hard to believe that Yuri and Finn's class would be graduating the following weekend from high school. The majority of them would be going off to college, their adult lives beginning.

I had kept my promise to all my classes that I would keep the letters they had written to their future selves. This year marked the first time I had former students graduating, and I was looking forward to mailing them back the letters that they had written when they were twelve.

I spilled out on the cement floor the contents of the folder labeled *Class of 2006*—Yuri and Finn's class—which had been stored in a filing cabinet in my basement. I gently fanned the letters across the floor. They say that a scent can trigger old memories that had remained dormant. But as a teacher, just seeing the names and handwriting of my former students now awakened a flood of memories. I saw Lisa Yamamoto's perfect penmanship and her drawings of flowers all over her envelope. I pulled out her letter, and three carefully folded paper cranes fluttered like paper snowflakes to the ground.

Dear Lisa,

Congratulations on being 18 and graduating high school. I hope when you read this you will have grown six inches and have gotten lots of college acceptances. I hope you wore a great dress to the senior prom and had the best date ever. I hope you have already traveled to Paris, but if you haven't, I hope you go there soon. I hope you have your driver's license too, so you can go to all the places you want without your parents having to take you. When you're 18, I hope you're on your way to being a fashion designer and that you never give up on your dreams.

From your 12 year old self,
Lisa Yamamoto

I smiled and placed the letter back in the envelope. Then I reached for another. Oscar Letino's was unmistakable. The boy had the worst penmanship in the class, but he always was full of energy and had a smile on his face. I opened his letter.

> *Dear Oscar,*
>
> *Congratulations on being 18. I hope when you read this you're six feet tall and have six million girlfriends. I hope you got to go to the homecoming dance with Stephanie Besuto and that she let you kiss her.*
>
> *I hope Ms. Topper doesn't really keep this letter because I'm going to be soooo embarrassed if she did.*
>
> *From,*
> *Oscar Letino*

Zach Gordon's was next.

> *Dear Zach,*
>
> *Congratulations on turning 18 and graduating high school! Hope you're having fun and getting ready to go to the University of Virginia, where you will be pitching and playing point guard. I hope your supermodel girlfriend treats you well when you two get married and have 5 kids. When you read this letter, I hope you're feeling awesome.*
>
> *From,*
> *Zach*

Rachel Mendelsohn's letter was covered in drawings. I had read in the school newsletter that she had been accepted to the Rhode Island School of Design. Her letter, written in purple ink, was short and sweet:

Dear Rachel,

I hope when you're 18 you're off to a better and more interesting life. I hope you rocked high school and got to take the AP photography class that you need to be recommended for. I hope you have the coolest art portfolio ever and that you got into a great art school. Here is a drawing of how I hope you look when you graduate from high school.

From your 12 year old self,
Rachel Mendelsohn

On the bottom of her paper, Rachel had drawn a picture of herself in all black clothes, holding a big portfolio exploding with artwork, and a paintbrush in her mouth.

Then I found Finn's letter.

Dear Finn,

Congratulations on graduating high school. I hope you had an amazing year and it would be great if you made the varsity basketball and baseball teams. Hopefully, you were team captain, too. I hope that you have made Mom and Dad proud and gotten into a good college. I hope that a surgery was discovered so Kelly doesn't need her brace anymore and can run with me outside. I hope when you go to college, you'll do well and then get into medical school and find a cure for Kelly if one hasn't happened already. I hope you'll become a doctor and improve people's lives.

Finn

I started to cry. There was so much in this letter that I hadn't processed when I first read it six years ago. Finn hadn't yet met Yuri when he wrote it, but his incredible empathy was there from the start.

YURI'S envelope was the only one that was sealed. It was covered in drawings of baseball players and Derek Jeter's number 2. I felt my baby kick when I touched the envelope. My pulse quickened as the rush of life whirled through me and an elbow pushed into my ribs. It hit me hard that as my own baby stirred inside me, I clasped an envelope written by the first little boy I had ever loved.

Sadness took over me. I picked up the envelope and studied the drawings. I read them as though they were a map guiding me back to Yuri. The happiness and enthusiasm of his spirit lifted off the paper.

I had forgotten, up until that moment, that I had neglected to tell him to leave his envelope unsealed. At that time, I hadn't had the heart to ask him to redo his art-filled envelope and had decided to just tuck his sealed envelope in with the rest of the letters from his graduating class. But now, as I held this letter in my hand, I wrestled with what to do.

I couldn't bear to tear open the envelope and destroy any part of those drawings, images that were one of the few permanent memories that came from Yuri's hands. And did this letter really belong to me? Was it mine to even read? All I could think about was Katya and Sasha. This envelope and whatever he had written inside were something that came from their beloved child. Didn't they deserve to have it?

And yet I was paralyzed to send it to them.

I hadn't spoken to Katya or Sasha since that terrible afternoon when, years earlier, her Russian words, angry and condemning, vaulted at me through the air. In another life, I would be able to call

Katya on the telephone and tell her that I had something precious that she should have. But all the calls made after Yuri's death had remained unanswered. How could I send a letter like this in the mail without letting her know it was on its way? The shock of receiving it would be unimaginable.

I pulled myself off the ground, pregnant and hot. I climbed up the basement stairs and found Daniel in the kitchen, replacing a burned-out bulb over the dinette table.

He took one look at me and knew something was upsetting me. "What's wrong, honey?"

I lifted the envelope toward the stepladder, showing him the outside without letting him actually take it in his hand.

"It's the letter Yuri wrote to his future self."

"'A Letter from the Past with a Message for the Future,'" he read aloud. "Oh, geez."

"It's the only one of the letters that's sealed," I told him.

He looked at the envelope in my hands. "If you want to read it, we could steam it open, Maggie," he suggested softly. "We could still keep all the drawings intact."

"But is it for me to read?" I started to shake as I stood there next to him. I felt my baby kick again; perhaps my heightened emotions were causing an increase in fetal movement.

"I don't know," he said gently. "But let's go sit down and try to figure it out."

I nodded and waddled over to the living room couch.

Daniel came over and nestled next to me, his large hand folding over my smaller ones, which still clasped the letter.

"Had you forgotten you even had it? You never mentioned it before."

I was quiet. The truth was those letters from Yuri's class were a time capsule. I always thought to myself that I still had years before

I would have to mail them back. And, all of a sudden, this year his class was graduating.

"I'm paralyzed about what the right thing to do is, Daniel," I said, my voice shaking. "Maybe if I was already a mother, I'd have more confidence."

"You could call your mom, Maggie. Ask her what she thinks you should do."

He tightened his grip around my fingers, and I felt another kick inside.

"Baby thinks that's a good idea," I said, lifting myself off the couch. I went upstairs to make the call.

70

"I think you need to let her know you have the letter, sweetheart," my mother told me. "But I also think you don't need to do that tonight or even this week. If anything, I think it's better if you wait. I'm sure she's already suffering knowing that his former classmates are all graduating this week. In the paper, they even mentioned some of the great colleges that many of the students are going to."

I knew she was right. I had seen a profile in *Newsday* that Finn had been accepted to Columbia on a scholarship, and I had made a mental note to write and congratulate him.

"Why don't you hold off a week or two and then reach out to her? You can leave a message and tell her that you have something that was written by Yuri and that she might want it . . ."

"But I don't know what's inside, Mom. What if it's something that will upset her?"

My mother was silent for a moment. "I have to believe, honey, that there isn't anything in the world I wouldn't want that was written by the hands of my child. And if I had ever lost you"—her voice broke—"I'd want it even more."

. . .

I had always planned on bringing the letters to school on the last day so the other teachers could look at them first and we could share our memories of the kids together.

I would keep private the fact that I had Yuri's letter, showing the envelope only to Suzie because I knew she would be touched to see the beautiful drawings he had done on his envelope.

In the faculty room, Florence marveled at Lisa Yamamoto's paper cranes, and Suzie reminded me how Oscar once spilled glue all over the floor and sealed one of Jackie's shoes to the ground. Everyone remembered Finn with great fondness, and Angela remarked how wonderful it was that he was off to Columbia in the fall.

After all the letters were read, I licked the envelopes and sealed them, bringing them back to my classroom to mail them later that afternoon.

My room looked painfully bare now. All the decorations had been taken down, I had returned the last papers to the students, and their writing journals were probably still in their backpacks. Most of them would likely throw theirs out when they got home, thrilled to put all the past year's work behind them and eager to begin their summer vacation.

It was hard to believe I wasn't coming back in the fall. I had elected to stay home for the first year of my baby's birth. Fortunately, Mr. Nelson had already hired my substitute teacher, Katherine, a twenty-four-year-old fresh out of graduate school who had been shadowing me most of the past week and could hardly contain her excitement that she'd gotten a full-time teaching position for the year. Looking at the packed-up boxes around me, I could tell she had made herself useful while I was reading the letters in the faculty room.

As I started to throw some more pens and Post-it pads into one of the bins, I heard Suzie's voice suddenly emerge.

"Do you want to go to McCann's and get an iced tea?" She looked at her watch. The kids had had an early dismissal, and it was now one thirty.

"Why not?" I looked around my classroom. I was in good shape thanks to Katherine. The walls were now bare. I had even taken down the large butterfly I had taped behind my desk and packed it gently away. The butterfly was something I had vowed to do every year after befriending Florence, as a reminder to myself just how important this job was.

"That's my girl! It's too beautiful a day to waste it inside, and you look like a dream in that blue dress." Suzie bubbled over with excitement. I smiled at her. I had always loved the happy feeling her own outfits had transmitted over the years. If my dress was the sky, her watermelon top and lawn-colored capris were certainly channeling the impending summer.

"Let's go. There isn't anything here that can't wait until we get back."

71

THE large iced tea with extra sugar had given me the boost I needed to transfer the last bit of my classroom items to my car. Suzie and I walked back to Franklin with big smiles on our faces.

"You'll have to come out to visit me and Joe in Montauk after the baby is born," she insisted. They had been dating for three years, and I knew she was hoping they'd get engaged soon. "I still can't believe that kid of yours will be here in mid-July."

"He could come sooner," I joked, patting my enormous stomach. Inside, I felt my baby move. His internal gymnastics had become constant at this point. Sometimes I felt as if he were going to literally kick himself out of my stomach.

"I'd like it if he came sooner. I feel like I've been pregnant along with you from the moment you took that First Response test."

What she said was true. She had been the fourth person I called. First Daniel, then my parents. Then Suzie. She had been my biggest cheerleader all along.

. . .

WE split up halfway down the hallway. "I'll come by your room before I leave," she promised. I smiled and waved before dipping back into my classroom.

I walked over to my desk and immediately felt that something was different, that something was clearly missing. I glanced over my desk blotter and saw that the pen holder I had emptied of all its contents an hour before was still there. But all the letters and Yuri's envelope were gone.

Panic swept through me. I opened every drawer in my desk and looked all around the room. Then I searched a second time, repeating in my mind every one of my movements since I had returned from the faculty room. I scoured the windowsill where I sometimes left my papers, behind the bookshelves, and around and under the children's desks.

But nowhere could I find the letters or envelope.

I began to think I had lost my mind. I patted the space on the desk where I had last seen them. I rummaged through every box, thinking maybe with my pregnancy brain, I had inadvertently placed them inside one of them. But I was still unable to find them anywhere. The letters had vanished without a trace.

Suddenly, as I was crouched on my knees, looking beneath my desk one last time, my belly nearly pushing against my chin, I heard a voice in the room.

"Maggie, I just wanted to tell you . . ." It was Katherine, the young substitute teacher who was replacing me in the fall. She was standing in the threshold, thin and beautiful in her tangerine-colored summer dress, her long chestnut hair gleaming. "I mailed those letters that were on your desk. I was heading to the post office anyway, so I sealed them and mailed them for you."

I felt the blood drain from my face. "What?"

"I thought I'd save you a trip to the post office." She pointed to my oversize belly. "I wanted to give you one less thing to do . . . I know how much you have on your mind."

"But . . . ," I stammered, trying to process what she had just said. "You mailed them, Katherine? All of them?"

"Yes." She looked at me, radiant and confident. She truly believed she had done a good deed.

"All of them?" I said it again. I could barely get the words out. I thought I was going to faint. "Even the envelope that was off to the side of the rest of them?"

"Oh, you mean the one with all the cute baseball drawings? Yeah, that one, too."

I immediately went pale, and my knees felt weak. All I could think of was that she had mailed Yuri's letter before I had a chance to alert Katya.

"It wasn't supposed to happen like this," I said, my voice cracking. I grabbed my purse and rushed out the door to find Suzie.

72

"WE need to get Yuri's letter back," I insisted to Suzie, frantically imagining Katya opening her mailbox and unexpectedly seeing the letter with Yuri's handwriting and drawings on the outside.

"Katherine thought she was doing me a favor, but she mailed all the letters, including Yuri's." I was hyperventilating. "Jesus . . . Suzie, what am I going to do?"

"You need to calm down." Suzie gripped my shoulders and looked straight into my eyes. She took a tissue from her sleeve and blotted my tears.

"Now you just need to breathe. We don't want anything happening to that baby of yours."

My eyes filled with tears. "Just help me make this right, Suzie. I can't cause any more pain to that family. I just can't . . ."

"First off, Maggie, this was an accident, so stop blaming yourself." She sucked in her breath. "Now I could just kill that toothpick, goody-two-shoes Katherine . . . Those goddamn first-year teachers are always trying to outdo us veterans." Suzie was doing her best to make me laugh.

"You and I both know she thought she was helping me out."

"And look how that worked out . . . But seriously, I have a buddy, Jack, who works at the post office. We're going to call him right now and see if he can pull some strings for us."

I tried to slow down my breathing. I didn't want to put any unnecessary stress on my baby, but the sense of panic was flooding through me. I couldn't get the image of Katya and Sasha out of my mind.

SUZIE pulled her cell phone from her purse and flipped it open, dialing the number of her friend.

"The letter's government property from the moment it leaves your hand and enters that box," Jack told her. "You will never be able to get it back. I'm sorry to be the bearer of bad news."

"Can't you call in a favor?" she begged. "Please."

"I wouldn't just lose my job," he answered. "We'd all probably go to jail, too."

AFTER Suzie hung up, she pulled up one of the art stools and sat down next to me.

"You told me you were going to reach out to Katya and tell her about the letter."

"I was . . ." I dabbed my eyes with the tissue. "But I was going to wait until after graduation week . . . I knew it was going to be a really hard time for her."

"Maybe this was meant to be, Maggie," she said, forcing herself to make sense of it all. "The letter needed to be sent, and this accident just set it in its rightful motion."

"I can't bear the thought of her seeing it without any warning.

You have to imagine what this will be like for her. The letter will be arriving in his twelve-year-old handwriting, with his drawings of stick-figure players and baseball diamonds. And even more upsetting, the letter is written to himself about his future . . . but he never got to have a future, Suzie. He was robbed of it."

Suzie was silent for a moment. Her hands reached for mine, and at her touch, my baby kicked again. "Do you want me to make the call for you?"

I loved her so much at that moment. She would have done it in a heartbeat for me, I knew it. But it wasn't her call to make. As difficult as it was going to be, it had to be mine.

73

I dialed the Krasnys' number slowly. I hung up the first time midway and then tried one more time to complete it in full. When the phone finally began to ring, I became so sick to my stomach, I thought I was going to drop the receiver on the floor.

Katya picked up, the sound of her voice pulling me back to the past. "Hello?"

The words halted in my throat for a second, but then I finally pushed them out.

"Mrs. Krasny, it's me, Maggie Topper."

"Maggie?" I could hear the surprise in her voice.

"I am sorry to bother you," I began.

"You're not bothering me, Maggie," she said softly.

"It's terrible it's been so long since you heard from me." My voice started to shake. I began to apologize for the last time I had visited them, and said that I felt that I had intruded upon them when they were still coping with their grief. I told her that I had never stopped thinking about Yuri, and her and Sasha, too. And only after I said all that did I tell her about the letter that had just been put in the mail.

She was quiet for what seemed like several minutes.

"Maggie, I would have wanted to see it. I want to read his words."

I began to cry on the phone, but she asked me to stop. "Please," she said, her voice almost stern. "No more tears. If you start now, I won't be able to stop." A painful blade of silence emerged between us. I stumbled to find the right words to fill the space.

Katya, though, found them first. "Why don't you come for tea next week? It's been too long, and by then I will have received the letter."

Her words were a huge relief for me. I knew the letter would probably be in her mailbox by tomorrow or the day after at the latest, so we made a date for the following Tuesday.

A few days later, as I drove the once-familiar back roads to their house, my mind flooded with memories of my year with Yuri. His face flashed in front of me. The bright blue eyes. The infectious smile. I had some difficulty remembering the sound of his voice, but I could recall with ease the memory of his laughter, the way its vibrations could immediately lift my spirits.

As I neared the Krasnys' house, I noticed three older boys playing street hockey. But when I pulled closer to the curb, I saw the small figure of a little girl in a pink tutu twirling on the grass, her slender arms swaying above her.

Katya was sitting on the steps outside the house, watching the girl, who looked to be close to three years old. Her eyes immediately struck me, for they were neither sad nor happy, but rather strangely calm. As though this was just another moment for her to soak in—like a ray of sunlight—to store for a rainy day.

74

THE house seemed different when I entered it. In the corner, where Yuri's chair used to be, was a pile of My Little Ponies and a box of pink and white plastic toys. Katya already had a pot of tea and a plate of cookies waiting for us on the small table by the sofa, just like she had when I used to visit years before.

The little girl came and sat down between us.

"This is Violet," Katya said as she pulled her into her arms and buried her nose in the girl's wispy blond hair.

"What a beautiful name," I said, slightly surprised by it.

Katya smiled. "Yes. Violets bloom even in the snow."

And now I understood. The name meant everything. "Such a pleasure to meet you, Violet." I extended my hand to her.

She took it and squeezed my fingers. Her big blue eyes pierced my heart when she looked at me. For they were the same as Yuri's.

Katya smiled. "And I see you are expecting a little one of your own as well. Congratulations."

I looked down at my enormous belly. "Yes, I'm due July seventeenth." She nodded, lifting the plate of cookies to soften the awkwardness between us. I took one of the shortbreads and put it on my plate.

Katya gave one to Violet, then patted the little girl on the bottom and told her to go fetch one of her dolls from her room. "It took us some time to find the courage to try for another baby. The genetic testing and the early sonogram helped me gain my confidence. But there isn't a day that I don't think of him . . ."

I looked outside. The birds were chirping. There were now three bird feeders on the deck, and suddenly my heart felt strangely full.

"I'M sorry the letter was sent by accident," I told her gently. "I wasn't sure what to do when I found it again. I was planning on calling you over the summer to let you know I had it and to ask if I should send it to you, but this mistake at school took it out of my hands."

"Please," she said, stopping me. Her voice cracked as she tried to force back her tears. "I just have to believe . . . that his letter was sent not by accident, but because he wanted to communicate with us again somehow. His words brought me so much comfort, you have no idea."

Her eyes wandered toward the corner of the room, the place where the big yellow chair had once stood. The old trophy from Finn was still there above the mantel, and on the bookshelves, I noticed several small framed photographs of Yuri. And by the sofa, on the end table, was an especially beautiful one of Sasha and Yuri wearing matching Yankees caps, their smiles radiant.

I could sense that she still felt Yuri's presence around her, and in a strange way, so did I. It was as if his spirit had remained here in the room along with us.

"I'm so relieved, Katya. I had no idea what it said inside, and I didn't want to cause you or Sasha any more pain."

The light in her face shifted. "Oh, you did just the opposite, Maggie." She reached for my hands and gripped them in her own. "You can't imagine how happy that letter made us."

A flood of emotions rushed through me. "I have always worried that you blamed me . . ."

Her face softened as I said that, and her fingers tightened around mine. "I was just so lost in my grief when you came that last time. I was drowning." She took a deep breath. "It wasn't anything you did, not at all. The loss was just so . . . so big." She brought a clenched fist to her chest.

"I want to show you the letter, Maggie. You will see how much peace it has brought me and Sasha." She pulled her fingers away from mine. "It's full of everything that made Yuri so special."

She left the room and came back holding the envelope.

"Please . . . ," she said, handing it over to me. "When you read it, you will see Yuri again. His need to make sure we're all okay. Not once thinking of himself."

I took the envelope in my hands, admiring the drawings one last time. Then I pulled out the letter:

Dear Yuri,

Congratulations on making it to 18 and graduating high school. I hope you are now six feet tall. I hope the Yankees are still champions and that Dr. Rosenblum found a cure for my heart defect and I am off to play baseball at college.

I hope my dad has won a lot of science prizes for his work at the lab. And I hope my mom has put on those ballet shoes she keeps hidden in her drawer and is dancing again. But the most important thing I hope for in the future is that we are always together as a family. Today, when Ms. Topper told us to write a letter to our 18 year old self, I looked up at the sky outside my window, and I thought: "I hope every family has its own cloud in the sky. Wouldn't it be nice if no matter what happens here on earth, that cloud is reserved for your family. When we die, we'll all go there, and wait for those we love to join us on the family cloud."

These are my thoughts.

Sincerely,
Yuri, 11 ½ years old. December 1999

I placed the letter down. I could hear Yuri's voice lifting off the page. Six years after his death, it returned to me as clear as a bell in my ears. There was a prescience to Yuri's words. As if he needed to know there was an alternate plan if something happened to him, I thought of the magical realism of *Shoeless Joe*, the fact that Yuri and I had discussed at length how Kinsella had dreamed up the possibility of a baseball diamond in the middle of a midwestern cornfield, populated by a team of all-star ghosts. "Anything is possible if you imagine it," I told him. And now as I read Yuri's letter, I saw he was dreaming of the possibility that a family cloud could actually exist. He needed to believe that one day, he would see everyone he loved again up there in the sky.

I put the letter back into its envelope.

Katya reached out to find my hand and squeezed it. "To think there might be a family cloud with him waiting there for us . . . It's just . . ." Her voice cracked. "It's just such a beautiful thought."

Minutes later, she stood up and went into another room. When she returned, she was carrying something I recognized immediately. Covered in tattered old magazine clippings and Magic Marker drawings on its front, it was Yuri's writer's notebook.

The timeworn images rushed through me. Strangely familiar, yet eerily from another time. I saw the faded yellow photograph of a ballet dancer. An image of a glass laboratory beaker. A Russian Orthodox saint. A Jewish star. An evil eye. All those Yankees baseball cards. Derek Jeter, now half-unglued and practically separated from the black-and-white marble cover. My eyes found the familiar slice of pizza, a chocolate sundae, the haunting sticker of a broken heart, and the boyish hopefulness of the cottony white clouds.

But there was another addition I hadn't seen before. At some point he had added a photograph of him and Finn on their graduation day from Franklin, their arms slung across each other's shoulders, their smiles radiant.

Katya came back to the sofa and sat down. "For years, this was one of the most precious items I had of Yuri. To see his words inscribed in the pages, his thoughts and his ideas preserved there. To have this tangible piece of him was such a gift. But now I have his beautiful letter, too."

Tears were falling down my face. I couldn't say the words I was thinking, because they were caught in my throat. But what I wanted to tell Katya was that everything about Yuri was beautiful—his laugh, his eyes, his words, and his soul.

Katya took Yuri's letter and slipped it into the notebook. "I will always have his words," she said, her voice breaking again. She patted the book's cover with her palms. "And it keeps me close to him."

And then she reached for my hand and covered it with hers. "I have you to thank for that, Maggie. Because of your teaching, I now have two things that came from Yuri that I can always take hold of and cherish. That I can reread whenever I need to feel close to him. You helped capture what was in his heart."

Epilogue

THE days pass in such a different way now that I've had Georgie. There are some afternoons when the hours go by so slowly, when the day slips into patterns of feedings, diaper changing, and maintaining a routine for an infant who depends on me for nearly everything to keep him clean, safe, and fed. When my father comes to visit, he brings the violin he made for himself, and he puts it on the ground so Georgie can touch the varnished top with his hands and run his fingers over the strings. I see age transforming my parents in a way that is in sharp contrast to my ever-changing son. With each passing month, he grows stronger and reaches more milestones, the gurgling sounds of infancy now replaced by a few monosyllabic words. But my mother hasn't been able to work in the garden because of back pain, and my father, still battling arthritis, seems to walk slower and more carefully now, as if he's afraid he might misstep. I tell Daniel I feel life's going in two directions, the aging of my parents against the miracle of our son's growth. Both equally fragile, both striking the chords of my heart. I want to cup my hands and hold everyone close and keep everyone safe and healthy, though I know there is only so much I can control.

Then there are days when I'm holding Georgie in my arms and I wonder how I will tell him about where he got his name, that in Russian his name would translate to Yuri. I want to tell him about a boy who loved baseball. Who had a heart so big and a smile just as wide. I want to tell him when he's older that we are blessed every day we are able to spend with the people we love. But I also want to tell him that, should we ever become separated, his mother believes the words of a twelve-year-old boy who once wrote them in a letter to himself—that in the sky above us, every family has its own special cloud.

Acknowledgments

The Secret of Clouds is first and foremost a love letter to all the teachers I've had in my life who contributed to making me the writer I am today. From my first-grade teacher, Mrs. Goldberg, who one day placed a blob of paint on a piece of paper and instructed me, "Write a story about what you see," to my creative writing professor at Wellesley College, Laura Levine, I've had so many wonderful teachers who helped to shape my mind and open my eyes to the world around me.

The late James Swink, my English teacher for all three of my years at Harbor Country Day School, was the first to encourage me to keep a writing journal. He always used to say to me, "Alyson, when you're a writer . . . ," and never "if you're ever a writer . . ." This year when my son, Zachary, was assigned *To Kill a Mockingbird* as the summer reading for his ninth-grade English class, I reread the novel and recalled Mr. Swink's voice in my head—his beautiful Southern accent sounding aloud the passages that he so loved. That is the thing about a good teacher; their voice and their wisdom become forever imprinted in us.

I came to have a new appreciation and even deeper respect for teachers after my two children, Zachary and Charlotte, started going to school. Every day I saw their teachers' selflessness and enthusiasm to instill the love of learning into young minds. Susie Meisler, Judy Biener, Ilene Brown, Erika Brignoti, Michelle Melara, Camille Tedeschi, and Kelly Krysinkski are just a few of the teachers my children have had over the years who awed me with their dedication to their profession.

The Secret of Clouds was initially inspired by a dear friend and teacher, Christina Tudisco, who described to me how every year she assigns her class to write letters to their eighteen-year-old selves, and that she holds on to the letters until the week that class eventually graduates high school. Although the character of Yuri is wholly a fabric of my imagination, I know there were situations where a few of Christina's students sadly did not make it to their senior year. Knowing that these letters could serve as a time capsule by preserving those children's hopes and dreams of a future that would never arise moved me deeply.

I am grateful to a handful of other dedicated teachers who shared their experiences with me and were kind enough to read and comment upon prior drafts of the book: Patricia Nowak and Angela Bruner shared with me their teaching experiences in 1999 and also introduced me to the work of the literacy educator Lucy Calkins and Teachers College Reading and Writing Project; I am especially thankful to Allison Von Vange and Michele Webb, who read several drafts of the novel and made sure it rang true. As well as early readers MJ Rose, Suzanne Sheran, Andrea Peskind Katz, Robbin Klein, Jardine Libaire, Victoria Leventhal, Nikki Koklanaris, Michelle Chydzik-Sowa, and my father, Paul Richman. An enormous thanks also to my agent extraordinaire, Sally Wofford-Girand, who has been a cheerleader for my writing for nearly twenty years, and to everyone at Berkley, especially my editor, Kate Seaver, who pushed me harder with this book than she has with any other. Also, as with all my novels, my husband, Stephen, is the first pair of eyes to read every chapter and serves as my sounding board. Without his love and support, none of this would be possible. You will always be the dark-haired, light-eyed boy in all my novels.

Also, I am indebted to dancer Nicoleta Moldavan for sharing stories about her childhood studying ballet in her native Romania when it was part of the Soviet Union's communist bloc. To Guy Fletcher and Philip Mollenkott, thanks for your assistance in helping me concoct a credible dance injury for my character Katya.

For assisting me in my research and understanding about Ebstein's anomaly, I wish to thank doctors David D'Agate, Sean Levchuck, and Doug Luxenberg. By sharing with me their knowledge of pediatric heart conditions, they helped to ensure that my descriptions of Yuri's experiences were as medically accurate as possible. And for relaying colorful details about their lives in Ukraine post-Chernobyl, I am very thankful to Lana Dovna and Vadim Shtrom.

Lastly, so much of my son is in this book. Without him, I would never have been drawn into the world of baseball that he so loves. I am indebted to Rob Steinert, who in teaching my son pitching over the years has also imparted to him many other worthwhile lessons about life and team sports. I also wish to thank Sam Menzin, who graciously detailed for me his childhood passion for baseball, which began the same time as my character Yuri's. His knowledge and enthusiasm were infectious, and I will always recall with great fondness our zealous wild-goose chase to fact-check some of the Andy Pettitte references in the story.

But it was my sweet, sweet Zachary who, after his great-grandmother passed away, whispered through his tears that he hoped every family had its own cloud and we would all end up on ours one day. He breathed the heart and soul into this book. I love you.

THE

Secret

OF

Clouds

ALYSON RICHMAN

Questions for Discussion

1. Maggie and Yuri's teacher-student relationship is the heart of *The Secret of Clouds*. Do you have a teacher who left a lasting impression on you or made a permanent impact on your life?

2. How do music and dance serve as different forms of language for the characters in *The Secret of Clouds*? Think about how music is embraced in Maggie's home and how it ultimately draws her to Daniel. How is it different from Katya's family's attitude toward her dancing? Does the fact that Katya is a ballet dancer influence her romance with Sasha?

3. How do the Topper and Krasny households communicate through food? What are the cultural differences? What are the similarities? Does food play a role in your family's traditions and holidays?

4. Maggie's mother tells her, "We can't be so afraid of experiencing pain that it interferes with the things we love." What are the different painful obstacles that the characters face, and how do they overcome them?

5. There are several references to butterflies in the novel. Why do certain characters identify with butterflies? Sasha also describes the butterfly effect to Katya early on in their relationship. Can you think

of an example in your life where one individual meeting changed your destiny?

6. Do you believe Yuri's heart defect was caused by the Chernobyl accident or was just a random case of bad luck? Does the author imply there were certain things that increased Katya's risk of having a child with a birth defect?

7. How do Katya and Sasha approach Yuri's diagnosis differently? How do their experiences as parents differ? How does each of them deal with the strain and fear of having a sick child?

8. How does Sasha's faith transform over time? How is the conflict between science and faith explored in the novel? How do Sasha and Katya's beliefs differ on this issue?

9. What role do sports play in *The Secret of Clouds*, and how do they unite the various characters in the novel? What makes baseball such an attractive sport for Sasha and Yuri?

10. Both Florence and Katya have family stories that they don't share readily with others, yet these histories impact how they are perceived by others. Did you have greater sympathy for these characters once you learned about their past experiences? Do you know people in your life whom you saw differently and more empathetically once you learned something they don't often reveal to others?

11. Do you think there are individuals who are destined to become teachers because of certain qualities that they possess? What traits do you think contribute to making some people more suitable than others for the profession? Is teaching a calling? Have you been drawn to a certain profession? What made you a perfect fit for that job?

Interview with Alyson Richman

1. In the past you've always written historical novels. What inspired you to a write a more contemporary story? What themes did you know you wanted to explore?

The Secret of Clouds is indeed my first contemporary novel, but I didn't consciously set out to write a more modern-day story. Instead, the material actually found me. Just like with my earlier novels, the book was inspired by a true-life story that haunted me and that I couldn't shake from my mind. A dear friend of mine who is an elementary school teacher told me about a letter she had kept for several years as part of an old class assignment. The letter, which was written by a sick child who later tragically died, was inadvertently mailed back to the boy's parents before my friend had had a chance to alert them that it was on its way. I felt that so much of that story warranted further exploration: the dedication and passion of an educator, the unique relationship between a teacher and a bright and curious yet physically weakened and isolated child, and the unforeseen comfort that a piece of paper—written in the since-departed child's hand—would later bring to all who had known him.

Because all my prior novels did weave in a historical theme, I again wanted to create a backstory of a part of history that I felt needed to be explored more in contemporary literature. When my son was an infant, his first babysitter was a former nurse from Ukraine who shared with me her stories of the accident at the Chernobyl nuclear plant near her hometown. I would never forget her describing how, for three days, no one knew about the accident, so they were all outside sunning themselves in the unseasonably hot weather and bathing in the unusually warm waters of the local river. Babies were soon born with rare cancers and heart defects akin to what my character Yuri had. Countless health problems related to the radiation leak still plague the Ukrainian population. I wanted to illuminate this trauma in my novel, and fusing these two stories of the letter and of Chernobyl was the perfect way for me to accomplish exploring the themes that were important to me.

2. You've always done a lot of research for your historical novels. Did you need to do the same amount for this novel? How was it different from and similar to the research you've done for your other books?

Because much of the book takes place in Long Island, where I grew up, there was a lot more "local" research than in my previous novels, so I didn't do as much traveling, which was actually very nice for me. I spent a lot of time interviewing teachers and listening to their stories about what had inspired them to become educators and the special bonds they had created with their students over the years. I also learned about how they themselves had transformed over the years, both as educators and as people, through the relationships they'd shared with their students.

3. Did you have a particular teacher who inspired you? Maggie feels a calling to be a teacher. Have you always felt a calling to be a writer?

My sixth-grade English teacher, Mr. Swink, was definitely the first teacher who treated me as though he knew I'd be an author one day. I will never forget him, and it's one of my deepest regrets that he died at such a young age and didn't learn that my lifelong friend and fellow classmate Jardine Libaire and I both became writers.

I think I always wanted to paint and write. So many of my early professional dreams were to be a children's book author and to illustrate my own stories. Years later, when I found myself majoring in art history in college, I realized that I loved writing stories about artists and exploring the psychological, historical, and cultural questions that art can inspire.

4. Are their certain characters based on real people? Who?

The character of Maggie's mother was inspired by the mother of my friend who shared her story about the lost letter with me. Her mother, Josephine, is the kindest, sweetest woman and an amazing Italian cook. She always has something cooking on her stove and is always gifting a lasagna, a tray of cookies, or something warm to the people she loves or neighbors in need of some comfort. I've included her famous lasagna recipe at the end of the book for those book clubs or readers who want to re-create some of her cooking.

5. Did you know a lot about baseball before you wrote the novel?

Before I had my son, I knew absolutely nothing about baseball. But ever since he was five years old, he has been a huge fan of the sport, and he also plays both on his school team and in a travel league. Like Yuri, my son gravitated toward the game not only because he enjoyed playing it but also because of the complex mental strategies behind it. When writing *The Secret of Clouds*, I interviewed women and men of all ages on why they loved baseball. It was really interesting for me to learn what made this sport so special to them, as it inspires such devotion and passion—and a wonderful sense of nostalgia—in its fans. But it can be a very long game, and I used to complain to my son that, when one of his doubleheaders took five or six hours, I could have flown to Paris by the time his games had finished! But after researching the novel, I found I had a new respect for baseball.

6. I love that both Katya's and Maggie's fathers are artists. Why did you choose those specific professions for them?

That's a great question. For those readers who are new to my work, this is a universal theme in all my novels. Because I grew up in an artistic home—with my mother being an abstract painter—I, too, dreamed of following in her footsteps. I've always channeled my love of exploring the creative process in my novels. In the past, I've written books about a mask carver, a painter, an actor, and a musician, but I had yet to write a novel about a violin maker or a ballet dancer. I love learning through my research, so it was wonderful to interview dancers who grew up during the Soviet regime and hear about their deep appreciation for how they utilized their artistic talents to try to overcome the bleakness of Communist life. The same was the case about learning about the craft of violin making. The baseball aspect of *The Secret of Clouds* came about because of my son's love of the game, and the violin part came from my husband's and daughter's love. Both of them are violinists, and my daughter takes lessons at a beautiful store in my town where there is an in-house luthier in the back. It was such a treat for me to see the behind-the-scenes work that goes into making violins, and I wanted to find a way to thread that into my novel.

Topper Family Lasagna

FROM THE KITCHEN OF JOSEPHINE MACRI

One of the themes in The Secret of Clouds *is how food is an expression of love. I've been lucky enough to be the recipient of the cooking of Ms. Josephine Macri, the woman who served as the inspiration for Maggie Topper's mother in my novel, and her cooking always feels like a warm hug. I wanted to share one of her signature recipes with my readers because there is nothing more comforting than some good food to accompany a good book. And for all my book clubs that Skype with me, I know you're often looking for dishes to accompany your discussions. So it's my pleasure to gift you the recipe for this magical lasagna. Enjoy!*

TOMATO SAUCE:

    1 medium onion, roughly chopped

    Olive oil

    Parsley and basil, chopped

    4 cloves garlic, finely chopped

    2 (1-pound) packages ground beef, pork, and veal combo

    1 pound Italian sausage meat (hot or sweet)

    Salt and pepper

    1 (6-ounce) can tomato paste

    ½ cup red wine

    1 (28-ounce) can crushed San Marzano tomatoes

RICOTTA FILLING:

    1 (2-pound) container whole-milk ricotta

    1 pound-plus whole-milk mozzarella, shredded

    Grated Pecorino Romano cheese

    ½ cup chopped fresh flat-leaf parsley

    ¼ cup chopped basil

    Salt and pepper

    Olive oil

    1 large egg

BÉCHAMEL:

    5 tablespoons butter

    4 to 5 tablespoons flour

    4 cups warm whole milk

    ¼ cup grated Pecorino Romano cheese

    Nutmeg

    Salt and pepper

    Package of no-bake lasagna noodles (buy 2 packages in case
       you need extra)

TOMATO SAUCE:

Sauté the onion in a couple tablespoons olive oil until golden. Add the chopped basil and parsley. Add the finely chopped garlic. Add the meat, sausage meat, salt, and pepper. Cook, breaking up the meat, until it is no longer pink. Add the tomato paste and cook for a couple of minutes. Add the red wine. Let the alcohol cook out, and add the crushed tomatoes, along with about a can of water. Simmer for about 45 minutes to 1 hour.

RICOTTA FILLING:

Put the ricotta in a large bowl. Add about a third of the shredded mozzarella, ¼ cup of the Pecorino Romano cheese, the parsley, basil, salt, and pepper. Drizzle with the olive oil. Add the egg and stir until smooth.

BÉCHAMEL:

Melt the butter in a heavy saucepan. Add the flour, and stir until it has the consistency of wet sand. Slowly pour in warm milk. Stir until the sauce is thick enough to coat the back of a spoon. Stir in the cheese, and sprinkle in a little nutmeg and salt and pepper to taste.

ASSEMBLY:

Lightly cover the bottom of the baking dish with the tomato sauce. Place the noodles over the sauce evenly, breaking if needed to fit the pan. Cover the noodles with the ricotta filling, pressing it evenly onto the noodles. Sprinkle more of the shredded mozzarella over the filling. Add another layer of tomato sauce, and top with more of the grated Pecorino Romano. Repeat, ending with noodles and sauce. Pour the béchamel over the top of the lasagna, cover the dish with foil, and bake at 350 degrees, until it is bubbling around the edges, 45 minutes to 1 hour. Remove the foil, and return the lasagna to the oven until the top turns slightly golden. Let the lasagna rest before cutting. Enjoy!

Ready to find
your next great read?

Let us help.

Visit prh.com/nextread

Penguin
Random
House